Cat Bearing Gifts

JAN -- 2013

DATE DUE			
Jw			

covered

ALSO BY SHIRLEY ROUSSEAU MURPHY

Cat Telling Tales

Cat Coming Home

Cat Striking Back

Cat Playing Cupid

Cat Deck the Halls

Cat Pay the Devil

Cat Breaking Free

Cat Cross Their Graves

Cat Fear No Evil

Cat Seeing Double

Cat Laughing Last

Cat Spitting Mad

Cat to the Dogs

Cat in the Dark

Cat Raise the Dead

Cat Under Fire

Cat on the Edge

The Catsworld Portal

Cat Bearing Gifts

A Joe Grey Mystery

Shirley Rousseau Murphy

HARPER LUXE

An Imprint of HarperCollins*Publishers*

CAT BEARING GIFTS. Copyright © 2012 by Shirley Rousseau Murphy. All rights reserved. Printed in the United States of America. No part of this book may be used or reproduced in any manner whatsoever without written permission except in the case of brief quotations embodied in critical articles and reviews. For information address HarperCollins Publishers, 10 East 53rd Street, New York, NY 10022.

HarperCollins books may be purchased for educational, business, or sales promotional use. For information, please e-mail the Special Markets Department at SPsales@harpercollins.com.

FIRST HARPERLUXE EDITION

HarperLuxe™ is a trademark of HarperCollins Publishers

Library of Congress Cataloging-in-Publication Data is available upon request.

ISBN: 978-0-06-220140-9

12 13 14 ID/RRD 10 9 8 7 6 5 4 3 2 1

For the cats who remember
their previous lives
in centuries passed and gone

There is a Celtic belief that cats' eyes are windows through which human beings may explore an inner world. In examining the power that the cat has to raise our feelings and to stimulate our imagination we can hardly fail to learn more about human nature in the process . . . The cat has not only been thought of as wholly good or evil, but has also been recognized as forming a bridge between the two. [Cat] has the power deeply to enrich our lives if, instead of obsessively loving or hating [him], we adopt a realistic attitude towards its paradoxical nature, and allow it to communicate its wisdom.

—PATRICIA DALE-GREEN, *Cult of the Cat*

Cat Bearing Gifts

1

The confusing events that early fall in Molena Point began perhaps with the return of Kate Osborne, the beguiling blond divorcée arriving back in California richer than sin and with a story as strange as the melodies spun by a modern Pied Piper to mesmerize the unwary. Or maybe the strangeness started with the old, faded photograph of a child from a half century past and the memories she awakened in the yellow tomcat; maybe that was the beginning of the odd occurrences that stirred through the coastal village, setting the five cats off on new paths, propelling them into two forgotten worlds as exotic as the nightmares that jerk us awake in the small hours, frightened and amazed.

The village of Molena Point hugs the California coast a hundred and fifty miles below San Francisco harbor, its own smaller bay cutting into the land in a deep underwater abyss, its shore rising abruptly in a ragged cliff along which Highway One cuts as frail as a spider's thread. Maybe the tale commences here on the narrow two-lane that wanders twisting and uncertain high above the pounding waves.

It was growing dark when Lucinda and Pedric Greenlaw and their tortoiseshell cat left their favorite seafood restaurant north of Santa Cruz. Lucinda had carried Kit to their table hidden in her canvas tote, the smug and purring tortie curled up inside anticipating lobster and scallops slipped to her during their leisurely meal. Now the threesome, replete with a good dinner and comfortable in their new, only slightly used, Lincoln Town Car, continued on south where they had reservations at a motel that welcomed cats—an establishment that even accommodated dogs if they didn't chase the cats or pee on someone's sandals.

They'd departed San Francisco in late afternoon, Pedric driving, the setting sun in their eyes as it sank into the sea, its reflections glancing off the dark stone cliff that soon rose on their left, towering black above them. The Lincoln took the precipitous curves with a calm and steady assurance that eased Lucinda's thoughts of the hundred-foot drop below them into a cold and churning sea. In the seat behind the thin, older couple, tortoiseshell Kit sprawled atop a mountain of packages, her fluffy tail twitching as she looked far down at the boiling waves, and then looked up at the dark, wooded hills rising above the cliff against the orange-streaked sky. The trip home, for Kit, was bittersweet. She loved the city, she had loved going around to all the exclusive designer's shops, riding in Lucinda's big carryall like a spoiled lapdog, reaching out a curious paw to feel the rich upholstery fabrics and the sleekly finished furniture that Lucinda and Pedric had considered. She loved the city restaurants, the exotic foods, she had rumbled with purrs when they dined grandly at the beautiful old Mark Hopkins Hotel, had peered out from her canvas lair secretly amusing herself watching her fellow diners. Part of her little cat self hadn't wanted to leave San Francisco, yet part of her longed to be home, to be back in her own village with her feline pals and her human friends, to sleep at night high in her own tree house among her soft cushions with the stars bright around her and the sea wind riffling the branches of her oak tree. Most of all, she longed to be home with her true love.

It had been a stormy romance since the big red tomcat showed up in Molena Point nearly seven months earlier, when he and Kit had first discovered one another, on the cold, windy shore. Pan appeared in the village just two months after Christmas, right at the time of the amazing snowstorm, the likes of which hadn't been seen in Molena Point for forty years—but the likes of that handsome tomcat, Kit had never seen. Almost at once, she was smitten.

Oh, my, how Pan did purr for her, and how nicely he hunted with her, letting her take the lead, often easing back and letting her make the kill—but yet how bold he was when they argued, decisive and macho and completely enchanting. Even as much as she'd loved San Francisco, she felt lost and small when she was parted from him. *Why can't I be in two places at once, why can't I be at home with Pan and Joe Grey and Dulcie and Misto and our human friends, and have all the pleasures of San Francisco, too, all together in the same place? Why do you have to choose one instead of the other?*

In the city, the Greenlaws had hit every decorators' showroom of any consequence, thanks to their friend, interior designer Kate Osborne, who had unlimited access to those exclusive venues. How fetching Kate had looked, ushering them into the showrooms, her short, flyaway blond hair catching the light, her green eyes laughing as if life were a delicious joke, and always dressed in something creamy and silky, casual and elegant. Kate's scent of sandalwood blended deliciously, too, with the showrooms' aromas of teak and imported woods and fine fabrics.

Lucinda and Pedric had made wonderful purchases toward refurbishing their Molena Point house. Ten new dining chairs and five small, hand-carved tables were being shipped down to the village, along with a carved Brazilian coffee table, three hand-embossed chests of drawers, and six lengths of upholstery fabric that were far too beautiful for Kit to ever spoil with a careless rake of her claws. The bundles of fabrics and boxes of small accessories filled the Lincoln's ample trunk and wide backseat, along with the Greenlaws' early Christmas shopping, with gifts for all their friends; Kit rode along atop a veritable treasure of purchases—to say nothing of even greater riches hidden all around her, inside the doors of the Lincoln where no one would ever find them.

They had stayed with Kate in her apartment with a grand view of the bay where, lounging on the windowsills, Kit could watch San Francisco's stealthy fog slip in beneath the Golden Gate Bridge like a pale dragon gliding between the delicate girders, or watch a foggy curtain obscure the bridge's graceful towers as delicately as a bridal veil. But best of all were their evenings before the fire, looking out at the lights of the city and listening to the stories of Kate's amazing journey:

tales that filled Kit's dreams with a fierce longing for that land, which she would never dare approach. Kate's adventure was a journey any speaking cat would long to share and yet one that made Kit's paws sweat, made her want to back away, hissing.

In her wild, kitten days, she would have followed Kate there, down into the caverns of the earth, and she would have ignored the dangers. But now, all grown up, she had learned to be wary, she no longer had the nerve to race down into that mysterious land, overwhelmed by wonder. Now only her human friend was brave enough to breach that mythical world with a curiosity at least as powerful as Kit's own.

It was just last June that Kate had phoned her Molena Point friends to say she had quit her job in Seattle and moved back to San Francisco. But then, after that one round of calls, no one heard from her again. Their messages had gone unanswered until two weeks ago when, in early September, she resurfaced and called them all, and this time her voice bubbled with excitement. She spoke of a strange journey but left the details unclear, she talked about a gift or legacy, a sudden fortune, but she left the particulars vague and enticing.

Now, Kit, safe in the backseat as Pedric negotiated the big Lincoln down the narrow cliff road, idly watched the white froth of waves far below glowing in the gathering night. She sniffed the wind's rich scent of kelp and dead sea creatures and she thought about the wealth that Kate had brought back, treasures Kate insisted Lucinda and Pedric share—as if gold and jewels were as common as kitty treats or a box of chocolate creams to pass around among her friends.

Though Kate made sure the Greenlaws took some of that amazing fortune back with them to Molena Point, she had in fact already sold much of the jewelry, traveling from city to city—Seattle, Portland, Houston— taking care that she wasn't followed, telling the dealers the most plausible of stories about her many European visits where, she said, she'd acquired the strange and exotic pieces. Though the gold coins she'd insisted on giving to the Greenlaws were common enough, she'd had them all melted down and recast into the tender of this world, they could be sold anywhere without question. "No one has followed me," Kate said, "no one has a clue. If anyone did, don't you think they'd have come after me by now? Someone would have broken into my apartment weeks ago, or intercepted me on my way to a bank or getting off a plane. And now," she'd said with a little smile, "who would suspect a respectable couple like you of carrying a car full of jewels and Krugerrands?"

Kate and Pedric together had removed the Lincoln's door panels, using special tools, one that looked like a fat, ivory-colored tongue depressor, and a long metal gadget that might pass for a nail puller or a bottle opener. They had tucked twenty small boxes into the empty spaces, taping them securely in place so they wouldn't rattle or become entangled in the wires and mechanisms that ran through the inner workings of the car. Pedric was as skilled in these matters as any drug smuggler, though his lawless days were long past. Kate said the coins were theirs to use any way they chose, and Lucinda suggested the village's cat rescue project, which the cats' human friends had organized early in the year to care for the many pets that had been abandoned during the economic downturn, cats and dogs left behind when their families moved out of foreclosed homes. There was enough wealth hidden in the car to build a spacious animal shelter and still leave a nice buffer for the Greenlaws, too, against possible hard times to come.

"I've seen what can happen," Kate said, her green eyes sad, "when a whole economy fails. That land, that was so rich and amazing . . . all the magic is gone, there's nothing left but the ugliest side of their culture, all is fallen into chaos, the castles crumbled, the crops dead, the people starving. Everyone is drained of their will to live, not even the wealth I brought back was of use to them. What good is gold when there's nothing to buy, no food, nothing to trade for? People wandering the villages scavenging for scraps of food, but with no desire to plant and grow new crops, no ambition to begin new herds or bring any kind of order to their ruined world. All their richly layered culture has collapsed, they are people without hope, without any life left in them. Without," Kate said, "any sense of joy or of challenge. Only the dark has prevailed, and it feeds on their hopelessness."

Now, as night drew down, fog began to gather out over the sea, fingering in toward the cliff as if soon it would swallow the road, too. As they rounded the next curve, Kit could see, far below, the lights of a few cars winding on down the mountain—but when she looked back, headlights were coming toward them fast, truck lights higher and wider than any car, racing down the narrow road. Then a second set of lights flashed past that heavy vehicle, growing huge in their rearview mirror, then the big truck gained on the pickup again, accelerating at downhill speed, the two vehicles moving too fast, coming right at them, their lights blazing in through the back window, blinding her. The truck swerved into the oncoming lane, passing the pickup, its lights illuminating the rocky cliff—then everything happened at once. The truck and pickup both tried to crowd past them in the left-hand lane, forcing them too near the edge. The truck skidded and swung around, forcing the pickup against the cliff, their lights careening up the jagged stone. At the same instant the cliff seemed to explode. Pedric fought the wheel as an avalanche of dirt surged down at them. Kit didn't understand what was happening. Behind them great rocks came leaping down onto the truck and a skyful of flying stones skidded across their windshield. She thought the whole mountain was coming down, boulders bouncing off the pickup, too, and on down toward the sea. Pedric crashed through somehow, leaving the two vehicles behind them. The stones thundering against metal nearly deafened her, a roar that she knew was the last sound she'd ever hear in this life.

And then all was still; only the sound of the last pebbles falling, bouncing across their windshield and across their dented hood.

2

Victor Amson's old gray pickup raced too fast down the steep two-lane, its bare tires squealing around the curves, its headlights glancing off the stony cliff, following the taillights of a big produce truck, drawing close on its tail. The truck driver swerved onto a turnout at the sheer edge of the drop, impatient for him to go on past. As Vic swung into the oncoming lane, he could see the round-faced driver giving him the finger. Prickly bastard. Moving on around him, Vic smiled, grateful that nothing was coming up the hill; though the narrow, winding road didn't bother him. Beside him, his passenger was hunched way over to the center, his eyes squeezed shut with fear. Didn't take much to scare Birely.

Once Vic was free of the truck he sailed right on down the mountain, driving one-handed, his tall, wiry frame jammed in behind the wheel, his lined face catching light from the dash in a cobweb of wrinkles, a thin face, narrow nose, his pale brown eyes too close together. Worn jeans and ragged windbreaker, rough, callused hands. Long brown hair streaked with gray, hanging down, caught on the back of the seat, loosely tied with a leather band. He drove scowling, thinking about those three cops in their patrol cars watching him when he came out of that fence's place.

The damn fuzz might not have been on his case at all but they sure as hell made him cranky, their marked units parked there in front of the Laundromat that the fence used as a front. That had made Birely fidget, too. Birely'd wanted to ditch the truck to get the cops off their trail, steal another car on some backstreet and then hit the freeway, he said they both should have had haircuts, that shaggy hair always set a cop off. Suspicious bastards, he said, and he was right about that.

Having passed the truck, Vic was coming down on a big sedan, shiny black in the wash of his headlights, maybe a small limo, its red taillights winking on and off as it negotiated the winding road, its headlights sweeping along the ragged cliff. When his lights hit it right, he could see a lone couple in the front seat, and what looked like a small dog perched up in the back. On past it, farther down the steep grade, occasional taillights winked, gearing down the steep curves, maybe trucks hauling their loads to one of the small coastal towns that stood like warts down there along the marshy shore. The truck behind gained on him again. Birely went rigid as a fencepost, glancing back, trying not to look down over the steep drop, his faded brown eyes turned away, his bony hands nervously clutching at his worn-out leather jacket that he'd probably picked up at some rescue mission. They had, until they hit the mountain road, been passing the bottle of Old Crow back and forth, but now, when Vic offered the bottle, Birely shook his head, glancing sideways toward the hundred-foot drop and scooting over even tighter against the middle console, his fists tight whenever their old tires let out a squeal. Made Vic wonder why the hell he'd linked up with Birely again after all these years, the guy was a total wuss, always had been. Scared of his own shadow, clumsy, always out of sync with what was going on around him, a real screwup.

Years back, when they were younger and ran together some, any time Vic had something profitable going, Birely managed to screw it up. Every damn time. Make a mess of it, blow the plan, and they'd end up with nothing for their trouble but maybe a night or two in the slammer.

He'd finally dumped Birely, didn't see him for years. Until three months ago, he'd run into him again. That was just after he'd confiscated this current pickup truck from a ranch yard north of Salinas, slapped on different license plates courtesy of a roadside junkyard, bolted on an old rusted camper shell he found dumped back in the woods. As he headed over to the coast, it had started to rain when he ran into Birely outside a 7-Eleven when he stopped for beer. Birely sat huddled on a bench out in front, under the roof that sheltered the gas pumps, sat eating one of them dried-up package sandwiches, and you'd think they were long-lost brothers, the way Birely went on. Bastard was broke, and happy as hell to see him.

Birely said he was headed over to the coast because his sister had died, how he'd read it in the paper. He still had the clipping in his pants pocket, all wrinkled up. Going on about the house she'd left to some stranger instead of to him, when he was her only family, how it ought to be rightfully his. How he meant to confront this woman who'd supposedly inherited Sammie's worldly goods, and how Sammie'd had a stash of money hidden away somewhere, too, way more than just a few hundred bucks, and he wanted to know what had happened to that. Listening to Birely's tale, Vic decided he was glad to see the poor guy after all, decided he'd give his old friend a lift and maybe help him out some. He knew that area pretty well, Molena Point and back up the valley, he'd used to grow a little weed back up in the hills there, break into a few cars now and then, never anything big time, and never did get caught.

Birely'd told him Sammie'd been shot to death, if you could believe it, her body buried right there under her own house. That hurt Birely, but mostly it was the loss of an inheritance, the loss of Sammie's love and confidence, that she'd leave everything to a stranger, that made him mad at the whole damn world. He didn't seem so much mad at the killer as he was mad at Sammie for getting herself killed and for leaving him nothing.

Birely needn't fret that the cops wouldn't find Sammie's killer, they'd already done that, the guy was doing time right now up at Quentin, some local Realtor there in Molena Point killed her, and that was a long story, too.

Well, the house she'd lived in wasn't much, but more than Birely'd ever had or wanted, until now. Sammie's death seemed to change him—he was Sammie's only family, but look how she'd gone and done him, she'd even made a regular will, leaving the big lot with its two small houses to, "Some woman friend of hers,"

Birely'd whined. "I'm her own kin. Why would she do me like that, leave it all to this Emmylou Warren? I met that woman once or twice when I came that way up the coast, stopped to see Sammie, just some dried-up old woman, nothing special about her. Who could be so special, over Sammie's own brother?"

"Maybe Sammie thought you wouldn't want a house," Vic had said, "being a hobo and all. You always said you couldn't stand to live under a roof, to be fenced in, you always said that."

"Maybe. But there's more than the house, there's the damn money, I never said I wouldn't want the money, I just never thought about her dying. Well, the newspaper didn't say nothing about no money, just a will leaving the property. Maybe," he said, frowning, "maybe this Emmylou Warren don't know about that."

"Where'd your sister get money?" Vic had said, watching Birely as alertly as a rattler onto a mouse.

"Old uncle left Sammie a wad. Even after all these years, she still had half of it, she told me that's what she lived on. Except for those times she worked at some job, housecleaning, bagging groceries. She was real tight with money. Told me she still had over half of it hidden away different places, right there in the damned house. Old bills left over from the middle of the last century. She never did like banks. Our old uncle, he stole it but she never would tell me much about that. Well, hell, she was just a girl when the old guy sent it to her, mailed it to her in a box, for Christ's sake, from somewhere in Mexico."

It was such a wild story Vic wondered if Birely'd made it all up, a pie-in-the-sky daydream because he wanted there to be money and maybe because he wanted a reason to be mad at Sammie. That would be like him, mixed up sometimes between what was real and what he thought was real. But hell, whatever was in the poor guy's head, what could it hurt to take pity on him and go have a look.

They'd come on over to the coast, got to Sammie's place, got a glimpse of the old woman who'd inherited the property, living right there in Sammie's house. They'd watched her for a few days, while they lived in the truck, hidden back up in the woods or moving the old pickup around the winding village streets from one small neighborhood to another, sleeping at night in the rusty camper shell and, in the daytime, approaching the old woman's house on foot. They'd watched her for over a week, doing some kind of carpentry on the house during the day but she went to bed early, the lights would go out at eight or nine, and they never once saw her go up the hill through the woods, to the old stone cabin on the back of the property; she seemed to have no interest in the old abandoned two-story farm building that was on Sammie's land, shed underneath, one-room stone shack on top. Birely said Sammie hadn't had much use for it, either, just left it there overgrown with bushes. Said the land was plenty valuable, if she ever needed more money she could sell it but she never had.

Late one night they'd moved into the stone shack when Emmylou was sound asleep, house all dark, and they didn't make a sound, didn't use a flashlight. Vic had picked the old lock, and had jimmied the padlock on the shed, too, hid the truck in there, fixed the lock back so it looked untouched, still hanging rusty against the peeling paint of the old, swinging shed door.

The single stone room had maybe been workers' quarters back in the last century, when there were mostly little scraggy farms up here. At some time, rough planks had been fitted up against the bare stone walls, nailed onto two-by-fours, most likely for warmth. Stained toilet and old metal sink in one corner. Stone floor, cold as hell under their sleeping bags.

It was some days before Birely, lying in his sleeping bag staring at the plank walls, said, "Money could be up here, where no one'd think to look. Maybe Sammie didn't leave Emmylou *all* of it, maybe she left some for me to find, in case I wanted to come looking. Sure as hell she didn't put it in any bank, she got that from Uncle Lee, he *robbed* banks. He told her, never trust your money to a banker. As little as she was, maybe nine or ten when he left for Mexico, I guess she listened." Birely shrugged. "Sammie lived all her life that way, hiding what she earned and hiding what Uncle Lee sent her. Lived alone all her life, stayed to herself just like the old man did, never got cozy with strangers—until this Emmylou person."

There were no cupboards in the stone shed to search, no attic, no place to hide anything except maybe in those double walls. They'd started prying off one slab of wood and then another, putting each back as they worked. Used an old hammer they'd found in the truck, had muffled the sound with rags when they pulled the nails and tapped them back in real quiet, moving on to the next board, and the next. Underneath the boards, some of the stones were loose, too, the mortar crumbling around them—and sure as hell, the fifth stone they'd lifted out, behind it was a package wrapped in yellowed newspaper. Unwrapped it, and there it was: a sour-smelling packet of mildewed hundred-dollar bills. Birely'd let out a whoop that made Vic grab him and slap a hand over his mouth.

"Christ, Birely! You want that old woman up here with her flashlight, you want her calling the cops?" But nothing had happened, when they looked out the dirty little window no lights had come on down at the house below.

"Hell, Vic, there's a fortune here," Birely said, counting out the old, sour-smelling hundred-dollar bills.

Took them several days to examine all the walls. They'd found ten more packets, and made sure they didn't miss any. They came away with nearly nine thousand dollars. But even then, Birely said that originally there'd been maybe two hundred thousand in stolen bills, and he'd looked down meaningfully toward the larger house.

Over the next weeks, whenever they saw the old woman get in her old green Chevy and head off into the village, they'd go down through the woods and search the house, and that tickled Birely, that he still had his key to the place, that Sammie'd given him years back, in case he ever needed a place to hide out from the law or from his traveling buddies.

While they searched her three rooms they took turns watching the weedy driveway so the old woman wouldn't come home and surprise them. Emmylou Warren was her name. Tall, skinny. Sun-browned face and arms wrinkled as an old boot. Long brown hair streaked with gray. She had a couple of cats, maybe more, there were always cats around her overgrown yard and going in and out of the house.

They'd see her drive in, watch her unload lumber that was tied on top the Chevy, all the while, cats rubbing against her ankles. Birely said, "You think that's Sammie's money she's spending for all them building materials? Or," he said, his face creasing in a knowing smile, "or did Sammie only *tell* her about the money, tell her it was hid, and she's looking for it?

"Sammie would do that," he said. "Not put anything in writing to keep from paying inheritance. Sammie didn't like the gover'ment any better than she liked banks.

"*That's* why she's tearing up the walls," Birely said, scowling at the nerve of the woman. "Tearing them up just like we're doing, and it's rightfully my money."

"If she's *found* any," Vic said, "why's she driving that clunky old car? I'd get me a new car, first off. And if she *is* looking for the money, why would she have help coming in, those two carpenters that are here sometimes, and that woman carpenter? She wouldn't have no one else around. That dark-haired woman's a looker, I wouldn't mind getting to know her better." Slim woman, short, roughed-up hair. Fit her faded jeans real nice. He'd heard the old woman call her Ryan, she drove a big red king cab, her own logo on the side, Ryan Flannery Construction. Pretty damn fancy. Well, hell, Vic thought, she was likely too snooty to give him a second look.

He did meet a little gal down in the next block, though, and she wasn't too good for him. Debbie Kraft, flirty little gal with two small children, both girls, light-fingered woman not too good to steal, neither, he soon found out.

They burned no lights in the stone house at night, and didn't cook none, or warm up their food. Just opened a can of cold beans, kept a loaf of bread handy and maybe doughnuts. He missed hot coffee. Even in the hobo camps they boiled coffee. And they didn't drive the truck, just left it hidden in the shed below and hoped she'd stay away from there. If they needed beer and food they'd walk up the hill through the woods and then down the next street to the village. Carried out their trash, too, dropped it in a village Dumpster, in one alley or another, always behind a different restaurant. Fancy place like Molena Point, even the Dumpsters were kept all neat and covered.

They'd kept on slipping down to the house whenever Emmylou went out, searching where she was starting a tear-out, fishing back between the studs, but then one night she came up the hill snooping around the stone house. They were inside sitting on their sleeping bags eating cold beans and crackers, they heard her come up the steps, saw her through the smeared window, and they eased down out of sight. They were sure she'd have a key, but she didn't come in. They'd stayed real still until they heard her leave again, her shoes scuffing on the steps, heard her rustling away down through the bushes, heard her door open and shut.

They'd waited a while after her lights went out, feeling real nervous. They'd opened the shed door real quiet, shoved some food and their sleeping bags in the pickup, with what money they'd found, hoping she wouldn't hear the pickup start. Had eased up the dirt lane and around through the woods, and moved on away from there. Had parked for the night way up at the edge of the village beside an overgrown canyon. Had waited until dawn, then had made a run back down near Emmylou's place, where Vic tended to a deal he'd made with Debbie Kraft. Had picked up some goods he'd told her he'd sell for her up in the city and some fancy, stolen clothes. A nice stroke of luck, when he'd seen Debbie and her older child shoplifting, and had got the goods on them. A nice little deal he'd set up with her: he'd make the sale and take his share, and not turn her in to the cops. He'd met with Debbie, picked up the goods, and then headed for the city. Let Emmylou think they were gone for good—if she ever *was* onto them living right there above her.

They were gone a week up the coast, boosting food from a mom-and-pop grocery or a 7-Eleven, and they'd gone on into San Francisco, where he'd made the business transaction. That turned out pretty good, except for the damn cops sitting out in front, there. Well, hell, the goons hadn't followed them, maybe it was just coincidence, maybe they were watching someone else.

He'd made a bit of cash off that, and who knew what other arrangements he might make with Debbie. Now, headed back down the coast to the stone shack, he hoped the old woman had settled down and they could finish looking for the money. Vic was daydreaming about what he'd do with that kind of cash, when the produce truck he'd passed came roaring down right on their tail, its lights so bright in his mirror he couldn't see the road ahead. Swearing, he eased over to let it pass. Truck hauled right down on them, riding their bumper. Let the bastard tailgate that big sedan up ahead, it was moving too damn slow anyway. That was what was holding him up, some rich-ass driver in that big Lincoln Town Car—one more curve, he was right on top of the Town Car, and the damn truck was climbing his tail. Swearing, he pulled over, pushing the big sedan closer to the edge. "Go on, you bastard!" Why the hell didn't the guy driving the Lincoln step on the gas, get on down the grade? Vic drew as close to the edge as he could to let the truck pass, tailgating the Town Car, then pulled toward the left lane. But the truck shot past him, rocking his truck, kicking up gravel, shaking the road with a hell of a rumble, and its headlights made the cliff look like it was moving— well, hell, the cliff *was* moving, rocks falling, bouncing across the road. He stood on his brakes but couldn't stop. The whole mountain was sliding down. The Town Car shot past, rocks thundering down across its tail. A whole piece of the mountain was falling. The big truck skidded, Vic smashed into its side and into the cliff. The front end of his pickup crumpled like paper, squashed against the bigger bumper. The passenger door bent in against Birely like you'd bend a beer can, Birely struggling and twisting between the bent door and the crumpled dashboard. Pebbles and rocks rained down around them. The produce truck lay turned over right in his face, one headlight striking off at an angle, catching the rising dust, its other light picking out the black Town Car on the far side of the rockfall, where it had plowed into the cliff. That

light shone into the interior where the driver and passenger were slumped, and picked out through the back
window the eerie green glow of a pair of eyes, he could
see the animal's tail lashing, too, and realized it wasn't
a dog, but a cat. Who would travel with a *cat*! A damn
cat, its eyes reflecting the lights of the wrecked truck
where it peered out, watching him.

3

Vic couldn't open the truck door, it was bent and jammed. The passenger side was pushed in, trapping Birely against the dash. Birely lay moaning, his face and neck covered with blood, reaching out blindly for help. The big delivery truck lay on its side among the fallen boulders, Vic's pickup crumpled in against the roof of the truck's cab, its right front fender jammed deep against its own wheel. Well, hell, the damn thing was totaled, was no use to him now.

But when he looked off across the rockfall at the Lincoln, it didn't look too bad. Looked like it had missed most of the slide, rocks and rubble thrown against it and scattered across the hood, but he could see no big dents in the fenders to jam the wheels, and the hood and front end weren't pushed in as if to damage the engine. The couple inside hadn't moved.

Reaching under the seat for the tire iron, he used that to break out what remained of his shattered window. Knocking the glass away, he crawled out and swung to the ground. Stepping up onto the unsteady heap of rocks, trying not to start the whole damned mountain sliding again, he worked his way around to the other side of the pickup, to have a look.

Birely didn't look good, sprawled limp and bleeding across the dash. Poor Birely. So close to finding the rest of his sister's money, and now look at him. What kind of luck was that? Vic thought, smiling.

Vic's one working headlight shot into the big truck's cab, casting a grisly path onto the driver. He lay twisted over the wheel, his head and shoulders half out the broken window, his throat torn open by a spear of metal from the dashboard, his blood coursing down pooling into the window frame. Dark-haired guy, Hispanic maybe. No way he could be alive with his throat slit. Vic turned his attention again beyond the fall of rocks, to the black sedan nosed in against the cliff. As the door of the Town Car opened, he stepped back behind the turned-over truck, out of sight.

The driver's forehead was bleeding. Vic watched him ease out of the car, supporting himself against the open door. The minute his feet touched the ground his right leg gave way. He fell, pulled himself up, stood a moment, his weight on his left leg, then tried again, wincing. Tall old man, thin. White hair. Frail looking. Easing out of the car on his left leg, clinging to the door and then to the car itself, he moved painfully around to the back of the car, making his way on around to the far side, to the woman. He stood beside her, reaching in, clinging to the roof of the car. She was as thin as the man, what Vic could see of her. She sat clutching the cat to her, mumbling something. The man reached past her into the glove compartment, found a flashlight and held it up, looking at her, and then looking at the cat, studying it all over, giving it more attention than he gave to the woman; but he was talking to the woman, mumbling something Vic couldn't hear over the crashing of the sea below. The man spoke to the cat, too, spoke right to it, the way someone'd speak to a pet dog. People made asses of themselves over their dogs. But a cat, for Christ's sake? He watched the old man flip open a cell phone. Speaking louder, now, the way people did into a phone, as if they had to throw their voices clear across the damn county. He was talking to a dispatcher, giving directions to the wreck. Hell, here he was, the truck no use to him, smashed too bad to get him out of there, and the damn cops on the way.

The old guy had turned, looking across the rock slide toward him, but Vic didn't think he could see him, there behind the truck. Guy told the dispatcher, "Nothing stirring over there. I'll have a look, see what I can do. Yes, I'll stay on the line."

He spoke to the woman again, dropped the phone in his pocket, and started limping across the rock slide. He turned back once, to the woman, his voice raised against the pounding of the surf. "You sure you're okay?" She nodded, then mumbled something as he moved on away. The old guy negotiated the rock pile half crawling, his white hair and tan sport coat caught brightly by the truck's one headlight. But Vic's attention was on the Town Car, on the big, heavy Lincoln. A car like that could take a lot of abuse. Even with deep dents and dings from the slide, it looked like it would move right on out and with plenty of power to spare.

Easing back around to the pickup, where the old guy crossing the rocks couldn't see him, Vic pulled the plastic bag of money out from under the seat and stuffed it inside his shirt. He didn't speak to his passenger; Birely was pretty much out of it, close to unconscious, gasping as if he wouldn't last too long. Vic watched the old man approach, balancing precariously, the pain showing in the twist of his long face. He moved on past Vic, never seeing him, and as he scrambled and slid down the unsteady boulders, Vic eased closer in behind the camper, hefting the weight of the tire iron. The old guy paused at the turned-over delivery truck, stood looking in at the dead driver. Shook his head and moved on, to the pickup. He still didn't see Vic until Vic stepped out into the truck's headlight, holding the tire iron low against his leg. The old man looked him over, took in the tire iron, and glanced into the cab of the pickup. "Your friend needs help."

"Best let him be," Vic said, "best not move him."

The old man nodded, watching him. "My wife's hurt. I called 911, ambulance is on its way. They'll both have help. I've got to get back to her, I think her arm is broken. You have any flares? I have two, I can set them down the road, at that end."

Vic didn't say anything. He nodded and stepped closer. The man was lean and, despite his look of frailty, Vic could see now that he was wiry, tightly muscled. He wore his white hair short, in a military cut, ice pale against his tan. The old guy was quick, he saw Vic's intention—the instant Vic swung the tire iron he lunged, grabbing for it despite the hurt leg.

But his timing was off, Vic stepped aside, hit him a glancing blow across the head. When he tried to break his fall, clutching at loose rocks, Vic kicked him hard. He went flat, didn't move again, lay bleeding onto the blacktop. Stepping around him, Vic saw Birely looking out at him, helpless and pleading.

He'd thought to leave Birely, the guy was already half dead, but some stupid softness touched him, he couldn't leave the dumb bastard. "Hoist yourself out of there, Birely." He didn't wait to see if Birely *could* get out, he headed on past the old man, who was bleeding bad now, past the turned-over truck and across the rockfall toward the Lincoln. He heard Birely struggling behind him, groaning as he tried to free himself. Hell, he wasn't jammed in there that tight, he could get out if he tried.

Approaching the driver's side of the Lincoln, Vic saw that the bumper was knocked loose on one end. It wasn't low enough yet to drag and make a racket, he'd find something to tie it in place. He didn't see much else wrong, he just hoped to hell the other side wasn't bashed in or that the other wheel wasn't bent. The passenger door hung open, the interior lights on. The woman sat holding her left arm, the damn cat still in her lap. He could see the keys in the ignition. He stood by the hood, watching her, holding the tire iron low and out of sight.

Kit watched him approach, the thud of his steps timed to the rhythm of the breaking waves. He paused by the hood of the car, and frantically she nudged Lucinda, her nose against Lucinda's ear. "Get out," she whispered, "get away. Now, Lucinda! Move!"

Slowly Lucinda climbed out, unsteady on her feet, shaking her head as if to clear it, cradling her hurt arm.

"Hurry," Kit hissed.

"I can't, I can't move faster."

The man stood watching. *Can he hear me?* Kit thought. *So screw him.* "You can!" she hissed, her fur bristling. *"Run, Lucinda. Run!"* her voice more hiss than whisper.

He stepped to the car, blocking Lucinda. Lucinda grabbed Kit with her good hand, catching her breath with the pain. She twisted awkwardly, threw Kit as far as she could, out toward the rock slide. "Run, Kit! Run!" Kit landed on rubble, spun around and leaped atop the car. Lucinda had turned, reaching in. She backed out holding the big flashlight where he might not see it. When he grabbed for her, she swung.

But again he was faster, he snatched her hand, jerked the flashlight from her, shoved her down against the fallen rocks. Kit leaped on him, landed in his face clawing and raking him. Lucinda rose awkwardly, turned, kicked him in the shin then in the front of the knee. He swung the tire iron hard across her shoulder, shoved her down again as Kit rode his back, clawing. He grabbed her by the scruff of her neck, swinging her out away from him. When she bit down hard on his arm, he threw her against the car. She tried to run, but staggered dizzily. Sick and confused, she backed away among the fallen rocks. He was a hard-muscled man, his arms brown and knotted and tasted unwashed. Long hair hanging down his back, dishwater brown, a short scraggly beard oozing blood where her claws had raked. Ice-blue eyes, cold and pale. He had moved around the Lincoln to the driver's side when, across the slide, she heard a car door open.

The passenger in the pickup staggered out. A small man with short brown hair, his face and plaid shirt slick with blood, his nose running blood. He came slowly across the rock pile, stumbling uncertainly, breathing through his mouth, wiping at the blood that ran from his nose. The man with the tire iron got in the Lincoln. "Get a move on, Birely." He started the engine, gunned it, paying no attention to Lucinda sprawled so near the front wheels. His friend stumbled on across, falling on loose rocks, clutching at the larger boulders, stepping over Lucinda as if she were another rock. Edging around the Lincoln, he crawled awkwardly into the passenger seat. The driver pushed the engine to a roar. Kit ran to Lucinda, Lucinda grabbed her and rolled away as he backed around narrowly missing them. He took off in a shower of rocks, heading fast down the mountain on the twisting two-lane.

Alone among the wreck with only a dead man to keep them company, Kit and Lucinda huddled together trembling with rage. Against the rhythm of the waves came the metallic ticks of the two wrecked trucks, settling more solidly into the highway. From higher up the mountain among the pine forest, a lone coyote began to yip.

"Cops will be here soon," Kit said, "and an ambulance."

"I'm fine," Lucinda told her. "Go to Pedric. Go and see to Pedric." Her color was gray. She held her left shoulder unnaturally, and her left arm hung limp. Kit pressed a soft paw against Lucinda's wrinkled cheek, pressed her face to Lucinda's jugular, listening. Lucinda's heartbeat was too rapid, faster even than Kit's own feline rhythm. She pawed into her housemate's jacket pocket, careful not to touch Lucinda's arm or shoulder, searching for Lucinda's phone. It seemed forever ago that Pedric had called 911, but she couldn't hear even the faintest sound of sirens down on the flatland, could see no flashing emergency lights below approaching up the two-lane, no one to help them. The shushing of the sea, with its eons-old assurance that all was well, that all of importance in the world would last forever, didn't comfort her much. She thought about a car coming down the mountain from above moving too fast as those trucks had done, the driver ignorant of the wreck ahead, not yet seeing the lone and disembodied headlight shooting up the rock slide. How far could such a light *be* seen, on that curving road? With no flares to mark the wreck, would an approaching car stop to help or would it crash into them? She found the phone, and before she raced to Pedric, she hit the key for 911.

She had no notion where central dispatch was located for these small coastal towns north of Molena Point, and she didn't know if they could track a cell phone. Some areas could, and some didn't have that equipment. When a woman dispatcher came on, Kit gave directions as best she could. She said Pedric had called earlier but that no one had come. She was so afraid of another car plowing into them that she was nearly yowling into the phone, her frightened words not much better than the scream of a common alley cat. "Hurry! Oh, *please hurry* . . . They've stolen our car, a black Lincoln Town Car, could you watch for it? Put out a BOL on it? Two men in it, one hurt bad." She described the men as best she could, all the while thinking about the treasure hidden in the doors of the Lincoln, wondering how soon the thieves would find that. The wealth was of no consequence, compared to her hurt housemates, but it enraged her to see it stolen. Clicking off, she stood looking down the highway wondering if, alone, she could drag Lucinda off the road and up among the boulders, safe from an oncoming car? Drag Pedric up, too, get them both higher up, away from further danger? When the dispatcher asked for her name, she said, "Lucinda Greenlaw. My husband's hurt, the man who took our car beat him." When the dispatcher told her to stay on the line, Kit laid the phone down, set her teeth firmly in Lucinda's jacket on her unhurt side, and began to pull. She *could* do this, she *had* to do this. Maybe the loose rocks beneath Lucinda would serve as a kind of rolling platform. Straining to get Lucinda up onto them, she fought as she had never fought, every muscle of her small cat body taut and stretched, crying out, her paws scrabbling for traction until her pads tore and became slick with blood that made her slip and slide. Lucinda tried to help, tried to roll with her, tried twice to get up but fell back, sweating with pain.

"Go to Pedric, Kit. You can't move me. Let me rest, then we'll try again. Maybe easier, once I've rested. Go help Pedric. Is he bleeding? Can you stop the blood?"

Kit licked Lucinda's face, her own face wet with tears, then headed fast across the rock slide, praying for the gift of strength, knowing that if she couldn't move Lucinda, she couldn't move Pedric, either, only knowing that she had to try, that she had to help them.

4

If ever Kit cursed her small size it was now as she raced across the slide to Pedric. Diving under the twisted delivery truck, its metal cab tilting over her, loose rocks shifting under her blood-slippery paws, she heard the coyote yodel again, high above her, and then go ominously still. Pedric lay in a pool of blood beside the crumpled pickup, his forehead running blood. Hesitantly she pressed her paw against the gash where it flowed hardest, telling herself that head wounds always bled a lot. Soon she was pressing with both paws, with all her weight, but still the blood pooled warm beneath her pads, mixed with her own blood. She tried not to think of the billions of cat germs she was sharing with Pedric, that might harm him, and about the gravel her paws had collected, that would become embedded now in his open wounds. He was conscious, but only barely, whispering vague little love words to her. The only other sounds in the empty night were the tick, tick of the settling vehicles, the voice of the waves far below, and the dripping of some liquid nearby that she prayed wasn't gasoline. Well, she didn't smell gas, so maybe it was oil or water.

Her paws grew numb with the pressure, but soon the bleeding did ease, and when the coyote yipped again she wondered if he smelled Pedric's blood on the rising sea wind. Pedric said, "Don't let me sleep, Kit, keep me awake. I need to stay awake." He talked vaguely about a concussion, then rambled on from one subject to another that had no connection to what was happening at that moment. When he went silent she nudged him and made him talk again. Once, as she shifted her weight over him, he startled and tried to rise, looking around fearfully as if expecting another blow from the tire iron.

"He's gone, those men are gone. Lie still."

"Lucinda? Where's Lucinda?" he said, pushing her aside, straining to get up.

"She's fine," Kit lied, trying to press him down. "She's only hurt a little, she . . ." She went still, listening, her heart quickening. She could hear, far down the mountain, the faintest echo of sirens whooping, she heard that thin ululation long before Pedric did. "They're coming," she said, "the cops, an ambulance." Rearing up, she could see lights flashing far down the mountain, red and blue lights disappearing around the curves and appearing again, accompanied by the approaching *whoop whoop* and scream of emergency vehicles that put the coyote's cries to shame. Now Pedric heard them, and he lay back, dragging her onto his chest, hugging and loving her.

But soon again he rose on one elbow looking past the turned-over truck, searching for the reflection of the Lincoln's lights that had been angled up the cliff, lights that would mark the wreck on the other side, for the approaching cars to see. "Lucinda," he said, struggling up. "They won't see her. I left the lights on . . . Did she shut them off?" He rose further, looking. "Where . . . ? Kit, where's the Lincoln?"

She looked at him, puzzled. Hadn't he seen and heard the Lincoln drive away? "It's gone," she said softly. "They took our car, those men took it."

He struggled up, the blood gushed harder again. *"Lucinda. Where's Lucinda?"*

"She got out before they took the car, she's fine." She nuzzled him, but as the sirens drew near she spun and raced away again, under the cab of the big truck and across the rockfall. Surely they'd see Lucinda lying there. How could they help but see her? The sirens blared, approaching up the steep highway, soon their lights would blaze along the side of the cliff. But Lucinda seemed so small, lying there unprotected and alone. *In just a second they'll be here, the world will be filled with their bright, swinging lights, they'll see her, there'll be uniforms all over the place, they'll see Lucinda and help her and comfort her. They'll help Lucinda and Pedric, cops or sheriff's deputies or whoever come, they'll have spotlights, they—*

Oh, she thought, *but what will they do with me?*

Or try to do, if they could catch me?

They sure wouldn't take her in the ambulance, that was probably against the rules, to contaminate their germ-free rolling hospital with kitty fur and dander. Maybe they'd try to lock her in a squad car, drop her off at the nearest animal rescue to be kept "safe" in a locked cage until someone claimed her, like a piece of baggage lost at some lonely airport.

And, if no one claimed her soon enough, if no one thought to look for her there, what, then, would they do with her?

No way! No one's taking me to the pound.

She found Lucinda several feet higher up the rockfall than she'd left her, lying huddled into herself, the phone abandoned beside her, her face white with the

effort it had taken to climb just that far. She licked
Lucinda's cheek and nosed at her worriedly. She
prayed to the human God or the great cat god or whoever might be listening, prayed for Lucinda, and then
the cops were there, the flash of colored lights, the last
whoop of the sirens, the powerful shafts of spotlights
sweeping back and forth. Patrol cars skidded to a stop,
cops spilled out, the flashing strobe lights blinded her,
strafing the highway and the fallen rocks, picking out
Lucinda and the two wrecked trucks. Lucinda clutched
at her, attempting to hold her safe. Kit ducked beneath
Lucinda's jacket, trying to decide what to do.

The thought of strangers' hands on her, even the
kindest of cops, the thought of barred cages that she
might not be able to open, of being locked in some
shelter all alone, the thought of possible clerical mistakes where she'd be put up for adoption before
anyone could come to fetch her, or consigned to a far
worse fate, was all too much. Cops knew how to care
for needful humans, but that might not extend to a
terrified cat. Snatching up Lucinda's phone between
her gripping teeth, she scrambled out from under the
jacket and ran.

"Oh, Kit, don't . . ."

She didn't look back, she fled straight up the cliff,
dodging between rivers of sweeping light, gripping the

heavy phone; it nearly overbalanced her as she scrambled up the sheer wall of stone. Only tiny outcroppings offered a claw hold until, higher up, an occasional weed or stunted bush kept her from falling. The phone grew heavier still, forcing her head away from the cliff. Twice she nearly fell. Scrambling in panic, she veered over into the rock slide where she had more paw hold, though the rocks were wobbly and unsteady. Moving up over the loose stones and boulders, she was afraid the whole thing would shift and go tumbling again, hitting her and raining down on Lucinda, who lay now far below her. Higher and higher she climbed, dodging away whenever a slab shifted, breathing raggedly around the phone through her open mouth, her heart pounding so hard that at last she had to stop.

High up on the lip of the slide, she laid the phone down on a stone outcropping. Below her, portable spotlights blazed down on Lucinda and two medics in dark uniforms knelt over her. Two more medics, one carrying a stretcher, the other carrying a dark bag that would be filled with life-saving medical equipment, were headed across the slide to Pedric. Young men, strong and efficient looking. The very sight of them eased her pounding heart.

Where will they take them? What hospital? I have to tell Ryan and Clyde, but what do I tell them?

A hospital somewhere in Santa Cruz, that's where we were headed. They'll know the hospitals, they'll call CHP to find out, Ryan and Clyde will know where to come, and they'll come to get me, too, she thought, comforting herself. *But how soon? Soon enough, before those coyotes up there find me, soon enough to save my little cat neck?*

Maybe she should go back down, slip into the medics' van while they were busy, and the cops were all working the crash scene. She watched another set of headlights coming down the mountain on the other side of the slide, watched a lone sheriff's car park beyond the wrecked truck. A lone officer got out and started across to join the others. The back doors of the white van stood open. In a flash she could be down the cliff and inside, hiding among the metal cabinets and oxygen tanks and all that tangle of medical equipment. *I could hide in there close to Lucinda and Pedric and, at the hospital—a strange hospital, a strange town—I could hide in the bushes outside and watch the door and wait for Ryan and Clyde or maybe for Charlie to come, and then . . .*

Oh, right. And if those medics spot me in their van trying to catch a ride, they'll try to corner me in that tight space. If they shut the doors, and surround me, and I can't get out and one of them grabs me, what then? They'll lock me up somewhere, to keep me safe? One of the cops will shut me in his squad car? No, she was too upset and uncertain to go back. Taking the phone in her mouth again, she moved from the top of the slide on up into the bushes that stretched away to the edge of the dense pine woods, damp and dark and chill. There she laid the phone down among dead leaves and pine needles and pawed in the single digit for the Damens' house phone. Crouched there listening to it ring, she watched the lighted road below as the medics slid Pedric into their van, working over him, attaching him to an oxygen tank. Lucinda sat on a gurney as the other two medics splinted and taped her shoulder and arm. The phone rang seven times, eight. On the twelfth ring, she hung up. Why didn't the tape kick in? The Damens' answering machine, which stood upstairs on Clyde's desk, was so incredibly ancient it still used tape, but Clyde wouldn't get a new one, he said it worked just fine, you simply had to understand its temperament. *Right,* Kit thought, with a little hiss.

She tried Wilma Getz, but she got only the machine. Where was everyone? She left a garbled message, she said there'd been an accident, that she had Lucinda's cell phone, that it was on vibrate so the cops wouldn't hear it ring. She hung up, disappointed by the failure of the electronic world to help her, and worrying about Lucinda and Pedric. What might happen to them on their way to the hospital, some delayed reaction that would be even beyond the medics' control? Or what might happen *in* the hospital? If ever a cat's prayers should be heard, if ever a strong hand were to reach down in intervention for a little cat's loved ones, that hand should come reaching now. This was *not* Lucinda's or Pedric's time to move on to some other life, she wouldn't let it be that time. Punching in the Damens' number again, she was crouched with her ear to the phone when she realized that, down on the road, Lucinda had awakened and was arguing with the medics, her voice raised in anger. Kit broke off the call, and listened.

"You can't leave her, you must find her. If I call her, she'll come to me. I won't go with you, neither of us will, unless you bring her with us."

The two medics just looked at her, more puzzled than reluctant. The taller one said, "You can't find a runaway cat, in the dark of night, it'll be scared to death, panicked. No cat would—"

The dark-haired medic said, "We'll send someone, the local shelter . . ."

"No," Lucinda said fiercely. "I want her with us. You can't take us by force unless you want a lawsuit."

Oh, don't, Kit thought, *don't argue. Let them take care of you.* But then she realized that Lucinda, in her anger, sounded so much stronger that Kit had to smile.

But stronger or not, Lucinda didn't prevail. Kit didn't know what the medic said to her, speaking so quietly, but soon she went silent and lay back again on the gurney, as if she had given up, yet Kit knew she wouldn't do that. *She knows I'll call Clyde and Ryan,* Kit thought. *She knows I can take care of myself.* She watched them wheel Lucinda to the van, her tall, thin housemate straining up against the safety straps, trying to look up the cliff. Lucinda was so upset that Kit thought to race back down and into the van after all, but before she could try, before she knew what *was* best to do, they had shut the doors, two medics inside with Pedric and Lucinda, and the other two in the cab. The engine started, the van turned around slowly on the narrow and perilous road, and moved away down the mountain, heading for a strange hospital where no one knew Lucinda and Pedric, where there was no one to speak for them.

Two black-and-whites followed them. The other two sheriff's deputies remained behind, one car parked on either side of the rockfall. Kit watched them walk the road in both directions, setting out flares, and maybe waiting to meet the wrecking crew that would haul

away the truck and pickup, maybe to wait for the tractors and heavy equipment that would arrive to clear
away the tons of fallen rock from the highway.

*When those earthmovers start to work, when they
start grabbing up boulders with those great, reaching pincers—like the claws of space monsters in some
old movie—I'm out of here.* Again she punched in the
Damens' number. *Come on, Clyde, come on, Ryan,
will you please, please answer!* Crouched in the night
alone, she looked behind her where the forest of pines
stood tar-black against the stars. The coyotes were at
it again, two of them away among the trees yipping
to each other. *When the machines come to move the
wrecked trucks and clear the road, I'll have to go higher
up in the woods away from the sliding earth, I'll have
to go in among the trees, where those night runners
are hunting.* She looked up at the pines towering black
and tall above her, and she didn't relish climbing those
mothers. The great round cylinders of their trunks had
no low branches for a cat to grab onto, only that loose,
slithery bark that would break off under her claws.
And what if she did climb to escape a coyote, only to be
picked off by something in the sky, by a great horned
owl or swooping barn owl? This was their territory and
this was their hour to hunt. She thought of great horned
owls pulling squirrels from their nests, snatching out

baby birds with those scissor-sharp beaks. The world, tonight, seemed perilous on every side.

She called the Damens seven more times before Clyde answered. "We just got in. I guess the tape ran out."

A temperamental machine was one thing. A run-out tape was quite another. Now, on the phone, Kit didn't say her name, none of the cats ever committed their name to an electronic device. They might use man-made machines, but they weren't fool enough to trust them. Anyway, Clyde knew her voice. She pictured him in his study, his short brown hair tousled, wearing something old and comfortable, a frayed T-shirt and jeans, worn-out jogging shoes. She started out coherent enough, "Lucinda and Pedric are hurt," but suddenly she was mewling into the phone, a high, shrill cry this time, in spite of herself, a terrible, distressed yowl that she couldn't seem to stop.

"I'll get Ryan," he said with a note of panic. She heard him call out, and then Ryan came on, maybe on her studio extension. Kit imagined them upstairs in the master suite, Rock and the white cat perhaps disturbed from a nap on the love seat.

"What?" Ryan said. "Tell me slowly. What happened? Where are they? Where are you? *Slowly, please!*"

Swallowing, Kit found her sensible voice. She tried to go slowly, to explain carefully about the wreck and to explain where that was. But try as she might, it all came out in a tangle, the kind of rush that made her human friends shout, made Joe and Dulcie lay back their ears and lash their tails until she slowed, but she never *could* slow down. ". . . boulders coming down the mountain straight at us and I thought we'd be buried but Pedric hit the gas pedal and the Lincoln shot through and the whole mountain came thundering down behind us and when the slide stopped the road was covered with boulders and rocks and there was a pickup on the other side crashed into the mountain and into a big delivery truck lying on its side and the driver was dead and . . ."

"*Slow down,*" Clyde and Ryan shouted together. Ryan said, "Tell us exactly where you are. Did you call 911? How badly are they hurt? *Did* you call the CHP? Where . . . ?"

"I called," Kit said. "They took Lucinda and Pedric away and Pedric's head was bleeding and Lucinda was conscious sometimes but then she'd fade and I think her shoulder is broken and the medics took them in the ambulance and I was afraid to hide in there because if they found me they'd take me to the pound and take the phone away and I could never call you to say where I was and if I couldn't work the lock on the cage . . ."

"Stop!" they both yelled. "Where?" Ryan said patiently. "Where are you, Kit?"

"Somewhere north of Santa Cruz but south of Mindy's Seafood where we had dinner. When the tractor gets here and starts moving the boulders . . ." She wanted to say, I won't be able to yowl and cry out to you, there are coyotes up here and owls who can hear everything. She wanted to say, When I'm up in the woods I'll be scared to make a sound. She said, "Can you bring Rock? To track me? Joe can find me, but Rock's bigger and . . . and there are coyotes and I love you both but humans are no good at scenting . . ." And she prayed that, this one time, no one was listening in on her call.

"We'll bring Rock," Clyde said. "We're leaving now. Be there in an hour or less, with luck. Please, my dear, keep safe."

Kit hit the end button, feeling small and helpless. She wasn't a skittish cat, she'd spent plenty of black nights prowling the dark hills above Molena Point and farther away than that, hunting and slaughtering her own hapless prey, but tonight the wreck and her fear for her injured housemates, and then the hungry cry of the coyotes, had taken the starch right out of her. She thought about her big red tomcat traveling all alone down this very coast, making his way from Oregon down into central California, *Pan traveled all that way and he wasn't scared, so why should I be?* But she was. Tonight she was afraid.

Pan had come to Molena Point following little Tessa Kraft, nearly a year after Tessa's father threw the red tomcat out of the house. Tessa's mother didn't want him, either, she didn't like cats. Pan hadn't returned, but he had watched the household. He knew when Debbie Kraft moved to Molena Point, and he followed the family, tracking his little girl and, as well, looking for his own father.

He could only guess that Misto, when he vanished from Eugene in his old age, might have returned to the shore of his kittenhood where he'd grown up among a feral band of ordinary cats; no other speaking cat among them, that Pan knew of, but the place was Misto's kittenhood home. And Pan had been right, he had found the old yellow tomcat there, and he had found Tessa. *And he found me,* Kit thought. *That's where we found each other.*

Where is Pan now, right this minute? Could he be thinking of me and know I'm scared, the way he senses me when we're hunting, the way he knows where I am even when he can't see me? Or is he crouched in Tessa's dark bedroom, as he so often is, whispering to her, ready to vanish if her mother comes in?

Pan isn't scared of Debbie, but if she catches him there'll be trouble for Tessa. Probably right now he's whispering away and laughing to himself because Debbie doesn't have a clue that he's anywhere near Molena Point. But no matter how Kit tried to distract herself, thinking of Pan, all she could really think about was that she was all alone and scared clear down to her poor, bloodied paws.

5

In the little wooded neighborhood below Emmylou Warren's house, the red tomcat was indeed crouched on Tessa's windowsill looking into the dark bedroom where she and her big sister slept head to foot in the one twin bed. The other bed was unoccupied. A light shone under the closed bedroom door, from the kitchen. When, approaching Debbie's ragged cottage, he'd looked in through the kitchen window, Debbie sat at the table sipping a cup of coffee, the dark-haired, sullen-faced young woman sorting through a stack of new purses and sweaters with the tags still dangling from them, items that he knew she hadn't paid for, beautiful clothes and gaudy ones laid out across the oilcloth as she clipped the tags from them.

At the bedroom window he reached a silent paw in, through a hole he'd made in the screen months before. Silently he flipped the latch and pulled the dusty screen open. Sliding in under it, he pushed the window casing up with infinite care and finesse so as not to make even the smallest sound and wake twelve-year-old Vinnie. Tattletale Vinnie, who would let her mother know at once that he had followed and found them.

Not even Tessa herself knew that he had arrived in Molena Point against all odds, like a cat in some newspaper story traveling across the country to follow his family. Pausing on the sill, at the head of the bed, he watched the two sleeping girls, listening for sounds from the kitchen. When he was sure that both children slept soundly, and that Debbie remained occupied sorting through her stolen bounty, he eased down onto Tessa's pillow, the tip of his red striped tail barely twitching.

He sat quietly watching her, the flicker of her dark lashes against her smooth cheeks, her pale hair tousled across the pillow. And softly, as she dreamed, he pressed his nose close to her small ear and began to whisper, to send gentle but bold words into the child's dreams, painting strong visions for her.

Tessa was only five, hardly more than a baby, and a silent one, at that, a timid little girl who seemed always fearful, never eager for life, a drawn-away, wary child.

Perhaps only Pan knew how watchful she was beneath the shyness, how aware of what occurred around her. Few grown-ups ever saw Tessa smile or saw her reach out to embrace the bright details of life that so fill a normal child's world, few ever saw her pluck a flower from the garden, snatch a cookie from the plate and run, laughing, or tumble eagerly across a playground screaming and shouting. Tessa Kraft clung to the shadows, bowing her head at her mother's voice, backing away from the overbearing tirades of her sister. Her father wasn't there to stand by her, not that it had ever occurred to him, even when he was home, that Tessa might have feelings that he should nurture, fears that he might have soothed and healed. Tessa's mother didn't bother to explain about her pa going to prison, or to help with her daughter's loss. Eric Kraft's final absence from their home, which had begun long before his arrest and sentence for murder, had left a deep hollowness within the child that, Pan thought, nothing in her future could ever erase. But he meant to try.

Since Tessa and her family had arrived in the village, and then Pan had followed them there, the other four speaking cats had come to know the child, too, and to care about her, as had their human friends. Maybe only they saw Tessa's hidden joy in life, saw the secret pleasures that she so carefully concealed from the dominance of her mother and sister. They watched and waited. They stood by Tessa when they could, hindered by a tangle of legalities specific to the human world, rules that no cat would pay attention to.

But Pan, with his own goal clearly in mind, sought to lead Tessa with his whispered suggestions, to slowly strengthen and transform the silent little Cinderella into a bold young princess. "Don't let their talk hurt you," he told her over and over as she slept. "Inside yourself, you can laugh at them. You are stronger than they are, that's your secret. You are your own strong person, and you never need to be afraid.

"You can be quiet and secret in your thoughts, but all the while you can see the world clearly. You can be wary of others but strong in yourself, and you will grow up stronger than they are. One day, you will pity their stubborn ignorance.

"You're little now, Tessa. But you grow bigger every day and already, on the inside, you're bigger than they are. You're stronger than they are, you have a wall of strength inside you that no one's meanness can hurt. Your mother and sister can't hurt you, they can't touch the part of you that's whole and bright and that loves the world around you."

As Pan whispered, reaching deep into Tessa's sleeping mind, he thought about his pa, too, and about that other little girl so long ago. That child far back in time who had also needed a special friend, the little girl Misto remembered from an earlier life among his nine cat lives.

How strange, Pan thought, the mirroring of father's and son's connections with the two little girls from two different times. Tessa here in this time. Misto's friend, Sammie, from sixty years past and from the other side of the continent.

How strange that Sammie, now dead, lay buried right here in this village, a continent away from where Misto had known her. Sammie Miller, found shot to death right there beneath her own house, that she had willed to Emmylou Warren. What a strange tale it was and a convoluted one, a saga of three generations, Sammie's part of it ending here, in this village.

It had been young Sammie Miller's photograph that had stirred Misto's memory of his earlier life, a picture that the yellow tomcat discovered when he visited Emmylou, a childhood picture that had drawn him back again and again to look at little Sammie, his visits generating a comfortable friendship with the old woman though he never spoke to her, he never breached the cats' secret.

The grown-up Sammie Miller, having no family but her wandering brother who could never stay in one place, had willed her cottage and the old stone building in the woods above to Emmylou. She told Emmylou more than once that Birely had no use for a house, that he preferred to travel footloose and free. Nice euphemisms, Pan thought, for a man with no ambition, for a drifter who let the world do with him as it would.

In the warm bed beside him, Tessa stirred suddenly and Pan drew back, crouching on the pillow. But the child only whimpered and turned over, dreaming. Often Kit came with him on his nighttime visits, she was his lookout, watching Debbie through the kitchen window, ready to hiss a warning if the woman rose and headed for the bedroom. But this night Kit was off up the coast with her humans, visiting the city. Or maybe they were already on their way home, after a week of shopping in what Kit said were "elegant stores that *smell* so good." How long it seemed, and how he missed her.

He had loved Kit since that first day he arrived in Molena Point, hitching the last leg of his journey on a tour bus, and then making his way through the small village to the sea cliff. Pushing through the tall, blowing grass above the sea, he'd seen the tortoiseshell hiding, watching him, her yellow eyes so bright with curiosity that even in that instant he knew that he loved her. Now he not only loved her and missed her but, as he crouched beside the sleeping child, his thoughts left Tessa suddenly and uneasily, the fur down his back stood stiff, his thoughts suddenly all on Kit. What was this shivering fear he felt, what was happening?

His ears caught no sound save Tessa's soft breathing, yet he heard Kit's silent cry. His fear made him abandon the child, sent him flying out the window knowing that Kit was in trouble, that she was afraid and alone. He sensed her crouched shivering in the black night and he was filled with her terror, he wanted to run to her but she was far away, she was in danger and far away and he had no way to find her or help her.

But maybe the disaster had already happened, he thought sensibly. Maybe he was feeling her fear from a moment already gone, maybe now she was safe. Maybe she and Lucinda and Pedric had already returned to the village, maybe he was feeling her residual fear telegraphed between them. Maybe if he raced up across the rooftops to her tree house he'd find her already there, safe and dreaming among her pillows. Willing this to be so, Pan scrambled to the roof and took off fast, racing through the night across the peaks and shingles, praying Kit was home and safe—but knowing, deep down, that she was not, that Kit was still in danger.

6

Crouched high up the rocky slide, having crept into a dark cavity between two jutting boulders, Kit shifted from paw to paw listening to the coyotes yipping back among the woods, and they sounded more focused now and intent. Nervously she watched the road below for the first glimpse of Clyde and Ryan's red king cab. Flares glowed along the narrow highway, those nearest to the slide reflecting sparks of light against the wrecked trucks. How lonely the night was, now that the medics had taken Lucinda and Pedric away. Who would look out for them and sign papers at the hospital, if Lucinda fainted from the pain of her shoulder, if Pedric passed out from the concussion? Who would make phone calls to their own doctor and to their friends, who would make sure that everything possible was being done to help them?

Ryan and Clyde will, she thought, trying to ease her worries. Down below her on the highway, even the two CHP cars looked lonely, one parked to the north of the rock slide, one to the south. She could hear their police radios' static mumbling and could smell coffee from their thermoses, each man cosseted in his small electronic realm, maybe talking back and forth on their cell phones as they waited for the wreckers and then the earthmovers to come and clear the highway.

She thought about their nice new Lincoln—a used one, but new to them and the first car Lucinda and Pedric had bought in ten years. The Lincoln gone, with all their beautiful purchases for their home and for Christmas. And Kate's treasure gone. Those men had a fortune hidden in the door panels, but they didn't know that. Maybe they wouldn't discover what they'd stolen, she thought hopefully.

Or do they know? Somehow, in San Francisco, did they find out what Kate had, did they spy on her, and then follow us here, follow us down Highway One?

Not likely, she thought. *I'm letting my imagination run. But,* she thought, *will they, for some reason of their own, remove the door panels anyway, and find Kate's treasure there?*

Whatever they did, they were sure to root around in the glove compartment, find the car registration with

Lucinda and Pedric's address, and they already had the house key, right there on the chain with the car keys.

But why would they go to Molena Point? They were probably headed miles away in the stolen Lincoln, maybe away from the coast where the cops might not be looking for them yet. Above her, the coyotes had eased nearer, through the trees, muttering among themselves. At a faint yip she crouched lower. They'd soon catch her scent, if they hadn't already, and come snuffling down among the rocks, hungry and tracking her.

If the beasts attacked, those two cops down there wouldn't help her. Why would they? A cat screaming in the night, they'd think it a wild cat, maybe hunting or mating, all a part of nature. All part of a world in which they had no call to interfere. How long before help *would* come, before she saw the lights of Clyde and Ryan's truck approaching up the road? It seemed forever since she'd called them. Hunkering down between the rocks, she stared up at the vast night sky, stared until the wheeling stars turned her dizzy, and made her feel so incredibly small. Tracing their endless sweep, she couldn't conceive of anything so huge that it went on forever.

What was *she*, then, in this vastness? Forgetting the innate cat creed that made each individual cat *know* that he was the center of all else, Kit thought, at that moment, that she was less than nothing, a speck of dust, a pinprick.

Except, I have nine lives to live, and that is not nothing.

And to a hungry coyote I'm something. I might be nothing in the vastness of time and space, but I'm something to those hungry mothers.

But then she was ashamed of her fear. *What if, right now, no one knew I was here, no one in all the world was coming to help me? What would I do, then? I've rambled all over on my own, I grew up alone without humans to help me, and ignored by the other clowder cats. I made out all right, then. I always outsmarted the coyotes, I didn't cower, then, shivering like a silly rabbit. So what's the big deal, now? I'll just hunker down here between the boulders where they can't reach me, and damn well bloody them if they try.*

But then she thought, *Maybe I have more to lose now. More than I did when I was a harebrained young-ster wandering alone. Now I have Lucinda and Pedric, I have all my friends, cat and human, I'm part of the human world now, as I never dreamed could happen. And best of all, I have Pan. I can't die now in the mouth of some slavering predator, and lose what we have together.*

From the moment she'd spied Pan up on the cliffs, heading for the windy shore searching for his father, she'd never doubted they were meant for each other, never doubted it even if, sometimes, their arguing grew volatile. *We always make up,* she thought with a little cat smile, and making up was so nice. *No,* she thought, *I don't mean to check out of this world now, in the jaws of some slobbering coyote. Screw the damn coyotes.*

Listening with renewed disdain to the beasts' yodeling, she backed deeper down between the rocks where she could lash out in safety, where they, if they tried to reach her, would meet only slashing claws. Curling up in a little ball, she deliberately made herself purr, and in a more sensible feline mind-set she imagined herself, as was proper to a cat, the very center of the vast universe. *She* was the center of all time and all space, one small and perfect cat, the universe whirling around her in endless veneration. This was cat-think, even nonspeaking cats knew in their hearts this assurance, and it made her feel infinitely better. Soon she felt whole again. Sheltered deep down among the rocks, too deep for a prying nose or reaching paw, Kit smiled to herself, and she slept.

But to Pan, tonight, the universe seemed unruly and fierce as he hurried from the last roof down a pine tree, and across the Greenlaws' dark yard. Scrambling up Kit's oak tree to her tree house, clawing up over the edge, he already knew she wasn't there, her scent was old, mixed with the aged smell of feathers from a bird she had consumed weeks ago. The high-roofed aerie was empty, its cedar pillars pale against the night, Kit's tangle of cushions abandoned, crumpled together and half hidden by browning oak leaves.

Looking back along the oak branches to the big house, he saw no light in any window. There was no sound, and no lingering whiff of supper. No faintest scent of exhaust from the empty driveway as if the Greenlaws had only now returned and perhaps already gone to bed, as if maybe Kit would be tucked up under the covers between them.

Maybe they're on their way. Maybe they stopped for supper along the coast, and will be here soon. Sand dabs and abalone, and Kit's making a pig of herself. Trying to reassure himself, he crept at last onto Kit's cushions. Burrowing among the leaves and pillows, he lay on his belly watching the street below, his whole body rigid with waiting and with his lingering sense of danger. He was so tense he couldn't rest; soon he rose again and began to pace, his heart filled with Kit's fear, his belly churning with her uncertainty and loneliness. He was pacing and fussing when the sound of leaves crumpled in the yard below by approaching paws brought his fur up, sent him peering over the edge, swallowing back a growl.

Earlier that evening, two blocks up the hill from where Pan would spin his whispered magic for little Tessa Kraft, Joe Grey and Dulcie had slipped down through Emmylou's ragged yard, departing the stone shack. Over the past weeks, whenever they found its two scruffy occupants absent, they had searched the fusty room, pawing behind whatever boards the men had loosened, sniffing the old stone wall so long concealed there. Early on, when the men first moved secretly into the stone shack, the cats, spying through the dirty window, had watched them searching and had pressed their noses to the glass wondering what could be of such interest, wondering why two tramps would tear the siding from the walls, removing it board by board and digging into the concrete behind, lifting out loose stones. What were they looking for?

What the cats had found was the oily smell of money, old paper bills, sour with mildew, but no money was there now in those spidery recesses. From the size and shape of the concentrated scent, they were certain thick packets of old bills had lain there. Hidden away for how long? Looked like the men hadn't finished searching, one whole wall was still boarded over. The cats took turns, tabby Dulcie crouched on the windowsill watching the woods and the weedy driveway below, while Joe Grey sniffed and poked behind the loose boards, where rocks were loose or missing. Was this Sammie's money, that had been hidden here? Did Emmylou know about it? In the six months since she'd inherited the place and moved in, they'd never once seen her near the stone hut.

It was Dulcie who first discovered the men slipping down through the woods and into the stone house carrying two grocery bags, a loaf of bread sticking out. She had been sunning herself on Emmylou's roof, deeply absorbed in composing a poem, when their stealthy approach made her fur go rigid.

"They've broken in," she'd said to Joe later. "Emmylou can't know they're there, she doesn't go up there, she's said nothing to Ryan though Ryan has been helping her with the lumber for her renovation." They were about to pass the word, see that it got back to Emmylou through human channels, when Joe saw the men as he was hunting rats in the yard below. From the looks of the smaller man, and from descriptions he'd heard, he thought that was Sammie's brother.

"Why would he be so secretive?" Dulcie said. "Why wouldn't Emmylou welcome him, Sammie's own brother?"

"Let's wait a while, and watch them."

"But . . ."

"Emmylou's perfectly capable of taking care of herself," Joe said. "You've seen her swing that sledgehammer, breaking up those concrete steps." Emmylou was tall, well muscled, despite her slim build and gray hair. "Besides, when she talked about Birely she made him out a timid soul, easygoing. Not like someone who'd make trouble."

"Humans don't always see others truly," Dulcie said with suspicion. They'd waited and watched, and of course the minute the men went out, they'd tossed the place.

Not much to toss, in the one room. An overflowing trash bag, half a loaf of stale bread, seven cans of red beans, dirty clothes thrown in the corner beside a pair of sleeping bags that were deeply stained and overripe with human odor, the few boards that had not yet been nailed back against the rock wall, and five loosened stones lying beside them. But tonight, something was off, tonight the room seemed abandoned. The sleeping bags were in the same exact position as when they'd last come in, but the two greasy pillows and the extra blankets had been taken away, and when they prowled the room there was no fresh scent of the men, even their ripe smell was old and fading. The canned beans were gone, too, the only food was three slices of bread gone blue with mold in the package. Dulcie said, "Is their old truck still down in the shed?"

There was no way to tell except by smell, no way to see into the shed, not the tiniest crack in or under its solid door, which fit snugly into its molding. When they trotted down the steps to investigate, there was no recent scent of exhaust. Any trace of tire marks in the gravelly dirt had been scuffed clean by the wind.

"Maybe they're having a little vacation," Joe said, "hitting the homeless jungles for a change of scene. But why did they leave their sleeping bags?"

"I would have left them, too," Dulcie said with disgust.

Trotting down through Emmylou's weedy yard, they'd scrambled up to the roofs of the small old cottages in the neighborhood below. Leaping from house to house, trotting across curled and broken shingles, they'd moved on down the hill until Dulcie, quiet and preoccupied, left Joe, heading away home to her own hearth. To her white-haired housemate and, Joe suspected, to Wilma's computer. Watching her gallop away, her tabby-striped tail lashing, Joe knew well where Dulcie's mind was. The minute she sailed through her cat door she'd head for the lighted screen, where she'd be lost the rest of the night, caught up in the new and amazing world she'd discovered, in the secret world of the poet.

7

It was earlier in the year, during that unusual February that brought snow to the village, when Joe found Dulcie in the nighttime library sitting on Wilma's desk, the pale light of Wilma's work computer glowing around her. When Dulcie turned to look down at him, the expression on her face was incredibly mysterious and embarrassed. How shy she had been, telling him she was composing a poem; only at long last had she allowed him to read it, to see what she'd written.

The poem made him laugh, as it was meant to do, and within the next weeks Dulcie produced a whole sheaf of poems, some happy, some uncomfortably sad, and the occasional funny one that made Joe smile. His tabby lady had discovered a whole new dimension to her life, to her already amazing world. That's where she would be now, sitting before the computer caught up in that magical realm where Joe could only look on, where he was sure he could never follow. Where he could only be glad for her, and try not to mourn his loss, of that part of his tabby lady.

To Joe Grey, words and language were for gathering information and passing it along—and for making certain your humans knew when to serve up the caviar. But Dulcie used language as a painter used color, and the concept was nearly beyond him, the inner fire of such expression quite beyond his solid tomcat nature. How many speaking cats *were* there in the world, living their own secret lives? And how many of *them* had found their souls filled suddenly with the music of words, with a new kind of voice that Joe himself could hardly fathom? Contemplating such wonders of the mind and heart left him feeling strange and unsettled, like trotting along a narrow plank high aboveground and suddenly losing his balance, swaying out over empty space not knowing how to take the next step, a devastating feeling to the likes of any cat.

Joe took a long route home, thinking about Dulcie and trying not to feel left out from this new aspect to her life; but soon again his thoughts returned to the two tramps, to questions that as yet had no answers, and to the paper money they were surely finding, money old and rank with mildew. Who had hidden it there?

How long had it lain within those damp walls? That stone building was more than a hundred years old, it had stood there since the early nineteen hundreds, when it was an outbuilding for the dairy farm that had once occupied that knoll of land. Ryan and Clyde had spent hours in the history section of the Molena Point library perusing old books and photographs of the area, when they bought the little remodel just two blocks down from Emmylou, where Debbie Kraft and her girls were now living. Had the money been secreted there since the place was built, or had a subsequent owner, Sammie or someone before her, stashed it away in those old walls?

Emmylou might not know about that hidden stash, but he didn't understand how she could fail to know that two freeloaders were camping on her property, not fifty feet from her. Yet she didn't seem to have a clue. Misto visited her often, he was sure she thought the old place as empty as a clean-licked tuna can.

It was strange, Jesse thought, that when he talked about the missing money, Misto grew silent and withdrawn and a curious look shone in his yellow eyes. As if he knew something, or almost knew but couldn't quite put a paw on what was needling him. As if some long-lost memory had surfaced but wouldn't come clear, leaving the old yellow tom puzzled and uncertain. Strange, too, that Misto spent so much time with Emmylou, visiting her and prowling her house, almost as if he felt a tie to the property.

Or maybe a connection to the dead woman who had owned it? If there were memories here, if there was a story here, either Misto wasn't ready to share it or he didn't remember enough to share, maybe could recall only tattered fragments. But this, too, unsettled Joe. Fragments of memory from when? Sometimes Misto talked about past lives, and Joe didn't like that, he didn't buy into that stuff. Even if they *did* have nine lives, which no one had ever proven, what made a cat think he could remember them, that he could recall those faraway connections?

As he crossed a high, shingled peak, the scudding wind hit him, thrusting sharp fingers into his short gray fur. Below him, the dark residential streets were black beneath the pine and cypress trees, only a few cottage windows showed lights, the soft glow of a reading lamp, the flicker of a TV. He was crossing a tiled ridge near Kit's house, just a block over, when he stopped and reared up, looking.

The windows of the Greenlaw house were all dark, with Lucinda and Pedric and Kit still in the city.

There should be no one about, certainly there should be no creature prowling Kit's tree house among the oak branches, but there against the starry sky moved the silhouette of a cat pacing fretfully back and forth across the high platform, an impatient figure, an interloper prowling Kit's territory where no strange animal was welcome. Joe sniffed the air for scent but the sea wind was to his back, heavy with iodine and the smell of a rotting fish somewhere. Heading across the interceding rooftops, he slipped silently down to the Greenlaws' garden and then up again, up the oak tree to Kit's high, roofed platform, his fur prickling with challenge.

Lights were on at the Damens' house, upstairs in the master suite, lights silhouetting hurrying shadows against the shades, the commotion stirred by Kit's phone call as Ryan and Clyde hastily pulled on jeans, sweatshirts, and jackets, grabbed up backpacks, stuffing in flashlights, cat food and water, and the first-aid kit. Rock, the big silver Weimaraner, was off the love seat and pacing; he knew they were going on a mission and he couldn't be still.

The upstairs lights went off again, the stair light came on, then the porch light blazed as the three of them headed out for the king cab, Ryan locking the door behind them. Rock bounded past Clyde into the backseat, lunging from one side window to the other with such enthusiasm he rocked the heavy vehicle like a rowboat, staring out into the night looking hopefully for the first hint of his quarry and then poking his nose in Ryan's ear or against Clyde's cheek, urging them to hurry, demanding to be out on the trail tracking the bad guys. The sleek silver dog had no clue that tonight his target would not be an escaped convict armed and dangerous, but one small cat, frightened and alone, a quarry who, if at last he found her, would snuggle up to him purring mightily.

But even to find one small cat, a tracking dog needs a sample of his mark's scent, a clear and identifiable smell to follow among the millions of odors he'd encounter along the high cliff. "Pillows," Ryan said. "Stop by the Greenlaws."

"Pillows?" Clyde looked over at her, frowning.

"Kit's tree house. Her pillows. I brought a clean plastic bag."

"You're going to climb the oak tree?"

"Ladder," she said, glancing up at the cab roof where, above it, her long construction ladder rode securely tethered on the overhead rack. "Just take a minute, we'll have a nice, fur-matted pillow for Rock to sniff."

"If we had Joe, he'd put Rock on the trail. Where the hell—"

"Even with Joe," she said, "I'd want a scent article, as you're supposed to have, so as not to spoil Rock's training."

"The one time Joe might be of help," Clyde said, ignoring her logic, "he's off hunting. Or off with Pan whispering in that little kid's ear. Talk about an exercise in futility."

"If Pan can help that little girl, we ought to cheer him on. Scared of her mother, bullied by her sister. Besides, Joe might not even be with Pan. He and Dulcie have been hanging around Emmylou Warren's all week, around that stone building up behind, whatever that's about."

"I don't want to know what that's about. More trouble, one way or another."

Ryan just looked at him.

"Name one time Joe went off on some crazy round of surveillance that he didn't stir a carload of trouble."

"Name one time Joe wasn't leaps ahead of the cops," she said. "That he didn't drop valuable information in Max Harper's lap, a lead that Max was grateful for, even if he didn't know where it came from." She sat scowling at him. "Don't be so hard on Joe, we're blessed to know him, and all you do is rag him."

Clyde grinned. "He loves it. Rags me right back."

"You don't realize how lucky you are just to share bed and supper with Joe, just to know those five cats. But," she said, "there is something strange going on at Emmylou's that Joe doesn't want to talk about. I guess, in time, he'll tell us," she said. "In his own good time."

Joe slipped up the oak tree and onto Kit's tree house ready to fight the intruder, his ears and whiskers flat. Only when the pacing cat turned, startled, and approached him stiff-legged, did Joe laugh and relax. Pan paused, too, tail twitching, his ears going back and up, edgy and questioning.

"What?" Joe said. "What's wrong?"

"I don't know." The big tom lowered his ears uncertainly. "Kit's in trouble, I can feel her fear, she's scared and alone somewhere out in the night."

Joe took a step back. "She's miles away, up the coast. You can't know what she's feeling, what she's doing." This kind of talk made his paws sweat.

Pan drew his lips back. "She's in some kind of trouble."

"Nightmare," Joe said. "You fell asleep and dreamed of trouble." Generally the red tom was a steady fellow, macho and straightforward—until he got off on this perception nonsense beyond all logic and reason.

But Pan's amber eyes blazed, he growled deep in his throat and spun around and was gone along an oak branch and in through the dining room window, through the cat door. "The Greenlaws, their cell phone . . ." he said over his shoulder. "Help me find the number."

Joe sighed. He was crouched to follow, knowing they'd sound like fools to the Greenlaws with such a call, when car lights came down the street below. They slowed, and Ryan's red king cab turned into the drive, headlights sweeping the front of the house and up through the oak branches, blazing in Joe's face. Squinting, he peered over, breathing exhaust as the engine died.

Ryan emerged from the passenger side, stepped around to the rear bumper and up onto it, reaching up to the overhead rack where the extension ladder was secured. He watched Clyde swing out the driver's door and move to help her. Why did they need a ladder? They *had* a key to the house, all the Greenlaws' close friends had keys. From the dining room, Pan shouted, "*You* picked up! Say something. Pedric? *Is this Pedric?*" Silence, then, "*Pedric, are you all right? Where's Lucinda?*" Another silence, then, "*Who* is *this? If this isn't Pedric, who are you? Why do you have Pedric's phone? Where's Lucinda?*

Speak up or I call the cops, they'll put a trace on you!"

Joe smiled. He didn't think MPPD was set up to trace the immediate location of a cell phone but it sounded good. He watched Ryan open the extension ladder, lean it against the edge of the tree house, and climb nimbly up. Joe waited until his housemate had swung up onto the platform and switched on her flashlight, then stepped out into its beam. The eerie night-glow of his eyes made her catch her breath.

"Did you have to do that, sneak up like that?" she asked shakily.

"*I'm* sneaking? What are *you* doing climbing up here in the middle of the night like some—"

"Like some cat burglar?" she said, laughing. She knelt and grabbed him up and hugged him. Her hugs always embarrassed him, but they made him purr, too.

Putting him down again, she fished a plastic bag from her pocket and reached across him to snag one of Kit's well-used pillows from the untidy pile. He watched her drop it into the plastic bag and seal it up with a twisty. He looked over the edge at the king cab where Rock was hanging out the open window, whining softly. He looked toward the house where Pan was on the phone, and looked again at Ryan. Now there was silence from the house. Joe watched Pan emerge through the cat door, ears back, tail lashing, his tabby forehead creased with worry, unsettled by that distraught phone conversation.

"Come on, Pan," Ryan said, swinging onto the ladder and down, frowning up at Pan there above her. "Come on, we're headed up the coast." She looked worriedly at the red tom. "It's Kit," she said softly. "She . . . We're going to look for Kit."

Pan leaped from the oak to the ground, sinking deep in the leafy mulch, fled to the king cab and up through the window past Rock. Joe followed, as Ryan descended the ladder clutching Kit's pillow. Inside the pickup, Pan was crouched on the back of the driver's seat, tail lashing. Joe, unsettled by the red tom's unnatural perception, hopped sedately up into the front seat beside Clyde, and snuggled close. Pan might indulge in these wild flights of fancy, but he could count on Clyde for a soothing dose of hardheaded commonsense.

8

Vic pulled down off the highway into the village, easing the Town Car away from the main street and through the darkest neighborhoods, the narrow lanes as black as the Lincoln itself. Molena Point streets were not lighted, and here among the crowded cottages only weak lampglow shone through a few curtained windows, vaguely illuminating the nearest tree trunks. Heading a roundabout way for the stone house, the big car slid through the inky streets nearly invisible except for its low beams picking out parked cars and an occasional cat racing across. In the passenger seat Birely huddled, his arms around himself, moaning at every bump and there were plenty of those on these backstreets, potholes, and warped blacktop where tree roots pushed up, jolting even the easy-riding Lincoln.

The trip down Highway One had been tense, watching for cops. There hadn't been much traffic and the Town Car stood out too clearly, making him jumpy as hell.

Leaving the scene of the wreck and moving on down the winding two-lane, they'd barely hit the flats, the highway straight and flat along the shore, when they'd heard sirens ahead. He'd turned off into a clump of eucalyptus trees, onto a narrow road that led away to a distant farmhouse. Pasture fences, faint lights way off up the hill. Waiting there on the dark dirt road for the cops and ambulance to pass, he'd done what he could for Birely, had cleaned the blood off his face with bottled water and an old rag. Birely's nose wouldn't stop bleeding, and he couldn't bear anything pressed against it. He couldn't hardly breathe, as it was. And the way he was holding his belly, whimpering, he was hurt more than a bandage could fix. When they'd left the wrecked pickup Vic had cleared out the glove compartment, had left most of the junk from the previous owner that he'd stole it from, but had pocketed a beer opener, an old pocketknife, and an out-of-date bottle of codeine prescribed in the name of the truck's owner. He'd given Birely two of those, had left the wreck trying to figure out what to do with him when they got back to Molena Point. He sure couldn't show up at a hospital emergency room driving the Lincoln; by this time, there'd be a BOL out. First thing was to get the Town Car out of sight, then decide what to do.

Waiting on the side road, he'd felt the inner pockets of his windbreaker, patting the one pack of bills he'd kept on him. Most of the money they'd found, that he'd been carrying, he'd stashed in the Lincoln itself. Rooting behind the stacked packages in the backseat, he'd pulled down the armrest and found a space lined with a plastic tray, the old folks had a couple of them little water bottles in there. Pulling the bottles out, he'd stuffed the packs of bills in, ten stacks of hundreds, all bound up in their little paper sleeves. One sleeve tore, spilling its contents, but he gathered it all, slipped the torn wrapper back on, and sandwiched it between the other packets. The hiding place, when it was covered up with packages again, would be easy enough to get to in a hurry. He still couldn't figure out if the woman Sammie'd left the place to, that Emmylou Warren, knew about Sammie's stash.

Had to, he thought, with all that carpentry work she was doing down there. Sure as hell she was going to find the money. Sammie'd told Birely, long ago, that she'd split the cash up, that she hadn't hid it all in one place. Sammie must have wanted Birely to have it, to tell him that—maybe wanted him to know about it, but not know too much, in case he turned greedy before she passed on, and came looking, nosing around maybe egged on by some "friend" he'd met on the road, Vic thought with a smile. Birely never was one to see he was being used. If she'd wanted Birely to have the money, but not while *she* was still around, she must've meant him to have the house, too. But something made her change her mind, and she wrote that will to the Warren woman instead. It didn't make sense, but people seldom made sense. He was just pulling off the street onto the dirt lane that led back through the woods to the stone building when the cell phone rang, the phone he'd taken off that old guy. It began to gong like a church bell. Birely sat up rigid, groaning with pain, staring around him like he thought he was about to receive the last rites. He came fully awake and grabbed up the phone.

"Don't answer it," Vic snapped. "Don't *answer* the damn thing." But Birely, groping, must have hit the speaker button.

"I didn't *answer* it," he said. "I just . . ." A man's voice came on, soft and quiet. "Pedric? Pedric, is that you?"

"I told you not to answer."

"I didn't, I only picked it up. What . . . ?"

"You punched something. Hang up." Vic grabbed the phone from him.

"You picked up!" the caller shouted. *"Say something. Pedric? Is this Pedric?"*

Vic stopped the car among the trees, couldn't figure out how to turn the damn phone off.

"Where's Pedric?" the voice shouted. *"Pedric, are you all right? If this isn't Pedric, who are you? Where's Lucinda?"* Vic started punching buttons. The screen came to life rolling through all kinds of commands, but the voice kept on. *"Who is this? Why do you have Pedric's phone? Where's Lucinda? Speak up or I call the cops, they'll put a trace on you!"*

"Sure it's me," Vic said. "Who did you expect?"

There was a short silence. *"This* isn't Pedric. I want to talk to Pedric."

Holding the phone, he wondered if the cops *could* use it to trace their location. Maybe some departments had the equipment to do that, he didn't know. But this little burg? Not likely. He tried to recall the soft, raspy voice of the man he had hit with the tire iron. Uptight-looking old guy, neatly dressed, tan sport coat, white hair in a short, military cut, white shirt and proper tie. Lowering his voice, he tried to use proper English, like the old guy would. "Of course this is Pedric, who else would have my phone? Could you tell me who is calling? We seem to have a bad connection."

There was a long silence at the other end. The caller said no more. Vic heard him click off.

The encounter left him nervous as hell, made his stomach churn. An unidentified call, coming over a stolen phone like the damn thing had ghosts in it. Birely had curled into himself again, as if the pain were worse. His smashed nose was bleeding harder, his breath sour, breathing through his mouth. Where his face wasn't smeared with blood, he was white as milk. Vic knew, even if he stashed the Lincoln out of sight, got some other wheels and hauled Birely to an emergency room, they'd start asking questions and who knew what Birely'd say? The little wimp wasn't too swift, at best, and in the hospital, drugged up for the pain, he might tell the cops any damned thing.

It had started out as a lark, when they'd first headed over to the coast to find that wad of money that Birely swore Sammie'd stashed away, a simple trip to retrieve Birely's own rightful legacy, and the whole damn thing had gone sour. It was that run up to the city that did it, their pickup totaled, and now the cops would be after them because they'd taken the damn Lincoln. But what else could he do? He didn't *have* no other way to get Birely to a doctor, he'd tell them that, with Birely hurt so bad, and all. And that truck driver dead, which would sure as hell send the cops after them, too. They'd be all over him for that, claiming you weren't supposed to leave an accident victim. Hell, the guy was dead, it wasn't like he could have helped him none. With Birely bad hurt, what could he do but take the one working vehicle to go for help? *He* didn't kill the truck driver, the rock slide killed him.

But the old man and his skinny wife, that was another matter. If one of *them* died he'd sure be charged with murder even if he didn't hit either of them very hard, not hard enough to kill them. If they died from shock or something, was that *his* fault? And there again he'd had no choice, had to get them off his back so he could help Birely. The law never took into account extenuating circumstances, they had no feel for a person when you were really up against it. Sure as hell those two people could identify him—and would swear he'd attacked them. And now, once he'd hidden the Lincoln, what was he going to do with Birely?

It was after they'd turned back on the highway, after the cops and ambulance went by, that was when Birely had started to talk. Rambled on as they skirted the little cheap towns along the peninsula, when the codeine took hold and loosened up his tongue. Talked about how strange Sammie was when she was a child, rambled on about their old uncle, the old train robber who was close to Sammie when she was small. All so long ago that Birely wasn't even born yet. He'd heard the stories from Sammie, how the old man had robbed some government office of big bucks, hid the money and got away clean, and the feds could never pin anything on him. Back to prison on other charges, and then a year later made a prison break and took off with the money, down into Mexico.

And then, some years later, maybe with a guilty conscience, he'd shipped a big share of it back to Sammie. Birely'd grown up knowing only those parts of the story that Sammie chose to tell him, he wasn't much good at filling in the spaces between.

Easing the Lincoln on down through the woods, Vic was about to pull around to the front of the stone shed, hoping to hell he could squeeze the Lincoln into that little space that had probably been built for cows or farm machinery, when he saw a light in the yard down below, saw Emmylou Warren descending the hill, heading down from the stone house. He killed the engine, watched to see if she'd heard the car. She made no indication, didn't pause or glance back. Had she been poking around inside there? Had she seen them before they left, knew they were staying in there? That would tear it. Was she looking for the rest of the money, maybe had found some down at her place, decided when she saw them that they were looking for it, too? Birely said the original theft was two hundred thousand, a big haul, back in those days.

But maybe Emmylou Warren didn't know nothing, was just out in the yard maybe feeding those cats that hung around her. Useless creatures, what were they good for? In the light from her porch he watched her poking around down in her yard and she didn't once look his way. Dark as hell up behind the pines and heavy bushes. He watched her head up the steps to her back door, that big yellow cat walking along beside her, following her like a dog, old woman talking to it, crazy as hell, walking around in her yard in the middle of the night gabbing away to a cat, talking as if the damn thing would answer her.

9

Misto glanced up twice toward the woods as he followed Emmylou up the back stairs and inside. He was quite aware of the black car that had pulled in among the trees high above the stone house, though Emmylou was not. He could smell the fumes of its exhaust drifting down, cutting through the scent of the pines, and on the riffling breath of the night he caught a whiff of blood that tweaked his curiosity. Accompanying Emmylou inside, he leaped to the sill where he could look back up the hill, studying the denser blackness among the night woods where the big car stood. Pretty nice car to be jammed in among the trees that way. He'd like to tell Emmylou to turn the porch light off so he could see better but he never spoke to her, she didn't share his secret, she was not among the few who knew the truth about the speaking cats, she was simply a kind and comfortable friend. Misto had, in fact, a number of secrets he didn't share with Emmylou Warren—though it was she who had, unwittingly, opened a new door to Misto. Had, by accident or by strange circumstance, pulled aside a curtain into the tomcat's ancient memory, had let cracks of light into a life he'd lived long before this present existence.

Maybe the memories began with the smell of the mildewed money there in Emmylou's house, often it was a smell of some sort that stirred a lost vision. The sour stink of those three packets of old bills she'd found had nudged him as if a hand had reached up from his past, poking at him, bringing back scenes from a life nearly forgotten. Or maybe it was the grainy photograph in a tin frame that had awakened those long-ago moments, the picture of a child who had, by now, already grown up, grown old, and died. Maybe that little girl's eager smile had stirred alive that lost time.

Back in February, when the cops found Sammie's body, Misto had no idea who the dead woman was but he knew her name, it stuck in his thoughts and wouldn't go away. He hadn't put it together until later, that *this* Sammie was the little child from his own past, from a life lived many cat generations before this one.

Emmylou usually left the back door open while she was working inside, replacing Sheetrock and sawing and hammering. Hearing her at work, he'd slip in for a visit with the stringy, leathery woman. With his own humans away for the week, Dr. John Firetti and his wife, Mary, off at a veterinarian conference, he'd been up here every day. He was staying with Joe Grey and the Damens, which suited him just fine: sleeping on the love seat with the big Weimaraner and little Snowball, or up in the tower with Joe. But Ryan and Clyde were busy folks, Clyde with his upscale automotive business and Ryan with her construction firm. And Joe was off at all hours with his tabby lady, following their lust for crime, hanging out with the cops at MPPD, waiting eagerly for some scuzzy human to be nailed and jailed. Sometimes, then, Misto would slip up to visit this homey and comfortable woman, to stretch out on her windowsill as she went about her work. He liked to watch her tear out cabinets and finish the walls with new Sheetrock, and Emmylou was good company. That was how he came on the picture of the child, she had moved it back onto the dresser after shifting the furniture around. He'd hopped up there to be petted, and there it was, the picture of a child that so shocked him he let out a strange, gargling mewl.

"That's Sammie," Emmylou had said, looking down at him. "Sammie when she was little, so many years ago. My goodness, cat, you look frightened. How could an old picture scare you?"

The photo was sepia toned, and grainy. The child was dressed in an old-fashioned pinafore, crisply ironed, and little patent-leather shoes with a strap across the instep, over short white socks. He had known this child, he remembered her running through the grass beside a white picket fence, he could see her bouncing on her little bed with the pink ruffled spread, he could hear her laughing. Those moments from another life crowded in at him in much the same way he remembered fragments from a long-ago medieval village, scenes so clear and sudden he could smell offal in the streets and the stink of boiled cabbage and the rain-sodden rot of thatched rooftops.

Here in Emmylou's house, the time of Sammie's childhood grew so real he could smell the bruised grass on her little shoes, could feel her warmth when he curled up close to her, the softness of her baby skin, the smell of little girl and hot cocoa and peppermints, the sticky feel of peanut butter on her small fingers. How strange to think about that lost time. How clearly he remembered the humid Southern summers, the buzz of cicadas at night, the days as hot as hell itself, and so muggy your fur was never really dry. How had he been drawn here to this place where, so many long years later, the grown-up Sammie had lived and died?

Soon he wasn't going off with Joe Grey at all, or even with his son, Pan, but heading up alone to see Emmylou and revisit those memories that so stirred him, to sit on the dresser looking at little Sammie while Emmylou hammered and sawed and talked away, and all the while it was Sammie's young voice he wished he could hear.

He wasn't sure how many of his nine cat lives he had spent, and he wasn't sure what came after. Some of his lives were only vague sparks, bright moments or ugly, a scene, a few words spoken, and then gone again. Only his life with Sammie was so insistent. As each new memory nudged him, another piece of that life fell into place, toward whatever revelation he was meant to see, another moment teasing his sharp curiosity.

But tonight, crouched on Emmylou's windowsill, a different kind of curiosity gripped Misto, too. He waited patiently until he saw the black car move on again down through the woods, following the lane that led to the old, narrow shed beneath the stone house. Misto guessed, with its wide, hinged doors, it was a kind of garage, maybe built for farm tractors or a Model A. Did the driver expect to fit that big car in there? Not likely, not that long, sleek vehicle. Though in the reflection of light from Emmylou's back porch he could see dents and scrapes in the fenders, too, and a loose front bumper. The driver stepped out, left the motor running, the taller of the two men he'd seen coming up there before, shaggy brown ponytail hanging down the back of his dark windbreaker.

He opened the heavy swinging doors, got back in and, amazingly, he pulled the car on inside. It was a tight fit, barely enough room for him to help his companion out, the shorter man stumbling, and that's where the smell of blood came from. Blood smeared down his face, soaking into the rag he held to his nose. Moving up the stone steps to the room above, he bore much of his weight on the wooden rail. The taller man closed the shed doors, replaced the padlock, and followed him up. Watched him struggle into the house but didn't help him. The door closed behind them. Misto heard the lock snap home.

No lights came on inside, except the faintest glow as if they had an electric lantern up there. Wanting to see more, Misto dropped from Emmylou's windowsill to the floor and trotted out through the old cat door that was cut in the back door. Emmylou's own three cats used it, wild creatures he thought might have been feral, who came and went as they chose. Galloping up the hill and up the stone stairs, through the men's scent, he leaped to the stone sill beside the door, peered in through the dirty glass.

10

Heavy fog hugged the coastal highway, slowing the king cab as Clyde negotiated the blind lanes following the dim taillights of the sheriff's car that led them, both drivers watching for unexpected obstructions in the heavy mist. He and Ryan and the two tomcats were all fidgeting, thinking about Kit alone somewhere on the cliff ahead, her little tortoiseshell face peering out from some stony crevice that could hardly protect her from larger predators, waiting for help to come rescue her. Kit might act brash and brave with her friends but tonight her voice on the phone had been shaky, scared, and uncertain.

"Good thing we have friends in the department," Joe said, rearing up on the backseat peering out the side window into the rolling mist. "*Someone* to get us through the roadblock back there. I wouldn't have wanted to climb up this damnable, fog-blind road ducking falling boulders you can't even see coming down at you."

"The rocks have quit falling," Clyde said. "Ryan and I will be climbing, carrying you and Pan."

Max Harper had called the Santa Cruz County Sheriff, who had, in turn, alerted his deputies to let them through the barrier down at the foot of the mountain. "Deputy will meet you," Max had said, "lead you on up." Now as they climbed above the flatland on the narrow, rising curves, the fog blew and shifted, arms of whiteness blinding and then revealing, playing with their senses, with their perception of place and balance. The streaming wisps made even the two cats giddy. Joe was glad they had the heavy king cab with its reliable four-wheel drive to keep them grounded. The only unsteadiness about the truck was Rock lunging nervously from one side of the backseat to the other, his eager weight rocking the heavy vehicle and, at each lunge, shouldering Joe and Pan aside.

"Settle down," Ryan told him, "you'll wear yourself out before you ever start to search." Rock gave her a sullen look, but he lay down, sighing dramatically, sprawling across the wide seat. Ryan had, long ago, filled the leg space of the backseat with empty boxes, and laid a thin pad over both boxes and seat to make a solid platform, preventing the big dog from losing his balance on the narrow bench. The resultant bed would have accommodated all three animals nicely if Rock wasn't hogging it all. Joe watched the deputy's disembodied taillights leading them up through the shifting blanket of white, watched the blurred reflection of their two sets of headlights move along the black cliff in their ethereal, half-blind world. The deputy leading them, plump and baby faced, had told them the wind was stirring higher up the mountain, "Maybe the night'll clear, make your tracking easier," but his tone had implied that this venture was nonsense, to bring a tracking dog all the way up here in this weather to find some lost cat. Maybe the fog *would* clear, Joe thought, but right now they couldn't even see the edge of the road where it dropped away to the sea; the muffled sound of the waves from far below seemed stealthy and threatening.

But central coast fog was notional, slipping along the base of Molena Point's coastal hills one moment, rising the next to leave the lowland clear and enfold only the tallest peaks. Many afternoons the cats, hunting across the high meadows, would watch a thin, white scarf of fog creep in from the sea just above the Molena River, down below the hills that rose bright green and clear.

And the next time they looked, the fog had expanded to cover all the hills and the sun, hiding the world around them.

Now suddenly Rock leaped up to pace again, and so did the red tomcat, the two shouldering past each other peering out one window and then Joe, too, caught a whiff of coyote mixed with the smell of the sea and of the pine forest. Pan's ears twitched back and forth, his striped tail lashing as he fretted over Kit, his every movement urging them to hurry. The red tom had traveled this coast, one small cat alone following Highway One from Oregon to Molena Point, he knew the bold beasts that hunted these coastal mountains, he knew the way coyotes tear their prey, and that was not a pleasant picture. He was aware of the bobcats and owls, too, the silent night hunters, and he was frantic for Kit.

Even as Clyde had backed the king cab out of their drive, Max had called them back to tell them that Lucinda and Pedric were safe in the ER, in Santa Cruz, but that both were driving the staff crazy, fussing about their cat. "They've refused to have the X-rays and MRIs that were ordered," he said crossly, "until they know someone's gone to fetch the damn cat." Max wasn't big on cats—though he had grown unusually fond of Joe Grey, brightening at Joe's presence on his desk or in his bookcase, and not a clue to the cat-sized detective lounging across his reports; to Max Harper the five cats were no more than housecats. "Why the hell did they take that cat with them? Try to control a cat, in a car? Why can't they have a nice little lap dog that they can keep on a leash?"

Joe imagined the tall, lean chief and Charlie, his redheaded wife, disturbed from an evening at home, tucked up before a warm fire in their hilltop living room maybe with an after-dinner toddy, maybe watching an old movie. The chief didn't get that many leisurely nights off without some emergency or another breaking in, too often taking him out again into the small hours. Max said, "You think Rock *will* track that cat?"

"Of course he will," Ryan said indignantly, "he's primed for the hunt."

"Charlie's making noises like she wants to head for the hospital. We may see you there, or she will," and he'd clicked off.

They were high up the mountain when, around the next sharp bend, a line of sputtering orange flares broke the thinning fog. The deputy parked beside two more black-and-whites. The landslide loomed beyond, a ragged hill of fallen boulders blocking the highway, the tons of rock lit like a movie set by three spotlights fixed to tall tripods, their blaze picking out broken glass and twisted metal, too, where the wrecked truck and pickup lay tangled together in a deathly heap. Clyde parked beside the patrol car that had led them, both cars backing around so their rear bumpers were against the cliff. The deputy got out of his unit and stepped over to talk with them, his round face pulled into a frown. "Town Car was on this side. It barely slid through, or they'd be dead. Strange what some people will think of, time like that. Worried about a *cat.*"

He didn't like bringing civilians up to a crash scene, he didn't like them tramping around the scene of a wreck, and didn't like the idea of these people going up the slide area with their dog, didn't like that at all. Most likely they'd get in trouble, fall down the cliff, and that would complicate matters, but orders were orders. "Well, at least the fog's lifted," he said dourly. "There's a hiking path on up the road another quarter mile. That'll put you up to the tree line, and bring you back there, right above us. I want you to stay in the woods. You're not to go down on the slide. Can you control your dog?" He looked doubtfully at Rock, who was huffing at the air, sucking in scent and staring up the tall, rocky cliff. "That cat could have taken off for anywhere. You ever try to catch a scared cat?" he said, backing away from Ryan's door so she could get out of the truck.

"We'll find her," Clyde said mildly. He reached over the seat for his backpack as Ryan strapped on her own heavy pack. Neither Joe nor Pan was in sight. The deputy looked at Rock, and reached a hand for the Weimaraner to sniff. "Nice hound. Trouble is, when that cat sees this big beast it'll take off like a bat in a windstorm, you never will find it."

"Dog and cat are friends," Clyde said, his voice slow and measured. "They eat out of the same supper bowl. Cat'll be happy to see him."

The deputy shrugged, unconvinced. "Wreckers and earthmovers'll be here at daylight. If the wind dies and more fog rolls in, you won't be able to see your own feet."

Not until he had moved away did Ryan make a rude face, and she and Clyde grinned at each other. Joe peered out of Clyde's pack, watching the pudgy officer depart, and from Ryan's pack Pan uttered a low, angry growl.

Climbing gingerly over the rock pile toward the upper road and the trail, they left the key in the king cab in case the deputies needed to move it. Negotiating the unsteady boulders, they tested every step, moving with infinite care despite Rock's eager pulling on his lead. Coming down onto the solid macadam again on the other side, past the wrecked trucks, they headed up the two-lane, passing two more sheriff's cars that had come down from the north. Rock pulled Ryan up the steep grade, straining on his leash. He wasn't expected to heel, he was working now, heeling and city manners weren't part of this program. In her left hand Ryan carried the plastic bag with Kit's scent. Once they'd left the rock slide, they didn't talk. Clyde swept his beam along the road ahead, lighting their way, while Ryan shone her light up the cliff, cutting back and forth through dried-up vegetation and ragged outcroppings, all of them hoping to see a pair of bright eyes reflecting back from the stony drop. Joe, half smothered in Clyde's backpack, didn't like the silence, he didn't like that there was no distant sound of coyotes yipping to one another, silent coyotes were bad news. Kit had *said* there were coyotes, he *smelled* coyotes, and their silence meant they were watching, well aware of them. But worse still, there was no sound from Kit, not the faintest mewl to tell them where she was.

Not likely she'd mewl with the coyotes so close, but I sure wish she would, wish she'd yowl like a banshee. Her silence made him shiver with dread.

11

The harsh ring of the phone woke Kate Osborne, but when she reached for the phone in the dark room, trying to sit up, tangled in the covers, she couldn't find the damn thing. Feeling around her, she realized she wasn't in bed; her bare legs were tangled in fur, making her shiver. She gingerly touched the animal feel of it, realized she was stroking the fur throw that she kept on the couch, that she'd gone to sleep in the living room. The phone was still ringing. Last night, she hadn't bothered to turn on the answering machine. She used it when she went out, if she thought of it, but since she'd returned to San Francisco from her long, dark journey, she'd found even that innocuous electronic gadget annoying. This change in her life, leaving her cozy and successful designer's position in Seattle, opting for unfettered freedom back in California with no obligations, taking the small apartment in the city, and then the amazing events that led her down through the cavernous tunnels into that terrifying other world, all of it had left her nervously intolerant of anything nonhuman speaking up for her. She found the phone on the ninth ring. Snatching it up, she pushed her pale hair out of her eyes, found the lamp, and switched it on. Her watch said ten o'clock, but it felt like way after midnight. "What?" she said. "If this is a sales pitch—"

"Kate, it's Charlie Harper."

She sat up, shivering in the cold room, pulled the heavy throw around her, shoved another pillow behind her. Beyond the open draperies the great, lighted span of the Golden Gate thrust its curves against the night.

"Wilma and I are in Santa Cruz, at Dominican Hospital. There's been a wreck. Lucinda and Pedric aren't hurt too bad, but—"

Kate came fully awake. "What happened? Are they all right? Where's Kit? *Charlie, is Kit all right?*" A wreck at night on that narrow, winding two-lane. "*Where's Kit?*" she shouted, imagining Kit thrown out of the car or running from the crash, terrified.

Charlie said nothing.

"*Where is she?*" She pictured Kit hurt, the confusion of cops and EMTs crowding in at her, Kit running from them in terror and confusion, the little cat who was more than cat but who, under stress, could revert to her basic feline instincts, running mindlessly, hiding even from the people she loved best, just as an ordinary cat might do.

"Ryan and Clyde have gone to look for her. She ran, but she's all right. She called," Charlie said, "called on Lucinda's cell phone. She's all right, Kate. They're taking Rock, he'll find her."

Kate kicked the fur cover to the floor. Carrying the headset listening to Charlie, she made for the bedroom. "Where's the wreck? Where *exactly* . . . ?"

"You can't do anything, Kate. They'll find her. I only thought you'd want to know—"

"I'm coming. Kit's all alone—"

"She's not, she . . . Rock will be there soon, Rock and Joe and Pan, they'll find her. You'd only . . . If you took Highway One, you couldn't get past the slide, you wouldn't be able to drive on down to the hospital. You'd have to leave your car there, walk across, and ride with someone."

"I'm coming. On my way. I'll take 280 . . ."

"Come to Dominican, then. In Santa Cruz, we'll meet there. I know a vet there, I've already called him, just in case. But she'll be fine, Kate, trust me. Kit's a resourceful little soul."

In the bedroom, pulling off her robe, she thought about getting a car in a hurry. She'd been taking cabs and cable cars since she'd returned to the city, didn't want to bother with a car, had rented one when she needed to. She thought about how Kit had loved the city, how only yesterday Kit had been right here shopping with them, the little tortoiseshell whispering secretly in her ear, letting no salesclerk see her, but so filled with joy at the wonders of the elegant stores and restaurants, and now she was lost, frightened and lost and maybe hurt. Oh, God, she couldn't be hurt.

Standing naked in the bedroom she called 411, got the number for the Avis office just down the block, made arrangements to have a car brought around. Pulling on panties and jeans and boots and a dirty red sweatshirt, she snatched up her purse and headed for the door. Whatever she needed, toothbrush, change of clothes, she'd buy somewhere. She stopped at her desk long enough to lock her safe. She checked the balcony glass doors, locked her front door behind her, and headed for the elevator.

The driver was at the curb, a tall, thin redheaded man, his long hair tied back beneath a chauffeur's cap. Kate drove him back to the Avis office over streets slick with fog, waited in the car for him to run her credit card, and then headed south, the city's narrow streets reflecting passing car lights and colored neon from the small cafés and shops. She pictured the city as a friend had described it from sixty years ago when Kate's grandfather was alive, her mother's father, Kate's link to her amazing journey. It was a friendlier city then, without the stark, tall buildings whose lighted offices thrust up into the night around her now like tethered rocket ships, dwarfing the cozy neighborhoods of an earlier day. A city that had somehow soured with the spoils of modern greed and degradation. A gentler San Francisco then, where you could walk the streets in the small hours unmolested, laughing and acting silly but never in danger; and where so many true artists had come together, living in the lofts and in the Sausalito houseboats, their work singing with the passion of life, Kate's own father among them. She had only recently visited his paintings again, in the San Francisco museums—but only his earlier works. Braden West, too, had gone down into the Netherworld, had lived there a long life with her mother.

She knew, now, that they had returned at least once, bringing their youngest child back with them, had made that last journey up to the city to put Kate herself into the care of a San Francisco orphanage. They'd had no choice. Even then the Netherworld was crumbling, they had wanted her away from its inevitable fall, wanted her to grow up in a city that would offer her some future, in a country brighter with promise than that decaying land.

As the tires of the rented Toyota sang along the wet macadam of the Embarcadero, she debated taking Highway One despite Charlie's advice. She moved on past the entrance to the AT&T Park. The traffic seemed light for this time of evening. Accelerating up onto the 280, she merged into fast traffic heading south between the clustered lights of the bedroom cities that ran one into the next, San Mateo, Palo Alto, the smaller communities separated like islands by short realms of black and empty night. The east hills rose invisible in the darkness, marked only by their scattered lights high up like gathered fireflies in the night sky. She'd be in Santa Cruz in less than two hours. She knew Charlie was right, that she could do nothing for Kit but get in the way of the searchers, slowing them and causing them added trouble. But she prayed for Kit, her own kind of prayer that had little to do with churches, she prayed for Kit and was filled with an aching fear for her, for one small and special cat shivering and alone among the vast, wild cliffs.

Kit lost her nerve when the coyotes drew too close. Crouched among the jutting rocks, she shot out of the dark niche at the last minute, scrambled back down the crumbling cliff where she hoped the beasts wouldn't venture. She still carried the phone, reluctant to leave her only link to the world of humans, but its weight was a hindrance, and put her off balance. Halfway down, sliding and clinging to the scruffy clumps, she heard the rush of the beasts above her, and when she looked up their shadows were too close, coming down the boulders. She scrabbled away across the face of the cliff, lost her balance and nearly fell, and it was then she dropped the phone. She froze, listened to it clunk end over end down the mountain.

When she looked up again a coyote stood just above her, peering over the top of the slide, his pale eyes narrow and hungry. She looked past him to the trees and knew she couldn't make that long run. He stank of spoiled meat, his smell made her flehmen, pulling back her lips with disgust.

He padded casually along just above her, easily keeping pace as she worked her way along the cliff's face, moving more easily now without the weight of the phone. She kept moving, seeking some fissure or shelter, until at last, ahead and below her, the black scar of a narrow crevice cut down into the earth. Zigzagging toward it, nearly falling, she slipped down into the four-inch crack. There was barely room for a cat, no room for the larger predator. The rough sides of the cleft was perfumed with the old, faint scent of skunk. She followed it deep, smug in her escape but terrified of being trapped in there if the earth should shift again. Above her, the coyote clawed at the stone, and she edged deeper down until she could go no further, until the rock closed beneath her hind paws. Above her the coyote's eyes shone in, reflecting light from the floods on the road below. He began to dig.

Watching his frantic, shifting silhouette, listening to the beast's scrabbling paws and smelling his rank breath, she longed to bloody that toothy muzzle. If ever the great cat god reached down with a helping paw, she needed him to do that now. Soon the coyote was joined by another and then a third, the beasts edging cleverly down the unsteady rocks and digging at the narrow crevice, panting and slavering, hungry with the smell of her. The night sky was milky, fog settling in again as the wind died, the thick mist easing down like a pale quilt over the shaggy beasts. She didn't know how long she cringed there wanting to leap out and attack and knowing she'd lose the battle. She was shivering with cold when the coyotes suddenly stopped digging.

Turning, they stood looking down toward the road; they shifted nervously, the faint hush of paws on stone. A new, moving light reflected up against the roof of fog and she heard a car's engine, heard tires crunching on the fallen gravel. Not one car, but two. She could hear voices muffled by the fog and the surf. The coyotes moved away and then back again, began to dig again. Still she heard voices, she listened for some time and then the talking stopped and she could hear someone walking up the road, two sets of boots tapping softly along uphill. Only then did the coyotes shift away, their shadows gone above her, but still she sensed them there, maybe crouched and waiting. She started up to look, scrambling up the narrow rift, straining, pulling herself up until she was at the top of the fissure again and could peer out.

Fog was thickening across the road below but she could see a long pickup. Ryan's king cab? Or maybe only the first of the cleanup crew, come to disentangle the wrecked trucks, preparing to haul them away? Looking along the cliff, she saw the coyotes crouched in fog at the edge, their backs to her, looking down the steep drop, too bold to back away, too familiar with the human world to fear the approaching hikers. Disdainful of mankind but still tensed to run, their ears moving nervously. Could she run now, while they were distracted? Streak away, and up that nearest tree that stood tall and ghostlike at the edge of the misty woods? Could she reach it before they were on her?

She was crouched on the lip of the cleft, poised to spring away, when one of the beasts turned, glancing back at her. She vanished down the hole again, scrambled down as deep as she could go. Now the beast blocked the hole, digging, his breath as rank as soured garbage. His frantic seeking stopped when a glare of light shone behind him, picking out his shaggy coat. She heard a roar—Rock's snarling roar, heard humans running, heard Rock's barking attack, and a cat yowled with rage, and another cat, the night rang with snarls and cat screams, she heard the thunder of boots on stone. Ryan screamed, "Hold, Rock. Back off!" Rock's roar was like a great wolf above her, a coyote screamed in pain, and she heard Pan's yowl of challenge.

Clyde shouted, "Not there, the cats . . ."

A gunshot thundered down the cleft, deafening her, accompanied by a pained yip. Another shot, another cry of pain, cut short. Running paws scrambling away across the stony escarpment.

Then, silence.

She peered up to the mouth of the cleft. Pan looked over, backlighted by the beam of a flashlight behind him. Joe Grey and Rock looked over. Ryan and Clyde crowded to peer down behind them.

"Come out," Pan said. "One of the beasts is dead, the rest ran off. Come out, Kit." The light swept away, out of her eyes, and she could see again. She scrambled out, bolted into Pan yowling and crying and talking all at once.

A dead coyote lay beside the cleft. Ryan held Rock away from it, the big Weimaraner fighting to get at the animal, but then he strained up toward the woods, too, where the others had vanished. He huffed and pulled at his lead, torn between the two prey, but held in check by Ryan. Kit backed away from the mangled coyote, its face torn and bleeding. She glanced at Ryan's revolver.

"I fired point-blank," Ryan said, "away from you, away from everyone." But Kit was hardly paying attention. Pan was licking her face, and she preened against him.

Ryan picked Joe up and held him in her arms, cuddling him, and she pulled Rock close, admiring them both, praising them both for their tracking, telling them they were the finest of SWAT teams. Joe Grey tried to look modest—not easy when he could still taste coyote blood, could still feel his claws in its rough coat, and felt more fierce than modest.

It was Clyde who had pulled Joe off the beast, forcing him away, and had grabbed Pan and somehow got hold of Rock's collar, too, and dragged them away so Ryan could fire and keep them from being bitten. Joe allowed Ryan to admire him until he heard someone coming up the hiking trail.

"The sheriff's deputy," he said softly, peering down the cliff where the trail angled up toward them, watching the law approach to see what the shooting was about. "You two better get your story together," he murmured. He wasn't sure whether shooting an attacking coyote, in California, like shooting any wild animal in the state, was a major crime, whether such an act was punishable by unrealistic fines and extreme jail time.

"He attacked me," Ryan said, "and he attacked Rock. Get in my pack, Joe. You, too, Pan. We don't need any extra cats on the scene."

Joe dropped from her shoulder into the pack, silent and obedient. Clyde scooped Pan up and deposited him unceremoniously in his own pack, then picked Kit up and cuddled her.

Settling down inside Ryan's pack, Joe thought about rabies, and about the red tape and bureaucratic confusion that was going to follow this little event, maybe even quarantine for all of them while the carcass was examined and rabies was ruled out. *Or not ruled out,* he thought glumly. Looking down at the dead coyote, he hoped this one was clean. Looking out through the netting in the side of the pack, he watched the baby-faced trooper step smartly up the trail, his hand poised lightly over his holstered weapon.

12

Vic got Birely into his sleeping bag, kneeling uncomfortably on the hard stone floor wishing to hell they had a couple of cots. The only light in the room, the only light they ever had, was the dinky emergency lamp with its six-volt battery, its glow so faint that from outside it didn't show at all. Even so he kept it under the sink to fully block it from the window.

"Can you pull the bag up higher, Vic? It's so cold."

Vic hauled the edges of the sleeping bag up around Birely's neck, immediately soaking it in blood. Guy must have lost a bucketful of blood, and it wasn't just his nose that got smashed. Every time he touched Birely, the little turd groaned and clutched his belly. When Birely began to retch, Vic snatched an empty fried chicken tub from the overflowing trash and shoved it under his face to catch the throw-up. That made Birely heave harder, maybe at the rancid smell. Dry heaves, but all he coughed up was blood. Christ, what had the damn fool done to himself? The way he'd been thrown across the dashboard, Vic guessed the dash had gouged some kind of wound in his belly. When Birely started begging for water, Vic found a paper cup that smelled of stale coffee, filled it from the tap at the sink. Water always ran rusty, there. He rooted through Birely's pack, found a neatly rolled-up pair of Jockey shorts that *looked* clean, used it to wipe the blood off Birely's face. Found a shirt to tie around his face, to soak up the blood that was still gushing. Bleeding would stop for a while but if Birely moved at all or talked too much, it'd start again. Vic left his mouth clear so he could breathe, that was the only way he could get air in. Once the blood stopped for good, he'd be all right.

Vic's own hurts from the wreck were mostly bruises, but he sure as hell was sore. Probably bruised all over, if he'd bothered to pull down his pants, pull up his shirt, and have a look. He knew there'd be a gash down his leg where blood was seeping through his jeans. He wasn't a bleeder, never had been, he expected it would stop in a while. Birely asked for water again, he was lucky the water was working. That had been a plus, when they first broke in. Turned the tap on expecting they'd get nothing. Vic thought maybe the indoor and outside water were all on one cutoff, maybe Emmylou had left it on so she could water the half-dead flowers down in her scruffy yard. When Birely began to moan again, Vic gave him another codeine. He kept whining that his belly hurt, but Birely'd always been a whiner.

"What're we gonna do, Vic, now the truck's wrecked? I need you to take me to a doctor," as if he'd forgotten they had the Lincoln. Though Vic sure didn't want to be driving it around, under the noses of the local cops.

"It's okay," Vic said, "don't worry about it. If you get worse I'll take you to somewhere, Doctors on Duty, one of them twenty-four-hour walk-in places." He got up from the floor rubbing his knees, waiting for Birely's codeine to kick in, so he'd drift off. Digging into one of the paper bags on the kitchen table, he pulled out a can of red beans, opened it with the rusty can opener, found the Tabasco and dumped some in. They hadn't eaten since Denny's on the outskirts of San Francisco, way early this morning, hours before they headed south. He stood scooping beans out with a plastic spoon, wolfing them down, filling his belly.

They'd spent the morning, in the city, looking up the fence he'd been touted on, taking care of business with him. Old man working out of a Laundromat. Guy had given him a fair deal, though. Birely'd been edgy about going in there, but hell, *they* hadn't stolen the stuff. That little chippie, Debbie, that was her haul. He wasn't sure why he'd helped her out. Maybe because she worked so damned hard at conning him. Well, hell, he'd take his thirty percent like he'd told her, give over the rest. Maybe something would come of it. Young, dark eyed, and feisty, she wasn't a bad looker.

Scraping the last of the beans from the can, he watched Birely drifting off, sucking air through his open mouth, the blood still running down staining his teeth red. Good thing they had the codeine, put him out of his pain for a while. But what if he got worse? And what would happen if he died? That would complicate matters.

The way things stood, he figured Birely had some kind of legal claim to this property and to the cash, too. He *was* Sammie's only relative, so he said. Maybe a claim they could make stick. All they had to do was find some softhearted defense group, a two-bit lawyer providing free legal help for the needy, making his money from some kind of federal grant. Guy like that, he went into court, he could get anything.

But if Birely died, what? In a way, that would free things up. He could just take off with the money, get the hell out of there, and who would know? Forget about the property that he'd thought Birely could sell, move on out with the cash, and the cops'd never think about any hidden money, how could they know? Sure as hell Emmylou wouldn't tell them, if she'd found any of it for herself. Not unless she could prove it was hers, which he doubted. Say she did tell the cops there was hidden cash, but couldn't prove she had some legal claim. Cops got in the act, she'd never see those packs of bills again, they'd vanish like spit in a windstorm.

Picking up the keys to the Lincoln where he'd laid them on the edge of the stained sink, he stood looking at the other five keys on the ring. Had to be a house key on there, and who knew what else? Little fat key that might fit a padlock or a safe. Moving to the far wall, he removed the last few planks they'd left loose, removed the loose stone behind them. Reached down into the disintegrating pocket of old concrete, fished out the last two packs of musty hundred-dollar bills they'd left stashed there. Turning toward the door, he saw Birely was awake.

"What you doing, Vic?" Little bastard had raised up on one elbow, groaning watching him, his breath wheezing in his throat.

"Going to hide this in the Lincoln with the rest," Vic said easily. "Maybe pull off one of the door panels.

If that Emmylou comes snooping, spots us in here and maybe calls the cops, we'll need to take off fast. I want the money stashed where they can't find it, ready to roll."

Birely retched and coughed and reached for the cup of water that Vic had set on the floor beside him. "What if the cops get their hands on the car, what then? We'll never see that car again, and there goes my money, every damn bit of it." Birely always put the worst spin on things, he never could see the positive side.

"I'll muddy up the license plates until I can steal some. Maybe I'll dirty up the whole car." Vic smiled. "A bucket of garden dirt, a little water. Don't look like the cops have a BOL out on the Lincoln yet, we passed three CHP units on the highway and two sheriff's cars, and not one of 'em even turned to look. Maybe that old couple didn't think to report the car stolen, maybe they were too far gone."

But Birely wasn't paying attention, he was real white. "I need a doctor, Vic. Otherwise I'm gonna die. You got to take me somewhere, to an emergency room."

"Codeine should have kicked in by now," Vic said. "I'll give you another pill, then you'll rest easy."

Birely was hugging his belly and wheezing for air, and Vic felt his temper rise. Birely was going to slow him down, was going to get in his way, going to give the cops time to start looking for the Lincoln, and maybe time to find it.

As Vic stood pondering what to do, Birely began to talk as he had earlier, as he'd been muttering on and off ever since the accident, snatches of his childhood, some of them repeated over and over, useless memories of his sister and their old uncle, that old train robber that he guessed was famous in his day. "It was our uncle, Lee Fontana, sent the money to her," Birely said now, "and Sammie only a kid, twenty-some, that old man sending her money like that, what was that about? He didn't send me none."

"Why didn't she put it in a bank?" Vic said. If Birely kept on talking he'd wear himself out and go to sleep again.

"Maybe she hid it all that time because it was stolen," Birely said, "afraid the feds had the serial numbers and would trace them if the money went in the bank, maybe thought the feds would want to know where she'd got it. Well, anyway she hated banks. Uncle Lee hated banks, she got that from him. I'm not so fond of banks, neither. Never have done business with one, all my life long." That made Vic smile. Birely'd never had no money to *put* in a bank.

Some of what Birely muttered about was things before he was born, that Sammie'd told him. Some man following their mother, coming to the house when her daddy was off in the war. World War II, and that was some long time ago. Birely'd said Sammie was about seven. This stuff Sammie'd told him years later, it got stuck in his memory and he'd keep repeating it, stories about the man following and beating their mom, and the cops wouldn't do anything, garbled stories warped by time and distance. Birely started whimpering again, as if the codeine hadn't ever taken hold. Vic didn't know how much codeine he could give him before he checked out for good, and he was torn about that. You had a dog this sick, hadn't eaten and couldn't eat, dog hurt like that, you'd put it out of its pain.

Sick man, dying man, what use did he have for two hundred thousand in musty bills? Nor did Emmylou, neither. What was she going to do with that kind of money? All she ever did was work away at her so-called remodeling project, and clump around in her scraggly yard talking to that mangy yellow cat. That in itself showed she didn't have good sense. Sure as hell she was seeking out the money little by little, down there, as she tore out the walls. What a waste, what would she use it for?

Outside, even as Vic headed over to open the door, the yellow tom dropped down from the window and was gone. He'd watched from among the trees as the man stared around into the night searching for a prowler he'd never find. He'd heard enough through the window to know that Birely *was* Sammie's brother, and to remember more clearly that moment from his earlier life. To remember that ex-con following Sammie's mother and beating her. The other guy was a classmate from her high school. Sammie's daddy off in the Pacific fighting in the war that was meant, once again, to end all wars, and this scum comes onto his young wife. Now, listening to Birely, that distant time came clear, the rooms of their tiny cottage in that small Southern town, the polished floors and handmade rag rugs, a gold-colored cross hanging over the bed; and then the old gas station and garage that Sammie's daddy bought when he did get home from the war, bought to make a living for the three of them. Birely's words woke in him sharp fragments of memory, each scene filtered through the eyes of the young and careless tomcat that he had been in that earlier life.

13

Lucinda Greenlaw's glass-fronted cubicle in the Santa Cruz ER was so tiny that Kate had to slide in sideways, pushing back the canvas curtain, joining Charlie Harper and Charlie's aunt, Wilma. The two women stood crowded against the wall between the water basin, the hazardous-waste receptacle, and Lucinda's hospital bed. But Lucinda was even more constricted, bound to her bed by a tangle of tubes and wires, as captive as a bird caught in a net, this active older woman whom everyone admired for her youthful outlook and vigorous lifestyle. Now, she slept, she was hardly a bump beneath the thin white blanket, so fragile, her breathing steadied by the oxygen that whispered through her mask. She wore a cast on her lower left arm, and a heavy white bandage around her left shoulder.

Charlie gave Kate a hug. "Sorry I brought you out in the night." Her unruly red hair shone bright in the overhead light, tied back crookedly with an old brass clip, caught across one shoulder of her brown sweatshirt, which she'd pulled on over what looked like a pajama top, pale blue with little white stars.

"I'd have been mad if you hadn't," Kate said. Her questioning look at Charlie brought a shake of the head. There was no word, yet, of Kit, then. Wilma took Kate's hand, trying to look hopeful. She wore a red fleece jacket over jeans and a navy sweater, had pinned her gray hair hastily back into a knot. Her canvas carryall stood on the floor beside her booted feet, looking so suspiciously lumpy that Kate knelt and peered in.

Dulcie looked up at her, the expression in her green eyes worried for Kit. Above them in the narrow bed, Lucinda stirred a little, muttered then was silent again.

"Still sedated," Charlie said. "They set the arm right away, and slipped her dislocated shoulder back into place. Thank God it wasn't broken. She's bruised all over, and scraped down her left side, where he jerked her out of the car. The nurse said she was still mad as hell, too," Charlie said. In the bright fluorescent light, Lucinda's skin seemed as thin as crumpled tissue, the veins of her wrists dark above the adhesive that held the invasive needles. She barely resembled, now, the slim, robust woman who walked the Molena Point hills several miles a day with Pedric, their Kit racing joyfully ahead leading them to the wildest paths and up the steepest climbs.

"She was able to describe what happened, then?" Kate asked, still kneeling and stroking Dulcie.

"Clearly," Charlie said. "We talked a few minutes, while they were preparing her for surgery. It's Pedric who doesn't remember much, and that's worrisome. Some moments come clear, but then he can't fill in the spaces between. That should come with time," she said. "Even so, he remembers enough to be raging mad, too. When they're awake and lucid, they're both impatient to talk to the CHP, to the county sheriff up there, and most of all, to Max." Max Harper, Charlie's husband and Molena Point chief of police, would most likely coordinate the Greenlaws' statements for the other law enforcement agencies. "He'll bring it all together," she said, "that will help ease Lucinda and Pedric from so many interviews. Multiple interviews are necessary, but it will wear them out."

Charlie watched Lucinda, sleeping so quietly. "You won't get these two down for long," she said hopefully. She filled Kate in on the wreck and the attack, repeating what Lucinda had told them. "There's a BOL out for the Lincoln. If those two men are picked up, they'd better be *locked* up, away from me."

"Away from all of us," Kate said, looking into Dulcie's own angry eyes. "By now, who knows how far away they've gotten. Headed where? Arizona? Oregon? Mexico?"

"Lucinda told us what's in the car," Charlie said. "If they dump the car or sell it, will they trash all those lovely purchases? But maybe," she said, "maybe they won't find the rest.

"At least Kit wasn't in the car," she said, thinking of what Kit might have tried to do, trapped in the Lincoln with those two men, and what they might have done to her.

"Have Ryan and Clyde called?" Kate asked. "Can you call them?"

"They called once," Wilma said, "when they parked up at the slide. They were just setting out to search." She touched Kate's shoulder, where she knelt beside the carryall. "Kit's tough, Kate. She's smart and quick—and she has Lucinda's phone. When she sees the Damens' truck, sees them start up the cliff, don't you think she'll use the phone or else call out to them, lead them right to her?"

"If she's not afraid to lead something else to her," Kate said. She wished she were there, she couldn't shake her fear for Kit, she felt as weak with fright as if she herself, in cat form, crouched small and lost up there in the black night, with only her claws and little cat teeth to protect her against whatever prowled, hungry and listening.

"Their house keys are on the ring with the car keys," Wilma said. "Ryan said that first thing in the morning she'll get her lock man out. I'll put holds on the credit cards. They have some blocks on them and on their bank accounts, but better to be safe.

"Pedric gave the hospital their insurance information, he still had his billfold, the guy missed that, too busy harassing Lucinda and stealing the Lincoln. When we got here, Lucinda's focus was all on Pedric and on Kit, she couldn't rest at all. She wouldn't let them take the X-rays until we assured her the Damens had gone after Kit, she just kept begging for Kit, fussing and trying to get out of bed. She made such a rumpus she disrupted the whole floor, the nurses had a time with her. We got here, talked for only a few minutes, told her Rock was tracking Kit. Finally they took her to X-ray, gave her a shot, and in less than an hour she was off to surgery."

The three women watched Lucinda and watched the lighted monitor above her bed with its moving graphs and numbers that mapped Lucinda's life processes, oxygen level and blood pressure and the slow steadiness of her heartbeat. "Once we've taken care of the credit cards and changed the locks," Charlie said, "we need to make arrangements for when they come home. Maybe they won't have to go into rehab, if we take turns staying at the house, have nurses come if they're needed. We *could* put someone in their downstairs apartment if . . ."

She shook her head. "I'd even thought of Debbie Kraft," she said with a wry smile. "She needs the job, and the Damens' would be thrilled to get her out of their cottage. But it would take more effort to ride herd on Debbie than to move in ourselves. To say nothing of the torment that older girl would dish out. There'd be no peace, with Vinnie in the house."

"I can stay," Kate said. "I'd planned to be with them for a while. I could stay, and you all could run the errands, pick up the meds and groceries. Would that work?" She wanted to be there, in part to watch over Kit, whose wild but vulnerable nature was so like Kate's own temperament. She longed to hold the little tortoiseshell safe, keep her close and safe. No one said, If Pedric comes home, if he heals from the concussion, and can come home. No one said, If Kit comes home, if Ryan and Clyde can find her. Wilma took Kate's hand and Charlie's, as if by touching, by all of them willing it, they could help to heal the older couple and could bring them home, and bring Kit home. It was in that quiet moment that tabby Dulcie crept out from Wilma's carryall and slipped up onto Lucinda's bed. Stepping delicately among the snaking tubes, she padded up beside Lucinda, on her unhurt side, slipped under the covers, laid her head on Lucinda's shoulder, and softly began to purr. Maybe Lucinda, deep in dreams, would imagine she held Kit in her arms, snuggling close, maybe that thought would help to heal her.

Leaving Birely half asleep, Vic headed out the door and down the stairs along the side of the stone building carrying a couple of rusty screwdrivers he'd found in the stone shack, an empty old bucket and a dirt-crusted spade he'd found in the yard, and a paper bag with four bottles of water, eight cans of beans, the rusty can opener, and the two packs of hundred-dollar bills he'd had on him. Maybe he'd find something useful among all that junk in the Lincoln, maybe a couple of blankets. The rest of the stuff he'd dump somewhere, all them fancy packages from the San Francisco stores. He should have had all this when he linked up with the fence, it'd be worth something. He didn't know much about upholstery material, if that's what those bolts of cloth were, but the fancy pictures and lamps had to be worth something—that old couple were big spenders. Had to be, driving a Town Car and all. Maybe when he headed out he'd swing through Frisco again and see what he could get for the lot.

Standing in shadow at the bottom of the stairs, he watched the house below. The old Chevy was parked off to the side on the dirt drive where that stringy old woman kept it. There was no light in the kitchen window, no reflection of lights from anywhere in the house, shining out against the pine trees. Moving around to the shed door, he removed the lock, eased the door back so it wouldn't squawk, and slipped inside.

He deposited the paper bag among the packages in the backseat, then carried the bucket outside again. Kneeling close against the stairs, he began scooping up loose garden dirt with the spade and with his hands. Filling the bucket, he turned back inside, poured in a bottle of water, and stirred the mess with the spade, into a thick mud. Earlier, leaving the wreck, he'd hidden the cash behind the back console. Maybe he could do better than that before he took off, maybe find a hiding place the cops wouldn't think to poke into with just a casual stop, a stop he might talk his way out of. If he changed his looks, got a haircut, cleaned up in different clothes, maybe he could slip by.

He thought how drug dealers pry off the door panels of a car to secure their stash, he'd watched a guy do that, once. Took special tools, which he didn't have. He sure didn't want to bend or crack the panel, not be able to put it back right. But he didn't want the money on him, neither. And if he decided to stay put here for a while, he didn't want to hide it again in the stone room. He had an uneasy feeling about Birely up there whining and carrying on. If that old woman heard him and came nosing around, who knew what she'd poke into that was none of her business?

Pulling down the armrest, he removed the packs of hundreds. The little metal tray beneath was screwed in place, with a small square hole in the front, along with two small connections where, he thought, people could charge their cell phones. When he poked the screwdriver down in the hole he could feel a space beneath, about an inch deep. Using the Phillips, he removed the screws and lifted the tray out.

The space beneath was big enough to stash most of the packs of bills. He stuffed the rest in his pocket, screwed the black plastic tray back in place, then got to work on the outside of the car. Stirring up the bucket of dirt and water, and using a wadded-up shirt from Birely's pack, he began to spread the mud on. First the license plates, and then the outside of the car, dirtying up the shiny black paint and the dents, just enough, not to overdo it. Working away humming to himself, he thought about a better place to hide the car, away from that old woman poking around. One thing, he'd have to lift a new set of plates, maybe from the far side of the village. But the car itself he wanted nearby where he could keep an eye on it.

There were plenty of empty houses down the hill, abandoned places, no one ever around, no furniture when he'd looked in through the dirty windows. Skuzzy neighborhood, foreclosures, empty rentals, the grass grown tall and brown, FOR RENT signs tipped crooked or lying on the ground. Their narrow, one-car garages, the ones he could see into, were empty. Stash the Lincoln for a few hours, steal himself another set of wheels or borrow them.

That little tart Debbie Kraft, she owed him one, the good sale he'd made for her. Maybe he'd use her old station wagon. Take the money he'd got from the fence down to her, and make nice. He'd sold everything she'd stole. When he handed over near three thousand in cash, that should make those dark eyes sparkle. Hell, she couldn't refuse the loan of her car, not when she knew he could finger her for stealing, tip the cops that she was boosting the local stores. She sure wouldn't want the cops to know she was using her daughter

Vinnie as a distraction and, sometimes, setting the kid up to heist small items herself, silk bras and panties, a few pieces of costume jewelry, while Debbie kept the clerks busy.

Judiciously Vic went on spreading mud, not too much, keeping it to the lower parts of the car, the wheels and fenders and bumpers. Spreading the slop, watching it splash onto the shed's dirt floor, he smiled. It was all coming together, his running into Birely like that, south of Salinas, the story Birely'd told that turned out to be true, the money in hand now, everything going real smooth. He had only a few more moves and he'd be out of there. Sell the Lincoln, get some shiny new wheels, not like Debbie's old heap, and head north out of California, maybe way north, up into Canada. Get lost up in Canada for a while and then off again, he could go anywhere he wanted now, with this kind of money.

14

"They're sure to stop us," Ryan told Clyde as they entered the hospital from the covered walkway. She avoided looking directly at the two guards in dark uniforms who watched them from within, through the wide glass doors. "We look like a couple of tramps, with our dirty backpacks, look like we're up to no good." Their wrinkled, stained clothes smelled of sweat and of dog, of gunpowder and maybe of coyote, too, to a discerning nose, maybe even the scent of animal blood. "And my mop looks like a Brillo pad," she said, pushing back her dark hair where it clung, frizzled into tight curls from their night in the fog. "Not to mention how your backpack is bulging. Be still, Kit," she muttered, leaning close to the pack, afraid the guards would see it move and want to investigate, would paw through the pack and find Kit staring up at them or scrambling to bolt away.

But no one bothered them, they received only a bored glance from the two uniformed men who were deep in conversation, totally uninterested in what they might be carrying inside with them. Maybe they looked too tired and limp to be bringing in a bomb, to be smuggling in anything that would take much effort. Or maybe Santa Cruz Dominican hadn't had any problems yet with bomb threats or petty vandalism, as the bigger city hospitals were experiencing.

But when they reached the emergency room, down an open flight of stairs, that area was more secure. The ER's doors were locked, they had to give a nurse their names, and provide Lucinda's and Pedric's names, and wait for another nurse to lead them in through the heavy double doors. The short, pillow-shaped woman in green scrubs escorted them past the inner nurses' station and on past rows of small, glass-walled rooms not much larger than a walk-in closet, some with the curtains closed, some open so they glimpsed patients within, sleeping or looking forlornly back at them. Lucinda's glass doors stood open, the canvas curtain drawn halfway across, the lights dimmed down to only a soft glow. Wilma Getz and a lean, dark-haired nurse in scrubs stood one at each side of her bed, frowning

as if they'd been arguing. Lucinda lay awake, scowling, but she seemed groggy, too. She smiled vaguely
at Ryan and Clyde. "Kate and Charlie were here," she
said. "Gone down to Pedric." And almost at once she
dropped into sleep again. The cast and bandage on her
left arm looked heavy and uncomfortable. Her right
arm lay across a red windbreaker, holding it posses-
sively. Wilma stood beside her, holding the red jacket,
too, keeping it firmly in place as the nurse reached to
remove it, apparently not for the first time. At Wilma's
angry glare, she paused and drew her hand back.
Wilma's gray ponytail was awry; she looked as if she'd
pulled on her jeans and navy sweatshirt while climbing straight out of bed. But she looked, even so, not a
woman to defy, with that steady and uncompromising
gaze. Wilma had intimidated her parolees for thirty
years, until she'd retired from the federal court system.
She didn't tolerate patronizing behavior from a person
committed to easing the suffering of others, particularly of helpless patients.

"Lucinda wants the jacket near her," Wilma said.
"She says it smells of pine trees, and of the hills of our
village. What harm, if it comforts her?" Her stubborn
grasp on the jacket, and Lucinda's own protective arm
across it, even in sleep, didn't hide adequately the little
mound beneath but, confronted by Wilma, and now

with Clyde and Ryan's presence, the dark, sour woman seemed reluctant to push the matter. She smiled woodenly at the Damens, shook her head as if there were little she could do about unreasonable patients or visitors, and turned away leaving the jacket in place.

Moving to Lucinda's bed, Ryan reached beneath the jacket, speaking softly to Dulcie, smiling up at Wilma.

Wilma grinned back at her. "Lucinda thinks Kit's cuddled next to her. She's much more peaceful since Dulcie slipped into bed with her. If the nurses will just leave us alone."

"The best therapy," Clyde said, slinging his pack off, resting it on the edge of the bed. "But there's no need for a stand-in now." And Kit peered out at them, her green eyes bright.

"Oh," Wilma said, reaching for her, pausing to glance out the door and then leaning to hug her. "Oh, you're all right, you're safe." She hugged Kit, squeezing almost too hard. "Pedric's been asking and asking for you, they've been so upset. That's made the doctor upset, he doesn't want Pedric stressed."

Ryan moved to the glass door and pulled it closed. She stood a moment looking out to the big, center island of counters and desks from which the nurses and doctors and orderlies could see into all the rooms. Only the canvas curtain offered privacy. When she closed that, too, leaving only a crack to look out, Kit slipped from the backpack, her dark coat stark against the white cover.

"Hurry," Ryan said, "she's coming back." Kit didn't crawl under with Dulcie, but returned to the depths of the canvas pack.

"Come on," Clyde said, slinging her over his shoulder. "We'll look in on Pedric. What time does the shift change, when does that nurse leave?"

"Twelve, I think," Wilma said, glancing at her watch. The clock above Lucinda's bed had almost reached eleven. Clyde and Ryan moved on out with their stowaway, leaving Lucinda sleeping happily with Dulcie as surrogate, and Wilma standing guard.

"How many cats," Clyde whispered, moving down past the nurses' station to the other side of the big, open square, "how many cats can you smuggle in, before you have Security in your face?"

"They let therapy dogs in," Ryan said softly. "If the cats wore those same little therapy coats, maybe . . ."

He gave her a lopsided grin. "Don't even think about it. This is dicey enough."

"What would they do if they caught us?"

He laughed. "What could they do? Two innocent little cats? At least we don't have to worry about Joe and Pan." They'd left the two tomcats in the king cab, both solemnly promising not to open the door, not to set foot outside, had left them pacing back and forth past Rock, who lay curled up asleep. Having completed his night's work, the silver Weimaraner didn't mean to be kept awake by a couple of edgy tomcats.

"I just hope those two are as good as their word," Clyde said.

"And how good is that?" she said nervously.

Pedric's room was brightly lit, the overhead fluorescents turned up high as if the softer lights of evening would too easily lull the patient to sleep when, with a concussion, he must be kept awake. Charlie and Kate sat crowded into folding chairs that they'd jammed between the wall and Pedric's bed. His head was wrapped in a thick white bandage. His thin, lined face was painted with black-and-blue marks down the right side and around his eye where Vic had hit him with the tire iron, bruises that made him look like a dignified clown halfway through applying his makeup. A young, redheaded nurse was fluffing his pillows, he was talking softly to her, the look on his face intense. Whatever he was saying made her uncomfortable. She turned away as Ryan and Clyde entered, bending to adjust the height of the bed. She glanced up embarrassedly at them and at Charlie and Kate, her face flushed, and silently fled the room. Behind her, Charlie and Kate exchanged a look of amusement.

"What?" Ryan said when she'd gone. "Pedric, what were you saying? You weren't coming on to her?" she said, laughing.

Pedric looked puzzled. "I was talking about the old country, the old myths, the old Celtic tales. I told her she looked like the princess from under the hill, but I guess she didn't understand. I guess I made her nervous." He looked vaguely up at them. "I guess if you're not into mythology, that might sound a bit strange?"

Charlie pushed back her red hair, where a loose strand had caught on her shoulder. "You got her attention, all right. Maybe nurses aren't into folklore. Maybe, when you work in a world of discipline and hard facts, slipping away into imaginary places can be unsettling." Though for Charlie that wasn't the case; she seemed, in her paintings and her imaginative writing, to live comfortably in both realms.

But Pedric's attention was on Clyde's backpack, which had begun to wriggle. When he saw Kit's bright eyes peering out through the mesh his face broke into a smile, he raised his arms to her as she struggled to get out to him. She was about to leap down beside him when another nurse, a blond, shapely woman, started across from the nursing station and Kit ducked down again. She was stone-still as the nurse entered. Her name tag said HALLIE EVERS. She opened the glass door wide, and opened the curtain.

"You can visit," she said, looking sternly at the four of them. "But not so many at once. One, maybe two if you're quiet. We don't want him excited, though we do need to keep him awake. We need to do that calmly, do you understand? Dr. Pindle will be in shortly. Are you all relatives of Mr. Greenlaw?"

"We're good friends," Clyde said. "The Greenlaws have no relatives. We came to do whatever we can for them."

She frowned. "He's been talking strangely, going on about some kind of fairy tale, about harpies and dragons as if they were real," she said doubtfully. "Maybe the concussion has stirred up some childhood fancy."

Kate hid a smile. Charlie frowned, looking down at her hands.

"That's not surprising," Ryan said, giving Nurse Evers her most beguiling smile. "Pedric's a folklorist, that's his profession. He *studies* the old, classical myths and folktales, he has an impressive collection of ancient literature, he tells wonderful stories. You should visit with him sometime, if you're interested in such things.

But you're right," she said, her green eyes wide and innocent. "Four of us is too many, all at once." She turned to Pedric. "We'll take turns visiting, then, seeing that you don't sleep," she said gently.

Kate grinned at Charlie and rose, and the two of them left, highly amused by Nurse Evers.

"We'll be quieter," Ryan told the nurse. "How long must he be kept awake?" Still smiling, she stepped back, easing against Clyde.

"Until the doctor has done an evaluation," Nurse Evers said, "possibly longer, depending on what is found. Dr. Pindle will give you that information. Mr. Greenlaw's hurt his knee badly, as well. He seems to want to wait for treatment on that until he returns home to his own doctors. He's very vague, most likely due to the concussion. The doctor may want to talk with you about that." All this as if Pedric were not in the room with them or as if he didn't hear or understand her. "Vague, and then he'll start in again on those strange stories."

Clyde pretended to adjust his backpack, where Kit had begun to wriggle with impatience.

"He seems able to remember only fragments of the accident, but that's to be expected. He remembers more distant . . . things. I suppose," she said doubtfully, "if these stories are his profession, I expect he would remember those." She gave them a brighter smile as if to humor them, and she left abruptly, leaving the door and curtain wide open behind her. Returning to the nurses' station, she moved directly to a computer where she sat facing them, keeping them in view.

Ryan moved to the door, smiled across at Nurse Evers, then closed the door and drew the canvas curtain. She turned to the bed, where Clyde had lowered the backpack and opened it. Kit's black-and-brown ears emerged. As her little tilted nose pushed up over the edge of the pack, Pedric reached in to her, such joy in the older man's face that Ryan had to wipe her eyes and Clyde turned away embarrassed by his own emotion. Quickly Pedric lifted the sheet and Kit crept under, tucking down so close to him that when he'd covered her again, she was barely a lump in the thin white blanket.

"After the wreck," he whispered, "where did you go? Where were you when they found you?"

"Above the landslide," Kit said softly. "Rock and Joe and Pan found me and Ryan and Clyde right behind them and Ryan had her revolver, one shot at that coyote that was trying to *dig* me out of the rocks, and *that* mother died, serves him right, trying to eat a poor little cat, and those other two ran like hell and then Pan was there and, oh my . . ." She stopped talking, purring so loudly that anyone passing might have heard her. But then, suddenly yawning, she went quiet beneath the blanket, all worn out. Snuggling deeper against Pedric's side, she drifted off into a deep and healing sleep—while Pedric, longing for sleep, for a forbidden nap of his own, lay watching over her, as their friends stood guard.

15

It was midnight when Vic crawled into his sleeping bag on the floor of the stone shack, careful not to wake Birely and have him start whining again. The little turd was finally sleeping deeply, despite having to breathe through his open mouth. Even in the dim glow of the battery light, he was pale as milk. Vic had tried to get him to eat but he didn't want anything, just sucked at the water in the limp paper cup. He'd woken up once and talked for a while, his voice slurry, rambling on about his childhood again and his sister, Sammie, and how she came by all that money. Birely'd never say why the old man would send that kind of money to a young niece, send it clear up from Mexico, maybe didn't know why. They'd already found over a hundred thousand, and sure as hell Sammie'd had more down in the house.

Weird, her growing old in that run-down place when she'd had enough to live high on the hog. Birely said she liked living the way she did. He said, look at Emmylou, her only friend, another recluse just like Sammie.

Strange, the change in Birely. He used to be a real wuss, a drifter, went right along with whatever anyone wanted him to do. But after Sammie'd given away what was his, now he was all anger, so mad at Sammie that he got moving, all right, looking for her hidden stash.

Birely never knew the old uncle, all he knew was what Sammie and maybe their folks told him. Old train robber did his share of prison time back then, Birely knew that much. Sammie was about nine when Lee Fontana made his big haul and lit out for Mexico, running from the feds, got out of the country shortly before Birely was born. Sammie called him the cowboy, Birely said. She claimed that sometimes she knew from her dreams what he was doing, knew what was happening to him even when he was halfway across the country. Well, you couldn't believe half what Birely told you. Birely said the old man's last robbery was big in the papers back then, and Vic could believe that, all right. Some kind of federal money, Birely didn't know exactly what. Said you'd get burned bad, back in them days, for a federal heist. Vic wondered if the feds kept records back that far. If, tucked away in some musty drawer of ancient files, some federal office had the serial numbers on those old bills.

But what the hell? Even if these cops here in Molena Point got their hands on the money, which wasn't likely, even if they figured out it was real old money, who would think to look back to the last century for some federal robbery? Who would even care?

Except, he thought, if that federal case was still open and he did take Birely to some hospital and Birely started talking, who knew what the dummy would blurt out? Enough to make some nosy cop curious, start him rooting around into the past? Birely could talk on and on, and Vic didn't want to chance that—there were times when a man had no choice, when he did what was needed just to save his own neck.

The Damens weren't night people, Ryan and Clyde were early risers, they were often in bed by nine or ten, but somehow in the small hours of this long night they managed to stay awake and to keep Pedric awake, taking turns, one dozing, one asking Pedric for details about the wreck to keep him from drifting off.

Charlie had gotten two adjoining motel rooms nearby at Best Western, so they could all take turns sitting with Pedric; Ryan had stayed with him while Clyde left to take Rock and the two tomcats there, to feed them and get them settled in. Kibble and dog food for Rock, a nice spread of takeout for Joe Grey and Pan, of rare burgers and fried cod. He praised the three trackers lavishly again for their night's work before he left to join Ryan.

Rock, having bolted down his supper, was tucked up with Charlie on her bed. Joe sprawled across Wilma's empty pillow while she and Kate and Dulcie were still at the hospital; Pan didn't settle but paced restlessly, leaping onto the daybed that had been set up for Kate, aimlessly wandering the two rooms, missing Kit, wanting to be with her, still suffering the aftermath of his worry over her. *How strange is that?* he thought. Kit was his first true love, and he didn't quite know what to make of the condition, of the intensity and turmoil that had descended to change his carefree life. *Kit is all fluff and softness—over slashing claws,* he thought, smiling, *sharp teeth, and a will more stubborn even than my own.* She was brave as a cougar one moment, dreamy the next, always volatile, keeping him forever off balance. All he knew was that right now he missed her; he paced until he wore himself out, and then settled down next to Rock and Charlie and, like the softly snoring Weimaraner, Pan slept.

It was one A.M. The lights in most of the ER rooms had been dimmed, only Pedric's lights shone brightly behind the drawn curtain. Ryan had left the glass door cracked open, but the few nurses and attendants visible were busy at their desks, able to get computer records entered, now that most of the patients were sleeping. At this predawn hour a quiet lull held the ward, perhaps before the next sudden round of broken legs and stomach cramps that would have nurses hurrying again to minister to the wounded and accident-prone. Quietly, Clyde pushed in through the canvas curtain.

Pedric was sitting up in bed, in his skimpy hospital gown, a white cotton blanket around his shoulders, looking relaxed despite the fierce headache he said still plagued him. Beneath the blanket he held Kit safe, so happy to have her there. Ryan sat beside the bed, Clyde's backpack near, in case someone came to tend to Pedric; nurses were never shy about waking patients from sleep to administer pills, to poke and prod and straighten blankets.

"I can remember only fragments of this week," Pedric was saying worriedly, "a breakfast of Swiss pancakes, a cable car ride in the rain. Kit stretched out on Kate's windowsill," he said, smiling, "watching fog slip in beneath the Golden Gate. Whole mornings and evenings are blank.

"I remember Kate's stories more clearly, the granite sky, those cavernous sweeps of stone lit by the green glow of the subterranean daytime, a winged woman with a . . ." He went still then as the canvas curtain moved and was eased aside.

A doctor in a white coat stepped in. "Dr. James Pindle," he said, rigidly watching Pedric. He didn't offer to shake hands with him, or with Ryan or Clyde. He was a thin-boned man, narrow arms and shoulders, small hands. Milk-white skin against ink-black hair, eyes so black you couldn't see the pupils.

"I left orders for only one visitor at a time," he said accusingly. "I don't want him talking away like this, I don't want him stressed. Didn't the nurse *tell* you that?"

Ryan had risen, pretending to straighten Pedric's covers as Kit slid deeper down; too late now to slip into the backpack, and they were terrified Pindle would lower the rail to examine Pedric.

"At least you didn't let him fall asleep," Pindle said. "I hope he hasn't slept. The nurse must have told you that much, if you were allowed to stay in here with the curtain drawn. You *must* have been instructed what to watch for." He glanced out toward the nurses' station, where Nurse Evers seemed totally preoccupied at her computer.

"You do understand," he said coldly, "that with a concussion he can't have drugs or painkillers or caffeine, and that he will try to escape the pain by retreating into sleep."

"We understand," Clyde said. "He hasn't slept. We've been very quiet, and he hasn't talked much."

"He just seems glad for the company," Ryan said. She didn't say which company had so pleased and calmed the patient. Pindle gave her a chill look and moved to the bed rail, forcing Ryan to step aside. He stood not inches from where Kit hid beneath the blanket, looking at Pedric. "One of you will have to leave. The patient is a bundle of nerves, surely you can see he's disturbed."

"Not at all," Pedric said, smiling easily at him, putting out his hand for a proper introduction. "In fact, I'm feeling better, the headache is less severe. I'd like something to eat, if there's anything available at this hour."

Pindle's face seemed frozen into scowl lines. "I'll tell the nurse. Maybe some crackers and applesauce." He looked at Clyde. "Is he still worrying about his *cat?*" he said with disgust. "This foolishness about a cat has him unduly upset. I can't have him worrying, certainly not over something so inconsequential. I'm moving him to the ICU in the morning, until he's stable. Blood sugar way too high, and that could mean any number of things. And the torn knee needs attending to. The hospitalist will be in shortly, he's the one who will admit him. I don't suppose either of you have a medical power of attorney?"

"We both do," Clyde said coolly. "As do Ms. Osborne, Wilma Getz, and Mrs. Harper. Ms. Osborne is down the hall with Pedric's wife. We are all listed on both of the Greenlaws' health care directives. Mrs. Harper signed him in, so that should be on the chart."

"Then there should be no problem if further tests are warranted," Pindle said. "His wife will be kept in ER overnight. If nothing else shows up, she can go home. I'm on my way to look at her. We'll keep Mr. Greenlaw until the concussion has healed and the torn meniscus in his knee is repaired, though we may find that other procedures will be needed."

What other procedures, Ryan thought, here in a strange hospital? And who said Pedric and Lucinda weren't alert enough to do their own signing?

"Maybe Dr. Carroll can deal with him," he said without explanation, and without any comforting word to Pedric, he left the room, the canvas curtain swinging behind him. Ryan looked after him, rigid with anger, then hurried to catch up as he moved along the hall toward Lucinda's room.

"I'm not sure," she said, walking beside him, "that it's wise to separate Lucinda and Pedric, to send Lucinda home alone." She kept her voice loud enough to alert Kate and Wilma. One close call was enough, they didn't need this man finding Dulcie. Dr. Pindle didn't respond, he didn't speak or turn to look at her. He pushed past her, was just entering Lucinda's room when Ryan, glancing back, saw another doctor leave the room next to Pedric's, heading for Pedric's door.

Praying Kate and Wilma had heard her warning, she turned back again, to help Clyde get Kit out of there unseen, or try to get her out. But, stepping in behind the doctor, he didn't alarm her as Pindle had; his movements were easier and unthreatening as he turned to look at her.

He wore the requisite white coat with its little brass name tag, same dark slacks as Dr. Pindle, soft-soled black shoes. But this man looked relaxed, he had an easy walk, a big man, big hands, tousled red hair framing a face that looked sunny and thoughtful. As he approached Pedric's bed she saw Wilma hurry out of Lucinda's room carrying her heavy tote bag, the canvas bottom sagging. Had Pindle seen Dulcie and angrily sent them packing? Or had Wilma moved fast enough to clear the premises before they found themselves in a nasty tangle of red tape and security guards, mired in a diatribe that would leave both the cats and humans shaken, leave the two patients sicker than they'd been when they were admitted?

Even before Ryan left Pedric's room Kit was digging her claws into the mattress trying not to squirm, not to burst out hissing at that Dr. Pindle person. She felt trapped by his cold voice, trapped by the bed rails and the tightly tucked blanket that hid her, trapped even by the tubes and wires that confined Pedric, that seemed to confine them both. Hidden in the near dark against Pedric's warmth, she couldn't see out; she'd listened with growing anger to Dr. Pindle, had heard Ryan follow him out of the room, heard her voice moving away down the hall as if to warn Kate and Wilma, but still she felt he might appear again, and the man made her fur crawl. But then, crouched there listening, she sensed Pedric start to fall asleep. She felt Clyde shake his arm, prodding him awake. "Talk to me, Pedric," Clyde urged.

Oh, don't talk about the Netherworld again, Kit thought, but already he was saying, "A world so green, like the green underworld of the old myths," and even as he rambled on again, to keep himself awake, she heard footsteps in the room next to them, a man's soft-soled step. "Green drifting out of the granite sky . . ." Pedric was saying, and she pawed at him to make him be still. She heard the next door slide open, the scuff of rubber-soled shoes approaching Pedric's door. She peered out searching for the backpack, but she couldn't see it. Yes, there, Clyde was holding it open. She tensed to slip out but she was too late. Another doctor had stepped in and with no time to hide she pushed closer to Pedric, her heart pounding.

He came to stand beside the metal rail. He would be looking down at Pedric, looking right at the covers where she hid. She tried not to move even a whisker, prayed not to sneeze or purr. Purrs weren't always controllable, sometimes they just slipped out.

He didn't smell like Dr. Pindle, he had a friendly scent, laced with a touch of spicy shaving lotion. His voice was easy, deep, and relaxed. "I was in the next room, Mr. Greenlaw. I'm Dr. Carroll. That was a fascinating tale you were spinning."

Kit swallowed. There was a long, awkward silence. She listened to Clyde and Ryan introduce themselves, standing near the foot of the bed. And Clyde launched into Ryan's explanation of Pedric's seemingly wild talk.

"Pedric's knowledge of Celtic folklore is remarkable," Clyde said, "he—"

Dr. Carroll stopped him. "Not necessary," he said. "I heard quite a lot, from next door." He smiled down at Pedric. "Dr. Pindle doesn't get it, does he?"

Pedric was silent, his body gone tense.

"The old tales are an interest of mine, too," Dr. Carroll said. "In my Scotch-Irish family, I grew up on the Celtic myths. Dr. Pindle seems concerned that you're delirious," he said, laughing. "I don't think that. Pindle has no feel for the ancient wonders. Maybe they frighten him."

There was another silence, Kit sensed the two men looking at each other. Dr. Carroll said, "Pindle seemed concerned that you are unduly distressed, Mr. Greenlaw. Over the loss of your cat? I understand she escaped from your car, after the wreck? I suppose he didn't understand why that would worry you. Has there been any word of her?"

Pedric's voice came stronger now. "She . . . she ran up the cliff, into the woods. But Ryan and Clyde found her, she's safe now, and that has eased my mind."

"I imagine it has," Dr. Carroll said, "and eased Mrs. Greenlaw, too." Kit felt him touch the blanket, and before she could slide away or think *what* to do he'd pulled the covers back. She stared up at him, stricken.

Dr. Carroll smiled. He looked straight down into her eyes, and it was a look she could never have feared. He reached to stroke her, his big hands gentle. His nails were very short, clean and neatly trimmed. His blue eyes were full of light, his red hair curly and wild, his freckles dark across his square cheeks. He spoke right to her. "The next time you hide," he told her, "you want to be sure you haven't left a tortoiseshell hair or two, on the white blanket."

Kit blinked, and then purred, but her poor heart was pounding so hard she knew he could feel it beneath his stroking hand.

He couldn't know that she understood him, but he spoke as if she did, he looked at her as if he knew what she was. He scratched her ears, then looked up at Pedric. "I'm glad she's safe, Mr. Greenlaw. I know you and your wife are relieved. Now that your little cat is here, I can already see the healing in your eyes, in your smile. This little lady," he said, "is the best medicine you could have. Don't be disturbed by people like Pindle. But," he said softly, "do keep her hidden."

He turned to look at Clyde. "Several of you came up from Molena Point to be with the Greenlaws?"

"Yes, my wife and three friends. Charlie Harper is the wife of our police chief."

"I know Max. We talked on the phone just a little while ago. You're not going back tonight?"

"Charlie got a couple of motel rooms, we plan to take turns sitting with Pedric, keeping him awake. If we're needed."

"It will be a big help. He mustn't sleep, yet." He gave Clyde a wink. "If you can keep their little cat close to them, maybe pass her back and forth, that will be good medicine for both patients.

"You've done well, so far, hiding her." He glanced up at the screen above Pedric's bed. "His vital signs are already stronger. Between the five of you," he said, "you should be able to keep the staff from discovering her."

"We're doing our best."

"Some of the nurses can get testy when a rule is broken." He scratched Kit's ears again, in just the way she liked. "If there's a problem, call my cell number. I'll be on duty all night, until six A.M." He jotted the number on two cards, handed one to Clyde, the other to Ryan. He winked at Kit, his blue eyes still laughing. He turned away, slipped out through the glass door, shut it, and pulled the curtain closed.

16

It was much earlier that night when Misto, wanting company, prowled the cool night looking for Joe and Dulcie or his son, Pan, to share the late and secret hours. Thinking that Pan might be visiting Tessa, he galloped away through paths of moonlight, through shadows as black as soot, trotted across rough oak branches above the narrow alleys, making for the crowded cottages that rose just above the village. Soon, from the roof of Tessa's small cottage, he looked down on the dark driveway where a reflection of light cut across from the kitchen window.

Backing down the pine tree by the front door and peering in, he watched Debbie at the kitchen table sorting piles of bright new sweaters and blouses and cutting the tags from them. He didn't scent Pan, and when he moved on to Tessa's window, there was no sign of him, no red tomcat. When he tried the screen, it was firmly shut and latched, and Tessa slept soundly. He wished she'd wake and talk to him.

He didn't hide from the child as Pan did, to keep Debbie from knowing he was about. But he didn't flaunt himself in front of the woman, either. Sometimes he'd come into the yard when Debbie wasn't watching Tessa, and the child would follow him, slipping away from her mother and sister up across the deserted streets into Emmylou's yard. If Debbie saw her, she'd drag her home again, she didn't want the child wandering off after "some stray cat. First that cat up in Oregon, that red-colored cat always hanging around. The fuss you made over it. And now this scrawny yellow one. What is it with cats, Tessa? Can't you play with one of your dolls and leave the dirty animals alone? I won't *have* it in the house, a dirty stray sneaking in and out carrying fleas and germs and dead mice."

But up at Emmylou's, the older woman was kind to Tessa, she liked the shy child, she talked to her just as she talked to Misto, never expecting an answer, just rambled on, and that put Tessa at ease. She would soon curl up on a chair or on the bed close to Misto, watching Emmylou and listening to her random comments and stories, and then she didn't look pale and pinched anymore. Now as he looked in at Tessa he heard Debbie's step, and saw the kitchen light go out. He dropped from the sill down into the bushes.

Heading away again, on up to Emmylou's house, he saw her windows were all dark, her lights already out, and he thought to curl up at the foot of her bed. It was lonely with his own family gone, even staying with the Damens sometimes it was lonely. Slipping in through the old, splintery cat door and through the dim house, he found Emmylou sound asleep. But before settling for a nap on her bed, he leaped to the dresser.

A finger of moonlight through the window reflected across the two pictures of Sammie. The little child. And the grown-up Sammie. Two photos taken sixty years apart, and that long-ago life nudged at him.

He thought about nine-year-old Sammie and how she had confided her fear of the man who followed her mother, and confided her dreams of her uncle Lee Fontana and his last big robbery, a lone bandit in the style of an earlier century making off with saddlebags full of stolen cash, never a hint of conscience or remorse, just a smug smile at the corner of his thin, leathery face. Was this, then, what these old musty bills were about, was this young Sammie's legacy from Lee Fontana that he'd sent her after he fled the country for Mexico? Misto's memory of that time was as fragmented as a shattered windowpane, only a few scattered moments coming clear, only a few snatches of that past life.

It was a noise outside from up the hill that drew him away, footsteps moving down the stone stairs from the little building above. Dropping to the floor and slipping outside again, he stood in the shadows of the porch, tail twitching, as the taller man eased down the stone steps carrying a bucket, a spade, and a heavy paper grocery bag. His jacket pockets bulged, too, and on the night breeze Misto caught the money scent. He watched him open the shed and disappear inside. The place was so small it was a wonder he'd gotten that long black car in there and been able to shut the door against its rear bumper. He came out again carrying only the spade and bucket. He knelt beside the stairs and began to dig, dumping crumbling dry earth into the bucket. There was a sense of hardness about him that Misto sometimes encountered in his travels, the cold brutality of some of the men around the coastal fishing docks that made him steer clear of them.

He expected the black car must be stolen, and he wondered what they'd done with their old truck. Maybe it had quit running and they'd traded it, in the way of thieves, for something far more grand. Easing down Emmylou's wooden steps and then up the hill for a closer look, he veered into deeper shadows as the man carried the full bucket inside and shut the shed door, shut it right in his face, never seeing him.

There was no way to see inside, no windows. The door itself, though ancient, was so tight a fit there wasn't a crack to peer through. The sounds from within were a dull clunking and gritty scraping, almost as if he were stirring the dirt in the bucket, and then a sliding, rubbing sound, then after a very long while there was another clunk and then silence. Waiting, he grew impatient, and at last he slipped on up the hill and up the stone stairs to the stone room to whatever he might see there.

The one window was crusted with grime, its screen fallen off, lying far away overgrown with weeds. The small pane of glass stood open to the autumn night, and he leaped up to the sill to look in. He could smell the stink of soured food in dirty cans, and of dirty clothes, could see a pile of clothes flung in one corner. The room smelled of the tall man, and of the smaller man and, sharply, the stink of sickness and blood.

Slipping in through the open window onto the short kitchen counter, he dropped as soundlessly as he could down to the grimy linoleum. The man lying in a sleeping bag didn't stir. He lay curled up like a hurt animal. This was Birely, the same man as in Sammie's grown-up photo of the two of them, still the same slanted forehead and fat cheeks as the tiny child he had known, same protruding lower lip caught in a permanent pout. His nose and face were a mess of blood and he was breathing through his mouth; he was doubled up in pain, he needed help, but apparently his tall friend didn't think so. He looked to Misto like he wasn't far from death. The old cat's instinct was to find a phone and paw in 911, to alert the medics. Leaping to the sill again, he was out the window racing down through the tangled yard to Emmylou's dark house, passing the shed where clicking sounds had begun again.

The phone was in the kitchen. He was through the cat door and up onto the counter. He could do it without ever waking Emmylou, he had only to whisper into the speaker, he thought nervously, hoping the call couldn't be traced, that the dispatcher wouldn't pick up Emmylou's number. Hoped Captain Harper and his detectives wouldn't start looking at innocent Emmylou Warren for the identity of the phantom snitch, for the source of so many informative phone calls over the years when, in truth, Emmylou hadn't a clue. The older woman had no notion about speaking cats or undercover cats who'd left their pawprints on so many village telephones.

But did Emmylou even have ID blocking? Not likely—why would she? This woman lived the simplest life, she didn't take a daily paper, didn't have a TV, didn't allow herself any amenities that he could see. Why would she pay for ID blocking? If her phone number *were* public knowledge, who did she have to fear? He had lifted a paw to the phone's speaker when Emmylou's bedroom light came on.

He heard her moving about and in another minute she came into the kitchen, in her robe and slippers. She glanced at him where he sat innocently beside the phone, and then moved silently out the back door. Stood on the porch looking up at the stone shed, listening to the faint scraping noises from within, then she moved silently down her steps, pulling her robe tighter against the chill. Moved up the hill in her slippers, the hem of her robe catching on weeds and on the overgrown bushes, stood to the side of the closed shed door, listening.

Two more taps, and then another long silence. When footsteps within approached the door, Emmylou ducked into the bushes, crouching comically, her tall form hunkered down among the tangled twigs, her long hair caught on the branches.

The door didn't open, the footsteps turned away again toward the back, and then again there was silence. So long a pause that Emmylou gave it up, just as Misto had done earlier. Rising, she looked up at the stone room above, stood listening, glanced back at the stone shed and then moved on up the hill as Misto had done, only pulling a small flashlight from her robe pocket and switching it on. The thin path of light picked out patches of wiry grass and the matted damp leaves trampled into a rough path. Twice she paused looking up at the house above her. The stone steps followed the ground only inches above it, and only near the top did she move from the yard up onto them, her damp slippers making no sound. On the little landing she switched the light off, and moved directly to the dirty window, again as Misto had done, and she peered in.

Even in the near dark she must have seen the figure doubled up on the floor, or maybe she heard Birely moan. She looked back down the long empty flight, making sure the man hadn't left the shed and was watching, then she shone her light in.

She stiffened when she saw Birely. Even with his bloodied nose, she had to know him from Sammie's pictures, and maybe she knew him, too, from when Sammie was alive? "*Birely?* Oh, my. What . . . ?" But even as she spoke, Misto saw the taller man slip out of the garage.

The doors had made no sound, only when he closed them was there the faintest scrape—but enough to startle Emmylou. As she turned, he saw her. He froze, then ducked into the bushes and was gone. Misto could hear him moving away, bumbling in the darkness crackling the branches, but then, as if gathering his wits, he moved on nearly silent as a cat.

Emmylou stood looking where he'd vanished, not where he was now. And then she ran, down the stairs and down the hill, up her own steps and into her cottage, and Misto heard the door lock behind her. Racing after her and in through the cat door, he watched her snatch up the phone and dial the three digits. He could hear the little canned voice at the other end, faint as a bee buzz, as the dispatcher questioned her.

When she'd hung up the phone, she fetched the crowbar, stood hefting it, looking out the kitchen window at the back porch. Misto rubbed against her ankles, wondering how Birely had been hurt so bad, wondering whether Birely would die, wondering why he still cared so much. Wondering why those lives, long past, had returned to haunt him so sharply, or why *he* had returned to this particular place and time. To play a part in Birely's sad life? Or, perhaps, so he could know the last, sad fate of his little Sammie?

17

Having left Pedric's room hidden in Clyde's backpack curled up atop his spare sweatshirt, Kit lay now beneath Lucinda's white covers pressed between the bars of the hospital bed and Lucinda's warm, familiar side. Her housemate seemed frail and vulnerable in her heavy bandages and cast, and wearing only the flimsy hospital gown. Whenever Lucinda slept, Kit drifted off, too. She woke when Lucinda stirred sleepily and stroked her back and head. Wilma sat close beside the bed in a folding metal chair, her brocade carryall hanging on a knob of the bed where Kit could slip easily down into it. Three times within the last hour, the nurse had come in. Each time, Wilma had risen to distract her, asking needless questions, going into useless detail about Lucinda's condition and care—maybe if she made a pest of herself the nurse would stay out of there for a while.

But nurses weren't easily distracted. This small, square Latina woman had answered Wilma's questions briefly as she checked and replenished the IV bottle and went about tidying up, picking up discarded tissues and adhesive tape and paper wrappers from the metal table, and then bringing Lucinda a fresh pitcher of water. Clyde was down the hall with Pedric, but soon someone would come to relieve him and to pass Kit back to Pedric again—like a library book forever changing hands. The time, by the big round clock above Lucinda's bed, was three A.M. and despite Kit's satisfaction at being with Lucinda, the predawn hour made her incredibly lonely.

This was the cats' hour, the shank of the night, the time when, if she were at home, she would be bolting out her cat door and down her oak tree to hunt the hills with Pan. Or they'd be lounging in her tree house listening to little animal sounds bursting suddenly out in the silent dark. But tonight, here in this strange town and strange building, shut in this small unfamiliar room among unpleasant hospital smells, she felt edgy and dislocated.

She knew that Lucinda and Pedric, lying bound to their beds, felt much worse, helpless and so far from home, felt far more displaced than she.

There were no windows in the ER—when dawn did come Lucinda wouldn't be able to look out at the sky, at the first hint of sun as she so liked to do. She always rose from bed when the sky was barely light, would put on the coffee and then, with the house smelling deliciously of that dark brew, she would sit at the dining table sipping her first cup, looking out through the big corner windows enjoying the sunrise, watching its blush brighten and then slowly fade again and daylight spill golden onto their little corner of the world, onto the round and friendly hills and the intricate tangle of rooftops spread out all below her.

And Kit herself, if they were at home, as they should be, would soon return from hunting. Another two hours and she'd bolt into the house as dawn broke, Pedric and Lucinda up and showered and in the kitchen making breakfast. She'd sit on the windowsill cleaning up, washing off the blood of the hunt. She'd long for a nap but breakfast would win, the three of them would enjoy waffles and bacon and then head out for a walk up the hills or through the nearly deserted village streets looking in the shop windows.

Would they do that ever again? Would her housemates come home healthy and well, ready to enjoy their long, free rambles and simple adventures?

But she knew in her little cat bones that they would, just as she knew the dawn was on its way, just as any cat at this hour would wake and begin to prowl restlessly—knowing something good was coming. Soon her housemates would be home again, as eager and hardy as ever; stubbornly Kit clung to that thought with a keen and sharp-clawed resolve.

She could hear, up and down the ward, little clinking sounds as late-night medications were prepared or other mysterious routines attended to. The smells of alcohol and human bodily wastes were not Kit's favorite scents; she longed for the smell of new grass and its sweet, cool taste. Around her the ER, though still shrouded in the hush of night, was slowly beginning to stir, the steps of the nurses quickening as they attended to late-night medications. Glass doors to several little rooms were slid open, curtains were drawn back. Whenever their night nurse left them alone, pulling the door closed as Wilma requested, the three of them talked in whispers. Lucinda sometimes slipped into sleep, but always when she woke she asked after Pedric.

"He's feeling better," Wilma told her, "the concussion's not a bad one. As soon as we get home, the knee will be repaired. Clyde's with him now, to keep him awake." And they talked again about that lost world where Kate had gone to learn about her forebears and had found only a dying civilization. All the anticipated magic was gone, only the cruelest creatures still blazing strong with their greedy hunger.

Wilma, like the Greenlaws, was comfortable with Kate's secrets. While Clyde, like Joe Grey, shied away from the tales. But, Kit wondered, what did Ryan think?

Ryan had cleaved easily enough to the knowledge that Joe Grey could talk, she hadn't been terribly shocked the first time the gray tomcat spoke to her—but still, Ryan had been raised in a hardheaded law enforcement family. Where were the limits of her sometimes willing imagination? What did she really think of a world teeming with remnants from the old Celtic tales that so embraced the cats' own history?

And what, Kit thought, *will Pan think, when he learns where Kate has been?*

She could imagine Pan's amber eyes blazing with a keen and hungry fascination, with a bold curiosity that would lead, *where?*

Kit herself had long ago come to terms with her own dreams of such exotic ventures, she had turned resolutely away from her own longing to descend down into the darkest pockets of the earth. When she was very young, when she first came to Molena Point, she had been drawn to Hellhag Cave that cleaved the hills south of the village, to its mystery, had sensed that dark fissure leading down and down, and down again deeper than any cat she knew had ever gone, she had longed to wander there, to discover whatever she might confront that would surprise and amaze her. Only fear—or a touch of good sense—had held her back. Then later she had been drawn to the cellars and caverns beneath the ruined Pamillon mansion that rose in the east hills above the village, intrigued by those dark clefts beneath the fallen buildings. But again she was afraid, she sensed evil there and a destruction she wouldn't dare to face.

But Pan was bolder. What would he do with Kate's secret? She thought Pan had never turned from danger. Her red tomcat had a hunger for adventure that had sent him traveling the coast of Oregon and half of California, one small cat alone never turning from a new and frightening adventure. *Oh,* she thought, *when he hears Kate's tale will he want to go there? Will he go away to follow the harpies and chimeras through that evil land, will he leave me for that adventure?*

Or would he want me to go with him down to that dying place that could destroy us both?

Vic watched Emmylou hurry down the hill tripping on the hem of her robe, watched her double-time up her own steps and inside. She was going to call an ambulance or call the cops, the damned old busy-body. He should have done Birely while he had the chance, and now it was too late. Unless he could stop her, push on in and grab the phone from her. Had she even locked the door? He'd started down, two steps at a time, but then he thought about the car.

He had to get the Lincoln out of there before the cops came swarming all over. Maybe he'd been foolish stashing the money there, but where else could he have hidden it? He thought about moving the money before the cops arrived because it was too late to move the car, but he didn't have time for that. He was reaching to open the shed when the whoop of the ambulance nearly deafened him, its flashing lights stabbing between the trees, a white medic's van pulling up into Emmylou's dirt driveway.

He eased back into the bushes as four medics in dark uniforms piled out and Emmylou came out her door onto the little porch and started down to them. He watched the shorter medic with the mustache follow her up the hill while the other three hauled out their trappings: stretcher, oxygen tank, black bags, and fancy stuff he couldn't name. Sure as hell, there'd be a patrol car right behind them. What he couldn't figure was, why would that old woman call the medics for a sick tramp? Why would she care?

And where would they take Birely? Some fancy emergency room? What if he started talking, if they gave him drugs for the pain and he got blabby, talking about the money, got some cop curious enough to start asking questions. Emmylou paused up on the stone porch while the medics hurried inside. That yellow cat had followed her winding around her ankles, damn thing gave him the shivers, he could see it there in the bushes, it kept looking at him, its yellow tail twitching in a way that made *him* twitch.

They took a long time in there. He grew cold in his light jacket. He crouched in the bushes hugging himself, antsy to get the car out. What had that old woman told the dispatcher? Had she said there'd been a break-in? Would she want them to search the whole damn property? Two medics came out of the stone house carrying Birely on a stretcher. Emmylou stood to the side, watching. Damned old do-gooder. A third medic, dark-skinned Latino, was asking her questions, writing down her answers on a clipboard. Vic watched her sign a paper when he passed the clipboard to her, and wondered what that was about.

She couldn't be making herself responsible for some tramp she didn't know, she couldn't be promising to pay his medical bill? Talk about a bleeding heart.

Or *did* she know Birely? Maybe Sammie'd had pictures, family pictures. Maybe this old woman recognized him and had got all sentimental over Sammie's
little brother? Or maybe she knew Birely from when
Sammie was alive? Birely had come here once in a
while but Vic couldn't remember if he said he'd ever
saw anyone but Sammie.

If this old woman had any sense, she'd let charity
or the government pick up the bill. The medics had to
take Birely to the emergency room, it was the law, and
the hospital had to treat him, the law said they couldn't
refuse. So why *pay* for it? Hell of a waste of money. He
watched the white van back around in the old woman's
driveway and move on down the hill again, heading
for some ER. Watched Emmylou head back down to
her house, her bathrobe pulled tight around her. The
black-and-white never had showed up. What had she
told the dispatcher? Just that there was a man sick up
there, and nothing about a break-in? Maybe said he
was renting the place—all to protect Sammie's little
brother? He waited a few minutes, was about to slip
back down to the shed when she hurried out again,
dressed in jeans and a sweatshirt, and got in her old
Chevy. Hell, she was going to follow the van to the hospital. What a patsy. When she started the car it belched
out a puff of dark exhaust. Yellow cat crouched on the

porch watching her back out and head away following the medics, and Vic thought uneasily about Birely there in the hospital blabbing about the money.

He waited until the Chevy had disappeared, then headed for the shed, smiling. Maybe he could silence Birely right there in the ER, and wouldn't that be a laugh. Shut him up before he spouted off about the money and the fancy Lincoln they'd stolen or, worse, about some of Vic's own, earlier ventures. If Birely died in the ER before he started bragging about Vic's successful robberies, and maybe about that store clerk he hadn't meant to kill, if Birely died right there under the care of a doctor, how could he, Vic, be responsible?

18

Heading for the hospital following two blocks behind Emmylou, her old green Chevy nearly bumper to bumper with the ambulance, Vic spotted the turn-in to Emergency but went on by. He drove on half a mile farther, turning into a wooded neighborhood with big, expensive houses set back among the trees, their grounds softly lit by fancy lanterns but only a few windows showing lights, at this hour. Rolling his car window down, he heard no barking dog. There was no one on the street, no night joggers with their fancy, lighted shoes, no reflective gear of a cyclist who might prefer the empty streets of night, no late partiers headed home. Big houses, three- and four-car garages, but most of the driveways empty. He drove until he found a place with two cars parked in front, a Mercedes and a Jag, and a Toyota sitting on the street. Pulling over beside the Toyota and killing the engine, he got out, slipping a short, oversized Phillips screwdriver from his back pocket.

In less time than it would take the householder to hear some tiny sound and turn on the lights, he was driving away again with his new license plates on the seat beside him. He stopped ten blocks away and switched the plates on the Lincoln, smearing on a little of the Lincoln's damp mud to make them match the rest of the car. Then he headed back to the hospital, following the big red signs to the emergency entrance at the mouth of the underground parking garage, easing the muddy, dented Lincoln along the first level to the back row where cops coming into the ER might not notice it.

Parking, he hit the lock button on the pendant with the key and walked back to the emergency room's wide glass doors, thinking about somewhere secure where he could hide the Town Car later for a few hours, get it out of sight. He couldn't take it back to the stone shed; the minute the EMTs filed their report with the PD, the cops'd be all over the place, the stone shack and Emmylou's house, too. And, in the ER, they'd be all over Birely, wanting to know how he got hurt, asking who else was involved, asking him why he'd been staying in an empty house with only a sleeping bag and where was his friend that the other sleeping bag belonged to?

Approaching the glass doors of the emergency room, he saw an ambulance parked down at a garagelike bay, which stood open but was dark inside. He saw no activity there, no sign of any medics, no stretcher or gurney visible. He moved on up the few steps to the glass doors of the admittance room; they slid open automatically for him. He was hardly inside, moving on past the clerk at the desk hoping she wouldn't try to stop him, when he spotted Emmylou sitting in a small glass cubicle to his left. Her back was to him, facing a desk where a young man in a white shirt and V-necked sweater was filling out papers. Turning away, he moved into the general seating area, sitting as near to Emmylou as he could, hoping to hear what she was saying. She didn't know him, she'd never seen him that he knew of, but he picked up a magazine to hide his face. He couldn't hear much through the glass, and their voices broken by the conversation of passing orderlies and nurses going in and out, carrying clipboards, pushing wheelchair-bound patients on into the ER. He'd catch a few words and then the meaning would be interrupted. He was pretty sure Emmylou was passing herself off as Birely's sister, he heard her clearly when she said there were no other relatives. He waited until the clerk led Emmylou down a short hall to a set of heavy double doors and used his ID card to open them. Quickly Vic followed, slipping in behind them, moving on down the row of small glass rooms as if intent on his own business. Center of the big space was all open, with an island of counters and desks. The clerk at the nearest desk gave him a look. He nodded at her and moved on past. Maybe his stained chinos and worn-out windbreaker got her attention, and his mud-stained jogging shoes. If he had to make another trip here, he'd have to do something about clothes, find something to wear that didn't make him stand out. Several cubicles down, he turned back to see where the clerk had led Emmylou, and nearly ran into two employees, right behind him. They were both in blue scrubs, with ID badges pinned to the pockets. They stood blocking his way, their expressions bland but businesslike. The white-haired woman's badge said NELLIE MACKLE, RN. Short hair, thin, a small woman, maybe a hundred pounds, and no physical threat to him, but her dark eyes set him back, hard and challenging. "Are you looking for a patient?"

"My neighbor. My neighbor was brought in," he said. "At least I think they brought him here. Birely Miller? I heard he was hurt in a car accident, all the lights went on at the house and then I heard the ambulance and

I thought . . . Well, he's kind of a loner, I wanted to know if he's all right, if there's anything I can do."

Nurse Mackle glanced back down the hall, where Emmylou stood in the doorway of one of the glass cubicles, number 12, then stepped behind a desk to a computer. She looked at the screen for a moment, returned to Vic, but said nothing. The man, whose hospital badge had no name, looked down at Vic from a healthy six foot four. Dark skin, dark brown eyes that looked soft and understanding, but with a gleam of challenge. Big hands loose at his sides, his fingers twitching just a little.

"Only family is allowed," Nurse Mackle said. "If you'll give us your name, we'll pass it on to his sister, she can let you know his condition."

Vic said his name was Allen James, that he lived four blocks down from Birely. He made up a phone number. She wrote down his information, nodded, and looked meaningfully toward the big double doors. Her dark friend's look, too, implied serious consequences if Vic didn't do as she suggested.

He left the two, feeling like a felon, turned away knowing their eyes followed him. He moved on behind another nurse who was headed for the big, closed doors just beside a unisex bathroom. Most California bathrooms were unisex like this one, the door marked with both his and hers symbols and, in this case, a picture indicating wheelchair access. When he glanced back, the two inquisitors had moved on away, but as he passed the last little room and was about to go on out through the big doors, voices made him turn back to a brightly lit cubicle.

Its glass doors and canvas curtain were open. The patient filled the whole bed, his broad shoulders crowded against the side bars, his feet pressed against the bottom rail. Beside the bed a small woman, round and wrinkle faced, fuzzy hair the color of old news- papers, stood talking with a dark-haired, white-coated doctor. "You might want to go on home, Mrs. Emory, and get some rest. In a little while I'll be moving Michael to ICU, I want to run some more tests, and watch him for a few days. That was a bad fall he took."

When he glanced up, Vic turned away, facing the door to the bathroom as if he were waiting his turn. "He can have one or two visitors at a time, Mrs. Emory, but they're not to stay long, you understand."

Vic turned his back to them, trying not to smile. With the patient's name, he had all he needed to get back into the ER without being interrogated. When the door to the bathroom opened and a woman stepped out, Vic stepped on in. He used the facilities, ignored the sign that said WASH YOUR HANDS, and left. Keeping his back to Michael Emory's room, he pressed his hand to the mark on the wall as he'd seen the nurse do, watched the big double doors swing open. He moved quickly out through the waiting room to the dim parking garage; he still had things to do. He needed a change of clothes, and a haircut. Maybe a barbershop cut, not just him snipping around his ears with a pair of rusty scissors, making a mess. A haircut could go a long way toward keeping the cops off your back.

He'd gone through the packages in the Lincoln again, there was some expensive stuff there, all right. Maybe he could add a few things to it, unload the whole lot with that fence. Them bolts of heavy cloth for covering a chair or sofa, fancier, for sure, than the kind of upholstery goods they used in prison industries to cover the cheap office chairs they turned out. He'd found the old folks' two suitcases in the trunk under all the other packages, and had gone through them. Maybe he could sell the clothes, the woman's stuff had labels so well known even he recognized the value. But among the old man's stuff there was nothing for him to wear, even if it would fit. Two dress suits, white shirts and ties, the kind of clothes that would call attention to himself in just the opposite way from his own stained jeans and mended windbreaker.

Maybe when he returned to the hospital he could lift a pair of blue scrubs like everyone wore in there.

He'd blend right in, except for the badge. Everyone he saw, nurses, orderlies, was wearing a badge. Did these people wear their scrubs to work, or put them on here? Maybe they got them from a supply closet, same as they'd get clean towels and sheets? And did they keep the closets locked?

He could think of a dozen ways to get tripped up, though, stealing hospital clothes. He kicked himself again for not snuffing Birely when they were alone and he'd had the chance. If he'd done him then, he'd be long gone by now, and wouldn't have all these details in his way.

But maybe Birely was so bad he wouldn't have to help him along, maybe before the night was over, the hand of fate would end the poor wimp's misery.

Heading upstairs to the main level, he glanced at his watch. Nearly four A.M. He found a phone, got the information he wanted. He was back down on the dim parking deck by four-thirty, easing the Lincoln out of the covered garage, turning down toward the freeway. Taking the on-ramp south, back toward the village, he wanted to get cleaned up, change his looks if he could, and get into some clothes that didn't make people stare at him.

He had the Lincoln's registration in his pocket giving the address, and now he had the phone number. One of the keys on the ring had to be the key to the Greenlaws' house, where the old man would have plenty of clothes. Let them two old folks give him a helping hand, it was their fault his truck was wrecked. If they'd been traveling at a decent speed he'd have been past the slide when the rocks fell, would have been well away from the damn delivery truck and would have never crashed into it.

Leaving the ER, he had wandered the main floor of the hospital until he found the courtesy phone on a little table in one of the seating areas. A nice amenity so patients' families like him, he thought smiling, could make local calls. Sitting down on the couch, he'd punched in 411, hoping Santa Cruz was in the same area code, because the phone sure as hell wouldn't reach long distance. Even these free spenders weren't going to let you call all over the country, at the expense of Peninsula Hospital.

But he'd lucked out, it was all the same code. He'd found the hospital pen he'd put in his pocket, jotted the names and numbers on a magazine, of the two Santa Cruz hospitals. He'd called Dominican first, asked for the room of Pedric Greenlaw, and he hit it right. The guy was there, secure in a hospital bed, maybe an hour away from Molena Point, and no way he'd be home tonight. He was advised that the patient was sleeping and that he should call back in the morning.

"And Lucinda Greenlaw?" he'd said, repeating her name from the car registration.

The operator would not disturb Mrs. Greenlaw, either, at this hour. "Try around eight in the morning, when the patients are awake," she'd said shortly.

Hanging up, he'd called local information again, for the Molena Point residence of Pedric Greenlaw. It was listed, all right—as if the Greenlaws had no idea someone would want their information for less than a friendly social call. When he was automatically connected, the phone rang twelve times before he hung up. He waited a few minutes and then called twice more, let each call ring a long time, but still there was no answer. Jingling the Greenlaws' keys, he'd headed back through the hospital and down the stairs, out through ER to the parking garage.

Before he pulled out, he'd gone through the glove compartment of the Lincoln again, found the local map stuffed in with a handful of Northern California maps, this one a colorful tourist edition meant for out-of-town visitors. He'd found the Greenlaws' street, and now he headed there, down the freeway and off into the hills above the village.

The neighborhood was wooded with scattered oaks, and dark as hell with no streetlights. He saw no light in any window. No house numbers in the village, either.

But higher up on the hill there were numbers on the curbs, in reflective paint. Driving slowly, he found the Greenlaws' place and pulled up in front.

The drive and garden were lit by low lamps at ground level, real fancy. The driveway and walk were of stone, a huge oak tree overhanging the garage. He could see a tree house up among the branches, as if maybe these people had grandkids. He sat looking and listening. There was no sound, no lights, no window open with curtains blowing, all was dead still.

He looked for a button on the car's overhead that would open the garage door. How much noise would that make, to alert the neighbors? Some of them doors were as loud as a stump grinder. At last he decided to risk it. If there was no other car in there, that was one more good indication he was alone.

He finally found the button in the visor. The door slid up with hardly a sound. He smiled at the empty two-car space, pulled on in, and killed the engine. Hitting the button to slide the door closed behind him, he fished his flashlight from his pocket and stepped out of the Town Car.

He tried three keys before he had the inner door open. Shielding the flashlight, he moved in through a hall that opened to a laundry and bath, and then on into a big, raftered living room, high ceiling, windows all along two sides. The drapes were open and through the tall glass he could see the lights of the village down below, all pretty damn fancy. Garden lights at the back, too, a level lower, picking out a narrow deck that probably opened to a daylight basement. No light shone from that level out onto the deck or bushes, but in case anyone was sleeping down there, he took off his shoes. Still shielding the flashlight, he checked out the living room.

Big, flat-screen TV hidden in a cabinet, that should bring a nice sum but would be a bitch to haul around, there wasn't room in the Lincoln unless he dumped what he already had in there. CD and DVD players and music system were small enough to tuck in the car. Nothing else of much value in that room, a wall full of old, worn-looking books along the back, cracked leather bindings, nothing worth taking. In the dining room they'd cut a cat door in the window, at table height, he supposed for that cat they'd had with them. People were weird about their pets. There was a kind of study in one corner of the living room, desk and computer and more books, floor-to-ceiling books, all of them old. The money these people had, why didn't they buy some new ones, buy some of them fancy best-sellers with bright covers?

There was just the one bedroom, but it was nearly as big as the living room, with a bath and two closets, his and hers. In the old guy's closet he tried on several pairs of pants and sport coats, looking at himself in the full-length mirror. Everything fit pretty good. He settled on a tweed sport coat, tan chinos, and a brown cotton turtleneck, a pair of soft leather Rockports that were stretched enough to fit his larger feet.

In the bathroom he dared a light, closing the shutters first, pushing their louvers tight together. Rooting through the drawers, he abandoned the idea of a barber, he didn't want to wait until one opened, and he didn't want some guy to ID him later. Small town, cops poking around, in and out of places, asking questions. He found a pair of scissors and set about trimming off his long hair, and that took him a while. Felt strange as his hair dropped away, made him feel naked. Belatedly he spread out a towel to catch the mess, sweeping what had fallen onto it with his hand, trying not to leave evidence. When he'd done as good as he could, he found a razor and shaved the back of his neck, holding a hand mirror he'd found on the woman's side of the cabinets, twisting awkwardly to see.

He shaved off his short scraggly beard, which never would grow thick the way he wanted. He took a shower, using a big thick towel on the rack. He slapped on the old guy's aftershave, which had a lime smell. He found clean shorts and socks in a dresser drawer, and pulled on the brown turtleneck. Posing in the full-length mirror, he thought he looked pretty good. Except for his white, newly shaven cheeks and chin and the back of his neck. He rooted around among the woman's things, looking in the medicine cabinet and in drawers, but couldn't find any bottle of colored makeup to disguise the pale marks.

It took him a while, in the kitchen, working by flashlight, to figure out the fancy microwave. In the freezer he found a package of spaghetti, read the directions, opened it, and shoved it in. While he waited, he put his own clothes in the washer, threw his canvas jogging shoes in, too. While the washer rumbled away, and with the spaghetti smelling good, he opened a cold beer from the refrigerator door.

Retrieving his supper, he found a plate to put it on, and sat down at the table where he could look down at the village lights. He even found a paper napkin, tucked it in the high turtleneck to keep it clean. How would it be to live like this, in a fancy house? Well, hell, with the money he'd stashed in the Lincoln, and maybe twenty thousand more when he unloaded the car itself, he could live any way he wanted.

But not in a house like this. Not in a tame village like this where he'd be bored out of his mind. The kind of money he had now would put him in Vegas or some

Caribbean island with plenty of action. Party all night, poker and roulette tables to help him double or triple what he had, and a choice of showgirls offering anything he could pay for.

Finished eating, he dumped his dish in the sink. He'd meant to make his way back to the hospital tonight, what was left of the night. Walk right on in, with his new, respectable look, take care of Birely and be done with it. But when he thought of going back there so soon, and maybe with those same goons on duty, he decided to hide the Lincoln first, maybe around Debbie Kraft's place, empty houses on the streets around her. He couldn't think of a better neighborhood. That woman contractor was around there some, but he could avoid her. Meantime, tonight, he wouldn't turn down a few hours' sleep, he thought, yawning.

Moving into the bedroom again, he undressed, folded his new clothes all neat on the upholstered bedroom chair, and climbed naked into the old folks' bed, sliding down under the thick quilt. Before he switched off the flashlight, its beam on the pillow picked out a couple of dark cat hairs. He flicked them off with disgust, turned the pillow over, got himself comfortable, and dropped into a deep, untroubled sleep.

19

Misto, having watched the four EMTs load Birely into the ambulance and head away for the hospital, sat now on Emmylou's porch, alone, pondering again Birely's presence there in the village, Birely whose grown-up photograph in Emmylou's house was neatly inscribed along the bottom with his name and Sammie's and the date the picture was taken, just a few years ago. Once when he'd hopped up on the dresser for yet another look, Emmylou had laughed at him. "You're an art critic now? I took that picture myself, with my old box camera, took it right out on the highway by the market where Sammie and I used to work. Took it one time Birely showed up, the way he did without ever letting her know, stopped off at the village from wherever he'd been wandering."

Misto had already died by the time Birely was born, the family already out in California, he was dead but he'd never left Sammie's side. Call him a ghost cat or whatever one liked, he'd stayed near her as they headed for the West Coast, stayed nearby through all that happened to her and to Lee Fontana, moving effortlessly in and out of their lives. Seeking to protect them, to face off whatever would harm the old man or the child. He'd been protective of Sammie's little brother, too, when Birely came along, and now in this different life he still felt protective of that little boy grown up and grown older. Birely was still irresponsible and maybe often useless in his ways but he was still Sammie's brother, lying alone in that cold stone house injured and hurting until Emmylou had discovered him and saw that he was cared for. When she'd left for the hospital behind the EMTs, Misto had paused at the edge of her yard, undecided whether to follow.

It was a long journey up to the hospital through tangled woods, down through a deep ravine, and across the busy freeway. Even if he could avoid the coyotes and occasional loose dogs, and dodge the fast cars, even if his aging bones didn't give out, it wasn't likely he could slip inside unseen through those bright halls, among so many people, and find Birely's room. Even if he got that far, how could he help Birely? He was only mortal, now. What could *he* do to help? He'd been more effective as a ghost without the limitations of a mortal body—and without the aches and pains. When he was spirit alone, he could appear suddenly wherever and whenever he chose, and more often than not he could subtly influence others with his whispers, just as he'd prodded tough old Lee Fontana.

He knew he'd had an effect on Lee's life, that he had hazed Lee away from some of the more shameful moves he'd considered. Even that last big robbery, when Lee held his forty-five to the head of the cowering postal clerk, Lee hadn't hurt the man. How much of that was due to Fontana's own sense of kindness, which he couldn't seem to escape, and how much to Misto's influence, would never be clear—though Lee's successful escape from the law was Lee's own sly plan. Misto couldn't take credit for that any more than he could be blamed for the darker presence that harassed Lee, and that Misto had sought to drive away.

But Misto's own ghostly power hadn't lasted long, and he found himself again among the living, encumbered again by a living cat's uncertain existence, by the forces of pain and of joy that the mortal world bestowed, and now by the pains and aches of old age descending on him once more; he didn't like that part of growing old.

Deciding against that perilous journey to the hospital, he left Emmylou's yard wanting companionship, wanting the other cats to talk with, Joe and Dulcie and his son, Pan. Scrambling up a pine to Emmylou's roof, he looked down upon the shabby neighborhood of small old cottages, to the village stretching out beyond, and to the vast expanse of lonely peaks and steep ridges that sheltered the coastal town. Tonight he had no heart for wandering, for roaming through the chill wind and the unforgiving dark, and he headed back to Joe Grey's house, to the most welcoming home he knew while his own two humans were absent. Maybe Joe was there now and would claw away his uncertain feelings, make him laugh again, and to hell with getting old.

Padding morosely over the roofs, the way seemed long tonight and the sea wind was unkind. He was deeply chilled by the time he reached Joe Grey's tower. Bellying in through one of the six windows, he found Joe's heap of cushions empty. Pushing on in through the cat door, leaving it flapping behind him, he crouched on the nearest rafter, looking over, down into the upstairs suite.

The big double bed had been slept in but was now empty, the covers thrown back in a heap. A fleece robe lay crumpled on the floor, a silk nightie flung over a chair. The doors to the walk-in closet stood open, a shirt dropped on the floor inside. Where had they gone, in such a hurry in the middle of the night? He looked down at Clyde's little office, his desk hidden by piles of papers, and through the open doors into Ryan's studio. The house smelled empty and sounded hollow, he had no sense of anyone there among the unseen rooms, not even Rock. The big silver dog, the minute he heard the cat door, would have been right there huffing at him, making a fuss. Rock was not in the house, the only living soul present was little Snowball, curled up on the love seat, so deeply asleep that even the flapping cat door hadn't woken her. The sleep of an aging cat, her sweet spirit floating deep, deep down among her hoard of dreams.

But what had gone down, here? Why had Ryan and Clyde risen in the middle of the night and left the house? Some emergency, someone hurt? Feeling a cold chill suddenly for his own humans, who would be traveling now on their way home, he dropped down from the rafter onto the desk, jolting his poor bones, and set about searching for a note or phone number jotted hastily, for some clue to where they had gone and, most important, for any hurried notation about John and Mary Firetti. Perhaps for some note from the veterinarian who was temporarily minding the practice and feeding John's feral band of shore cats.

He found nothing. Slipping down to the floor, he looked for some bit of paper that might have fallen. Again, nothing. He padded into Ryan's studio beneath its high rafters and tall, bare windows. Trotting beneath the big drawing board, circling the solid oak desk and blueprint cabinet, he looked out the west window, down at the drive where he had not thought to look before while he was still on the roof.

The king cab was gone, only Clyde's antique roadster was there, parked to one side and shrouded in its canvas cover. He circled the studio again, then prowled the bedroom, tracking Rock's scent back and forth as he'd followed close behind Ryan and Clyde from bed to bath to closet, back again to the stairs, and down. But then he thought, not only his own family was headed home. So were the Greenlaws and Kit. Could something have happened to them, on the road or before they left the city? He leaped onto the desk again, eyeing the answering machine.

He'd never used one of these. He nosed uncertainly at the flashing red light. Warily he punched the play button, hoping he wouldn't erase whatever was there.

Nothing happened. He punched again. There was a long, annoying buzz and the red light flashed and then died. The green light blinked twice and died, too. No lights now and only silence. He hissed at the uncooperative lump of plastic, hoped he hadn't erased anything, and turned away. His medieval life—what he remembered of it—might have been harsh, but one didn't have to deal with machines. And the machines of young Sammie's time had been simple ones, even cars had been slower and more predictable. Leaping from the desk to the file cabinet and across to the love seat, he climbed into Snowball's crumpled blanket close to her, and curled up. She woke only a little, looking at him vaguely. He spoke nonsense to her, as much to comfort himself as to comfort her. He washed her face and licked her ears, talking to her as Clyde and Ryan or Joe would do, telling her what a fine cat she was.

But soon she began to grow restless, to glance toward the stairs and toward the kitchen below. Leaping down, he led her down the stairs to her kibble bowl, which of course had been licked clean. He hopped from a chair to the counter, pawed open the cupboards until he found her box of kibble. With considerable maneuvering, and spilling quite a lot, he managed to tip the box on its side and send a cascade of little, aromatic pellets raining down over the side, some of it into the bowl. He sat atop the counter looking over, watching her gobble up the dry little morsels, watching her drink her fill at the water dish, her curved tongue carrying water into her pink mouth like a little spoon. She didn't offer to jump up on the counter, her arthritis was worse than his. Snowball's face was getting long, her belly dragging with age.

But she still handled the stairs all right, and when they headed back up, she settled into the exact same spot on her blanket again. When, purring, Misto stretched out near her, she looked at him expectantly. He looked back, puzzled—it was frustrating that his feline cousins couldn't talk to him, that, despite a vast repertoire of body language, they couldn't communicate their desires exactly, as a speaking cat could.

But he could see she wanted him to talk again, wanted to hear his voice. Snowball, too, was lonely, she wanted to hold on to the rambling cadences of a speaking voice. Clyde and Ryan often read to this little cat, the same way the Greenlaws read to Kit, or as Wilma Getz read to Dulcie, in bed at night. Just as Mary and John Firetti read to Misto himself, though John's reading too often involved veterinary journals that put him right to sleep. The difference was that the speaking cats understood all of the tale, while, for Snowball, the excitement and drama of the story lay in the tone of voice, in the emotion that one could impart.

Now, tonight, Snowball needed a story. To please her, and to distract himself from his own worries, too, he told her about his kittenhood in that long-ago Georgia time, about the steamy summers, playing in the grassy yard with small Sammie behind the white picket fence, playing with a little rubber ball she threw for him, or climbing together up the twisting oak tree that shaded the little front lawn. He left out the bad parts that happened later; and he left out the way he himself had died. He gave Snowball a happy tale, nothing angry in his voice to spoil her dreams, no dark shadow of Brad Falon stalking Sammie and her mother. Where was Sammie, now that she was gone from this world? Did humans, like cats, return to experience more than one life on this earth? Or did human spirits go on somewhere else altogether, wandering farther than Misto himself could ever imagine?

And what about a cat, once his nine lives were finished? Did he move on, too, as a human might? Did a cat at last rejoin his human companions? So many questions, and not even the wisest cat or human could know the true answer. All Misto knew was, there were more adventures to come than one could see from the confines of a single life. And that, from the other side, looking back, one saw many more patterns to the tangles of mortal life than were apparent while you were still there.

But, speaking his thoughts to Snowball and telling his tale, half his mind still worried uneasily at what had taken Clyde and Ryan out in the small hours. He didn't like the absence of the other cats, either, when usually one or another would come wandering in through Joe's tower, or he'd see someone silhouetted out on the rooftops, someone to race away with and laugh with. Thankful for Snowball's presence, he pushed closer still to the white cat and closed his eyes, and tried mightily to purr, to lull himself into a soothing sleep, too.

20

Birely lay beneath the bright lights in the operating room, sedated but awake, his nose numbed by a local anesthetic as Dr. Susan Hunter leaned over him working swiftly, carefully rebuilding the shattered bone. With normal breathing impossible, with the breath sucked through his mouth too ragged and labored, she could not administer a general anesthetic. She was a thin woman, wiry and strong. Pale dishwater hair barely visible beneath her blue cap, long, thin hands, long fingers, a light, sure touch with the surgical instruments. Birely lay relaxed, deeply comforted by the welcome cessation of pain, his waking dreams happy ones; he was a little child again safe between his parents, not a grown man tramping some dusty road to nowhere, with no home to come to at the end of the

day. No watchful traveling companions waiting to separate him from any small amount of cash he might have
in his jeans, no overnights in a strange jail for some
petty crime that, usually, his buddies had committed.
His childhood memories were far different and more
comforting—until the last memory grew frightening
and he became restless, fidgeting on the table.

Sammie had told him this story many times, it happened when she was just nine and Birely wasn't born
yet. Her daddy was gone away in the Second World
War, her mama working as a bookkeeper in their small
Georgia town. The town had three gas stations, one of
which their daddy would later buy, when he returned
from the war. Sammie and her mother lived in a small
rented house that would have been peaceful if not for
an old schoolmate who, the minute her daddy was
sent overseas, began to pester Becky, coming around
the house uninvited wanting to spend time with her,
a pushy man who frightened young Sammie with his
cold eyes and slippery ways. Sammie had a cat then,
a big yellow tom who liked the man no better. On the
night Brad Falon came there drunk, knocking and then
pounding, not beseeching anymore but demanding to
be let in, it was the cat who at last drove him away.

When Falon pounded, Sammie's mother bolted the
door and ran to the phone. Falon broke a window,

reached in, and unlocked it. He swung through, grabbed the phone, and threw it against the wall. He threw Sammie hard against the table, shoved Becky to the floor, and knelt over her, hitting her and pulling up her skirt. As Becky yelled at Sammie to run, the big yellow cat exploded from the bedroom and landed on Brad Falon's face, raking and biting him. When Falon couldn't pull him off, he flicked open his pocketknife.

The cat fought him, dodging the knife. Becky grabbed up a shard of broken window glass and flew at Falon. He hit her, he had her down again, cutting her, but the cat was on him again. He leaped away when a neighbor man, hearing their screams, came running, a wiry young fellow. He saw the broken window and climbed through, but already Falon had fled, banging out through the front door. Their poor cat lay panting where Falon had hit him.

Now, on the operating table, Birely woke hearing Sammie weeping, the dream always ended this way, her weeping always woke him; but he knew the cat had survived, Sammie always ended the tale the same way. Groggy now and filled with the dream, he was jerking on the table. Dr. Hunter had drawn back. She waited, trying to calm him, until at last she could proceed.

After surgery, Birely was taken back to the ER for the rest of the night. The next morning he would be moved to ICU or to the observation ward. The ER doctor on the floor said that, with whatever emotional trauma he'd suffered there on the table, he could have no visitors. "Only his sister, and only if he calms down sufficiently." It was that order from the attending physician which, had it been strictly heeded, might have saved Birely's life.

Vic woke before dawn in a real bed, under smooth sheets and real blankets, and it took a moment to think where he was. Then, when he looked around at the big, fancy bedroom, he had to laugh. It was his room, now. Last night the bed had smelled of soap or maybe of that old woman's face powder. Now, did it smell of him? If those old people came home again to sleep in it, would they smell that he'd been there, and be frightened? He guessed that cat would smell him if they let it inside. Well, of course they let it in, they'd had it right there in the car with them. Good thing that cat couldn't testify how he'd roughed up those two, he didn't need no witnesses.

Climbing out of bed, he stood naked to the side of the open drape, looking out at the faint glow of pre-dawn lights from the village. Watching the sky grow light in the east, he went over what he had to do before he made a last trip back to the ER, or to wherever they took Birely, if they meant to fix his smashed nose. He wondered again if Emmylou was paying for all that.

Maybe if he didn't go back too soon, they'd put Birely in a regular room where there'd be fewer nurses going in and out, and more visitors allowed. People wouldn't notice him so much; with his new "look," he'd blend right in, could take care of business without being bothered. Birely's final business. What more natural place to die than the hospital? You were there because something was wrong, people went to the hospital to die. He wondered how many folks had been done in there with help, and no one the wiser. How many cadavers did they haul out of there in a week, and no one suspicious that one or two hadn't died natural?

He went over, again, the way that paperback book had laid it all out, a book he'd picked up at the Goodwill when he was buying a pair of jeans, waiting for Birely to find a shirt he wanted. He'd got real interested in the story, had read that part four or five times, off and on, had carried the book in his pack for a long time. Well, it was sure as hell the foolproof way. How would you ever get caught? With a little adaptation, you could use it on a druggie, too. Just one more needle puncture. A little creativity, you could use it on just about anyone.

But in the book, this guy had died in a hospital exactly like he meant for Birely. All you needed was a 30cc or 50cc syringe, and he was sure he could pick that up around the nurses' station, there'd be syringes there somewhere, in a drawer or cupboard. If he couldn't find any, he could put on those rubber gloves he'd seen handy in the wall dispensers in the rooms, slip on gloves, dig a syringe out of the hazardous-waste bin right there in the room, too. Hospital was all organized for fast work, they made everything easy.

The way they did it in the book, you do the injection, the guy goes into some kind of fit or trauma, half a second later he's dead. Touchy part, you had to get out fast. Book said the minute the injected air hit the heart, the dials went crazy, alarms going off, the whole damn staff running in to save a life and you'd better be long gone.

Moving into the bathroom, he brushed his teeth with the old guy's toothbrush, and even took a shower. Felt strange to be so clean, didn't seem quite comfortable. First, before he went back to the ER and did Birely, he had to hide the Lincoln. Then he'd need wheels to get back to the hospital, Debbie's station wagon would do for that. How could she refuse, when he'd sold that stuff for her to the Frisco fence—that, plus what he had on her.

When he and Birely'd first moved in, up the hill, he'd seen her down there around her cottage, and then seen her twice in the village market, light-fingered and quick. He'd drawn back into the shadows, to make certain, knowing he'd find the information useful, one way or another.

Two days later, he saw her come out of a village dress shop pushing one of them fancy baby carriages. She didn't have no baby that he'd ever seen, just the two girls. She came out of the store with the sun hood pulled over, the "baby" all covered up with a blanket, and the older girl walking beside her.

After that, a couple times he'd watched her return home, haul the carriage out of the station wagon all folded up, no sign of a baby, but she always carried four or five bulging shopping bags inside. For a few days he'd followed her, too, walked into town when she left. It wasn't far, and it was never hard to find that old brown Suzuki station wagon, the village was so small. She liked to park beside the library where there was more shade than on the street. She often had the twelve-year-old with her, but never the smaller girl. He'd see Debbie take off with both girls in the morning, come back without them as if she'd dropped them at school, but in the afternoons, she'd have only the older one in the car again. Or maybe the little one was in the back where he couldn't see her. The older kid, Vinnie, she was a smart-ass, but when she shopped with her mother she was quick, fingers nearly as slick as a professional.

He'd gotten acquainted with Debbie, walking down there of an early evening as her kids ate supper, walked the roundabout way, coming up from below. When he'd let her know he knew what she was up to, that had scared her. She'd denied it until he told her exactly what he had seen. The woman was feisty but she was easy enough to intimidate. He got her to show him what she had, and some of the stuff was high-end, from the Neiman Marcus and Lord & Taylor stores in the village plaza, and that had surprised him. Molena Point might be small, but there was money here, and Debbie had gone right for it.

Once he'd complimented her on her skill, she came around real nice, got real friendly. He noticed that, heading out for those high-end stores, she dressed real slick, tried to look like she belonged in there. She said she was selling what she lifted through a consignment shop up in San Jose, the guy was a second-rate fence, using the shop as a front. Said she'd drive up there once a month. She'd told him what they paid, and after a couple conversations, they'd struck a deal. He said he knew a fence in the city—well, he knew *of* him. Said he could get way better prices, that he'd sell what she stole, keep his share, and still make more for her than she was getting. He wasn't sure why she trusted him. Or why he bothered. Except she was a looker, and she had a snotty little way that he liked. Who knew, maybe something more would come of that.

Out the bedroom windows, the sky was growing lighter. He dressed in his new clothes, folded up the old ones, clean now from the washer. Carrying those, moving into the living room, he looked down from the front window to make sure the street was clear, then moved on through the laundry into the garage. Locked the door behind him, and slipped into the Lincoln. He'd thought to eat something, there in the house, but he wanted to move on out of the neighborhood before people came out to walk their dogs, take kids to school or go to work. Starting the engine, he hit the button to open the big door, checked the street for cars as he backed out, closed it again fast. On the street he saw only the same three cars that had been parked there the night before, their windows fogged over. Moving on away, down the hill, he studied the houses as he passed. No one out in any of the yards, no kids, no one on their porch or looking out a window, that he could see. He had a good feeling about the day ahead. By tonight he'd be miles away from the coast headed inland and north with the Lincoln and the money, and he wouldn't have to worry about Birely anymore. By tonight, Birely would be history.

It was the next morning that Pedric was transferred down the coast from Dominican Hospital in Santa Cruz to Molena Point's Community Hospital. Joe peered through the mesh in Ryan's backpack as she walked along beside Pedric's gurney, approaching the ambulance. Wilma stood with Clyde, Dulcie looking up over the edge of her carryall. Clyde's backpack bulged with Pan and Kit crowded in there—a four-cat entourage to accompany Pedric's careful transport home.

But in Clyde's pack beside Pan, Kit couldn't be still. Fidgeting and staring out, her gaze followed Pedric worriedly as he disappeared into the ambulance. "He's so hurt. All that talk about MRIs and arteriograms, whatever they are, and about maybe a tumor and more blood work to do and—"

"Those are just tests," the red tom said, his tail twitching irritably. Did she have to fuss so, in the confined space? "Only tests," he said, "precautions. They don't necessarily mean anything."

"But Dr. Carroll said Pedric's blood sugar's high, and he's having trouble with his eyesight, and—"

"He said there could be any number of causes. It doesn't *mean* anything, Kit. He just wants to be sure. Will you settle down?"

"He said there might be something going on in Pedric's *brain*," she said, her voice quavering. "He talked about a *brain scan*. *That* means something, *I heard* him say they'd look for a tumor, maybe a pituitary tumor, whatever *that* is, and an abnormality in an artery, and—"

Pan hissed at her impatiently. "Those things can be fixed. Would you rather they *didn't* look, and missed something important and Pedric got worse?"

"I'd rather he wasn't hurt at all and we hadn't been in that wreck and that *scum* hadn't hit him in the head and we were all home right now, all safe at home and they had never been hurt," she said, shivering.

Pan fixed her with a hard gaze. "You can't help Pedric by crying, and you can't help Lucinda if you're all weepy." Reaching out a paw, he tucked it around her paw, and licked her ear. "They're lucky to have you, and they're lucky to have good doctors. Now can't you settle down?"

Kit settled, glancing sideways at him, and together they peered out through the mesh, watching the ambulance pull out of the parking area, to the street. They watched a nurse wheel Lucinda out from the ER in a wheelchair and help her into Kate's rental car, which was the newest and most comfortable of their three vehicles. When Lucinda was settled inside and the nurse had gone, Clyde leaned in and Kit and Pan slipped out of his backpack onto Lucinda's lap. Lucinda was a bit groggy from the pain medication; she smiled sleepily at the two cats. Kit licked her hand, which tasted of disinfectants. Through their open car door, they watched Charlie settle Wilma into her Blazer, setting the carry-all by Wilma's feet, watched Dulcie emerge and climb up into her housemate's lap. The rented Lexus and the Blazer pulled out, with the Damens' red king cab behind them, Joe Grey and Rock peering out the side window, the little parade moving through the quiet morning, heading home.

21

The click, as Clyde unlocked the Greenlaws' front door, echoed hollowly in the deserted house. Outside in the drive, Kate's rented Lexus stood next to the Damens' red king cab. Charlie had gone on to the hospital, to offer moral support as Pedric was admitted. She would swing by Wilma's first, drop Wilma and Dulcie at home where the two meant to tuck up for a mid-morning nap; their all-night vigil in the motel, broken by only a few hours of sleep, had left both woman and cat yawning, and a bit fuzzy in their thoughts.

Clyde and Lucinda moved on inside, Lucinda leaning on his arm, still groggy and unsteady from the pain medication. The room was chill and smelled musty even after only a week's absence. Ryan and Kate followed them in, but tortoiseshell Kit hung back, looking off where Joe and Pan had raced away. The moment the two vehicles came to rest in the drive, Pan had taken off for the rooftops, his amber eyes flashing with anger. Joe Grey had followed him, perplexed, uncertain how to think about Kit and Pan's sudden conflict.

In the car, driving down, Pan had been fascinated by Kate's tales of the Netherworld, but Kit had soon gone sullen and cross. She'd always been drawn to the thought of mystical lands that might link to their own history, but this morning suddenly, faced with Pan's enthusiasm, she hadn't wanted to hear about Kate's journey.

Now, she watched the two toms race away, and then quietly she entered the house. There she paused, shivering at its neglected feel. The kind of gloom that makes folks hurry to flip on the lights in the middle of the day and open the windows, as Ryan was now doing, to let in the fresh ocean breeze. But Kit, entering, sensed more than abandonment. Nervously she scented out and backed away, curling her lip at the smell.

She watched Clyde settle Lucinda in her chair before the hearth and then turn to lay a fire, arranging logs from the stack in the wood box, and striking the gas starter. She could hear Ryan in the kitchen filling the coffee maker, and taking a lemon cake from the freezer, as Lucinda had asked her to do. Kate settled in Pedric's chair, near Lucinda, looking questioningly at Kit when she didn't leap up into Lucinda's lap.

With the smell of that man in the house, Kit turned away to prowl the empty rooms—hopefully empty. *He used Lucinda's keys to let himself in,* she thought. *If he's still here, he's cornered, and he's even more dangerous.* Giving Clyde a look, she moved off toward the bedroom. Watching her, Clyde picked a short length of firewood from the stack behind Lucinda's chair, and followed. Kate looked after them, frowning, then rose to tuck a lap robe around Lucinda.

"Kit's just in a mood," Lucinda said. "All this stress. She'll be all right, in a while."

"That was my fault," Kate said, "that argument in the car, my fault for telling Pan about the dark world. His interest didn't sit well with Kit."

"They'll have to work it out," Lucinda said sadly. "They were so happy. But it wasn't your fault at all, Pan had to hear the story sometime. How could he not, when Joe and Dulcie both know about your journey."

The drive down from Santa Cruz had started out pleasantly, the morning bright and cool, the sea on their right a deep blue beneath stacks of high, blowing clouds. Pan had curled up on the seat between Kate and Lucinda, while Kit snuggled in her housemate's lap, her tortoiseshell coat dark against Lucinda's white bandages. But then as Kate spun her tale, Pan sat up straight, listening eagerly, and soon he was asking excited questions, his tail twitching—and soon Kit grew restless watching him, her ears back and her own tail lashing hard when Pan talked about going down himself, about going there with her. Kit had once dreamed of that land, but not the way it was now, she didn't want to go there now. What was Pan thinking? Kate had had a reason to go, searching out her mother and father's own history, but Pan had no such excuse.

It was in San Francisco that Lucinda had asked Kate, "Your journey down into that world? It was your father's old journals that led you there?"

Kate nodded. "Yes, the diary he left me. And the jewelry I found there and brought back, it's so like the pieces he left me. The same ancient Celtic jewelry style that has haunted me. And so many pieces with cats worked into the design."

"I remember you sold a few pieces, those without cats."

"Those lovely pieces stashed away for nearly half a century, in the back of a walk-in safe."

It was the grandson of the attorney who gave Kate the first pieces of jewelry, who had journeyed with her down through the caverns. He had found her again, up in Seattle, got her address from the San Francisco designer firm she'd worked for. He meant to retire, to leave the firm, and he had the trip all planned. He'd wanted her to go because of what her parents had done in trying to save that land. "He wanted to know if I'd like to join him."

"You said yes, just like that," Lucinda said.

"Oh, I did some research on him, as much background check as I could, by myself. I didn't want to involve anyone else. From what I found—mostly what I didn't find—from the holes in his own family background that were so similar to mine, I decided to trust him."

She moved into the right lane; they were making good time. The sea wind had turned warm now, as the sun rose higher. "I knew it was risky, but I was burning to see where my mother was raised." She had described for Pan the vast caves of the Netherworld, the rich veins of gold reaching down miles below California's own depleted gold fields. And then, in the car, when she talked about the shape-shifting beasts and the winged lamia, Pan's paws kneaded with excitement— and Kit's claws kneaded with unease, and as they'd passed Seaside, just north of Molena Point, the two cats had begun to argue.

Pan wanted to descend down into those dark tunnels despite the dangers, and he expected that Kit would go with him. Kit said that if *he* went, that would be the last adventure he'd live to see, and Pan didn't see why she was suddenly so timid. Her hissing refusal sent them into a snarling argument, the matter ending when Kit leaped into the backseat, curled up in a dark little ball with her back to them all. In the front seat, Pan had crouched forlornly between Kate and Lucinda looking helplessly from one to the other, not knowing what to do, not wanting Kit's violent anger, but unwilling to give in to her.

The minute they pulled into the Greenlaws' drive, and Kate parked and opened her door, Pan leaped out and took off across the yard, vanishing among the neighboring oak trees. Kit dropped to the drive and headed for the house, looking at no one, her ears flat to her head, her eyes blazing, her fluffy tail lashing with rage. Glancing back once, she saw Joe jump out of the Damen truck and follow Pan and she hissed at him, too. Joe didn't know what had happened but he was with Pan all the same, as if he were certain that it was her fault.

Now as Kit explored the house, Kate looked after her, dismayed. "I thought Kit loved my stories. It wasn't until this morning that I saw the truth."

She hurt for Kit, and for Pan; she had no idea how this clash of feline stubbornness would resolve itself.

They could hear Clyde in the bedroom opening the closets and cupboards. They watched Kit return, her nose to the carpet, moving on through to the kitchen.

"What?" Lucinda said. "What is it?"

Kate shivered, listening to Clyde's movements as he investigated the house. Someone had been in there but was gone now, she'd heard Clyde open every closet, every door. Their assailant had Lucinda's car and house keys; and Lucinda's muzzy, sedated condition had left her without her usual sharp perception.

Kit, returning from the kitchen, looked up at Lucinda, lifting a paw. "The man who hurt you and Pedric, he made himself at home. He ate, he messed up the kitchen, he rummaged through your closet. He slept in your bed," she said, hissing indignantly.

Ryan appeared from the kitchen, wiping her hands on a dishtowel. "There's a dirty plate in the sink, an empty container from frozen spaghetti, a crushed beer can."

Clyde came out of the bedroom. "He took a shower, left wet towels on the floor. Hair all over the floor, long hair, and more wrapped in a towel. As if he's cut off a pigtail. Left a hell of a mess."

Lucinda rose, and they followed Clyde back to the bedroom. She looked with disgust at the mussed bed, which she had made carefully before they'd left for San Francisco. She inspected the dresser drawers, and then the closet. "Pedric's tweed sport coat's gone," she said. "He didn't take that to the city. His tan slacks, too, with the stain on one cuff."

"And the dark brown Rockports," Kit said, "that he wears to walk the hills." She looked up at Clyde, her ears flicking uncertainly. "If he wanted clothes, the suitcases were right there in the Lincoln. Did he have to come in here, invade our house, mess it up, and leave his smell everywhere? What a pig."

"What else has he done?" Lucinda said. "What else has he taken?" She moved back to the dresser, began opening drawers to examine them more carefully, lifting layers of sweaters, socks and underwear, leaning awkwardly with the weight of the cast.

Kate opened the carved pine armoire, but the big, flat TV and the DVD player were in place, the rows of CDs lined up on the shelves beside them. Ryan, stepping out to the living room, opened that armoire but returned shaking her head. "TV, music system, looks like it's all there."

"He means to come back," Lucinda said.

Ryan put her arm around Lucinda. "I'll call the locksmith again, get him on out here pronto." But Kit looked worriedly at Lucinda. Even if the locks were changed, Lucinda and Kate would be alone tonight.

With only me to guard them, she thought with dismay. Despite the angry, predatory twitch of her claws, despite knowing she'd do her best to protect her humans, she was no hundred-pound police dog. *Even with new locks,* she thought, *he can break in easily enough.* Now, since the accident, her housemate seemed so frail, hindered by the cast and the pain, her senses dulled by the drugs that were meant to ease her pain.

Ever since she first met Lucinda and Pedric, up on the grassy slopes of Hellhag Hill when she was a very young cat, she had looked on them as invincible. She'd never before known a human in her short, wild life. She'd had no idea they could be like these two, so wise; two humans who understood her, who saw at once her true nature as a speaking cat, and delighted in their discovery. That first day as she spied on Lucinda and Pedric while they enjoyed their picnic, as she listened to Pedric recite the same ancient Celtic tales that she herself loved, Kit had felt as one with them. It hadn't taken long for them to coax her out with gentle questions and with smoked salmon, and that was the beginning of their friendship. Despite Kit's wild and independent life roaming the hills alone, she soon went home with them. She had never left again, they were her family, two strong humans she could trust with any problem, any secret, could trust with her very life, the two humans who would be there for her forever, wise and indestructible. But now suddenly she might have to protect Lucinda, or try to. Now suddenly Kit had a hard glimpse into human mortality, and she didn't like it much.

She listened to Ryan calling the locksmith back, watched her hang up the phone, looking at Lucinda. "He'll be here within the hour. I'll call the department, they can photograph, and run prints."

"Do we have to?" Lucinda said. "There's nothing else missing, a jacket, a pair of pants, and a pair of shoes. Clothes that Pedric *could* have packed and forgotten though I know he didn't, clothes he might have left in the city. The TVs and computer are still in place."

"It's vandalism," Ryan said. "Whatever they find, including prints, might help as evidence later, if . . . when they recover the Lincoln."

"Call them," Lucinda said at last, resigned. She didn't want to be disturbed, she only wanted her house to herself again, cleaned of every trace of the man, wanted to wipe away every invading trace of him with scrub rags and disinfectant.

As Ryan made the call, Kit watched Clyde pack a duffel bag to take to Pedric's hospital room. She showed him where Pedric kept his robes and pajamas, his shaving things. She watched Kate put fresh sheets on the bed, throwing the used ones and the bed pad in the washer, with Clorox that made the whole house smell. Ryan brought Lucinda a bed tray with coffee and some lemon cake, helped her change into a nightie and tuck up under the covers. It had been a long morning, Lucinda was yawning and already half asleep; everything was hard for her, with the use of only one arm. When she was settled in bed with the tray and her snack, Kit lay down close beside her, daintily accepting small bites of icing; and only now did Kit let herself think about Pan again, let the whole sorry episode fill her heart.

She told herself that maybe Pan never thought about danger. Maybe, traveling all over Oregon and down the California coast, cadging rides with strangers, maybe he'd just done what he wanted, fought when he needed to, and then gone happily on his way again undeterred by worries. So now, he expected her to do the same, to follow him on what he said would be the greatest adventure of a cat's life. She tried to think about it from his viewpoint, but lying close and safe beside Lucinda, Kit's anger burned anew when she thought about the fiery pit that Kate had approached, the flaming mouth of hell itself, and about the beasts that had crawled out of it to attack anything mortal. She loved Pan, but she was sickened that he blithely expected her to go there, into that dark and deathly realm.

How is it that when I was younger I would have leaped at such a journey, would have longed to go there—how close I was to venturing down into Hellhag Cave and, later, down alone among the dark Pamillon caverns—how is it that now I'm so afraid?

She told herself she was grown up now, that she wasn't so foolhardy anymore, but all she really knew was that Pan wouldn't give in, and she wouldn't give in, and his shortsighted stubbornness hurt her clear down to her very cat soul, to her frightened and uncertain soul.

22

It took Vic a while to hide the Lincoln. On leaving the Greenlaw house he had detoured past the village market, parked on a side street, and walked back. Bought a jar of peanut butter, a box of crackers, and a cup of machine coffee that tasted like boiled sawdust. The market wasn't two blocks from the PD, and that gave him a thrill of fear. But who was going to recognize him, all shaven and cleaned up? The cops had never even seen him, all they knew was what that old couple told them: two men, shaggy hair, old wrinkled clothes, and him with a ponytail. No one was going to look at him twice now, dressed all proper like some village shopkeeper on his way to open up the store.

He'd eaten in the car parked under some low-hanging eucalyptus trees, then headed for Debbie's place. Passing Emmylou's, he'd checked for her green Chevy. Just as he'd hoped, it was still gone as if she hadn't returned from the hospital, had stayed there all night worrying about that little wimp, about her friend's baby brother.

Easing on by, he turned down onto the cracked streets of the neighborhood below among the small, ragged cottages, expecting the streets to be empty as they usually were. Not so. Here came a fat woman walking a skinny old dog and, overtaking them, a pair of joggers dressed in tight black spandex like earthbound skin divers, and from the other direction a young boy in a blue jacket cruising on a bike, the whole damn neighborhood suddenly crowded with people. He circled through, parked on a side street. Waited until the streets were empty again, then headed back to Debbie Kraft's place. Her station wagon was gone, and that annoyed him.

Passing on by, he turned into the drive of the place he'd spotted earlier, house and narrow garage sat way at the back, all secluded back there, bushes rangy and tall; the dirt-crusted Lincoln looked almost at home there. He pulled clear on back to the garage. Cracked gray paint, heavy wooden garage door hinged at the side. Getting out, he tried to open it but it was securely locked. He moved around to the side. That door was locked, too, but this was one of them old-fashioned skeleton-key jobs, older than dirt. Fishing out his pocketknife, it didn't take him long, he had it open. The power to the place was shut off, and with no windows it was dark as hell in there. Moving to the big door, he turned the knob for the lock and pushed it open, lifting where the door wanted to sag and scrape on the cracked cement drive. Jury-rigged kind of arrangement, only one door and not two, even if this was just a one-car garage. Good thing he hadn't heisted a *stretch* limo to hide here, he'd be flat out of luck.

By the time he'd finessed the Lincoln inside and had the door closed again, he was sweating like a pig. Shutting the big door, leaving the place looking as deserted as he'd found it, he'd walked on over toward Debbie's place hoping she'd got home, meaning to give her the money and talk her out of her car. But when he came in sight of the house, the drive was still empty. Walking on up her drive like he belonged there, he looked in the garage window.

Garage was empty except for some boxes of junk, kids' broken toys, some dried-up paint cans. If she was out "shopping," light-fingered and involved, she might be gone for hours. Turning away, he headed on up the hill, past Emmylou's. Her car was still gone. He moved on up the stairs of the stone house thinking to pick up the sleeping bags, stash them somewhere up the hill in the bushes, clear the place out before them cops showed up. Maybe even wipe the place down of fingerprints, he thought, amused. Like some big-time criminal. When all he ever did this time was borrow a car and lift some money that was *already* stolen, for Christ's sake.

Pan and Joe, having raced away from Lucinda's house as their human friends moved on inside, were wandering the rooftops above the center of the village, Pan still grousing about Kit's stubborn nature, when they saw Debbie Kraft walking down Ocean Avenue wheeling her empty baby stroller. The interior, as usual, was swaddled with a concealing pink blanket. They watched her approach the drugstore and wheel her "baby" inside; they had watched this routine before, they knew too well what she was up to. Joe, pausing on a shingled peak, his paws in the damp gutter, looking down at Debbie, wanted badly to nail her. This was the first time in his life he had turned his back on a thief, the first time he hadn't called the department the minute he saw a crime coming down. Shoplifting might seem like a minor offense, but even in their small village hundreds of thousands of dollars of merchandise vanished every year. The local shop-keepers were having a hard enough time, with the sharp failure of the economy. They didn't need any light-fingered visitors trashing their livelihood; he itched to snatch her up like a struggling mouse, and turn her over to the law. He didn't like Debbie any-way. He had bristled at her nervy attitude when she'd moved in with Ryan and Clyde uninvited and had dis-liked her even before she first arrived in the village just from her pushy letter. It would be a real treat to see her cooling her heels in Max Harper's jail—but if he turned her in, what would happen to Tessa? To both her little girls?

Beside him, Pan had already tuned Debbie out; all his anger, for the moment, was still directed at Kit, at her puzzling disdain for adventure. "Even my pa never explored such a land. If Misto ever once set paw there, he'd be bragging about it, rambling on so you'd never shut him up."

Joe said nothing. The Netherworld made him ner-vous, he knew exactly how Kit felt. What was so invit-ing about a dark world that had decayed and fallen to ruin? No way *he'd* venture down there into those crumbling caverns. Maybe their heritage did have its roots among the ancient Celts, and maybe some strain of those races *were* down there beneath their own coast, emigrants from an ancient time, but so what? That didn't mean he had to launch himself into some nightmare encounter with a world that should be left to complete its own destruction. The very thought made his paws sweat.

They watched Debbie emerge from the drugstore, tenderly arranging the pink blanket over her baby, taking care that the little tyke was warmly covered. She smiled sweetly at two uniformed officers coming out of the coffee shop, heading for their black-and-white. The younger officer smiled back at her, but Officer Brennan was busy brushing crumbs from the ample front of his uniform.

"She's going to get caught," Pan said softly, finally paying attention. "Caught without any help from us. Are those guys taking a second look at that stroller? Did you see Brennan glance back? Maybe," the red tom said, smiling, "Debbie's little operation is going to hit the fan. But then," he said, dropping his ears, "where does that leave Tessa? If Debbie's arrested and goes to jail and has to do prison time, what will happen to Tessa?" He didn't mention Vinnie, he didn't give a mouse's ear what happened to that little torturer. Too many times up in Oregon Vinnie had poked and teased him, tormented him until he raced out of the house, often into the snow and rain, and it would be a long time before he came creeping back—only to be with Tessa, with his own small human.

"The girls have one aunt," Joe said. "Debbie's older sister. I guess by law they'd go to her, if she'd even take them. That would be a pity for Tessa. Sour woman, no use for kids." They watched Debbie move on up the street leaning over the stroller, whispering tenderly to her baby. "Tessa has a half brother," Joe said, "but Billy's only twelve. He'd take her if he was older, just like he adopts stray cats and cares for them."

Billy Young had lived with Charlie and Max since his grandmother died, an arrangement they'd made when his father went to prison for the murder of Billy's mother and, later, of Sammie Miller. Billy was a caring boy and dependable. Ever since his mother died when he was eight, he'd worked on the neighboring ranches, he was trusted with their horses, and proud to help in his own support, as boys did in past generations, taking pride in doing a man's work. Then when Billy's grandma died shortly after Christmas, and neither Debbie nor her sister wanted him—not that Billy wanted to live with either of them—he had moved up to the Harper place. Had gone where he was wanted, had taken over the Harpers' stable work before and after school in exchange for his room and board and "a little to put aside in the bank," Max had told him. But now, for the Harpers to take in two little girls as well, both with emotional problems, would be, in Joe's view, an exercise in calamity.

The two officers still sat in their black-and-white, Brennan in the right seat filling out paperwork, the rookie in the driver's seat talking on the radio, both men watching the street only casually, barely glancing at Debbie as she passed. Whether Brennan's instinct alerted him was hard to say, neither Debbie's amateur ruse nor her body language seemed to touch the older man. The cats, trotting away over the roofs, followed Debbie's progress on the sidewalk below, watched her looking covetously into the shop windows. Over the cool rooftops, they moved through shafts of sun and through pools of shade, beneath twisted oak limbs and splayed pine branches that overhung the shops. When Debbie turned into the little village market they eased down a bougainvillea vine, deftly avoiding its thorns, dropped to the sidewalk and followed her. They had, looking back, seen the black-and-white move away from them, heading toward the shore.

The village grocery kept two cats of their own, assigned to rodent control. The customers were used to seeing them wander among the shelves, so why would they be surprised at a visitor or two? Slipping along through the aisles, and through the shadows at the base of the produce bins, they found Debbie in the canned goods, dropping one can of soup or beans in the little basket she'd picked up, and easing two more in under the pink blanket. By the time she headed for the checkout, the padded vehicle was so full she had a hard time pushing it along between the narrow aisles.

Easing into the shortest of the three checkout lines, she arranged the purchases from her basket on the moving belt and then set the basket on the floor beneath. Pushing the stroller along ahead of her, she paid for her groceries and moved quickly on out, looking smug with the success of her morning's venture, both in resaleable merchandise and in food for her little family. Carefully arranging the three grocery bags down onto the lower shelf of the stroller, she headed around to the small parking lot at the side of the store. The cats saw, only then, that she'd left her station wagon at the back beneath a row of low-growing pepper trees that sheltered the adjoining building. Vanishing in among these, they climbed a few feet until they were hidden beneath its foliage.

Debbie set the grocery bags on the ground by the tailgate and then opened the side door. Leaning in, she retrieved some additional paper bags from under a tangle of toys. Opening them, and rolling the stroller close, she began to unload her take from beneath the pink blanket. When the bags were full she put a few groceries, a loaf of bread and packages of chips, in on top to hide the telltale new clothes and handbags. As she opened the tailgate and folded up the stroller the cats peered in at the tangle of toys, small sweaters, and empty drink cans. Lifting the stroller in, she laid it on top, squashing a cloth bunny and a sandal caught in the folds of a plaid blanket. Even as the cats watched, the blanket moved, a thin little arm flopped out, and Tessa turned over, a hank of pale hair straggling across the plaid cover, her dark lashes shadowing her soft cheeks. Waked by the intrusion of the stroller, she looked up at her mother, groggy and flushed. Her nose was running. Debbie fished into her own pocket for a tissue, reached in as if to blow the child's nose, but Tessa turned away, turned over again, sniffed loudly, pulled the blanket higher around her, and closed her eyes. Had Debbie left her alone in the car all the time she was shoplifting? At least the vehicle was in the shade, and she'd left the windows down a few inches, apparently unconcerned that anyone would want to bother the child.

Had she kept Tessa out of nursery school because of a cold but, because she was sick, didn't want to leave her home alone as she so often did? That was more motherly concern, Joe thought, than Debbie would normally exhibit. When she turned away from the open tailgate the two cats dropped down onto it and slipped inside, fast and silent. Pan hid at once among the rubble, concealing himself from both Tessa and her mother. They wanted to see where Debbie was headed and, of even more interest, to see if Brennan's patrol car might show up again, if the two officers were, indeed, watching her.

At the Getz house, as Wilma slept away her mid-morning nap, Dulcie sat alone on the desk in the soft glow of the computer, her restless mind too busy to let her sleep. Last night as the cats and humans crowded into the two motel rooms, the human contingent taking turns napping and one then another return-ing to the hospital to keep Pedric awake, Kate's tales had filled Dulcie with such wonder that the pictures and words just crowded in. The grimness of that world had turned her incredibly sad; the pictures that filled her head grew dark, and this poem, now, was not like her usual ones, not sly and humorous verses that would make Joe laugh. She didn't know what her tomcat would think of this effort but she didn't care, she needed to get the words out, to make sense of what she felt for that lost land. Just as Joe was driven to slaughter the wharf rat, and catch the thief, her words must be brought to life. Needs were needs, and a sensible cat attended to those urges.

Down and down on silent paws
Deep into the earth I go
Down and down through caverns black
Stones hang like spears above me

Green light glows from granite sky
Harpies fly above me
Castles fall around me
Farms lie dead around me

Herd beasts dead around me
Bones all white around me
What was grand is lost
Twisted into ruin
Magic shattered now
Used too long for evil
What was loved is lost

Gone, that earthen magic
Gone, those magic people
Used too hard for evil
Used by greed and power
By the cold hard lust of evil

She didn't know if it was a good poem or without value. She didn't care, she needed to write it. She wrote quickly, changed a few words, and then sat reading the lines back to herself, her small cat being filled with sadness for that land where, now, neither she nor Kit would ever want to venture.

23

"I ran over to look at the leaky plumbing," Ryan said, pulling into Debbie's weedy driveway beside the station wagon. The dark-haired young woman was unloading her grocery bags, and at Ryan's voice she turned, startled, a secretive look crossing her face, replaced at once by a too bright smile. Ryan smiled back, and killed the engine. She had, for the last few minutes, been sitting up the street in her truck beneath some overhanging juniper branches, watching Debbie haul a baby stroller out of the back, open it up and pile grocery bags into it. She had also seen, the instant Debbie opened the back of the wagon and turned away, a flash of red and of gray leap out, the two tomcats streak across the drive behind the woman and disappear up the pine tree near the front door. What was that about? Now the cats crouched on Debbie's roof, peering over; Ryan didn't dare look up at them, she kept her eyes on Debbie.

"You came to fix the leak now?"

"I came to look at it," Ryan said. "To see what's needed."

"Go on in, then. It's the kitchen sink," Debbie said, turning away, busying herself with the stroller.

Ryan went in, watching through the kitchen window, pretending to be occupied with the faucet as Debbie wheeled the stroller up to the little porch. Hauling it backward up the three steps with its heavy load of groceries, she passed on by the kitchen and parked it in the bedroom. She returned with three bags of groceries, leaving the rest in the stroller. Outside the window, the two tomcats seemed just as interested as Ryan was. She watched them scramble down the pine again, to pause among the lowest branches, intently looking in. Ryan, herself, had no chance to look at the remaining bags, under Debbie's gaze.

Returning to the truck, she let Rock out, snapped on his long line so he could roam the yard, and tied that to the pine tree. He didn't like being tethered; but she didn't like his propensity to take off suddenly on some track he considered too urgent to ignore. Already he was sniffing over some scent, his ears and tail up.

Maybe a deer that had been in the yard, or a raccoon. Whatever had crossed the dry grass, Rock had that look in his eyes that told her she'd better keep him under control. The Weimaraner's long generations of breeding for a powerful and single-minded hunter and tracker had produced a strong-willed individual. This, plus his lack of any early training, had produced a dog eager to outstubborn human orders in deference to his lust for the hunt.

Rock was eighteen months old when he and Ryan had found each other; he'd been roaming stray in a wild stretch of country north of Molena Point. Unclaimed and untrained, his habits already indelibly formed, he came to her defiant and headstrong, with a burning power to do as he pleased. She had worked hard to redirect his talents, sometimes with the help of the gray tomcat. It was Joe Grey who had taught Rock to track on command, to heed to his handler and stay irrevocably on the scent when seeking a felon or a lost child. Joe's method of tracking with nose to the scent himself as he gave his commands, could not have been accomplished by any human trainer. Now when the gray tomcat spoke, the big dog paid attention; though still, Ryan's own commands were not always heeded.

As she moved on inside again, Debbie was just coming out of the bedroom. Saying nothing, Ryan stepped past her into the little room crowded with its twin beds. The loaded stroller stood against the far wall, five grocery bags lined up on the floor beside it, a loaf of bread sticking out, and boxes of crackers. Behind her, Debbie had returned nervously to the kitchen as if hoping she would follow. Ryan gave the bags a cursory look and followed her back into the kitchen where she turned her attention to the sink. She knew what was in the bags, but right now she was too tired to play games; it had been a long day, after a sleepless night.

She and Clyde, after leaving Lucinda's house, had dropped Pedric's duffel off at the hospital. Charlie was still there, waiting with Pedric for the ICU doctor, and she seemed to have everything in hand. Pedric was in better spirits, now that he was back in the village, and soon Ryan and Clyde had gone on, stopping for a bite of lunch in the hospital café before heading home, sitting at a small table beside the café's big reflecting pond. They'd left Rock in the truck, snoring away in the backseat. The shallow water and plashing fountain shone brightly where the sun struck down through a great, domed skylight. Waiting for their order, they'd watched the red and black koi fish, as strikingly patterned as Japanese kites, dashing mindlessly through the water from one onlooker to the next, hoping for a handout. After lunch she'd dropped Clyde at the shop and headed on for Debbie's, having promised to look not only at the faucet but at an electrical plug that had stopped working.

She had never been fond of Debbie, she hadn't seen her since their art school years in San Francisco, then suddenly Debbie had gotten in touch. She wrote that she was moving down from Eugene, was divorced and claimed to be destitute, and was needing a place to stay. Joe Grey said, "Demanding a place to stay," and that was closer to the truth. It was Joe who discovered Debbie wasn't broke at all but had a nice wad of cash tucked away in her suitcase. Between Debbie's patronizing ways, and Vinnie's rudeness and loud tantrums, her sojourn in the Damens' guest room had lasted one night. Neither Ryan, Clyde, nor Joe himself wanted her there. Rock, who liked most children, kept his distance from Vinnie, his lip curling in warning, though he let Tessa climb all over him.

Unwilling to put Debbie out on the street, in desperation they had offered her the empty cottage which, later in the year, they intended to remodel. She was to clean up the cottage and the yard, and do as many repairs as she was capable of, under Ryan's direction. So far, she had pulled a few weeds, which she'd left lying in a limp pile in the driveway, and had made a poor stab at painting the one bedroom, abandoning half-used paint cans in the garage with their lids off, leaving the unused paint to grow dry and rubbery. As for any temporary plumbing repairs, the woman was sullen and evasive. "A busy mother," she told Ryan, "with two children to support and care for shouldn't have to be doing a man's work." Ryan wasn't sure what a man's work consisted of, but Debbie seemed to know, and the prospect of pliers and wrenches didn't appeal.

She glanced in again at the loaded grocery bags. If they had held only groceries, one would have to wonder where Debbie had gotten the money for such a large purchase. Debbie'd said she was looking for work, and sometimes Ryan did see her go out dressed as if for an interview. But so far no job had materialized, not even the most menial employment—though Debbie didn't think much of cleaning houses or bagging groceries, those pursuits didn't fit her idea of a suitable lifestyle.

It was Joe Grey who had first told her about the shoplifting. "How long," he'd said, "before someone peeks under that pink blanket, baby-talking, and finds themselves prattling on to a pile of soup cans and designer jeans?" But neither Ryan nor Joe wanted to blow the whistle on Debbie. There seemed no way to nail her and yet leave Tessa unscathed. Examining the faucet, she saw it would be better to replace it. The thing was shot, several parts loose, its joints rusting beneath the chrome. Knowing how particular her men were, she thought maybe she'd do this job herself, just a temporary fix. She and Clyde had bought the house to remodel, they expected to replace the ancient plumbing at some point.

The building was old but solid, its frame was good and the ceilings were nice and high. It was hard to lose money on a spec house in Molena Point, particularly in a hillside location with a view down over the village— hard to lose, she thought, once the economy turned around. She hoped that *would* happen soon. Stepping outside, she fetched her tool belt from the backseat of the truck. Moving into the garage, to the junction box, she turned off the master breaker so she could look at the malfunctioning wiring. As she stepped out again, Debbie came down the steps headed for her car. Leaning in over the open tailgate, she dragged a rumpled blanket heavily toward her. Ryan saw Tessa stir within, knuckling at her eyes as if she'd been asleep, heard her grumble as Debbie lifted the child out.

"She was in the car all the time you . . . shopped?" Ryan asked.

"I parked in the shade, she slept the whole time," Debbie said innocently.

"How long?"

"How long, what?"

"How long was she in the car? She looks flushed."

"She has a little cold," Debbie said. Saying no more, she headed for the house carrying the child, the blanket dragging behind her along the drive. Ryan followed her into the bedroom, watched her tuck Tessa under the covers, and then move to the kitchen where she poured canned orange juice into a glass. Moving to the bed, Ryan put a hand on the child's forehead. She was warm from the car but didn't seem fevered. Behind her, Debbie had set the juice on the dresser and was rooting in the closet. Turning, she threw a blanket over the stroller as if that were a handy place to put it down, letting it trail across the grocery bags.

"Shall I give her the juice?" Ryan asked.

"I'll do it." Debbie grabbed the glass, pulled Tessa up, propped her against the pillow. The child drank sulkily, but she drank it all. Looking past her mother, up at Ryan, her resignation was far beyond her years. When Debbie spoke to her she didn't respond. When Debbie turned away, Ryan smoothed the child's pale, damp hair. Tessa gave her the tiniest smile and reached to touch her hand.

But then she turned over again and burrowed down beneath the cotton spread. As Ryan stood watching her, Pan appeared at the window, looking in and glancing warily toward the kitchen where Debbie had disappeared. Deciding the coast was clear, he remained there watching the sleeping child, disappearing only when Debbie's footsteps approached again, vibrating on the hard linoleum. Standing by the dirty window Ryan could see him below her on the brown lawn, but instead of racing away he stood frozen, looking up along the side yard to the street in front, his ears twitching uneasily.

When she looked along the side of the house, all she could see was a slice of empty street and part of a ragged cottage on the other side, crowded by overgrown cypress trees. Below her Pan turned and looked up into her eyes with a smug little cat smile, and when she looked at the street again, the nose of a squad car was slipping into view, the black-and-white moving slowly along, the young officer at the wheel scanning the driveways and cottages. Beside him she could see Officer Brennan's heavy profile.

When she turned, Debbie stood behind her, occupying herself with the child. "It's just a cold," Debbie said, "she'll be better tomorrow." She leaned to straighten Tessa's covers, and when Ryan looked back out the window, Pan had gone and the squad car had moved on, she could see it moving away up the hill toward

Emmylou's. She spotted Pan and Joe two roofs over, keeping pace with it as it cruised slowly along.

Turning to Debbie, she said, "I guess nursery school doesn't want Tessa there, with a cold."

Debbie nodded. "So much sickness."

"She'll be going back, when she's well?"

Debbie looked up at her, her expression flat. "The nursery school's too expensive, I took her out. Why doesn't the village have a free preschool? Not everyone can afford . . ."

"So, you take her with you when you . . . shop," Ryan said, "and leave her in the car?" Moving toward the stroller, she lifted the loaf of white bread and a box of Sugar Pops from the nearest grocery bag. Beneath, neatly folded, lay an assortment of cashmere sweaters, cherry red, turquoise, lime green, all still bearing their sales tags.

"Why would you buy so many sweaters, when you don't have a job, Debbie? When you can't pay for nursery school, or pay rent?"

"They were on sale, they were really a great bargain."

"Debbie, you have a choice here. Do you think that squad car was cruising this street by accident?"

Debbie just looked at her.

"You can clean up your act, take these things back to the store, and stop any further stealing. Or you can move out, find somewhere else to live. We can't let you stay here," she said, trying to be gentle, "when we know you're shoplifting, when Clyde and I are connected to MPPD. Our friendship with Chief Harper and Charlie, and the fact that my uncle Dallas is one of Harper's detectives, doesn't leave any choice. You will quit stealing and return every item you stole to the store it came from. You can beg them not to report you, not to press charges. If you don't do that—and I'll know whether you did—you will be out of here by the end of three days.

"If you do neither, I'll report you. You'll be arrested and most likely held, unless you can make bail. Your two girls will be taken to Children's Services." It broke Ryan's heart to say that, to think of the children being taken away. She didn't tell Debbie she meant to talk with the store owners. She knew several of them and was hoping, if Debbie followed through, they wouldn't press charges. Turning back to the grocery bags, she went through them all, writing down in the back of her purse calendar every stolen item, its brand, and the name of the store as it was printed on the price tag. Maybe those two officers already had that information, maybe they had already made Debbie when they'd followed her, or maybe not. Maybe they were just cruising, keeping an eye on this problem neighborhood with its empty cottages and foreclosures.

She said nothing more to Debbie. She left the house disturbed equally by Debbie's thieving and by her neglect of Tessa—and with no idea at all how to resolve Tessa's plight, how to prevent Debbie's foolishness from coming down hard on the forlorn little girl.

24

From high above the stone cottage among the cypress trees Vic watched that woman contractor, that Ryan Flannery, back her red pickup out of Debbie's drive and take off. He'd stashed the sleeping bags deep in the bushes, their dirty clothes rolled up inside, had pushed the bundle under the tangled branches of a deadfall. Now, the minute the pickup left, he moved on down through the woods, watching for that cop car that had pulled by Debbie's place, half expecting it to come back.

But maybe they weren't looking for him, were just cruising the area, a mindless routine while they sucked down their doughnuts and coffee. They hadn't stopped at Emmylou's, and hadn't looked up toward the stone house—but after Emmylou called that ambulance, you could bet your bippy MPPD would show up sooner or later, nosing around.

Moving on down onto the empty streets of the small neighborhood, he turned up Debbie's driveway, pausing beside her station wagon to look it over. Old Suzuki was ready to fall apart. He looked in to see if she'd left the keys but she hadn't. The car was a mess inside, even to him, and he wasn't real picky how he kept a car. He was wondering if the old heap would hold together for the few hours he needed it when movement above on the garage roof startled him and he swung around to look.

Couple of cats up there pawing at something in the metal gutter, maybe a dead bird. Nasty beasts. Turning away toward the front door, the only door, he saw a light on in the kitchen but, approaching the window, he couldn't see Debbie inside. He didn't knock or call out, he moved on up the three steps, tried the knob, found the door unlocked, and pushed on through.

Joe and Pan watched the man enter. On the little fitful breeze they couldn't catch his scent, but they looked at each other, puzzled. He was familiar, but different. He was well dressed and his clothes were familiar, too. Even from the roof they could hear the scuff of his loafers across the linoleum of the cottage.

They heard him pause at the kitchen and then head for the bedroom, his rubber soles grating across something gritty. Quickly they scrambled down the pine tree to the ground, and only then did they find his scent. "The guy from the stone shack," Joe said, "the one with all the hair." And, as they sniffed around the door, a mix of familiar smells hit them that made their fur stand up: the ripe male smell from the stone house overlaid, now, with the smell of lime shaving lotion and, making them hiss in consternation, the personal scent of Pedric Greenlaw, distinctive and familiar. From within, they heard Debbie yip, the beginning of a startled scream.

The man's voice was low and flat. "It's just me."

Debbie's voice was cranky. "You could have knocked," she snapped. "What do you want? You scared me half to death."

The cats, pushing the door in, slipped on inside, past the kitchen and into the shadows outside the bedroom door. The two stood in the middle of the bedroom, the man's back to them. Debbie had turned from Tessa's bed, scowling up at him. She didn't seem frightened, just annoyed. "You have my money?"

"I got it."

Joe studied the guy. He was wearing Pedric's tan slacks with the spot on one cuff, Pedric's tweed sport coat. The guy's brown hair was newly trimmed, the skin at the back of his neck as white as a baby's bottom. His cheeks and chin were pale, too, and he'd used too much of Pedric's Royall Lyme shaving lotion.

"You got yourself cleaned up fancy," she said. "What's the occasion?"

"You like it?" he said, leaning close to her.

Debbie laughed, a squeaky little giggle. "I hope you didn't spend my money on that fancy sport coat!"

"No way, baby. The money's all here." He sat down on the edge of the bed, crowding the sleeping child as if she were only another pillow. The cats, crouched beside the door, watched him remove a wad of greenbacks from his jacket pocket. Using the bed as a table, he began to count out hundred-dollar bills, fanning the stack like a deck of cards and then dealing them out across the covers. Debbie moved closer, watching greedily. Behind them, the cats slipped through the room into the shadows of the baby stroller, beside the five grocery bags—a swift flash of gray and red, their paws silent on the grainy floor. Behind the cats, the closet door stood just ajar. With a silent paw Pan eased it open, preparing for escape, watching Vic warily.

Dealing out the bills, Vic said, "Like to borrow your car."

"Why would you need my car? Where's your truck?"

"Just for a little while, an hour or so. Had some trouble with the truck."

"Where is it? What kind of trouble? You wreck it?"

"It's in the shop."

"So why do you need my car?"

Laying down the last hundred-dollar bill and smoothing it out, he drew her close to the bed and put his arm around her. "Just for an hour or two, baby. Some errands I need to run." He picked up the stack of bills, tapped it against his palm to align the edges, and handed it to her. "Twenty-four hundred bucks. I did pretty good. Agreed?"

"I'd hoped to get more than this," Debbie said crossly. "Those Gucci bags . . ."

"Those Gucci bags were last year's models. I did a hell of a lot better than you'd have done, trying to peddle that lot to someone here in the village or trying to sell it through some consignment shop. Or on eBay. That'd bring the cops down on you."

Behind the stroller, Joe and Pan smiled at each other. The actual sale of the stolen luxury items put a nice footnote to Debbie's thieving ways.

But what the cats didn't understand was the connection. How did Vic and Debbie know each other? He and his friend couldn't have moved here to the village

260 · SHIRLEY ROUSSEAU MURPHY

just to act as her go-between, where was the profit in that?

Had they just happened on her, down in this adjoining neighborhood, and got acquainted? Maybe Vic liked her looks, started coming on to her. One thing led to another, and first thing you know, he's easing in on her profits. They listened to Debbie argue about the amount of money he'd offered, but then rudely she snatched it up, pulled up her sweater, and stuffed it in her bra.

"What about the car?" he said. "Just for a little while, baby."

"I don't think so, I need it for the children, I need to pick Vinnie up at school."

"School's four blocks away. Vinnie can walk." Vic hugged her close, his voice teasing. "Come on, baby. You got to have more stuff for the fence by now, with your clever ways. What's in them grocery bags over there, under the bread and cookies? You want me to handle that lot? I will if you loan me the car."

He argued and wheedled until at last she gave in. "On one condition," she said, and now there was a smile in her voice. She turned, indicating the bulging grocery bags. "Load those in the back under the blankets, get them out of here until that contractor's done nosing around."

"And them cops," he said. "You wouldn't want them cops to see all this, the ones that were cruising up here."

Debbie shrugged. As if she wasn't worried about cops.

"Will you be going back up to the city again, when you get your truck?"

"Might."

"When will that be?"

"Two, three days for the truck to be ready."

"Take that lot with you, sell it for me like you said, and you can borrow the car for two hours. No more."

In the bed, the cover stirred and Tessa peered sleepily out, watching Vic and her mother. The little girl, Joe thought, observed more than people imagined. Vic said, "When I get the truck, what if I head for the city with your stuff but don't come back this way for a while?"

"Send me a money order," Debbie said smartly.

"You trust me with the money, baby?"

"You brought me this much," she said softly, picking up her car keys, looking toward the stroller.

Panicked, the cats slid into the closet. From among the tangle of shoes and dropped clothes, they watched Debbie hand Vic the bags, loading four into his arms, piling the last atop the others in the stroller, watched her wheel the stroller out, escorting him to her car.

Slipping out of the closet, Joe Grey followed. But Pan leaped up onto the bed beside Tessa, worrying over the child, sniffing at her to determine just how sick she was.

Outside, skinning up into the branches of the pine, Joe watched Vic load up the grocery bags and cover them as Debbie had instructed, watched him back the station wagon out, turning downhill in a direction that would put him on Highway One, and watched Debbie turn back to the house with a smug and self-satisfied smile. No stolen goods on the premises now, no evidence to any crime.

Was this the last of her shoplifting, had she paid attention to what Ryan had told her? Or was she thinking Ryan would get busy with other matters and forget her threat? Was it possible that Debbie, now that she'd been caught red-handed, *would* stop stealing and look for a job?

Not likely, Joe thought. *Not bloody likely.* Clawing farther up the pine tree to the roof, he watched Debbie head for the garage with the empty stroller. Maybe she meant to fold it up and stick it in the corner behind her trash and boxes, get it out of the way, too. Behind her, Pan slipped out the door and scrambled to the roof beside him.

"Why does he need her car?" the red tom said. "Has he already sold the Lincoln? Sold it with Kate's treasure inside, with millions of dollars hidden in there just inches from his greedy fingers and he doesn't have a clue, no idea he's dumped a fortune for a few hundred bucks, to some scuzzy dealer?"

"You find that amusing? You think that's funny, if he let Kate's hoard get away where no one will ever find it, where not even the law might get a line on it?"

"I didn't mean it that way," Pan said contritely. "MPPD will find it. If he *has* sold it, it'll just take them longer."

"Or maybe," Joe said, "maybe he found the jewels before he sold it, took the door panels off himself to hide his stolen money, and found everything. Maybe right now he has Kate's treasure stashed somewhere else. Or," he said, "is the Lincoln still here somewhere with Kate's treasure still in it?" He looked up the hill to the woods, where the narrow dirt drive led down to the stone shack. "*Could* he have gotten the Town Car down through the trees? *Would* it have fit in that narrow shed?"

"Like a rat stuck in a jam jar," Pan said. "None of us were here to see him hide it, we were all up at the wreck. Except my dad," he said. "Except Misto."

"Vic's hardly had time to sell a car," Joe said. "Maybe everything *is* in the shed, and he's afraid to drive the Lincoln, afraid Harper's men will spot it, maybe that's why he wants Debbie's car. Let's have a look before he and his pal take off for good."

"Maybe the other guy's too hurt to travel. Kit said the man in the wrecked truck never stopped moaning, as if he were injured real bad."

Approaching the shed, looking up at its solid door, Joe leaped up at the padlock, striking and pawing at it. The big lock swung heavily but was closed tight. Pan tried, but with no better luck. Together they clawed at the door itself, trying to pull it away enough to see under or see through a crack at the side, but the heavy construction of bolted planks wouldn't budge. But then when they sniffed along the molding they caught Vic's fresh scent, and when they pressed their noses to the thinnest crack between door and molding they could smell a faint breath from within that made them smile: a distinct new-car smell, the smell of fine leather seats, the same comforting aroma as when they'd ridden in there with Kit, the smell of the Greenlaws' Town Car.

And when they examined the dirt apron of the drive itself, the faintest tire tracks led up to the shed door, the sharp tread of new tires just visible on the hard earth. Another set led away again to vanish where the narrow drive was covered with rotted leaves, where only vague indentations compressed the damp mulch. And only now, sniffing along the ground, did they catch Misto's scent where the old yellow cat had indeed padded along following the track of the Lincoln.

"Did they bring the Lincoln directly here from the wreck?" Pan said. "While we were headed up the mountain with the Damens, did my pa see those two men hide it in here?" He lifted his nose from the old cat's scent. "While you and Dulcie and I, and Rock and the Damens, were setting off to find Kit, did Misto know all along where those two men had holed up? He couldn't know who they were or what they'd done, and he couldn't know the Lincoln was stolen, but he knew where it *was*," he said, smiling.

"He knew they'd put a car in there," Joe said. "But would he recognize the Greenlaws' nice Town Car if it has heavy damage, dents and crumpled fenders, dirt and gravel from the landslide? And now," he said, "is it still parked in there behind those plank doors, or is only the smell there, and the Town Car gone again?"

"Secrets within secrets," Pan said as they moved away, wondering where else to look for the stolen vehicle. "This old place reeks of secrets. Only a few months ago, you and Dulcie find Sammie's body buried right down there under her own house. Then Emmylou inherits the house and starts finding money

hidden in the walls. Those two tramps come here looking for it, too. And then those same two men wreck
the Greenlaws' car or are involved in the wreck, one
of them attacks Pedric and Lucinda and could as well
have killed them both."

"And," Joe said thoughtfully, "even Sammie's death
itself might be tied in. It was her money."

"Tied in how?

"The department's file on Sammie says she was
killed because she saw Debbie's husband, Erik Kraft,
kill Debbie's younger sister after he got her pregnant. Killed his own wife's little sister. But did Erik
kill Sammie because of the money, too? Could he have
known Sammie had hidden money? If he found out
somehow, could he have tried to find it himself, tried to
force her to tell him where it was? When she wouldn't,
he killed her?"

"Maybe," Pan said thoughtfully. "I guess we'll
never know. Whatever happened, Erik Kraft is scum, I
always hated him. With a father like that and a mother
like Debbie, it's no wonder Tessa has problems. Do you
think," he said, "Vic hid the Lincoln nearby, where he
can get at it in a hurry?"

Both cats glanced down the hill where the little cottages stood crowded close together beneath their overgrown cypress trees. "Come on," Joe said, "it's worth a

look, half those places are empty." And off they went, past Debbie's house, down among the FOR RENT signs and the neglected foreclosures, to peer into garage windows and under doors, searching for a car worth maybe twenty thousand but loaded with treasure worth many times more.

25

Ryan drove home from Debbie's feeling dead for sleep and out of sorts, wishing Debbie Kraft had never returned to the village, and cursing her stupidity that she'd allowed Debbie to entrench herself rent-free in the little spec cottage. She had no idea whether her ultimatum to Debbie would have any effect on the woman. If it didn't she'd give the department a heads-up—if they weren't already watching Debbie. She hated that this would jeopardize Tessa. Even rude little Vinnie didn't deserve to be swept into the maw of Children's Services. Looking at her watch, she saw it was only mid-afternoon, just after two, but she'd love to crawl under a quilt for a few hours. Last night's desperate phone call from Kit seemed like weeks ago, a whole lifetime seemed to have passed since Kit's lonely cry for help.

Racing up to Santa Cruz, searching the dark cliffs and then that business with the coyote, their relief at finding Kit unhurt and then hurrying to the hospital and their long vigil there, had left her limp with fatigue. Their trek home this morning behind the ambulance, getting Lucinda settled, and finding that lowlife had been in there pawing through their personal things, stealing Pedric's clothes, that was enough without Debbie's sour defiance to top off the long and exhausting drama. Was she getting old? she thought crossly. But no long day on the job, no amount of hard physical work on a construction project, exhausted her as these stressful hours had done. Now, pulling into her own drive and killing the engine, she glanced in her side mirror to see Clyde turning in behind her, in one of the shop's loaner cars.

He had put in less than an hour, since she'd dropped him at work to clear up some irksome detail about Jaguar parts lost in shipping. She watched him step out of the silver Mercedes, yawning. Despite his aggravation at a delay in the repair schedule and, consequently, an annoyed client, it was nice to own your own business, to feel comfortable taking some time off when you needed to. The minute she opened the truck door, Rock bolted out and straight for the house, nearly upsetting Clyde as he unlocked the front door. When he pushed it open, swinging it wide, Rock bolted through heading for the kitchen.

Grinning, Clyde put his arm around her and they followed Rock in, found the big silver dog checking the kitchen floor for stray food. They stood watching him lick Snowball's empty bowl clean then sniff along the countertop—whatever enticing trail he found led him out of the kitchen again and up the stairs to the master suite. They moved up behind him, Clyde carrying their duffel and backpacks, to find Rock had followed the scent of the old yellow cat.

On the love seat in Clyde's study, Misto and Snowball woke only a little, curled together sleepily. On the desk the message light was flashing, but neither Ryan nor Clyde wanted to listen to messages. They watched Rock nose at the two cats, licking them all over. The little white cat was used to the big dog's attention, his wet caresses made her smile. Misto batted at Rock with velvet paws, hissing halfheartedly—but then the yellow tom caught a whiff of the backpacks where Clyde had set them on the floor. He rose to investigate. He smelled the canvas with a puzzled look, then looked up at Ryan, questioning. He sniffed the ocean smells the canvas had collected, the scent of fresh pine needles, the scents of Kit and Joe Grey and Pan. He dropped his ears and backed away.

"Coyote," he said, scowling up at them. "And blood," he added, drawing his lips back at the metallic scent.

"The Greenlaws had a wreck," Ryan said. "They're in the hospital. Kit ran off and was lost and called us, and we went after her. We found her, she's fine, but . . ."

Behind her, Clyde had flicked the replay on the answering machine; she paused until it had played its messages. The first two were about problems with the house she was just finishing, but nothing serious. The third call was from Dr. John Firetti; his recorded voice brought Misto to full attention. Leaping onto the desk, he nosed at the machine.

"We're home!" Firetti said.

"We're home," Mary chimed in, "shall we come get Misto? We so missed him, could we—"

But Misto was already on his way, leaping up to the rafters like a young cat and through Joe's cat door, his yellow tail vanishing as he bolted out through Joe's tower. They heard him thudding across the roof at a dead run, his gallop soon fading and then gone; they imagined him flying across the peaks above Ocean, making for the veterinary clinic and the cottage that stood beside it, making for home.

He'd left the Damens' without knowing much at all about the wreck or about Kit's fearful adventure, and with no idea the Greenlaws' car had been stolen, that the black car he'd seen pulling into the stone shed did, indeed, belong to Lucinda and Pedric. He left Ryan and Clyde equally ignorant, as well, of where the Town Car might now be hidden.

Debbie's cluttered and smelly station wagon was a big change for Vic, from driving the pristine new Lincoln. He'd quickly grown used to the heavier, smoother ride, and even with the Town Car's dents and coat of mud its interior had been better suited to his new, cleaned-up persona. Though in truth the Suzuki, stinking and littered, was more what he was used to, more like the comfortable old truck with trash on the floor, discarded socks, the smell of accumulated dust, stale crackers, and empty drink cans.

Heading for the hospital, he meant to use patient Michael Emory's name to enter the ER through the locked doors, to be admitted without a hassle. He planned to head for Emory's cubicle as if to visit, but then move right on by to Birely's room. It wouldn't take a minute to do Birely, inject the air the way the book said, bending the IV tube to keep air from going up into the bottle—just stick the syringe in below the bend, and push the air in. As simple as that, the air goes down through the IV, through the vein and up into Birely's heart. Half a second and he's dead, his life snuffed like a match in a blast of wind.

Vic knew he'd have to move fast, get out in that split second before the alarms went off and the place exploded into action, nurses and doctors running in with their expertise and their machines to bring Birely back to life; that part worried him, hoping he could escape before anyone saw him or realized he'd been in Birely's room at all.

And who knew how long it would take before he could even be alone with Birely without them nurses going in and out? The hour he'd spent in there before dawn, when he'd followed Birely's ambulance and pushed on in, the place had been pretty quiet. But now later in the day he imagined it might be real busy, people in scrubs hurrying every which way, phones ringing, maybe gurneys pushing by him coming or going from X-ray, white-coated doctors moving with deliberation from one cubicle to the next. If it was like that, he'd be lucky to get half a minute alone. He could hardly hang out there for hours waiting for the right moment without someone asking questions.

Pulling into the underground, he found a parking slot near the glass doors into the ER. He figured no one would take a second look at the old Suzuki, would think, just one more patient with no money and no insurance, going into the ER with the flu or a back-ache, going for help where the doctors wouldn't refuse to treat you even if you couldn't pay. The wide glass doors opened automatically. At the admitting desk, he gave his name as James Emory, told the nurse he'd come to see his cousin Michael.

"Mr. Emory has two visitors, that's all we allow at one time. If you'll have a seat here in the waiting room, we'll call you when you can go in."

"No problem," Vic said. "You got a Coke machine handy?"

"There's nothing on this floor. You can go up to the cafeteria, they have Cokes, coffee, and sandwiches." She pointed down the short hall, where he could see the lower steps of a stairway leading up. "That's the shortest way. At the top just keep going to the big central atrium."

He didn't know what an atrium was but he guessed he'd know when he saw it. He went up the steps into a wide, bright corridor, glass walls on his left looking out to manicured trees and gardens. Passing well-dressed people who looked like they belonged there, he felt out of place until he remembered he looked just like them now, no more shabby clothes, he was so cleaned up it took him a minute to recognize his own reflection in the tall windows. Hell, he looked pretty damn good, for a hobo.

The atrium was high ceilinged, with a towering round skylight at the top, and a big indoor fishpond with a small tree growing in the middle. He bought a Coke in the cafeteria, sat down at a table beside the pond. All kinds of space led away into bright halls and more open spaces, and he could see two more sets of stairs leading down. All so damn clean it made him uncomfortable. What kind of money did it take to build a fancy place like this? Molena Point was even richer than he'd thought.

He drank his Coke watching some kind of large, brightly colored fish swim back and forth, then got himself a sticky cinnamon bun and a cup of coffee. How long would it take for those people down in the ER, visiting Michael Emory, to get tired and leave? He felt edgy to get back down there and get this over with, and nervous, too, not wanting to go back. What time did the nurses change shift? Maybe better to wait until then, when they were hurrying to go home, others hurrying in to work, looking at records, playing catch-up to which patients had checked in or checked out or died—best to get down there when they were all distracted, do the deed, slip out to the parking garage again and vanish.

He got more coffee and settled back, watching the circling fish, checking his watch every little while. Just before four, several young women dressed in scrubs hurried out, and several others double-timed in from another parking lot that lay beyond the gardens. Young women walking fast, all businesslike, they knew where they were going and were in a hurry to be on time. Rising, he left his trash on the table.

He was headed for the stairs when he saw that woman contractor come in through the glass front doors, and he stepped back, frowning. No mistaking her, same jeans and red sweatshirt she'd had on at Debbie's, only now she was wearing one of those backpack purses, an expensive leather model. Looked like, the way she held her head, she was talking to the damn purse, but then he saw she was talking on her cell phone. He turned away and sat down at the table again. Did she recognize him from around Emmylou's place?

As far as he knew she'd probably never noticed him there—yet when he glanced around again, she was looking straight at him. She saw him looking, said something into the phone, and went on past the pond toward a set of stairs that descended on the far side. Well, he'd seen *her* for sure, around Debbie's and up at Emmylou's, too, helping out with the old woman's carpentering. Were these women all friends? He didn't rise until she had disappeared, moving on down the steps, making him wonder where she was headed, what was down there in that direction. He waited a while and then descended the other way, to the ER, trying to calm his jumpy nerves.

Ryan had awakened in late afternoon to the ringing of the phone. Clyde, sprawled beside her on the king-sized bed, hadn't stirred. An afternoon nap was a rare occurrence in their lives, she didn't like being woken up. Grabbing the ringing instrument, she'd eased out from under the coverlet that she'd tossed over them.

"It's Kate. I hope I didn't wake you."

"Only a little."

Kate laughed. "I'm sorry. Pedric called, he's feeling better, he asked if I could bring Kit over, he misses her, he wants to know if I can smuggle her in. I don't want to leave Lucinda alone yet when she's on the pain meds, but he sounded so forlorn. I think Kit's ordeal up on the cliffs has left him more upset than she was, he wants her close to him, he asked if Lucinda could spare her for a while. Could you . . . ?"

"Of course I'll come, I'll take her over there to him." Beside her, Clyde turned over, mumbling but hardly waking; Clyde had sat up the longest last night with Pedric, he deserved to be sleepy.

"I'm just running Kit up to the hospital," she said, "Pedric's asking for her."

"Take the Mercedes," he said, waking fuzzily. "Keys are on my desk. I'll drop the truck off at the shop before the mechanics go home, I don't like the way it's running."

She thought it was running fine, he was so picky about their cars. She grinned at him, nodded, pulled on her boots, and found her purse. She dropped her keys on the desk, took the Mercedes keys, and told Rock to stay home. The Weimaraner, having hauled himself from sleep and surged off the love seat, was more than ready to go with her. She told him, "No," and hugged him, but he looked after her ruefully. She moved on down the stairs and out, slipped into the silver Mercedes, and headed for Lucinda's house.

When she pulled up into the Greenlaws' drive, tortoiseshell Kit was waiting on the steps shifting from paw to paw, lashing her fluffy tail with impatience. Ryan set the emergency brake and then opened the driver's door. Kit leaped up into her lap, her expression a strange mix of eagerness and sadness.

"What? What's wrong? Lucinda's all right?"

"Fine," Kit said, snuggling down close to her, pushing her head into Ryan's ribs.

Ryan rubbed Kit's warm little ears, but she didn't start the car. "Tell me." She sat frowning down at Kit. "Is it Pan? Is it because you argued?"

"Because . . ." Kit pawed at a tear seeping into the dark fur of her cheek. "Because the most important things to Pan are so different from how I see things. I didn't know that about him. We can never . . ."

Ryan took Kit in her arms. "You're not opposite at all. You're perfect for each other. You're male and female, that's all. That's what makes the world work. Females go more for security, they'll fight tooth and claw to protect their home and kittens but tomcats' hearts are strung for adventure. They go searching for challenge, that's the way *they* protect their brood. That's the way you're made, you and Pan."

Kit looked up at her and her pink tongue came out, licking at another tear.

Ryan looked down into Kit's wide yellow eyes. She didn't know what else to say, she didn't know how to resolve this. Their story was as old as the very concept of male and female. "Maybe," she said, "if you could talk without hissing and spitting at him . . ."

"Pan does all the hissing," Kit said untruthfully. Ryan gave her a sideways glance, settled Kit in the seat again, put the car in gear, and headed for the freeway.

"Maybe I hissed a little," Kit said, "but he was so—"

"If Pedric sees you all teary, you'll make him feel worse than he does now."

"I know," Kit said contritely. She crept up into Ryan's lap again, curled up in a tight little ball, shivering. She was being so dramatic Ryan wanted to scold her, but this was the way Kit reacted, the little tortoiseshell was a born drama queen. This was the way she was made, her wild little spirit knew no compromise, her wild heart blazed with the passion of an unruly youngster, and Ryan knew she would never change. Taking the off-ramp for the hospital, she headed up the hill, made a right, and a left into underground parking. Cruising the first level for a space, she passed Debbie's old station wagon pulled in beside a pillar. What was she doing here? Had one of the children been hurt? Or maybe Debbie had brought Tessa to emergency for some free cold medicine, that would be her style. But then when she did find a parking place, she was two cars down from an old green Chevy that was a ringer for Emmylou's car, so much like it that, telling Kit to wait in the car, she walked back and looked in.

She could see Emmylou's ragged tan sweater on the front seat, no mistaking the tear in the sleeve. The presence of the two familiar cars there at the hospital unsettled her. Uneasily she returned to the car, where Kit was standing on the dashboard, peering out. "Debbie's car, and Emmylou's?" Kit said. "What's that about?" And neither of them could answer.

Opening her small leather backpack, Ryan watched Kit climb in and curl up at the bottom. Kit didn't like this pack because she couldn't see out, like the big canvas one with the net insets, but to Ryan the oversized purse seemed less obvious. She buckled the flap loosely enough so Kit could crawl out if she had to, she would never confine any of the cats beyond escape. "Smile for Pedric," she said, "he needs you now, even more than Pan does." She slung the pack over her shoulder. "Who knows," she said, "maybe Pan will get some sense and change his macho mind, maybe he'll look at your side of the argument."

Kit didn't answer.

"Maybe," Ryan said, locking the Mercedes, "if Kate describes her journey in more detail, if she tells him more graphically exactly why she will never, ever return to the Netherworld, maybe he'll listen. Maybe," she said, "he'll think a little more about the dangers to his beautiful lady." Heading for the elevators, stepping in and pushing the button for the main level, she took her phone from her pocket so she could talk with Kit in public looking perfectly natural. Stepping out of the elevator onto the open terrace, she crossed to the glass doors, moved inside into the vast, airy court with its sun dome and pond, its information desk and cafeteria, its light-filled corridors leading away to the various hospital wings. The hospital walls were made of white concrete in a bas-relief pattern that made her think of Aztec monuments, the occasional paintings hanging against them offering rich islands of color, oils and watercolors by well-known local artists, dating back into the last century. The smell of coffee and of onion soup rose sharply from the cafeteria kitchen. A man stood beside the pond half turned away seeming to watch the red, black, and white fish swimming aimlessly, but in fact he was watching her, a furtive sideways glance. Did she know him? The back of his neck was so white he must have only recently decided to change his hairstyle. Pale cheeks and chin, too, when he turned.

But he was no one she knew, and she headed past the fishpond, for the far stairs that descended to the ICU, hoping she *could* slip Kit into Pedric's room without getting caught. The nurses in the ICU stuck pretty close to their patients. They'd pushed their luck enough, up in Santa Cruz. Their own Peninsula Hospital, being larger, seemed somehow more intimidating. Who knew what contempt a furry feline visitor, discovered in the ICU against all bureaucratic regulations, would stir among the medical staff—what lack of sympathy that would generate for a needful patient?

26

Ryan descended the stairs, not talking to her hidden passenger even with the ruse of her cell phone. The scrutiny of that man by the pond had made her edgy. Light from the main pavilion shone from behind her down the wide stairs; she imagined Kit peering out beneath the leather flap at the sunny vistas and at the paintings spaced along the walls, oils and watercolors, many of the bright California coast. At the bottom of the stairs she followed the signs through a long waiting room; three women sat at a little round table at the far end, all talking at once. Passing them, she moved on down the hall to the ICU. As she entered, no one paid any attention to her, the nurses were all busy with patients or at the computers. When she found Pedric's glass cubicle, the clear doors and the canvas curtain were wide open. His hospital bed was empty, the white covers neatly turned back. When she turned, a slim, dark-haired nurse stood behind her, green scrubs, gold earrings, hair sleeked into a bun at the back.

"Where's Pedric? Mr. Greenlaw? I thought he was in room 7."

"You are . . ."

"Ryan Flannery," she said. "I'm a friend, I'm on his health care directive." Did they keep *lists* of those permitted in the ICU? The nurse moved to a desk within the open nurses' station, peered into a lighted screen and pushed a few keys, then glanced up at Ryan. "Mr. Greenlaw is having an MRI. Later today, sometime after he returns, he'll be moved over to the west wing, into a room there."

"Why is that? He's not worse?"

"Oh, no, his own doctor wants a few more tests, that's all. And he wants the surgeon to go ahead with the arthroscopy on his knee, for the torn meniscus. That's usually an outpatient procedure, but with the other complications, Dr. Bailey wants it done while he's here, wants him to stay for at least a day or two."

"Can you tell me where the new room will be? What number?"

"We don't have a number yet, they're still cleaning the rooms. If you want to come back in, say, an hour, we should know."

Ryan nodded, and left the ICU, glancing in at the rows of bedridden patients, each tethered to their iron bed like a prisoner, she thought dourly. Heading for the waiting room, she thought that Pedric must not have known he would be having another scan and then would be moved, or he wouldn't have called the house asking for Kit.

In the lounge she chose a love seat as far from the three noisy women as she could. The room was furnished with dark rattan chairs, small rattan tables, and three leather love seats. Potted schefflera plants the size of small trees cast the room in gentle shadows. The place smelled of coffee, from an urn sitting on a console against the longer wall. Paper cups, a basket full of artificial creamer and fake sweetener, all the accompaniments a health-conscious hospital would want to furnish. Setting the backpack down beside her on the cushion of the love seat, she fished out her cell phone. The pack shifted only slightly as Kit peered out the top, scowling at the boisterous women, at their frantic exchange as each tried to get in one more word. "Why do women go on like that," Kit whispered, "tearing their husbands apart? *You* don't do that, none of *my* human friends do that."

Ryan shrugged, holding her cell phone to her ear. "*You* said a few things about Pan," she pointed out.

Kit said nothing. Inside the pack, she curled up again, closed her eyes, and tucked her nose under her paw. Maybe, Ryan thought, after her long and arduous night she would sleep now, would drift off into happier dreams and would wake less angry. Ryan closed her own eyes, but the women's too-loud voices racketed into her thoughts as sharp as hail on a metal roof; when she did doze off, her dreams were filled with fog and craggy cliffs, with the gleam of a coyote's eyes and the sharp smell of gunpowder, with regret at the kill but with deep satisfaction that Kit was safe.

When Vic came down from the cafeteria into the ER, the nurses were too busy to pay attention to him. He moved on past the nurses' station glancing into each glass cubicle trying to look like he knew where he was going. He walked the entire square, all four sides, but Birely was not in any of the rooms. At last, revving up his nerve, he asked a nurse.

"I'm his neighbor, I stopped in to see how he's doing."

The little blonde was young, her hair tumbled up atop her head like a bird's nest and secured with a strip of white bandage. "Mr. Miller just returned from surgery, he's over in the ICU. They repaired his nose. It'll be some time, after that heals and his breathing's steadier, that he'll be ready for surgery to remove the spleen."

This had to be more than the nurses were supposed to tell a stranger, and Vic smiled at her in a friendly way. "Sounds like he's getting good care. I'll stop over there a little later, then, when he's feeling stronger."

Leaving the ER, he had a time finding his way to the ICU. The halls led every which way, and many of the heavy double doors were locked. By the time he found Birely his hands were sweating with nerves. The layout was pretty much the same as the ER, big room maybe fifty feet square, nurses' station in the middle fenced off by open counters with their ever-present computers.

Big chrome machine on the counter near him with spigots for hot and cold water, another machine for brewed coffee, regular and decaffeinated, just like a fancy café. Again he circled the nurses' station but when at last he found Birely there was too much traffic around him, nurses moving in and out of the other rooms. Beneath the white blanket, Birely looked small and weak. He had a white bandage across his nose, a tube sticking out of each nostril so he could breathe, and the usual IV tube attached at his wrist, held in place by heavy tape. His eyes were closed, as if he slept. Even as Vic watched, a nurse moved past him and inside followed by a white-coated doctor. Vic glanced at them casually and stepped on along as if heading for a room around the corner. Damn place was crawling with doctors and several of them glanced at him, looking him over as if he had no business there. He moved along paying no attention to them, as businesslike as he could manage, until an older nurse stopped him, an overweight redhead in blue scrubs, braces on her teeth, asked what patient he was looking for. He gave her Michael Emory's name. She carried a trench coat over her arm, and a brown leather purse as if she were headed home. Stepping to a computer, she said Michael Emory was over in the ER, and she told him how to get there. She was pretty nice, she didn't treat him like scum. It had paid to get cleaned up and wear expensive clothes. It was nearly five, and he was sure the shift had already changed. Eight to four, four to twelve, midnight to eight, that was the way most places broke up their time. He waited until he saw the redhead leave, hurrying down the hall carrying her trench coat and jingling her car keys. When he was sure no one was looking, he slipped into an empty room where he could see they hadn't cleaned up yet, bedsheets wadded in a heap in the middle of the mattress, trash can overflowing with blue plastic pads of some kind and lengths of used tubing. Metal table cluttered with pieces of bloody gauze and used tape, and two used syringes with no needles in them.

He found the rubber-glove dispenser on the wall beside the door, pulled a pair from the section marked LARGE, worked one onto his right hand, and dug into the trash. When he couldn't find a syringe he turned to the hazardous-waste bin, which was also attached to the wall.

The first three syringes were useless, just the blunt plastic end. Digging deeper, he found one that someone hadn't broken off the needle. Retrieving it, he hoped to hell he wouldn't pick up some kind of lethal disease that'd put *him* in the ER or leave him sick and helpless.

Well, hell, if he didn't pull this off he'd be looking at worse than a hospital bed, looking at a lumpy metal cot behind steel bars. If the cops went nosing around Emmylou's after she'd called the ambulance, if she told them she'd had a break-in and they were camping up there, and the cops came up here to the hospital asking Birely questions, and the dumb little twerp started talking about the money, that would put him on the hot seat. Cops picked up even one fingerprint in that stone shack, ran it through the system, they'd have his whole damn record.

Dropping the syringe in his pocket, he left the ICU still trying to look casual. Made his way out to the stairs, thinking to wait a while until maybe there was less action in there and until people forgot they'd seen him looking in the rooms. He was passing the waiting room to the ICU when he saw her again, that dark-haired woman contractor sitting right there only a few feet from him, and he stepped back out of sight.

She sat in there drinking a cup of coffee and talking on her cell phone. Sounded like she was talking to a carpenter, going on about door sizes and the delivery of some kind of flooring. She sat turned away from him, and silently he slipped on by. What was she doing here?

Well, hell, people got sick. Birely didn't have a corner on the market. He moved on down a long hall to another part of the hospital thinking to wait a while until people forgot about him, then go back and take care of Birely. He knew he was putting it off, he told himself he was being cautious, that he wasn't scared. He wandered the halls until he'd got himself thoroughly lost again and began to feel shaky.

Finally, passing a big, glassed-off garden right in the center of the building, he saw the cafeteria ahead, and knew where he was. He stopped off there, had himself another cup of coffee to steady his nerves, and another one of them cinnamon rolls. Jangled nerves always made him hungry. That garden he'd passed, big as a city lot, hospital rooms and glassed hallways facing it on all four sides, garden had a big rock formation with a waterfall, three stories of rooms looking out on it. Pretty damn fancy, he wished he had half the money it'd taken to build this place. What couldn't he do with that kind of cash?

Finishing his coffee and sticky roll, he headed back to the ICU. Moved on in past the nurses' station and across to Birely's room. He was about to step inside when he saw a nurse in there and another doctor. He moved on by, glancing around, and into the room next door. The patient was sleeping, snoring softly. Slipping past him to the connecting wall, he stood listening.

The doctor's voice was deep, it reached him easily, he must be standing right there on the other side. The glimpse Vic had had of him, he was a big man, his shoulders rolled forward as if maybe he had a weak back. He was talking about the IV, giving the nurse instructions. "Keep him on fourteen milligrams of Demerol every three to four hours, until his nose is less painful. I want him to lighten up a little now, not so deep under. I want only nurses in here, no trainees, I want him handled with care. I don't want any pressure on the abdomen. None. Do you understand?"

Vic couldn't make out what the nurse said, her voice was too soft. He was so intent, listening, he almost missed seeing Emmylou pass by, he barely glimpsed her through the crack between the curtain and the wall as she turned into Birely's room.

Had she seen him out there, coming into the ICU? But hell, *she* didn't know him, either. He was too edgy. Just because he recognized someone didn't mean they knew him. If Emmylou'd ever seen them and knew they were living up there, she'd have called the cops long ago. And with his change in looks, his long hair gone, why would she recognize him now? The doctor was telling her that when Birely's nose had healed some, he'd go back into surgery and they'd take out his spleen, same as that nurse had said.

"If the spleen doesn't rupture," Emmylou said, "before you get him back into surgery?"

"We're taking the best care we can," the doctor said coldly. "You have no idea what happened to this man?"

"None," she said. "I found him hurt like that, lying in a sleeping bag half-conscious and moaning."

"Found him where?"

"In an old vacant house at the back of my property, no one was supposed to be in there."

"You reported it to the police?"

"I called the ambulance. I don't plan to file a complaint, so why call them?"

There was a long silence. The doctor said no more. Emmylou said, "I'll come back in a while, see if he's awake. He . . . I'd like a word with him, when he wakes."

Vic watched through the crack as she left. Soon the doctor left, and then the nurse. He watched the nurses' station as personnel moved back and forth, going about their business, all so damned organized. The ward grew quieter, some of the nurses disappeared into patients' rooms, the pace seemed to slow. Vic moved out of the room past the sleeping patient, his rubber-gloved hand in his coat pocket, caressing the syringe. He was about to slip into Birely's room when two nurses came around the corner wheeling a gurney, came straight toward him. He stepped away, looking with curiosity at the patient, his head all wrapped in white like a turban, his face white as death itself. They turned into a room two doors down, both nurses looking up at him. He smiled at them and nodded, annoyed that they looked right at him, that they could identify him in a damn minute entering Birely's room. Angrily he moved on out of the ward, down the hall and out of sight. He'd wait a while and go back. Or come back tonight after another change of shift, when maybe the ward would be quieter?

Right, and when every visitor would stand out all the more. Best to walk the halls a while and then go back again, get it over with, this time, before he lost his nerve altogether. Strolling the hall pretending to look at the pictures on the walls, he stopped at a picture of boats in a stormy harbor, the water wild with whitecaps that made him cold just looking at them. He walked on, feeling shaky, and at last headed back to the ICU. Passing the waiting room, he saw that carpenter woman was still in there, and Emmylou had joined her, she sat right there beside her, talking earnestly. Moving on beyond the open door past the big leafy plant beside it, he paused in the shadows to listen.

27

Kit was so warm inside the backpack she couldn't help but squirm, she had to poke her nose out for one breath of cool air. She ducked back when Emmylou appeared in the doorway. What was she doing here? "Come sit," Ryan said, moving Kit's leather pack off the love seat, setting it on the floor. "Have you come to see Pedric?"

Emmylou crossed the room with a soft scuffing sound, and sat down. "Pedric Greenlaw's here? Oh, my. What happened? What's wrong?"

By the time Ryan had explained about the wreck, Kit had crawled halfway out of the backpack again, listening. Ryan explained how Kit had run off from the wrecked Lincoln, which was the natural thing for a frightened cat to do, and how they had gone to search for her.

"Poor little thing," Emmylou said. "How lucky that you found her, up in those dark woods. She must have been terrified."

I was terrified. And ready to bloody those damned coyotes.

"She came to us," Ryan said. "She had the good sense to do that."

Well, of course I did.

"And you spent the rest of the night at the hospital up there? You must be dead for sleep. And they're here, now, in the hospital? Pedric and Lucinda?"

"Pedric is," Ryan said. "They brought him down in an ambulance. They'll be moving him over to the other wing for a few days, but Lucinda's at home. Our friend from San Francisco is staying with her. Lucinda's happy to *be* home, and so is their little cat."

"I'm sure of that," Emmylou said. "Cats don't take well to that kind of stress. But now they're both safe in their own place, and that will help to heal them." Emmylou had a special fondness for the concept of *home*, for a safe haven of one's own, having recently lived homeless in her old car, and before that in a wind-riddled, one-room shack from which she had been evicted. Her work on her snug house, as she remodeled, was thoughtful and loving. Was, in its own way, deeply restorative to the lone woman, a home at last that no one could take from her.

But, Kit thought, *we're not all home, Pedric's not home yet. And I feel like I've spent half my life in hospitals hiding under the covers having to be quiet and still and my very fur smells of hospital. Pedric has to feel just as trapped, all the bandages, the needles stuck in his arm, the nurses doing things to him he'd rather do for himself. We're not all home yet, we're not all three of us back together yet.* The brush of a footstep in the hall, the silence as it paused startled her. She rose up out of the leather pack, to look.

Beyond the open door a shadow shifted where someone stood listening, his shadow half hidden by the big floppy leaves of the schefflera plant that hid, as well, most of the hallway. Emmylou was saying, ". . . squatters. Two sleeping bags, empty cans of beans, beer cans, trash. They left a mess. Well, this man that I've come to visit, he was in there in his sleeping bag on the floor, and he was hurt real bad. I don't know what happened but he was all alone, moaning and bleeding, the minute I saw him I hurried down to my place and called the ambulance."

Listening to Emmylou, trying to make sense of what she was saying, Kit watched the shadow shift again, and when she breathed deeply she picked up the sweet smell of sugar and cinnamon, and then . . . What? What was that she smelled?

Pedric? The faintest scent of Pedric? But then even stronger, over Pedric's scent and the smell of sugary cinnamon, came a familiar odor that made her swallow back a growl. It was all she could do not to bolt out of the bag and leap at him, slash him as she had up on the mountain when he'd hurt Lucinda. Why was that man here at the hospital? The same hospital where Pedric was. What did he want, what did he mean to do?

"Well, to make a long story short," Emmylou was saying, "the hurt man is Sammie's little brother, Birely. Can you believe it? Her homeless brother who came around once or twice a year. Birely who never admitted to being among the homeless, who called himself a hobo. Whenever he showed up, she'd take him a sandwich or a hot supper from the deli. Sometimes I went with her, we'd sit under the Valley Road bridge, the three of us like homeless folks, having our picnic."

"Was Birely here for her funeral? I don't . . ."

"No," Emmylou said. "He probably didn't know she'd died, until now. Came back all these months later, after Sammie was buried, came up to the property but didn't tell me he was here. Broke into that stone shack with one of his cronies. How long have they been there, and I didn't have a clue? Not until I heard some noises up there last night, and went up to see and there was Birely, lying there only half alive."

The shadow had moved closer, pressing against the door, Kit could see the flap of his jacket now, through the crack between the wall and the open door. His smell came stronger again, hiding Pedric's scent. Emmylou said, "Days earlier, I *had* wondered, when Misto started watching the place, sitting in the yard, looking up there. And then when I saw your Joe Grey and little tabby Dulcie up there, saw them come down off the windowsill as if they'd been inside. I thought, then, there were rats up there, there are wood rats all over these hills. I decided they were hunting in there, and I thought no more about it."

In the shadow of the love seat, when Ryan turned away, Kit slipped on out of the backpack, to the floor. Ryan said, "When he learned Sammie had died, why didn't he come to you? Was he too shy, did he move in there out of loneliness but was too shy to let you know he was there? But then," she said, "what happened? How did he get hurt?" Behind her Kit fled belly down across the dark tile floor and into the shadows of the potted schefflera tree. "Last night," Ryan said, "when you called the ambulance, why didn't you ask for the police, too?"

"Those two hadn't *hurt* anything," Emmylou said. "They were trespassing, but nothing more. My concern was all for Birely."

"Emmylou, you don't know anything about the other man, or, in fact, about Birely . . ."

"Oh, Birely isn't mean, just irresponsible. Maybe a little dim. Sammie always tried to take care of him. She was nine when Birely was born. She said he was always shy and rather slow, that the other kids teased and harried him. Their parents did their best to see he wasn't bullied and to teach him to fend for himself, but then their father was killed. Birely was seven, Sammie sixteen. After that, I guess they all had a hard time.

"When Sammie died she left me everything she had, the house and the money. She asked me to take care of him if I could, so of course I feel responsible for him, I couldn't betray Sammie, I have to help Birely."

"She left you money? I hope enough to pay the taxes and insurance."

Emmylou smiled. "Oh, my, yes. She . . ." She glanced down the room at the three women, but they were still talking all at once, as frantically energized as sparrows on a pile of bread crumbs. "She left money hidden in the house," Emmylou said softly. "Quite a lot of money."

"I'm glad of that," Ryan said. "That helps with the refurbishing, too. I hope you have it safe in the bank, now. But, Emmylou, if Birely's friend knew he was hurt, why didn't *he* get Birely to the ER? He just went off and left him? Doesn't that tell you something?"

Kit, hidden among the leaves of the schefflera, wasn't six inches from the man who'd hurt Pedric and Lucinda, who'd gone into their empty house and trashed it. He looked different now, smooth shaven, with short, neater hair—having left his pigtail scattered across their bathroom floor, she thought, twitching a whisker. He was wearing Pedric's sport coat, the missing tweed sport coat, and Pedric's missing Rockports that, when she sniffed them through the crack, still smelled of the Molena Point hills, of bruised grass and damp leaves. He had used Lucinda and Pedric's house key to steal Pedric's clothes, and now he was here at the hospital. Come to visit his hurt partner? Or to nose around Pedric's room? For what reason?

Emmylou said, "Maybe Birely's partner didn't have any money to take him to the hospital, maybe he left Birely to go for medicine, to help him the only way he could, maybe—"

"You know better than that, Emmylou. Medicine, for a smashed nose? Everyone knows you can check yourself into the ER with no money, that, by law, they can't refuse to treat you. Where *is* this friend, who couldn't bother to bring Birely here?"

The man beyond the door had turned away, moved silently, heading down the hall toward the ICU. Silently Kit followed him. Bellying out from under the schefflera and out the door, she hoped no doctor or nurse came along the hall and made a fuss, called security to chase that cat out of the hospital. Behind her the voices faded as Kit streaked across an intersecting hallway close behind the man's heels. The floors were no longer dark so he blended in; the linoleum was white now, against her black-and-brown coat as she followed him into the big, open expanse of the Intensive Care Unit.

In the waiting room, Ryan knew she should be returning to the ICU, to see if Pedric was back in his bed. She imagined Kit sound asleep in her backpack, worn out from last night's excitement. Emmylou was saying, "I read Sammie's letter over and over. I kept it for only a few days and then I burned it. I was afraid someone might find it, and find the money. Sammie had invested some of it, and she did all right, enough to live on, and to work only when she wanted to. She kept most of the original money at home, she said her uncle'd taught her never to trust banks.

"After he left the states, Sammie thought he was afraid to write or call, afraid that might put the Mexican

Guardia on his trail, afraid of being extradited back to the U.S. He must have been a tough old guy; he was one of the last legendary train robbers, a man right out of the Old West, and he was a real hero to Sammie. She prayed he'd come back, but he didn't, not until she was nearly thirty. Came back to California to die.

"She was living up in the Salinas Valley then, working as a bookkeeper, when the uncle showed up again. He was real sick, lung disease. He was bone thin and weak, and could hardly breathe, she was surprised he had made it up from Mexico, came by train all the way. She got him into the hospital," Emmylou said, "but he only lasted a week, lying there white and helpless, she said, and then he was gone. Dead from emphysema and pneumonia.

"Her letter was with her will. I was surprised she had a lawyer, she lived such a simple life, was so reclusive." Emmylou laughed. "Like me, I guess. Well, the lawyer gave me the sealed letter, and the newly recorded deed in my name, a check for what little she had in the bank, and the letter he'd sent her with the money some years before he died."

"That's why you were tearing into the walls," Ryan said, "that's why you're remodeling, looking for the money. Oh, my God, Emmylou. What if there'd been a fire?"

"It was wrapped in sheets of asbestos," Emmylou said, "some kind of insulation, maybe what they used to use in houses before the laws got so strict."

Ryan closed her eyes, imagining packets of old, frail treasury bills, wrapped in asbestos that probably wouldn't help much if those ancient, dry studs went up in a hungry blaze. She wondered if, in those simpler days when every crime was more newsworthy, that robbery had been in the California papers. She wondered if the case was still open, perhaps, was still on the books after all these many years—and if the feds would still like to get their hands on those old bills? It was only after Emmylou had left, and Ryan reached down to pick up her backpack and head for the ICU, only when she felt the pack swing up too light, light and empty, that she panicked.

28

Making sure he had the rubber glove, Vic patted the syringe, safe in his pocket. At the door to the ICU he tried to look casual, walked on in past the chrome coffee machine, scanning the glass-fronted cubicles. His plan was to use patient Michael Emory as his cover, pretend to be visiting him. The nurse had said he was being moved over there from the ER. With luck he'd be there already and maybe asleep, sick people slept a lot. If the wife wasn't in there he could sit in there himself, like a visitor, could watch Birely's room from there until the coast was clear. It would take only a second to do Birely, bend the tube, inject the air, and get the hell out—and talk about luck! There she *was*, that Mrs. Emory, coming out of number 15, the same small dumpy woman with the round, wrinkled face and yellowed fuzzy hair. Congratulating himself on his perfect timing, he watched her leave Emory's room pulling the canvas curtain halfway across as if maybe Emory *was* sleeping. As she passed the nurses' station and moved on out the double doors he stepped over to the coffee urn, filled a white foam cup with coffee, added sugar and cream. Carrying this, he headed on around the nurses' station to the other side. If anyone questioned him, he was here to visit with Michael Emory. He smiled and nodded when one or another of the nurses glanced up at him. They were all busy, no one paid much attention to him, busy doing their routine chores of one kind or another, oblivious to Vic's purpose there.

Stalking the man was an exercise in fast judgment and heart-thumping panic. Kit made it down the hall and around the corner into the ICU having to dodge only twice into open doorways, where she barely missed being seen. Slipping behind his heels into the ICU, she was engulfed by the smell of alcohol, adhesive tape, disinfectants, and human urine. The ward was brightly lighted, and on the white linoleum she stood out like a raven on a white bedsheet. There was not one dim recess near her in which to hide, to camouflage her dark coat, not one shadow except, yards away, where the occasional cart or wheeled cupboard was parked against the open nurses' counter. Twice she dodged behind rolling electrical equipment that looked like it could shock her straight into cat heaven.

If this man was visiting his wounded friend, wasn't it a little late? Why would he care about Birely after leaving him to suffer and maybe die all alone? Her sense of Birely, after listening to Emmylou, had softened, had left her feeling only sorry for Sammie's pitiful brother. It wasn't Birely who had hurt Pedric and Lucinda and stolen their car, it was Birely's visitor.

The soft pad of a nurse's approaching footsteps sent her behind a stainless steel machine with a cord hanging down like a noose. Next to it against the counter stood three rolling storage cabinets, polished steel carts with doors and drawers, with who knew what inside them? Towels and warm blankets? Or lethal and radiating medications that could sear a cat's very liver at this close range? The carts stood on casters, four inches off the floor, leaving narrow, bone-bruising spaces beneath. Flattening herself, she crept under.

Squeezed against the cool linoleum floor, concealed within the cupboard's shadow, she peered out at the man in Pedric's sport coat. He stood with his back to her looking in through a partially open glass door, the canvas curtain drawn halfway across. She watched him move on in, to disappear inside. Whatever he was up to, his body language and his nervous smell made the fur along her back stand stiff.

But this wasn't Pedric's room, his was around the corner near the double doors, she'd seen it earlier from Ryan's backpack. Relieved but curious, she looked both ways as if crossing a busy street, and slipped behind him across the wide walkway to the open glass door. She crouched there frantic to hide herself before a nurse spotted her, but she was afraid to push inside where *he'd* see her.

The canvas curtain didn't reach the floor; whoever had designed the flimsy barrier hadn't envisioned anyone interested enough to peer underneath from a four-inch vantage. When she looked under, his back was to her. She crawled under and crouched against the glass beneath the curtain's edge.

The patient was either asleep or unconscious. He lay unmoving, his eyes closed, his nose covered with a thick white bandage. A thin plastic tube snaked out of each nostril, she could hear him breathing through them. The man she'd followed stood over him. She had to force her tail to be still, not switch with anger. He stood looking down at the tube that ran from a vein in Birely's wrist up to the hanging jar that was the IV dispenser. He reached to examine the tube and then looked up at the screen, watching its moving graph and changing numbers. When he fished a syringe from his pocket, she shivered at the long needle.

He took the IV hose in his other hand and bent it double, stopping the flow of liquid. She watched him lay the needle along the tube as if preparing to stick it in—for what purpose? All Emmylou's sympathy for Birely hit her, and all her own hatred of the man who had hurt her humans. She leaped screaming at him, landed on his shoulder clawing hard.

He hit and grabbed at her trying to pull her off, then swung around as if to run. She clawed down the side of his face, down his neck. When he raised the needle to jab her she dropped off and dove under the bed, up onto its heavy metal stand. He leaned over, looking. He kicked at her, swearing. Even as she dodged away, she saw him drop the needle, straighten up, and draw back his fist over the patient.

His fist struck straight down with all his weight, into Birely's stomach. Birely screamed a gurgling cry and then was still. Bells went off on the monitor, the graph of Birely's heartbeat went flat, the gauges blinking in distress. An alarm shrieked from the nurses' station. Birely's attacker was gone, racing away, dodging nurses who came running. He shouldered through them shouting, "Help, someone help . . . Get a doctor, call the doctor." Pointing and shouting, he fled through the open double doors and vanished. Kit flew through behind him, flicking her tail away as they swung closed.

Racing past the surprised clerk at the admittance desk, she could see him out beyond the glass doors running through the dim parking garage, nearly trampling three children coming in with their heavily pregnant mother. His running feet echoed on the concrete, heading for an old brown station wagon. Debbie's car? Puzzled, she raced for it. The instant he jerked the door open she streaked behind him into the back, into the dark tangle of Coke cans, mashed food, and little stray shoes. As he started the car, grinding the engine, she barely heard, behind them, a little child's voice, "A cat, Mama . . . a cat chasing . . ." He took off with a squeal of rubber, the concrete roof passing over them, but at the entrance he slowed, easing sedately out of the covered parking into daylight.

Turning left on the tree-lined highway, she knew he was headed toward the freeway. She braced into the right turn, up onto the south on-ramp as if heading back toward the village. She heard no siren behind them, and there'd been no one in the parking lot to note his frantic flight, no one she'd seen except the woman and three children. She couldn't believe he'd escaped past the running nurses without alarming any of them.

Couldn't they see what he'd done? Crouched behind him among the litter of toys, she scared herself thinking she could have been crushed in the slamming ICU door and then in the slamming car door. She scared herself even worse, knowing she was alone with this man whom she'd twice attacked and bloodied, who might do any terrible thing to her if he got his hands on her.

29

Emmylou had headed back to the ICU when Ryan reached down to her backpack, found it empty, and panicked. She stared around the lounge, rose to look behind the two chairs in the corner, behind the other three love seats, all unoccupied, behind the green scheffleras that spread out as lush as small trees. She studied the three loud women down at the end, scanned the shadows around their feet, but there was no darker shape, and why would Kit be there? She looked out to the hall, and with an uneasy feeling she headed for the ICU. She was halfway up the hall when she heard women shouting ahead, heard some kind of alarm go off. She ran, saw someone roll a machine across the ICU to a cubicle on the far side where nurses were crowding in. "He's flatlined . . ." Two white-coated doctors pushed inside, shouldering Emmylou away where she was stretching up trying to see over the crowding nurses.

"Birely," she was crying, "let me in, let me by." Ryan saw a running man disappear out through the open double doors and—her stomach sank—a dark cat chasing him, leaping through the closing doors behind him. She ran. They disappeared in the direction of the admittance desk, the closing doors clicked together in her face even as she fought to open them. Had they locked down automatically, like prison doors? She remembered a nurse touching the wall earlier, just there where that little black hand was painted. Maybe an electric eye? She hit the wall.

Slowly the doors swung out again, so slowly. She threw her weight against them, squeezed through, raced across the reception room startling a red-coated volunteer pushing an empty wheelchair. Dodging him, she was out through the wide glass doors into the dim underground parking garage, nearly falling over a woman and three children. They stood staring after him, the taller girl pointing and shouting, "A cat! Look, Mama, a cat chasing that man." Tires squealed, she saw Debbie's station wagon pull out fast and then slow as it moved up the ramp, as if the driver didn't want to attract attention. Dodging past the children, racing for the Mercedes, Ryan barely glimpsed the man driving. Whatever he'd done back there had enraged Kit. She had no notion what happened or why he had Debbie's car, only that something violent had occurred and Kit didn't mean to let him get away. Had she leaped inside his car? Yes, a pair of pointed ears were visible for an instant, then gone again. Starting the Mercedes, she followed, glad she didn't have her truck. A red pickup with a ladder on top wasn't so good as a tail. The Suzuki turned onto the freeway. She entered the heavy traffic two cars behind, sliding into a narrow slot. Whatever emergency had brought the nurses running, the patient in trouble had to be Birely Miller, the way Emmylou was yelling.

Was this man Birely's traveling partner? What had he done to Birely? Had he stolen Debbie's car? She tried not to think about Kit in there with him, she could picture her hiding in the back among the children's cast-offs, and she was sick with fear for her. She was angry as hell, too. After they'd searched for her half the night up among the cliffs thinking she was dead, why did the crazy little cat have to launch into another crisis? Moving in and out of traffic, changing lanes while following the Suzuki, she was needled by too many questions. Had Kit gone back to the ICU looking for Pedric, seen the commotion, was startled by the cries of distress, saw the man running headlong and guilty, and had impetuously given chase?

Ryan played back Emmylou's talk about Birely that had made her feel sorry for him and would have made Kit pity him, too. Or did Kit already know the man, and maybe know Birely? Was this the man who had broken into Lucinda's house? Kit would know him by smell, if nothing more. She thought about Birely camping in the stone house. Was this his partner? Were they, and the men at the wreck on the cliffs, the same? Was this the man who had hurt Pedric and Lucinda, and who now had apparently hurt Birely? No wonder Kit was angry. Up ahead a car pulled out of her lane moving to the left, and she was right behind the Suzuki. She looked for a lane to dodge into, but already he was watching her, studying her in his rearview mirror, glancing ahead and then back at her. She was still trying to cut into another lane, away from him, when a siren whooped behind her.

She tried to nose over into the right lane to let it pass but horns honked and no one would let her in. Easing precariously near the car on her right, she barely let the emergency van squeeze past, giving her an angry blast of siren. Ahead, the Suzuki managed to swerve across, nearly hitting a blue convertible; tires squealed and a horn blasted as the station wagon spun off onto Carpenter Street. The traffic surged on, bearing her with it, she couldn't get over to turn and follow. By the time she managed to change lanes she was at Ocean. She swung off there, knowing she'd lost him. Nothing ahead of her now but a green panel truck. Taking a chance, she made a right onto a small, wooded street, heading for a tangle of narrow, twisting lanes where it might be easy for the driver of the battered old station wagon to get lost among a maze of similar cars tucked into every narrow drive and wooded crevice. Moving as fast as she dared on the little residential streets, she scanned every side street, every hidden drive, praying for Kit and shaky with fear for her.

Rocking along in the back of the station wagon, crouched in between a dozen loaded grocery bags, Kit peered out between them watching the driver. Earlier, coming down the freeway, she'd watched him look repeatedly in the rearview mirror at the cars behind him as if he were being followed. She could only hope he was, and hope it was a cop. She couldn't creep up again to look, he'd be sure to see her—but when he'd swung fast off the freeway almost getting them creamed, she'd glimpsed a silver Mercedes and the driver was a dead ringer for Ryan. But then, screeching off the freeway onto Carpenter, he must have lost her.

Still, though, he checked behind him as he negotiated the narrow and twisting residential lanes, and at last he pulled over onto the shoulder beneath a clump of eucalyptus trees, the car hidden by the overhanging branches of the dense trees in front of the small, crowding cottages.

He must have taken a cell phone from his pocket, must have punched 911, she listened to him describe a silver Mercedes four-door, "Moving south on the freeway," he said, "headed for Ocean or maybe on beyond. A woman driving. Dark, short hair, red sweatshirt. I saw her pick up a man running out of the hospital, looked like he was being chased. I thought . . . Looked like there'd been trouble in there, that maybe he'd robbed someone. He jumped in the backseat of the Mercedes, ducked down so you couldn't see him. The way he acted, I thought maybe you'd be looking for him . . ." He paused, listening.

"A sport coat, I think. Maybe brown, sort of rough . . . like tweed . . ." He listened again, but then abruptly he hung up. Maybe the dispatcher had asked for his name, maybe asked him to stay on the line. He sat looking around him into the wooded neighborhood as if planning what to do next. She wondered if he'd borrowed the car from Debbie, or stolen it? Swiped it before she had a chance to unload her groceries, Kit thought, amused. But when she nosed at the paper bags, she realized they didn't smell like groceries, no scent of cereal boxes or fresh fruit. Maybe everything was canned, that would be Debbie's style. Feed the kids on cans of soup and beans. She tried not to think about being trapped in there with him, tried not to scare herself. Trapped until he opened the door, or until she opened it herself behind him, fought the handle down, leaped out and ran like hell.

But she wasn't ready to do that, she wasn't finished with him yet, she wanted to know where he was headed. If he'd killed Birely she meant to see him pay one way or another. Maybe he'd hole up somewhere for a while. Then, when he thought he was safe, she could slip out, find a phone, and call the department. She just hoped he didn't take off for good, putting long fast miles between him and the cops—and between her and home.

She wasn't sure why she cared so much that he'd hurt Birely. Except she'd felt bad when they'd found poor Sammie's body, and now it didn't seem fair Sammie's little brother would be murdered, too. Not fair the killer would get away with it, just as Sammie's killer had almost gone free. She didn't like when human criminals didn't pay, she wanted to see them face their accusers and squirm, wanted to see them suffer due consequence. *That's the way the world's supposed to work, that's the right balance,* she thought angrily. *If you have to live among the dregs and put up with their evil ways, then you should see some retribution.*

30

Having lost Birely's attacker, Ryan still didn't call the department. She wanted Kit out of there first, and safe, before the cops descended on him; they wouldn't be polite in taking down a killer, if in fact Birely was dead. They'd run his attacker off the road if they needed to, fire at him, do whatever necessary to take him into custody, and Kit would be right in the middle.

She could keep on cruising the village backstreets looking for the Suzuki among the winding, wooded residential lanes, which would, she thought, be an exercise in futility. Or she could go back to Debbie's, park the Mercedes out of sight, and watch. See if he showed up there—perhaps to return the car, if he hadn't stolen it. If Debbie had let him use it, then did Debbie have a role in this, whatever it was? Was she into more than shoplifting? Ryan thought angrily. Moving on through the village and up the hill, she parked two blocks above Emmylou's on a narrow backstreet roofed over with its giant cypress trees, their lower branches reaching out across the street half covering the Mercedes. Getting out and locking the car, she walked on down to Emmylou's.

The Chevy was still gone, Emmylou would still be at the hospital. Maybe she was being questioned by the police, or maybe she was asking questions of her own. Was she mourning poor Birely now? Ryan wondered. Moving up the back steps, she tried the door but found it locked. She sat down on the top step, in the shadows where she could see down across the street into Debbie's scraggly yard. Into *her* scraggly yard, that Debbie had never bothered to clean up. She could see the full expanse of Debbie's empty drive but no sign of Debbie, no light on in the kitchen. Was Tessa still in there alone, tucked up in bed?

Watching the shadowed bedroom, she began to make out a silhouette, a small figure looking out. As if Tessa were kneeling up on the bed, looking out watchfully at the neighborhood, much as she herself was doing.

She was scanning the empty streets, the empty yards, when Debbie's station wagon came into view slipping slowly along a side street. The driver didn't turn onto Debbie's street, he paused at the corner and then turned, circling back, moving down along a stand of pines. She watched him turn into a narrow, over-grown property two blocks to the south. He pulled down the long, weedy drive to the back, where a one-car garage stood beside the forlorn gray house. Parking at one side of the drive, two wheels on the yellowed grass, he nosed the Suzuki into a pile of scrap lumber, gray with age. The minute he opened the driver's door a dark streak exploded out behind him, fled across the lumber pile and up into a pine tree. Ryan eased back with a sigh of relief. Among the dark foliage, she could barely see Kit slip out onto a branch, to peer down.

Stepping out of the station wagon, the man moved to the old-fashioned garage door and stood fiddling with the lock. She could imagine the hinges rusted, the cracked driveway beneath stained with scrape marks where the old door swung out. With his attention diverted, Ryan moved on down the stairs, had started down the hill, heading in his direction, when she heard the ratcheting squeal of wood on concrete as he eased the door open. Within, beyond the open door, some-thing dark loomed. The hood of a dark car, its lines sleek but its narrow chrome and its headlights dulled as if with dirt; they were the smooth lines of the Lincoln.

Snatching her phone from her pocket, she punched in 911.

She ended the call just as fast, clicking off.

She didn't want the law there, taking over the stolen car, declaring it out of bounds to everyone but the department, impounding it for evidence. Not with what was there—what she hoped was still hidden there behind the door panels. Instead, she hit Clyde's number.

When she got no answer she left a message, irritated, and clicked off. Turning away among Emmylou's trees, she headed back to the Mercedes, through the overgrown yards. Slipping in behind the wheel, she hoped he wouldn't hear the engine start, or would think it was just some neighbor pulling out. Easing down the street and onto his street, she couldn't see the garage now, it was on the other side of the forlorn gray cottage; not until she was level with the house did it come into view again.

As she turned into the drive, the dropping sun was in her eyes, it was hard to see inside past the Lincoln. She could sense him watching her, as if maybe he stood deeper in, where the shadows were dense. Letting the engine idle, she hit Clyde's number again.

Still no answer. She eased on down the drive toward the garage, glancing up toward the pine tree where Kit crouched among the thin branches. *Stay put, Kit, just stay where you are.* He came out of the garage fast, heading for her car as if he meant to jerk the door open. She didn't kill the engine, she let it idle. As she hit the master lock she dropped the phone, felt frantically along the seat for it. When she looked again he had moved to the edge of the drive. She watched him grab up a short length of two-by-four, and turn. He came at her fast, swinging at the window, his pale eyes flat and mean. She ducked, fishing under the seat for some weapon, maybe a wrench left by one of the mechanics. She found nothing, but then scrabbling deeper she found the phone. He swung his makeshift club, and she covered her face. The window shattered, crazing into a pattern like snowflakes. She gunned the engine, put it in gear, gave it the gas again as if to back away from him up the drive.

Instead she sent the Mercedes leaping forward, braking only as her front bumper rammed the back of the Town Car, solidly blocking it. He came at her again, striking at the broken window, glass flew around her in a cascade of particles. He hit it again and reached through, grappling for the lock. She snatched up the phone, brought the end of it down hard on his wrist. He yelped and drew back and then lunged at the door. He had reached in, grabbing for her, when darkness exploded from above him from the roof—and the world was filled with cats, a tangle of clawing, screaming cats.

Earlier in the day, having searched the neighborhood for the Lincoln, Joe and Pan had given up at last and headed away into the village. Their fur smelled of juniper bushes, every garage they'd investigated stunk with overgrown foliage crowding its old walls. Where they'd been able to find a thin crack beneath a tight-fitting door, they'd detected only the smells of empty oil cans, caked dirt, and mice. When they'd leaped up at dirty garage windows they'd seen nothing within but a broken chair, old cardboard boxes filled with who knew what refuse, and a rat-eaten couch, the cotton stuffing leaking out across the concrete. They'd searched for the Lincoln until both were cranky and hissing at each other, then they hit the rooftops hoping to see the Town Car parked on some farther-off, out-of-the-way lane. But soon, growing discouraged even with that futile effort, they simply ran, working off their accumulated frustration. In the center of the village they raced up the stairs of the courthouse clock tower, to the parapet high above.

Leaping to the rail, they had prowled along it looking down at the rooftops and crowded streets, focusing

326 • SHIRLEY ROUSSEAU MURPHY

on each long black car they spotted, but knowing that this, too, was an exercise in futility. They were circling the rail yet again when Dulcie came racing up the stairs, looking up at them. She paused on the little tile balcony.

"There's been a murder," she said, "at the hospital. Those men staying up behind Emmylou's, looks like one killed the other. Killed him right there in the ICU. Emmylou'd found the one man hurt, lying in that stone house behind her place, she called the ambulance and . . ."

The two toms dropped down to the tiles beside her, giving her their full attention.

"Pedric heard it all from Emmylou when they took him back to the ICU before they moved him to his new room. He got a glimpse of the man from his gurney, he was just being tucked up in bed again when the whole place exploded in an uproar and Pedric saw him running out. Pedric swore the guy was wearing his sport coat, the tweed one. He and Emmylou called Lucinda, she called and told Wilma, and I came to find you. Emmylou said Ryan ran out chasing the guy, that a nurse just coming back from her break saw them, she knew Ryan, she said the man took off in a battered brown station wagon. Debbie's car? The nurse said Ryan chased him in a silver Mercedes, I don't know where she got that car but the nurse swore it was Ryan. If he has Debbie's car and goes back there, and Ryan follows him there, if that's where he was headed, and Ryan's all alone . . ."

"Come on," Joe said. He leaped down the stairs hitting every fourth step, but halfway down the last flight, before he hit the street, he sailed onto the adjoining roof. The three cats, racing away over the peaks, their heads filled with questions, made straight across the village and up the hill toward Debbie's hoping he *was* going there, where they could help Ryan if she needed help, and where they could summon the law. They were a block from Debbie's cottage when they saw, between the pines, Kit crouched on the edge of a roof looking over, precarious and intent.

Leaping the chasms between cottages, they gained the roof beside her, to the accompaniment of breaking glass below as the man in the tweed coat swung his crude club, then yelped and drew back, then lunged at the door, reaching in grabbing for Ryan. The cats sprang, exploding down on him in a whirlwind of teeth and claws.

He twisted, shouting and flailing, and dropped the two-by-four. Fighting them off, reaching down for it, he lost his balance. Ryan was out of the car, pounding at him. He went down under her blows. She snatched the two-by-four away, and kicked him in the groin. He curled into a ball, whimpering. She yelled at the cats to back off, but Kit kept at him, raking and biting, she stopped only when Ryan pulled her away, forcing her clinging claws out of his arm.

Kneeling, Ryan held the end of the two-by-four hard against his throat as she frisked him. He looked at the four cats crowding over him growling, their teeth bared, and he lay still. She had pulled two packets of hundred-dollar bills from his pockets, stuffing them into the front of her zipped jacket, when he struck out again, hit Ryan in the face, and struggled to his feet. He ran—but not to the Lincoln, it was useless to him, blocked by Ryan's car. He headed for the station wagon, jerked the door open, Ryan could see the keys dangling in the ignition. She grabbed Kit away as he swung in. Clutching Kit, she moved away fast as he gunned the engine, dodging the car as it shot backward burning rubber, careened the length of the drive, racing backward into the street, and took off.

Ryan held Kit tight against her, both of them shaking with rage. He was gone, but the Lincoln was safe. Her heart pounding, Ryan flipped open her phone.

This time, Clyde answered. "Sorry," he said, "I was talking to the supplier, he thought he had the part, but he doesn't."

"You're at the shop?"

"Just leaving."

"I'm a couple of blocks south of the cottage, down from Debbie's. Old gray house with the garage way at the back? Can you bring me those two tools your body guys use, to take the panels off a car door?"

"You found the Lincoln."

"We did."

"You okay?"

"Fine," she said.

"You call the department?"

"Not until you bring the tools."

"On my way."

"Pick up some gloves," she said.

He laughed, and hung up. It wasn't twenty minutes until he pulled into the drive in her king cab. The cats, crowding into the dim garage behind them, peered up into the Lincoln as Clyde, putting on a pair of cotton gloves to prevent leaving fingerprints, removed the door panels. Lifting them off one at a time and reaching in, he began to remove the small white boxes, and he lifted out the little plastic containers of coins, too, all tightly sealed. Ryan placed each item carefully in a stained paint bucket that she'd taken from the back of her truck.

But it was Joe and Pan together who, leaping up into the backseat of the Lincoln, rooting among the tightly packed bundles, found the scent of the old musty bills. Sniffing at bolts of fabric, at boxes and bags scented of far places, the two tomcats rooted down under the Greenlaws' diverse and expensive purchases, and came up grinning.

"Try here," Joe told Clyde.

Pulling packages away until he was able to examine the center console beneath, Clyde pulled down the armrest, revealing the small black tray with its cell phone connections.

"There," Joe said, sniffing at the small square hole in the front. "Musty. The money's there. Take the screws out." Already Ryan was headed for the truck. She returned with a Phillips screwdriver, which she handed to Clyde. He unscrewed the tray and lifted it out.

There it was, the rest of the money, thick packets of hundreds stuffed tightly into the small space. He handed them out to Ryan, she packed them in the stained bucket atop the little boxes, filling it to the dented edge. Turning away to the king cab, she locked the bucket in one of the metal tool compartments along the side, arranging heavy coils of electric drop cords in front. Only then, locking the compartment, did she call the dispatcher.

She told Mabel they'd found the Greenlaws' stolen Lincoln, and gave her the location. But as they talked, she watched Kit and Pan, up on the roof again sitting near but not looking at each other, both staring away into space—looking as if they *wanted* to make up, but both still too stubborn. She could see only a touch of Kit's superior "I'm right, you're wrong" expression. Pan, though he glanced sideways at Kit, sat tall and macho, still with a "I'm not changing my mind" look in his amber eyes. Both cats so hardheaded, Kit refusing to understand Pan's hunger for new adventure, Pan just as obstinate, wanting Kit to thrill to *his* view of the world. Neither cat, even after their bold and concerted attack on the thief, willing to understand the other. And Ryan could only watch, disappointed with them both.

31

Kit lay sprawled on the dining table among the last pieces of jewelry that Kate and Lucinda had not tucked away in one bank or another, the gold and sapphires and emeralds reflecting bright shafts of light where the setting sun slanted in through the oak trees. With a soft paw she patted at the brooches and pendants, feeling like a queen counting her wealth, though it wasn't hers at all. Lucinda was in the bedroom napping, Kate in the kitchen making a light supper, filling the house with the scent of grilled cheese on rye and herb tea.

It had taken Ryan and Clyde only a few minutes, yesterday, to strip the jewelry and money out of the Lincoln before they called the department, before the police were all over the car, lifting fingerprints, taking blood samples, and impounding the vehicle itself for closer inspection. But it had taken the two women all this morning and most of the afternoon to rent seven safe deposit boxes, each requiring them to open an accompanying bank account, to take the necessary cards and papers up to Pedric at the hospital to sign, and then return them to the banks. And then at last to retrieve the treasure from the Greenlaws' padlocked freezer and tuck it securely away where, they hoped, the banks would keep the gold and jewels safe.

It was last evening after the police arrived to meet Ryan and Clyde at the small garage and go over the Lincoln, that Kit had trotted home shaky from their attack on Vic, and had made a follow-up call to the department. Talking to Max Harper himself, she had laid out in every smallest detail Vic's murder of Birely Miller there in the hospital. She had hung up abruptly, of course, when Max asked for her name, as he always asked. Both knew he didn't expect an answer to that question. Secrets upon secrets, she thought, pawing at the mysterious jewelry, and smiling.

Kate and Lucinda, after finishing with the banks, had kept back just this handful of antique pieces that lay scattered around her, now, each one featuring a cat or some mythical creature in its design. Patting at those Netherworld images, Kit thought about Pan's hunger for that world, and she wondered if he would go there without her. But, then she wondered, would his attachment to Tessa keep the tomcat from leaving, after all?

That very morning when Ryan returned to Debbie's, to put in the faucet herself, Tessa had whispered to her all about the man with the black car. It was the morning after the cats' attack on Vic, and Tessa had told Ryan all about that, too, she had seen it all from the window above her bed. She had, much earlier in the day, seen him hide the Lincoln, too. The child had seen more than anyone guessed. "I didn't tell Mama," she whispered.

"Why didn't you?" Ryan had asked her.

"She'd say I was lying. I'm not, that's what I saw, that's what happened. My Pan and those other three cats attacked that man to save you. My Pan is back," she had said, smiling. "But, where is he now? When will he come to live with me again, to be my cat again?"

To that, Ryan had no answer.

No one owns a cat, and yet Kit knew that Pan, in his secret spirit, was indeed Tessa's cat, just as Tessa was his person. *Maybe,* she thought, *maybe Pan will stay here for Tessa, if he won't stay for me.*

But how will I feel about that? she thought, and she wasn't sure.

She lay watching as Kate set the table around her, arranging the jewelry in a wicker basket that she put on the buffet. Kit watched her bring in the teapot and cups, watched her go to call Lucinda and help her get up; Lucinda's cast was heavy and cumbersome, and was tiring to haul around. Walking out with Lucinda, Kate seated her in her own chair and brought in the sandwiches, steaming hot and oozing pale cheese with slices of salami peeking out.

Kate cut Kit's sandwich in small bites and set the plate on Kit's own place mat. Over supper they talked about Pedric's knee surgery, a noninvasive laser technique that was scheduled for early the next morning; they discussed Birely Miller's simple burial, which would also take place in the morning. Not until after supper did Kate read to them from her mother's diary, from the later pages that she had found hidden among the moldering Netherworld volumes in the library of a fallen palace, the long passage disconnected from whatever the previous pages had told, from whatever had gone before or after those faded lines.

> . . . all along. We have done our best to battle the royal families that would bring this world down. Inconceivable that the very rulers who benefit most from the labor of the peasants are now destroying

their only source of food and goods, of the labor to produce what they need. Hatred, not logic, drives them. Hatred and greed. An evil drives them that comes straight from the hell pit and, in the end, will drag them down into the pit themselves. Soon we must get the baby out of here, must make the journey up into the surface world and find a home for Kate. I pray our one friend there, with Netherworld connections, can watch over her until she's grown. Will there be any Netherworld left, when Kate is grown? I cannot bear to leave her, but we must return here and rejoin the battle, we must keep fighting.

There Melissa's journal pages ended, the last page torn at the bottom as if whatever came after had been ripped away. "Maybe buried somewhere among the rubble of the palace," Kate said, "buried in a world where no one reads books anymore or hardly knows what they're for.

"Do you remember, Kit, the year I was given that other jewelry, by the old lawyer, the pieces he'd held so long for me in his office safe? That big old walk-in safe, the box hidden way at the back containing my mother's journal, too? Do you remember how excited you were when you first learned of another world, how you had dreamed of such a place?"

"I remember," Kit said quietly. "But that world was bright and happy, not crumbled and cold, it was not a dead world, then."

Kate said, "You remember, Lucinda."

Lucinda said, "Most of the earlier entries in your mother's journals were bright. There was destruction even then, failure of the magic, but the world still held much of wonder. That was only the beginning, the failure of that magic that your parents tried so hard to prevent."

Supper ended in sadness, which none of them had intended. Kate rinsed the dishes, and they sat for a long while in the living room before the fire, Kit curled in Lucinda's lap. She looked up often at Kate, still caught and grieving in the remains of that sad world where her parents had died.

Birely Miller's funeral, early the next morning, was indeed simple, only a few words spoken by a funeral director who had never known Birely nor, if he had, would have approved of him. A few words and then without further ceremony Birely's casket was lowered into the ground next to the grave of his sister, Sammie. Only a handful of people attended: Max and Charlie Harper, the Damens, Emmylou Warren, and Kate Osborne. Lucinda was at the hospital with

Pedric. Those were the human mourners, if one could call their solemn attendance a kind of mourning. The five cats sat at attention, exhibiting varied degrees of pity, sat concealed behind a headstone featuring the image of a praying angel with lifted wings. Six humans and five cats silently attending Birely Miller's last contact with the souls of this world. The day had turned heavy, with a wet, gray overcast that made the women's hair curl willfully, and made the cats lick their fur to try to dry it. What Joe Grey wondered, as he watched Emmylou drop a handful of dirt onto the casket, was, *Where's Birely's old uncle buried, old train robber Lee Fontana? Where did he end up, carrying with him the secret of that final robbery— escaping without restitution and most likely without remorse?*

But maybe now Fontana would make restitution of a kind more valuable than the U.S. courts demanded. Emmylou, like Kate and the Greenlaws, had decided to give some of her newfound wealth to CatFriends, their local rescue group that Ryan and Charlie and a raft of volunteers had helped to start. Money to pay for cat food and supplies, to pay Dr. Firetti, who so far had donated all his services and all the needed medications. There'd be money, too, to build a central shelter where volunteers could care for the abandoned animals that were brought to them. Joe thought about the starving cats the group had trapped when, at the first downturn in the economy, so many householders left their homes with back rent or mortgages overdue, and left their pets behind.

What would Lee Fontana think of this use of his stolen money? Maybe, from the stories Misto told of Fontana—if Joe could bring himself to believe Misto's tales—maybe the old train robber would like that choice just fine. If the old yellow cat *had* been Fontana's ghostly confidant as Misto liked to say, guiding Fontana safely through his self-inflicted troubles, then Fontana must have a warm place in his spirit for a cat, maybe he'd be pleased and amused by his unwitting gift to catdom.

Vic had fled from Ryan badly shaken by the attack of the cats. Headed for open country, he had parked the Suzuki on the berm of the narrow dirt road, as far under a drooping willow tree as he could get it without tilting over into the drainage ditch; the willow was already shedding its small yellow leaves down onto the hood and, in the light evening breeze, its stringy branches dragged back and forth across the metal, scraping annoyingly. It was nearly dark inside the car, shaded by the tree and with the windows blocked

340 · SHIRLEY ROUSSEAU MURPHY

by his makeshift curtains; bright-colored cashmere sweaters with their store tags attached hung down from the two lowered visors, and along the driver's side he'd secured a blue sweater into the crack of the rolled-up window. He sat sprawled in the back where he had pushed the clutter aside, no room to put the backseat up, the whole seat was in one piece, but at least the resultant platform was low, giving him some headroom. He sat bare to the waist, his bloodied shirt wadded up, the ripped tweed sport coat already discarded, resting ten miles back in the trash can of a FastMart where he'd stopped for a dry sandwich, some salve for the scratches, a bag of corn chips, and a Coke.

He'd parked, for that quick shopping trip, at the back of the FastMart building among some scraggly trees. That area up along Molena Valley road was a mix of scattered fields, sad old houses and new ones, pastures with horses, scraggly woods, weedy unused land all mixed together. He'd got in and out of FastMart as quickly as he could, keeping his head down just a little and the collar of his ripped coat turned up. He'd bought a brown sweatshirt, too, off a rack by the refrigerator. There'd be a BOL out on him, with Birely lying dead back there and probably, by this time, Debbie Kraft hollering up a fuss that her old car'd been stolen.

Leaving FastMart after making his purchases, a café two doors down had smelled so good he'd been tempted to chance it, go on in there for a hot meal. But even as he paused, looking down that way thinking about scrambled eggs and potatoes and sausage, wondering if it was worth the risk, a pair of sheriff's cars pulled up right in front, couple of deputies got out, moved into the restaurant hardly looking around them. Mid-morning snack, he guessed. They didn't glance his way, didn't make the Suzuki or they'd have skipped their meal and come after him. As soon as they disappeared inside he'd hightailed it to the Suzuki and got on out of there. As he turned out onto the two-lane highway a cat ran across, he gunned the car but missed it. He'd like to cream every damn cat he saw, his back still stung like holy hell. He'd driven on watching the side roads, look-ing for a place to get out of sight, to stop and smear some of the salve on, see if that would help. He wasn't far from Molena Point, maybe only ten miles, he knew he should get on over the grade to Highway 68, head for Salinas and onto the faster freeway.

But then again, maybe not. Maybe not hit the free-way until full dark when the cops couldn't make him so easy. Maybe hole up until then close to the village where they wouldn't think to look for him. Lay low for a few hours and then move on. He could use some sleep, catch a couple hours before he headed for the 101, if he planned to drive all night. Up through Eureka, on up to Bremerton, he knew a guy up there he could stay with, place way back in the boonies. Dump the Suzuki, pick up some decent wheels.

Now, bending awkwardly, he smeared salve on his bare back, on the scratches and bite wounds. Damn friggin' cats jumping down on him like that, as vicious as that cat up at the wreck. He never had liked cats, sneaky and mean. The bloody wounds stung, but then in a few minutes the salve began to ease the pain and burning. And why would that cat *chase* him, there in the parking garage? Dark, ugly cat, just like the others. He'd never have seen it except for that kid shouting. He'd got one glimpse of the cat racing across the concrete right at him, piled in the car, slammed the door, and when he looked back the damn thing was gone. Shivering, he'd started the engine and peeled out of there, then slowed so as not to call attention to himself.

And then when that contractor woman got in his way blocking the Lincoln and them cats jumped him for no reason. Twice attacked by cats, and chased by another one. Spooky as hell, still made him sick to think about it, unnatural, bloodthirsty beasts. Pulling the brown sweatshirt on over his salve-smeared wounds, he lay down in the space he had cleared. The bed of the station wagon was hard as hell. He pulled an old, torn blanket over him that smelled of peanut butter and sweaty kids. He wondered if Debbie had ever had the backseat down all the time she'd owned the heap. The sun had set now, the car dim under the tree and under his jerry-rigged curtains. He lay there a long time, he didn't sleep until heavy darkness drew in around him.

32

It was early evening, nearly eight hours since Pedric's knee surgery. He sat up in bed, a blue cotton robe pulled over his skimpy hospital gown, his bandaged leg propped up on two pillows. The general anesthetic had worn off. The bandage around his head had been removed. The red scar across his forehead looked raw but clean, the four stitches standing out like four little fly legs, Kit thought. Bruises still marked his forehead and down his cheek, but his short gray hair was neatly trimmed and brushed, and he looked bright, happy to have his surgery over with. Kate sat on a built-in daybed by the window, Lucinda sat in a folding metal chair beside Pedric's bed, holding his hand with her good, right hand, comfortable to be close to him.

The room was spacious and quiet, a great improvement from the crowded little cubicle in the noisy ER. The view through the wide wall of glass had sent Kit bolting to the windows, forgetting that a nurse or orderly might come barging in. She had returned only later to Pedric's amused embrace—he was mending, he was safe and happy and she loved him, but right now she wanted to be out there in the amazing garden that rose up the hill just beyond the glass.

The two huge windows were framed by heavy white pillars jutting out into the room, part of the superstructure of the strongly built hospital. The big garden beyond was softly lit, and was enclosed at some distance by the glass walls of the three-story hospital. Kit crouched on the wide sill, her nose to the glass, her heart lost to the garden, to its cascading waterfall that tumbled down beneath the trees and past the flowering shrubs. Bright plashes of water fell and were lost within the rough escarpment of granite blocks—giant, rough-cut stones piled one on another, towering high above her looking as natural as nature's own casual toss of rocky elements; the water fell down the stone in clear cascades, she wanted to dabble her paw in, to splash at the little pond below where the last rays of the sun reflected, she wanted to leap up the rocks, race up the little trees, she wanted to play out there in that small Eden.

The big windows were fixed in place, there was no way to open them. It would not be until later, as night fell, that Kit would discover, down beyond the end pillar, a narrow, hinged pane with a hinged screen and with handles that would open both. Now, Pedric watched her from his bed and watched the closed door, wary of a nurse's intrusion. Kit would find the opening later, he thought, smiling, find it sometime in the dark hours and would slip out there in a wild bid for freedom just as Alice had once finessed her way through the first locked door into Wonderland. Watching her, he and Lucinda exchanged an indulgent smile.

This was Lucinda's third journey out of the house since they'd arrived home, but she was pale still and felt weak. Yesterday's banking transactions had tired her, as had standing for even that short time at Birely's funeral. The aftermath of the wreck and attack, the theft of their car and the intrusion into their home, had left her feeling incredibly fragile and vulnerable, quite unlike herself. But now, with Pedric's surgery behind them, the torn meniscus in his right knee repaired, and with his head injuries healing, she was beginning to feel easier. Pedric's blood work showed normal levels of sugar, the swelling in his brain had subsided, and he would come home in the morning. The anticipation of having him home so lifted her spirits that when Max

Harper and Charlie knocked at the door and peered in, Lucinda's smile was bright and she was filled with questions.

Both the Harpers were dressed in jeans, boots, frontier shirts, and smelled comfortably of horses. Maybe Max had taken off early, and they'd had a late-afternoon ride. Even before the tall couple stepped in, Kit had hidden herself in the carryall, not sure what Max would think of her there. She peered out for one look as Kate tucked an edge of the brocade down, hiding her from the police chief.

Charlie's curly red hair was tied back with a leather thong. Leaning over the bed, she hugged Pedric. "Glad the surgery's over with, and that it went so well."

Max grinned down at Pedric. "Glad all this mess about the car is pretty much over, too. We've impounded it at Clyde's place, locked up in one of the back shops. As soon as forensics finishes, Clyde's crew will clean it up and start work on the scratches and dents. Forensics will be going over your packages, too, for fingerprints and to see if any stolen items are mixed in with your own things." He looked at Lucinda. "Could you give us an inventory, and then come down later, to identify what's there? Make sure it's all yours, and maybe go through some of the packages?"

Lucinda nodded.

"Clyde thinks the blood stains should come out of the leather all right," Max said. "He hopes not to have to reupholster. Blood type matches Birley's blood in the wrecked pickup, and that on the sleeping bag up at Emmylou's place. Forensics has particles of paper from the old bills, from the cubbyhole beneath the back console where Ryan and Clyde found Emmylou's money."

There had, in the end, been no way for Emmylou to avoid reporting the stolen money, reporting at least part of it when forensics found part of a torn wrapper and two musty hundred-dollar bills that had slipped down among the packages. Emmylou had told Max the money was hers, that it had been left to her by Sammie with the house, and had given Max a copy of the will, leaving her, "All contents within the house or on the property," and she had told him about Sammie's letter. Some recluses were like that, Max had said, guy lived in poverty all his life, he died and was discovered to have been worth several million, usually with a handwritten will leaving it all to a favorite charity, Salvation Army or animal rescue or a church that had been kind to him.

Pedric said, "Birely Miller is dead, but no sign of the other man, of Vic Amson?"

"Not yet," Max said. "We have a BOL out on him. He's wanted for Birely's murder, for his attack on you two, for theft of your vehicle, and leaving the scene of the wreck. There are several old warrants for him, including a person of interest in a murder over in Fresno.

"Both Vic and Birely have records," Max said. "Though Birely's didn't amount to much, most of his offenses the result of overenthusiastic bad judgment. Going along with one pal or another, and then left holding the bag. Acting as lookout during a gas station robbery, and he's still sitting there watching for cops when the other guy slips away. By the time Birely realizes he's all alone, two sheriff's deputies are pulling in, to cuff him and book him. Maybe just born a loser," Max said with a shrug. "Poor guy just couldn't get it together."

"If Vic Amson escaped in Debbie Kraft's car," Lucinda said, "then was she involved with them?"

"Not sure, yet," Max said. "Except for what we know from the child." He smiled. "Debbie's little girl ratted her out."

"Vinnie?" Lucinda said, surprised.

"No, Tessa. The little, quiet one. Detective Garza stopped by the house, wanted Debbie to come down to the station to file a report on her missing car. She'd made enough fuss about it, called the department three times since she reported it stolen, wanting to know if we'd found it yet, demanding faster action. Said we'd have to furnish her a loaner, claimed it wasn't her fault the car was stolen," he said, smiling. "Said that was due to our failure in protecting her property.

"In fact," he said, "street patrol was about to haul her in, the day she reported her car missing. Brennan had been watching her, off and on, but he was reluctant to come down on her because of the kids, with their daddy already in prison."

"What did you tell her when she said you owed her a loaner?" Pedric asked, grinning.

"What I told her," Max said, "isn't recorded in the department memos."

Lucinda laughed. "But little Tessa, what did that shy, silent little child say? I can't imagine her speaking up and defying her mother."

"She said quite a lot. Debbie was reluctant to ask Dallas in, finally offered him a chair, in the kitchen. She was making up excuses why she couldn't come into the station, when Tessa came out of the bedroom, sniffling, bundled up in an old pair of oversized pajamas, maybe her sister's. She looked up at Dallas, and sniffled, and for some reason, she took to him. Came right to him, climbed up in his lap, snuggled right up to him. Maybe because her mother was being rude to him, maybe the kid didn't like that.

"She told Dallas her momma loaned that man her car, and that Debbie had made him put all the stolen clothes in there before he took it. Debbie tried to shut her up, said there were no stolen clothes, wanted to know where she got that idea, said, why would she have stolen clothes? She told Tessa she had it wrong, that it was the car that was stolen, not clothes. Said, 'You know that. You've got yourself all mixed up.'

"Tessa might be a quiet little thing," Max said, "but not this morning. This morning she had her back up. I guess when she wants to let you see it, she does have a mind of her own."

Maybe with Pan's coaching, Kit thought, listening unseen, her whiskers curved in a satisfied smile.

"When Tessa said her momma gave the man her car, she pointed away across the neighborhood. 'Drove down to *that* house,' she said, pointing straight in the direction of the gray house where we found the Lincoln. Dallas could see she wanted to say more, but Debbie pulled her off his lap and hauled her back into the bedroom."

From outside in the hall they could hear the clink of metal on metal as the dinner trays were delivered, and the smell of boiled beef and overcooked vegetables seeped in under the door.

"If they pick Victor up," Pedric said, "you have proof enough to hold him, proof he killed Birely?"

Pedric rubbed gently at his knee, as if it were beginning to hurt now that the local anesthetic had worn off.

"We have Vic's fingerprints from the rubber-glove dispenser in the adjoining room," Max said. "Particles of cinnamon and sugar icing on the edge of the dispenser and on the floor under it. Sugar and cinnamon scattered across Birely's blanket, where Vic punched him in the belly. Vic might have been wearing gloves, but he didn't think to brush off his clothes, to get rid of the crumbs down his front.

"Dallas talked with the volunteers who work in the cafeteria. Two of the women remembered Amson, from our description. When Dallas took them the mug shots, once we'd run the prints and got photos, they gave us a positive ID. They said they don't serve anything there with cinnamon icing except for their cinnamon buns. They had a couple of stale ones from the day before, and forensics has those.

"And that fits in with the phone tip," Max said. "That's not admissible evidence in court, and we don't know who she is, but—"

"A phone call?" Kate said innocently. Maybe, she thought, if no one asked, Max would wonder why they didn't. Beside her, Lucinda and Pedric had stiffened only a little.

Max said, "The woman described Victor, said she saw him punch Birely. Said before he hit him, he was fiddling with the IV tube, bending it, that he had a syringe, looked as if he meant to pierce the tube, plunge the needle in. Said suddenly he dropped the needle as if something had changed his mind. Instead he pulled back his fist, landed Birely a real hard one in the stomach, and ran. She said the dials went flat, alarms went off, he passed the nurses yelling at them to help the patient, ran straight through the crowding nurses shouting for someone to help Birely, and not one of them thought to nail him."

It was just another anonymous call, Kit thought, *no different than any other, and we do have ID blocking, Pedric checks it every week to make sure it's working. Just another phantom tip,* she thought nervously, *even if I was still shaky and mad, after jumping Vic, and even if I did almost* yowl *into the phone! Well, not exactly a yowl.*

"And we have one witness," Max said, "who was in the parking garage, who saw Vic burst out through the glass doors, running. After she got home, she caught the murder on the local TV, and she called in. Said she and her kids were just going inside, into the ER to see her sister, when a man ran out, nearly ran over them. She described Vic, described Debbie's station wagon, saw him pile into it and take off. Dispatcher who took the call, she said the woman seemed to have more to say, but then she changed her mind. She was reluctant to leave her name and number, but Mabel talked her into it." Max shook his head. "People afraid to get involved. Can't say I blame them, sometimes."

On the windowsill, Kit breathed easier. She'd gone rigid, thinking that woman would have described the whole chase. She guessed the great cat god *was* watching, to stop her from mentioning the cat or her kids' excited shouts. *Maybe that upset her, to see an angry cat chasing a running man. Maybe she didn't want to talk about that and come out sounding like a nutcase,* Kit thought, smiling. And maybe the great cat god was smiling, too.

33

It was full night when two hobos, dressed in dark clothes and bearing heavy backpacks, had come walking down the winding grade that cut through from Highway 68 down onto Molena Valley Road. As they turned right onto the shoulder of the dark two-lane, the light of a half-moon illuminated the surrounding bushes and trees as if ragged and ghostly figures were watching them in the night. Heading west along the dirt shoulder, moving in the direction of the ocean some twelve miles beyond, they watched for a deserted side road, somewhere to get off the highway and camp for the night, maybe a denser woods than these scraggly, stunted oaks, or maybe some deserted old house or barn where sheriff's deputies wouldn't come nosing around to hassle them.

They'd parted from the slat-sided farm truck they'd hitched a ride in, up at the top of the grade, the driver hauling crates of chickens, coming over from Salinas. Truck stunk real bad of caged chickens, the smell still clung to them—or maybe it was the dead chicken they carried, dangling by its feet. Riding in the back in the truck bed, they'd slid open the nearest crate, hauled out an old brown hen and wrung her scrawny neck, her squawks hidden by the rattle of the truck's old engine and loose body. Now, by the time they'd hoofed it down the grade, they had their dinner already bled, cleaned, and plucked.

The narrow road was dark as hell, no car lights streaming by, no houselights off to the sides, and none of them fancy overhead vapor lights out here in the boonies to pick them out moving along the blacktop. In their dark old clothes, they were part of the night itself, blending into the hill that rose steeply on their right. Half a mile down, they crossed the two-lane and stepped off into the shadows of the berm, moving along beneath another stand of scraggly trees. When they came on a battered station wagon sitting there on the berm, they stopped to look it over, watching for movement within.

Nothing stirred beyond the dark, partially covered windows. They approached warily, with a

keen and predatory interest. The oddly shaped curtains blocked their view through the windshield and
through the driver's window. They tried the doors
but they were locked. Cupping their hands to peer
into the back, they couldn't make out much more
than a long, dark lump in the darkness, a bundle of
some kind, but then they snickered and pressed their
ears to the glass.

"Guy asleep in there, snoring. Dead to the world."

"Here, hold the chicken. Hell, don't lay it down, you
want gravel in our supper?" Slinging off his pack, the
taller man reached down into it and fished out a long,
heavy wire that he kept in the side pocket, a carefully
recycled coat hanger fashioned for just such emergen-
cies. Hauling a flashlight from his coat pocket, he
shielded its light, moved to the driver's window, peered
down where the beam led, and got to work.

Deeply asleep in the car, Vic's dreams carried him
through scattered stirrings from a bumbling childhood, as his father moved them all from one small
town to another, one sorry job to another, one miser-
able grammar school to another. His father was sometimes absent altogether, while he did a short stint in
some two-bit jail, but mostly he was traveling, dragging the nine kids and wife behind him like cans tied

to a stray dog. The dreams were always the same, of a sorry and muddled past without shape and without hope. Maybe it was the scuff of footsteps in the gravel outside the Suzuki or maybe the faint scrape of the coat hanger as it slid in through the crack in the window that stirred him, that sent his dreams careening down into the dark nightmare chasm where one twitches and moans and cries out, where one would try to pry himself awake again, if he'd *known* he was asleep.

He woke feeling hands tightening around his throat. This was not part of the dream, cold hands and rough, cold air sweeping in through the open car door, and the ripe stink of an unwashed body and unwashed clothes, and a bright light blazing in his eyes so he couldn't see.

"You got money, hand it over." The guy had his knee on the blanket, gouging into his ribs, leaning his body full over Vic, close and threatening.

"I got no money. If I had money, would I be sleeping in this heap?"

The other door opened, second guy flashed the beam over the mess of broken toys. "Where's your woman and kids?"

"I got no woman and kids. I borrowed the car." He had no weapon handy, either. He'd been asleep, for

Christ's sake, peacefully minding his own business—
and with what little money he had left, that that contractor woman hadn't found, tucked deep in his pants
pocket. He should have hid it better before he went to
sleep but he'd wanted it on him in case the cops showed
up and he had to leave the car, make a run for it. He
tried to sit up, tried to push the guy's clutching hands
away from him, and it was then that he saw the knife.
The guy with the flashlight had a switchblade in his
other hand, the knife open and gleaming.

"Take the car if you want," Vic begged. He fished
in his pocket for the keys then knew he shouldn't have
done that, maybe the guy thought he had a weapon.
The knife flashed in the beam, he felt it go into his
throat, it went in so easy, like slicing butter. He felt
nothing more for a minute, then pain exploded.
He heard himself screaming and then he couldn't
scream. He felt the blood bubbling up and he couldn't
breathe . . .

Vic's own scream was the last sound he ever heard,
the last sound he would ever make. He lay dead in the
backseat of Debbie Kraft's battered Suzuki. Blood
spurted for a minute more and then stopped, his heart
no longer pumping. The bleeding subsided to a dribble
like a faulty tap, and stopped. He lay in his own blood,
his own bodily wastes seeping out as his killer picked

up the dead chicken from the front seat, and fished in Vic's pocket for the car keys.

Before anyone knew of Victor's death, the cats waited hopefully for the law to pick him up, for a sheriff or the CHP to spot the Suzuki and pull Vic over, cuff him, lock him behind bars, and transport him back to Molena Point for arraignment and to stand trial. None of the cats allowed that justice might go awry and that Vic might walk, cats are ever hopeful, they didn't want to think about failures of the U.S. justice system, they expected ultimate punishment for Amson. Maybe it was the cats' expectations, sparked by divine fate, that had prompted Victor's own peers to deal out his retribution, to provide his last judgment in this world, in a far more decisive manner than the law would have done.

But now, at this moment, Kit wasn't thinking of retribution. Having just heard the current police report on Amson, and sure he would soon be apprehended, she smiled with satisfaction but then set those thoughts aside as she sought a way from Pedric's hospital room out to the waterfall.

Max and Charlie Harper had just left, heading back to MPPD where a call had come in from a horse rancher up in the Molena Valley. His teenaged boy, out riding one of the yearling colts, had come on the Suzuki in the dark, the scent of death sharp to the colt's senses so the young horse would not approach the car. Curious, the boy remembered a TV newscaster's description of the Suzuki, and of Amson. He didn't pause to see if Amson was in there, he hurried his horse home and dialed 911. The county dispatcher had routed him through to the sheriff's office and then to MPPD. At once sheriff's deputies had moved in that direction, and now were searching again along the two-lane roads though they had driven that area the night Vic had fled. Kit prayed the sheriff would find Amson and treat him as he deserved. But once she'd wished the worst for him she'd dismissed him and turned her attention to the garden again and to slipping out into it.

Able to prowl the room now that the Harpers had left, she had quickly followed the thin draft of cooler air that teased her from the far end of the room. Padding down to look, she found the narrow window, half concealed beyond the last pillar. Eagerly she set about opening it.

The room lights had been turned low. Lucinda and Kate sat by Pedric's bed, the three of them deep in conversation as Kit slipped up onto the sill, finessed the hinged screen open with a soft paw, and pulled at the window handle. Yes, it flipped up. Pushing the glass out four inches, she was through and out into the night, into the damp and sweet-scented garden.

Beyond the small trees and scattered bushes the hospital building rose up on four sides, some windows dark, soft lights shining in others behind drawn shades. Did sick people prefer privacy over a glimpse of the more fascinating world? Only in Pedric's room were the shades still up, the room as bright as a lighted stage. Pedric in his bed, Lucinda and Kate huddled close, the three of them lost in conversation. She smiled at the little tableau, then spun away, leaping up the rocky escarpment beside the waterfall. Pausing, she patted her paw in the falling water and then danced away; she spun, she bounced up the rough ledges to the very top where she crouched in shadow among the highest crags then raced away again down the rocks, ducking beneath cascades of falling water and out the other side, wet and giddy.

She played among the falls for a long time but then at last came down the escarpment again slowly, stepping daintily now, dropping from one level down to the next, quiet and thoughtful—wishing she were not alone. Where the thinnest sheet of water slid down over a little rocky cave, she slipped in through the clear curtain, into a small and secret aerie; looking down into

Pedric's room through the fall of distorting water, feeling her fur grow damper, she saw Pedric's door swing open.

In the square of brighter light she saw Ryan and Clyde step inside to join them, they stood by Pedric's bed next to Kate and Lucinda, Ryan talking excitedly. Clyde had placed his backpack on the floor, she watched Joe Grey slip out, heading straight for the windowsill. Leaping up, he made a dark silhouette looking out into the night, marked by his white chest and white paws. But another shadow slipped out, too, and, nose to carpet, he moved across the floor to the narrower window, where he slid through into the garden and disappeared among the bushes. Watching him, she drew back beneath the waterfall and remained still.

He stood in the darkness of the bushes looking up the little hill, taking in the wooded glade and the tall rocky escarpment and the bright, falling water. He looked intently at one part of the garden and then the next, scanning each, and lifting his nose to taste the air. Seeking her? Oh, she hoped he was.

At last he moved on, following her scent up the rough stones, up and up he went over the tumbled rocks and down again, leaping a fall of water where she had leaped but then he stopped, looking around.

Did he wonder if she was hiding and sulking, if she was still angry? The water plashing down before her sang softly; its sliding gleam distorted the garden and distorted Pan himself into a phantom image as he stood scenting out.

Suddenly he headed fast straight up the rocks to disappear above her. She listened but heard only falling water; she lay behind her watery curtain, her paws crossed, and then sat up nervously. Where had he gone? Had he given her up and turned away?

He burst in through the falling water, pounced on her like a lion capturing its prey, he cuffed her, boldly laughing. She struggled free and rolled him over and cuffed him good, too, and he let her. Battling and laughing, pushing each other out into the water, they were soon soaked.

"Let up," he said at last, but she didn't. "Let up! Listen! They found Amson."

She stopped battling him. "They got him? He's in jail?"

"No need." Pan smiled. "He's dead. Knife blade through his throat."

"Oh, my," she said. "Who did that? Oh, not Debbie?"

"Not Debbie, but they picked her up, *she's* in jail. Charlie called Ryan and Clyde, and we came over to tell Pedric and Lucinda."

"If Debbie's in jail, what about Tessa?"

"She's fine," Pan said. "She's more than fine, I'll get to that. On the way over, we stopped by Wilma's." Kit imagined the homey scene as they pulled up in front of Wilma's stone house, Pan and Joe galloping through Wilma's deep English garden to the carved front door.

"Come in before the fire," Wilma said, opening the door, "what can I get you? Coffee? A drink? A snack for you two tomcats?" She bent down to stroke Pan and Joe.

"Nothing," Ryan said. "We can't stay." Joe leaped to the couch beside Dulcie, thinking a small snack wouldn't take much time, but Ryan said, "We're on our way to tell Pedric, we thought you two would want to know."

"What?" Wilma said, pulling back her loose gray hair and tying her plaid robe tighter around her.

"They found Amson," Clyde said. "Sheriff's deputies found him out on Valley Road, dead in Debbie's car, his throat cut. Looks like he was robbed. No other fresh tire tracks on the dirt shoulder, maybe someone traveling on foot, maybe some homeless person. They found grocery sacks in the car full of cashmere sweaters, upscale costume jewelry, new handbags, all with the tags still in place, and all too bulky for a person on foot to carry away."

"They picked Debbie up at home," Ryan said. "Her prints match those on the store tags—from four upscale village shops, and even two small pieces from Melanie's, and their security's pretty tight."

"It'll do Debbie good to cool her heels in jail," Wilma said. "But what about the children?"

"Emmylou has them," Ryan said. "We took the girls up to her, helped her fix them some supper. Left both girls tucked up in Emmylou's bed, Emmylou making up a bed on the couch for herself. Every time Vinnie opened her mouth to sass her, Emmylou scolded her. By the time we left, the kid wasn't saying a word, she'd crawled into bed and curled up around her pillow, real quiet."

"They'll be all right with Emmylou," Wilma said, smiling. Though what the girls' future held, no one could say.

It was after the Damens left, that Wilma returned to the computer to read Dulcie's newest poem, and the lines made her very sad. But one doesn't choose a poem, the poem chooses the writer. Dulcie couldn't help that this one left them both filled with a dark mourning, a strange uneasy balance, tonight, to the sadness of Birely's unfocused life that was now ended, and to their satisfaction that Vic Amson would not torment and hurt anyone else.

A shadow in the somber stillness
Sways serenely.
The river in its roaring race
With the waning, woeful wind
Laughs loudly, luxuriously at the loser.

A mockingbird, moved by the midnight moon,
Trills tender notes
To the shadow standing silently now
Before a ruined barbican and bail
Now dead, decayed
Only the devil left within its fallen ranks.

The shadow sways,
Slumps sadly to the dark and hoary ground.
Nothing left but emptiness.
No bird sings now
No castle stands
Where ran the laughing river.

Dulcie herself didn't know what to make of the poem. It just happened, a shadow of the lost Netherworld. Wilma put out the fire, stifling the cheery gas logs, and they tucked up in bed, Dulcie stretched out quietly on her own pillow. "What will happen to the children now? The law won't let Emmylou keep them, an older woman without a husband. And their aunt won't want them."

"If the court lets Debbie out on her own recog," Wilma said, "and then if she gets probation, maybe Emmylou would keep the girls during the day. Debbie will have to get a job, or try to, that will be a condition of her probation." Stroking Dulcie, Wilma smiled. "Tessa would have a little more love in her life, with Emmylou. And Pan would be there for her, too. Emmylou won't throw him out."

"Maybe," Dulcie said, "if Pan has his little girl back where he can be with her, maybe he won't long to travel so far away. He knows Tessa needs him."

"And Kit needs him," Wilma said. "What's that sigh about? What are you thinking?"

"Thinking how strange life is. Still thinking about that dark world where Pan wants to go, so different from our world—and thinking about that long-ago time in *our* world, where Misto once lived, that was so different from today. Two strange and different places," she said, "but each is only part of something bigger. So many centuries, so many chains of life, and each one unique and different. So much we don't know," she said, "and in the end, what's it all about?"

"It's about the *wonders*," Wilma said. "That's what it's about."

Dulcie looked at her, purring.

"Wonder, and joy," Wilma said. "No matter where you are in time or place, joy and wonder are what stand between you and the evil of the world. That, and love, are all we have against our own destruction."

And away in the night, in the dark garden, there was wonder, too. Kit and Pan, coming out from beneath the waterfall, sat on a rock away from the mists, licking themselves dry. "Maybe," Pan said, looking around the garden, "maybe *this* world *is* pretty amazing, maybe what Joe Grey says is true."

"What does he say, that pedantic tomcat?"

"That the greatest adventure of all is right here in our world," Pan said, twitching the tip of his tail. "That the biggest thrill of all is to outsmart the bad guys right here, not go chasing off somewhere that's already destroyed and beyond help." He looked deeply at Kit, his amber eyes gleaming. "Maybe Joe's right that it's more fun to work the system right here, take down the bad guys right here. 'Hold the fort,' Joe says, 'and make our own world better.'"

"Maybe," Kit said. "But what if somewhere in the Netherworld, down among those dark caverns, some

370 · SHIRLEY ROUSSEAU MURPHY

small portion of those lands did survive undamaged, as Kate thinks might have happened? What if there *is* some small country there that's still strong, some hidden village that managed to escape the dark?"

Pan said nothing. They sat thinking about that. Maybe it was the enchantment of the garden that made everything seem so different tonight, that made them come together in their thoughts, that helped the two resolve their conflict. Sitting close together looking around at the garden and down into Pedric's lighted hospital room watching their human friends, they no longer bristled at each other; they sat thinking about the amazing world around them, and about their roles in it. And when, at last, they returned through the narrow window, their ears were up and they were ready to move on, to trot boldly on into whatever amazements waited, there ahead of them.

THE NEW LUXURY IN READING

We hope you enjoyed reading
our new, comfortable print size and found it
an experience you would like to repeat.

Well – you're in luck!

HarperLuxe offers the finest in fiction and
nonfiction books in this same larger print size and
paperback format. Light and easy to read, HarperLuxe
paperbacks are for book lovers who want to see
what they are reading without the strain.

For a full listing of titles and
new releases to come, please visit our website:

www.HarperLuxe.com

marked for murder
A SHELBY NICHOLS ADVENTURE

Colleen Helme

Book Cover by Damonza.com ©2019 – Colleen Helme
Book Layout & Design ©2017 - BookDesignTemplates.com

Marked for Murder/ Colleen Helme. -- 1st ed.
ISBN: 9781095581209

To Mike and Don
For the love and happiness
You each give to my daughters.

The Shelby Nichols Adventure Series

Carrots
Fast Money
Lie or Die
Secrets That Kill
Trapped by Revenge
Deep in Death
Crossing Danger
Devious Minds
Hidden Deception
Laced in Lies
Deadly Escape
Marked for Murder
Ghostly Serenade

Devil in a Black Suit ~ A Ramos Adventure
A Midsummer Night's Murder ~ A Shelby Nichols Novella

NEWSLETTER SIGNUP
For news, updates, and special offers, please sign up
for my newsletter. To thank you for subscribing you
will receive a **FREE** ebook.

ACKNOWLEDGEMENTS

These books wouldn't be possible without all of you, my wonderful readers and friends. Thanks so much for your encouraging emails and fantastic reviews! You keep me writing. I'd also like to thank my wonderful family for your continued support, love and inspiration. Thanks again to my great editor, Kristin Monson, for making this a better book. Thanks to the amazing Wendy Tremont King, for producing the audiobook, and doing a fantastic job of bringing Shelby to life. You rock! I love Shelby and the gang, and I hope to continue with many more adventures!

Contents

CHAPTER 1

My phone began playing, "Here Comes the Bride," right in the middle of an important meeting. My eyes widened, and I frantically dug the offending electronic device out of my pocket.

I quickly declined the call and glanced up. Four men sat around the conference table at Thrasher Development, each staring at me with undisguised amusement. Uncle Joey, the local mob boss for whom I worked, raised a brow, unhappy with the interruption.

"Uh... sorry about that," I said, giving them my best smile.

A split second later, it started up again. This time, I jumped out of my chair. "Please excuse me. I'd better take this." I grabbed my notes and rushed into the hall for privacy. I hoped Uncle Joey wouldn't be too mad at me for ditching him. But since the phone call was from Billie Jo Payne, who was getting married on Saturday, I figured it had to be important.

She and Detective Drew Harris, aka Dimples, were both friends of mine. In fact, Dimples was my partner on the police force. Since I'd had a hand in getting them together, I had a vested interest in their upcoming nuptials.

"Hey Billie," I answered, walking down the hall toward my office. "What's up?"

"Shelby! I need your help. Something terrible has happened."

"What?"

"Can you come to my office at the newspaper? I'll explain everything then."

"Uh... I'm kind of in a meeting right now. Can it wait?"

"No," she replied, her voice filled with alarm. "Please. I need you."

"Okay. I'll be right over."

She disconnected without even saying thanks, and my heart filled with dread. I'd never heard her sound so frantic before. Did that mean the wedding was off? She didn't usually panic, or beg for my help on such short notice, so I knew it was serious.

I let out a sigh, knowing I had to go, but what about Uncle Joey? It didn't seem like a good idea to poke my head back in the conference room and tell him that I had to leave. But I could let Jackie, his secretary, tell him for me. Since she was married to him, she wouldn't get in trouble for it.

I rushed inside my new office. Moving behind my desk, I set my notes on top and pulled open the drawer holding my purse. As I slipped my purse over my shoulder, I paused to glance at the painting Uncle Joey had picked out for me. He'd told me the abstract art reminded him of me and how I'd changed his life for the better. I hoped he remembered that when he came in to get my notes.

I hurried out the door and paused at Jackie's desk to let her know I was leaving.

"Is something wrong?" she asked, noticing my heightened color. "Is the meeting over?"

"Uh... no, but I have an emergency. Tell Uncle Joey that my notes about the meeting are on my desk, and that I'll be back as soon as I can. Thanks!" I ran out before Jackie could ask me any more questions and pushed the call button on the elevator.

The doors opened, and relief filled me to find the elevator empty. Now all I had to do was make it to my car without running into anyone, and I'd be home free.

On the parking level, I stepped out of the elevator and started toward my car. Hearing the roar of a motorcycle, I glanced up to see Ramos, Uncle Joey's right-hand man, driving toward his spot behind the pillar next to the elevators. Not sure if he'd seen me, I ducked my head and hurried on.

Usually, I liked running into Ramos, especially when he was on his motorcycle, since that meant I might get to go for a ride. He was one sexy, hunk of a man and gave most women shivers just to look at him. But since I'd run out on Uncle Joey, I didn't want Ramos to know. He wouldn't approve, especially if he knew the reason.

As I reached my car, I heard the motorcycle change direction to head my way, and I knew I'd been caught. Ramos pulled up beside me. His eyes narrowed with suspicion that I'd tried to leave without speaking to him. Why was I in such a hurry?

Since he was one of the few people who knew I could read minds, I answered his thoughts. "Oh, hey Ramos. You're right. I'm in a hurry, but it's nothing life-threatening, so you don't need to worry." I gave him my brightest smile and pulled open my car door.

"What's going on?" he asked.

"Uh... just a minor emergency, but I'll be back."

"Involving Manetto?"

"Oh... no. Not about him. It's something else."

"Like what? Maybe you'd better explain." He leaned forward on the bike and waited, not about to let me go without an explanation.

I let out a sigh. "Oh, all right. I got a phone call from Billie Jo Payne. She's getting married to Dimples on Saturday, and she sounded frantic. I told her I'd come right over."

His eyes widened. Was I putting the police detective and his fiancée ahead of Manetto? "Did you just ditch the big boss?"

How did he know? "Well... sort of. But I picked up enough from the meeting to know what those guys are thinking about the deal, and I left the notes on my desk for him. So in a way, I'm not ditching him at all, see?"

As a mind reader, my job for Uncle Joey was pretty straight-forward. He invited me to sit in on his meetings, and I reported all the pertinent details that his associates forgot to mention.

Ramos frowned, not about to let me off so easy. He couldn't fault me for being a good friend to Billie, but Manetto wouldn't be happy that I'd left like that. Then he thought it was a good thing Manetto had a soft spot for me. No one else would ever get away with my antics. Still, he hoped I didn't make a habit of running off.

"I won't. Like I said, it's an emergency. And I'll be back as soon as I'm done."

He nodded, thinking that trouble had a way of finding me, and he hoped this wasn't one of those times I got involved in something that was way over my head. Had I remembered to get the tracker in my watch replaced? With my record, I'd need it.

"Good grief! I'm sure this is not going to be dangerous. I'll be fine."

"And the tracker?"

I rolled my eyes. "I took my watch to Geoff." I raised my wrist to show him. "It's all good."

His lips quirked up in a lop-sided grin, and my heart did a little flip-flop. He had that effect on me, especially taking in his dark good looks, black leather motorcycle jacket, and the total hotness of a Harley Davidson. Add to that the glint of danger in his eyes, and it was enough to make any warm-blooded woman drool.

He was thinking about the time I'd accidentally called him Romeo, mostly because I had that same goofy look on my face, and his smile widened. "Go on. I'll catch you later."

As he drove away, I shook off the trance he'd caused and climbed into my car. Ugh! Romeo! How embarrassing. He didn't even have to say it out loud to tease me about it, and I knew I'd never hear the end of it.

I slipped on my seatbelt and backed out of my parking space, but couldn't remember where I was going. Oh yeah... Billie. She needed my help. Focusing on her dispelled the Ramos-caused fog in my brain, and a shiver of disquiet caught my breath.

I fervently hoped her problem was nothing to worry about. But if this was about the wedding, I had to do my best to make sure everything worked out for Billie and Dimples. That should be easy for a mind reader like me, but I'd been wrong before.

Ever since that fateful day when I'd gone shopping for carrots at the grocery store, I'd had to adjust to my new life as a mind reader. I'd gained this crazy ability when I'd been shot in the head by a bullet from a crazy bank robber. Some days it was great, and I felt like a super hero.

But on other days, like when I was coerced into working for a mob boss, it didn't go so well. Of course, in the long run, that hadn't turned out so bad either, although recently, Uncle Joey had claimed my family as part of the Manetto clan. Since I couldn't stop it from happening, I tried to ignore the pangs of unease that twisted my stomach into little knots, and concentrated on all the perks.

My husband, Chris, was now a partner in his law firm, mostly because Uncle Joey was his biggest client. That wasn't all bad, right? Among other things, Uncle Joey had used his influence in getting my fifteen-year-old son, Josh, a job at the ritzy country club as a lifeguard this summer. It was a dream job for a kid his age, so how could I complain?

I'd also been sent to New York in his private jet to help him out. Staying in a swanky hotel in New York was awesome. To find out he owned the place, and then to meet his extended family, had nearly given me a heart attack. But I'd managed to fit in as Uncle Joey's newly discovered niece, even though it was all a lie.

But how could I stop working for a mob boss when both he, and more directly, Ramos, had saved my life more times than I could count? I couldn't turn my back on them now. They'd even helped me out when they didn't need to, and I owed them more than I could ever repay.

Still, as deeply as I was involved with Uncle Joey, I tried to balance things out by helping Dimples and the police department. I'd even been to D.C. to help the CIA stop a terrorist attack, so that had to count for something.

Of course, the CIA didn't know the truth that I could read minds like Uncle Joey, Ramos, and my husband, Chris. Dimples had figured it out because we worked so closely together, but I'd told everyone else, including my kids, that I simply had premonitions.

Sure, helping all those people had brought me close to death a few times, but somehow I'd always managed to survive. So how bad could it be to help Billie today? I guess I'd find out soon enough.

I pulled into the parking lot across the street from the newspaper offices and hoped Billie would spring for a parking pass so I wouldn't have to pay. I'd never been to the newspaper's offices before, so this was a new experience.

I crossed the street, glancing at the towering glass walls before entering through the sliding doors. A long desk stood between the glass walls and the elevator bank. I stopped to tell the receptionist I was there to see Billie.

She checked a list and nodded, then motioned me toward security. I had to walk through a metal detector and send my purse on an x-ray conveyor belt. The security guard made me wait while he pulled out my stun flashlight. He examined it, thinking that, since it wasn't a gun or a knife, I could keep it.

Billie's office was on the third floor, so I took the elevator up and wandered around until I found her cubicle. Unfortunately, it was empty. As I stood there wondering what to do, Billie spotted me from a nearby office and hurried out.

"Shelby! You made it. Let me tell you what's going on." She pulled me into a conference room for privacy and began to explain. "I've been doing a series of special interest pieces on single mothers, and I've run into a big problem. One of the women I've reported on has been trying to get paternity support from the child's father, but it's all gone wrong."

"So this isn't about your wedding?" I asked, interrupting her.

Her brows creased together. "No. Why would you think that?"

"Well, I don't know, maybe because you're getting married this weekend?"

She smiled, brimming with excitement, and then her shoulders dropped. "I guess it is, in a way, because I'm on a deadline, and this last article is supposed to be done by the end of the day today. Now I'm not sure what's going to happen."

"Okay. So there's something wrong with the paternity test? The guy isn't the father?"

"Actually it's not with the father... but with the mother. I can hardly believe it myself, but the DNA test clearly shows she is not the mother of her baby."

"Are you kidding me? How does that even happen?"

"That's what I've been trying to figure out," she responded. "I mean, surrogacy is about the only way it could happen, but the mother, Claire, is devastated. She's insisting that she's the baby's mother.

"I'd like to believe her, but how does a DNA test lie? And this is the second one they've done. They're from different labs, but they're both showing the same result. It's conclusive that she's not the baby's mother. So, not only can they take the baby away, but, because she's been getting assistance from the state, they can arrest her for welfare fraud."

"Dang," I said. "That's not good."

"Exactly. That's why I need you. I'm hoping you'll be able to pick up if she's lying so I'll know how to help her."

"Okay. I'll see what I can do." I was surprised that Billie even considered an alternative. That meant the mother, Claire, must be pretty convincing to pull one over on Billie. I mean, how can a DNA test lie?

Billie and I have a shared history. Even though she doesn't know the truth that I can read minds, she's seen enough to believe in my psychic ability.

She let out a relieved breath. "Thanks Shelby. She's in my boss's office. I'll take you there."

As I followed Billie, I caught her concern that time was running out. In fact, Claire had run from a social worker and a police officer who'd come to her house earlier. They'd come for the baby and, most likely, to arrest Claire. She'd managed to dodge them and had come to Billie for help.

Sheesh. That didn't sound good. What had Billie gotten me into here?

We came to a corner office that had all the blinds pulled. Billie opened the door and ushered me inside, discreetly checking to see if anyone had noticed.

A petite, young woman, with long, sandy hair, sat in the chair in front of the desk. As we entered, she clenched the baby to her chest in fear, but calmed to see it was Billie and me.

"Hi Claire, this is Shelby, the person I told you about," Billie began. "She just needs to ask you a few questions."

I smiled and focused on the baby. "She's so cute," I said, hoping to get Claire to relax. "What's her name?"

"Riley. She's almost seven months old." Claire glanced at me with fear in her eyes. "I don't know what's going on, but I am her mother. Somehow the test got messed up, and it's all a horrible mistake. Please. You can't let them take her from me."

Claire's eyes glistened with tears, and regret filled her heart. "I never should have tried to get the support money from Ray. He doesn't even want her. Now it looks like they can take her away from me. How did this happen? If they take her because of the test results, I might never get her back. She's mine. You have to believe me!"

I swallowed back my emotions. As a mother myself, I knew just how Claire felt, and it was killing me. "Tell me about you and Ray. Was getting pregnant a mistake?"

"I guess you could say that." She told me the story of how they'd met and fallen in love, and how she'd thought they were perfect together. Then she got pregnant. "The idea of having a baby scared him off. Ray left me the next day."

She was telling me the truth. She was definitely the baby's mother. So why was the test wrong?

"I believe you, Claire. I don't know what's going on with the test, but I believe you're telling the truth. It might take some time to figure this all out, but we'll do it, okay?"

Tears of relief sprang into Claire's eyes. "Thank you. Thank you so much."

Billie sent me a grateful nod, knowing it had to be true if I believed her.

"What do we do now?" Claire asked.

"I hate to say this," I responded. "But if it comes down to it, you might have to let social services take Riley for a few days until we can figure it out, but we will."

"No, I can't do that. There's got to be another way."

Billie had an idea that sent alarm spiking through my chest. I glanced at her and shook my head. "Billie, don't."

Her brows rose, but she pursed her lips with determination and turned to Claire. "I'll hold them off until we can prove it."

"How?"

"I'll put you up for a few days. If they can't find you, they can't take Riley."

"Billie," I said. "You could get arrested for that."

"Not if they don't find out. Don't worry. She won't be staying at my place." Billie turned to Claire. "There's a motel not far from here. You can stay there until we get this sorted out. I'll pay for your stay."

A knock sounded at the door, and we all jumped. The handle turned, and a man poked his head inside. I picked up from Billie that he was her co-worker, Ben, and he wasn't happy. He took in the scene, and his brows drew together. "Billie, there's a social worker and a police officer downstairs looking for Claire Hadley." His gaze traveled to Claire. "Is that you?"

Before she could answer, Billie spoke. "Stall them for me." She turned to Claire. "Come on. Let's go out the back. The motel's just a block away."

"Billie. No," Ben said. "I can't do that, not even for you."

Billie wasn't about to let that stop her. As she brushed by him with Claire and the baby in tow, he called out, "They know she's here."

Ignoring him, Billie continued out of the newsroom and into the hall. She passed the bank of elevators and rushed to the stairwell. As she opened the door, the elevators opened. A police officer and a heavy-set woman stepped out.

They caught sight of Claire before she disappeared through the doorway and ran toward her. Billie firmly closed the door and stepped in front of it, blocking their way.

"What do you think you're doing?" the woman asked.

"Oh... did you want to use the stairs?"

"Get out of my way."

Billie stood her ground, so the woman continued. "You're interfering with an ongoing investigation."

"I am?" Billie asked. "Maybe you should take the elevator? I'm sure it's faster."

The woman turned to the officer. "Arrest this woman for obstruction of justice."

"What? No." I jumped to Billie's side and grabbed her arm, tugging her away from the door. "You don't have to arrest her. She's not in the way now."

The officer didn't want to arrest anyone, let alone a news reporter. The chief would hate the bad press.

The woman shook her head, thinking we should both be arrested. She turned to the officer to tell him that, but before she could get the words out, he dashed to the door and pulled it open. "I'll get her," he said, then hurried down the stairs.

"Oh, for Pete's sake!" the woman said. She set her steely-eyed gaze on Billie and shook her index finger. "This is all your fault. I'm going to file a complaint. You won't get away with this."

With pursed lips, she pulled the door open and hurried down the stairs after them. Before the door closed behind her, we heard the wail of a baby, and the echo of stomping feet.

Billie glanced my way. "Let's take the elevator. We might still beat them." We pushed the call button and jumped inside. The doors swished shut, and Billie stabbed the button for the lobby.

I picked up that Billie was still hoping to whisk Claire and the baby away. Alarmed at her single-mindedness, I caught her gaze. "Billie, this is crazy. You can't interfere. You'll get arrested."

That didn't seem to faze her, so I continued. "What about Dimples? You're getting married in a few days. This would ruin your wedding." She let out a groan of defeat, knowing I was right, but hating it. "It's okay," I continued. "We can still help Claire, just not like this."

The doors opened, and Billie burst out, running toward the staircase. I followed, but there was no sign of Claire or the officer and social worker. Billie pulled the door open, and sounds of echoing footsteps came from above.

Claire came into view, with the officer beside her, holding her by the elbow. To Billie, it looked like he'd caught her in a tight grip but, in reality, he was helping her down the stairs because he didn't want her to fall with the baby in her arms. He felt bad for Claire, thinking that this was one of those times he hated his job.

Filled with disappointment, Billie held the door open for them, then glanced upward for the social worker. Since she lagged behind, Billie let the door shut and hurried to Claire's side.

"Don't worry, Claire," Billie said. "We'll find out what went wrong and fix this, I promise."

Inconsolable, Claire could only nod while tears poured down her cheeks.

The social worker came through the door huffing and red-faced. She caught sight of Billie and took a breath to scold her, then had second thoughts. Claire's tears touched a soft spot in her heart and she frowned, then hardened her jaw and reached for the baby.

"No," Claire said. "She's my baby."

The social worker pursed her lips, hating this side of her job, but she had no choice. Before she could reach to take the baby away by force, the officer intervened. "Why don't you let her hold the baby until we get to the car? We'll have to put the baby in a car seat anyway, so what's the harm?"

He was thinking that the lobby of a newsroom was no place to make a scene. Sure he was supposed to arrest the woman, but she wasn't in any shape to resist, and getting her to the police station in cuffs wasn't necessary.

"It's Claire, right?" he asked. She nodded and he smiled. "Everything's going to be fine. No one's going to hurt the baby, all right?"

Claire turned her pleading gaze to Billie.

"You have to go," Billie said. "But we'll figure this out. I promise." Resigned, Claire hugged Riley to her chest and stepped toward the exit.

On impulse, Billie turned to me. "Do you think you could get Chris to take her case? I'll help pay his fees."

I raised my brows, knowing that Billie had no idea how much that would cost. I knew it was way above her pay grade, but what could I say? "I'll see what I can do."

"Thanks, Shelby." Billie caught up with Claire at the exit. "I'm getting you a lawyer. It's Shelby's husband." She motioned toward me as I came to her side.

Claire's eyes brightened with hope. "Okay. Thanks. Thanks so much." She swallowed her distress and stepped out of the building with the officer and social worker.

Through the glass walls, we watched the social worker take the baby while Claire got in the police car. Hearing the baby's crying tore at my heartstrings, and I hated that this was happening. Sure I knew that Claire was her mother, but how did that compete with a DNA test?

Billie had the same struggle, so she focused on the next step to get Claire out of jail. She thought that, with Chris's help, it shouldn't be too hard. While Claire got the legal help she needed, Billie would have time to investigate the whole DNA fiasco.

Then she thought about how crazy all this sounded; the mother that DNA said wasn't the mother. Stuff like this was unheard of... but... wasn't that what made a good story? And here she was, right in the middle of it. Her mind cleared, and her heart filled with excitement. Maybe this wasn't so bad after all? From a personal interest point of view, this story could be epic.

She'd have to work quickly to get to the bottom of it before the wedding. But she'd learned that, most of the time, there was a reasonable explanation for everything. She just had to dig deep enough to find it.

She glanced at me, wondering why I wasn't calling Chris. I quickly pulled the phone from my purse and placed the call. Since I had no idea what Chris's schedule was like today, I called his cell number and waited for him to pick up. After several rings, he finally answered. "Hey there," he said. "What's up?"

"Hi honey. Hey... I'm at the newspaper with Billie. She's helping someone who just got arrested and needs a lawyer. Can you help us out?"

"What happened?"

I explained the story as succinctly as possible, but when I got to the DNA part, Chris jumped in. "Wait. The DNA shows she's not the mom? That's not good. As an attorney, I have to tell you that it's a losing battle to fight DNA evidence. I'm not sure we can take the case."

"But she is the mother, I'm sure of it."

He sighed before answering. "Okay. I'll send Ethan over to represent her... for now. What's her name again?"

"Claire Hadley."

"Okay. Got it."

"Thanks Chris." We said our goodbyes and disconnected. Glancing at Billie, I repeated what Chris had told me about the DNA. "This is just weird. I know she's the mother. Maybe we need to get a different lab to run the test again?"

Billie shook her head. "Maybe, but it has to be something else."

"Like what? Aliens?"

Billie grimaced, but I knew she'd considered aliens since I'd picked it up from her mind. "Yeah... right," she said, smiling at the joke. "I guess I'd better get to work."

I opened my mouth to respond, but a distinguished looking man I didn't know stepped to Billie's side. He wore a blue dress shirt and charcoal slacks. His dark hair had streaks of gray on the sides, and silver, wire-rimmed glasses sat on his nose. "Payne... what's this I hear about resisting arrest? You almost gave Ben apoplexy."

Billie's eyes widened, alarmed that he knew, and I picked up that this was the editor-in-chief of the newspaper. "Uh... just a story I'm wrapping up. Shelby's helping me. Have you ever met?"

He glanced my way, and she continued. "Shelby, this is Michael Lewis-Pierce, our editor-in-chief. And this is Shelby Nichols. She consults for the police and has her own P.I. business."

"Hi," I said, smiling. "Nice to meet you."

We shook hands, and the muscles around his eyes tightened. "I've heard of you. Aren't you that psychic? You've helped Billie out a few times, haven't you?" He was thinking that I was something of an enigma, mostly because I hadn't wanted a lot of attention in Billie's stories.

"Uh... yeah. That's me."

He smiled, thinking that it could make an interesting piece to follow me around for a few days. He was sure Billie was up to the task. He'd have to pitch it to her and see what she thought. Even if I wasn't the real deal, a special interest story like that could sell a lot of print, especially if it got picked up by the big syndicates.

"Billie's helping a single mom," I said, wanting to get his mind off me. "It's a crazy story, right Billie?"

"Uh-huh." She hadn't wanted to tell him about it since he might not approve, especially the part about hiring Chris's law firm, but she could leave that part out for now.

I tried not to smile while Billie explained what was going on. I caught that Michael was on his way to lunch, but Billie's story fascinated him. Since we stood in the lobby, lots of people passed us on their way to lunch. In the rush, I noticed a woman who'd come inside.

She stopped to focus on our little group, and I caught her staring at Billie and Michael. She wore jeans and a deep-pocketed coat that seemed too warm for an early summer day. Her stringy, dark hair looked unwashed, and she wore no make-up, but her eyes held an unhinged intensity that caught my breath. I listened to her thoughts and picked up word fragments that hardly made sense.

The whispering voices chilled me to the bone, reminding me of something dark and sinister, like how I imagined a deranged mind would sound. But, under all that noise, it wasn't hard to pick up the anger driving her.

Then I caught the words of the loudest voice: *it's him, right there in front of you, now's your chance—kill him—kill them all, you have the gun—do it.*

My blood turned cold. What the freak? A shooter? Right here in the lobby? What should I do? Should I rush her? Yell "shooter?"

With my heart racing, I slipped my hand into my purse and wrapped my fingers around my stun flashlight. Knowing I had only moments to act, I pulled it out and stepped away from Billie and Michael into a group of people exiting the building.

With her attention still focused on Michael, I managed to get closer, coming at her from a side angle. As hate flooded her mind, she pulled the gun from her pocket. I rushed toward her, plunged the stun part of my flashlight against the side of her neck, and pushed the button.

One million volts of attack-stopping power slammed into her, and she jerked with spasms and choking gasps. The gun went off, sending a loud echo through the lobby. Then she slid to the ground in a heap, and the gun fell from her hand, clattering to the floor. I cringed, but luckily, it didn't go off a second time.

A space cleared around us, and people started screaming about the gunfire. Amid cries of panic, one guy glanced my way thinking I'd shot her, and his eyes rounded with horror. I held up my stun flashlight and he ducked, screaming a little.

"It's a flashlight," I said, hoping to calm him.

"Drop it!"

To my left, the security guard held a gun on me. His breath came fast, and he was thinking he'd pull the trigger if I moved a muscle. My breath caught, and I slowly raised both of my hands in the air. "Don't shoot me! I'm unarmed!"

"Put the gun away," Michael said to the guard. He hurried to my side. "Shelby's not the shooter. It's the person on the ground."

It took a few seconds before comprehension entered the guard's mind, shortening my life span by about three years. He lowered his gun and hurried toward the woman on the ground. As she came to, he pulled her arms behind her back and slipped cuffs around her wrists.

Billie joined us, along with several people who had witnessed the event, taking up the space around us.

"Is anyone hurt?" Michael asked, glancing around the room.

"I think the bullet hit the floor," Billie said, pointing to the damage. She got down on her knees and examined it more closely. "Yeah. It's lodged in there."

Michael exhaled with relief. "Did anyone call nine-one-one?" Someone answered in the affirmative, and Michael nodded. He thought about picking up the gun, but he didn't want his fingerprints on it. "Give us some room, please." He motioned for everyone to step back.

Sending a glance my way, he thought I'd probably saved his life. After I'd stepped away from him and Billie, he'd noticed me walking toward the woman. Glancing at her, it only took a fraction of a second to see the deranged look on her face and realize that she was staring right at him.

After that, everything had happened so fast it made his head spin. Somehow, I knew her plans ahead of time. I'd saved him and probably many others. How did I know? It had to mean that my premonitions were real. Yeah... that was the only thing that made sense.

He wondered how my premonitions worked. Did they come in a vision, like seeing the future? Or was it just a feeling that I'd learned to act on? With all the people standing around, now wasn't a good time to ask, but he was determined to find out.

"How did you know she had a gun?" the guard asked, not having the same problem as Michael.

I shrugged. "Something about her seemed off."

He didn't buy it. Without evidence of a gun, zapping her like that was taking a big chance. I must have seen it, or I was in on it. While he pondered that, a police car with sirens blazing pulled in front of the building.

Two police officers rushed inside. Spotting our little group, they quickly took charge. By now, the woman had regained consciousness, and she began to spout expletives and jerk at her bound wrists.

One of the officers stood guard over her, while the other bagged the gun. Several more cars pulled up, and I wasn't surprised to find Dimples running into the building. He caught sight of Billie and rushed to her side, pulling her into a quick hug.

"Are you okay?" He stood back to look for signs of blood.

"I'm fine. Just a little shaken."

Dimples glanced my way, relieved to find me unscathed as well. "What happened?"

He'd asked me, but Billie answered. "She had a gun, and Shelby zapped her. It went off when she fell." Billie turned her gaze to me. "Was she going to shoot me?"

"Uh... I think she had her sights set mostly on Michael, but she wasn't going to stop there. Do either of you know who she is?"

They both turned to look at her more closely. With her hair covering her face, it wasn't obvious, but something clicked with Michael, and he drew in a breath. Instead of voicing her name, he just shook his head. "I don't think so."

By now, the officers had the woman standing and held her arms tightly to keep her steady. She'd quit swearing and swayed in a stupor. I caught her wondering what the hell happened. One minute she was getting ready to shoot, and the next, she was lying on the floor.

Glancing up, she saw Michael staring at her. Sudden anger caught her breath, and her face turned red. Michael was supposed to be dead, along with everyone who worked for him. Her perfect chance to kill him before turning the gun on herself was ruined. Now look at her... at him... this had all gone wrong.

She squeezed her eyes shut, like she could make it all go away, thinking she'd just pretend he was dead. She'd done it. Now the voices in her head would finally stop. One of the officers asked for her name, and she jerked away from him.

"Leave me alone. I didn't do anything wrong." Agitated and upset, she glanced up, catching sight of a living, breathing Michael. A high-pitched scream came out of her throat. "You murderer! You should be dead." She lunged at him, but the officers held her back. She struggled and yelled at them to let her go, but they held firm. Kicking and screaming, she was dragged out of the building.

Mesmerized by the spectacle, we all watched through the glass as they pushed her into a patrol car. After they drove off, the tension left, and we turned to each other. "That was nuts," Billie said. "She's nuts. I wonder who she is."

Everyone glanced at Michael, expecting him to answer, but he just shrugged. It wasn't something he wanted to own up to, but I picked up plenty of guilt. Her shout of "murderer" had shaken him to the core, and he knew exactly what she'd meant.

Before I could pick up more, Dimples turned to Billie. "I've got to go." He glanced at me and Michael. "I'm glad Shelby was here and that everyone's all right."

"No kidding," Billie agreed, sending me a grateful nod. Turning back to Dimples, she said, "I'll walk you out."

As they left, a police officer approached us, wanting our statements about what had happened. After getting Michael's name and my own, he zeroed in on me, mostly because everyone else he'd talked with had told him I was the one who'd stopped her from a killing spree.

In fact, several of the bystanders bunched around us, hoping to hear my explanation. It didn't help that most of them were reporters, and I picked up that more than one of them had recorded some of the action on their cell phones.

I noticed another guy taking pictures with an actual camera. Was he with the newspaper? This was getting complicated, and here I was, right in the middle of it. I did not need this attention.

Michael stood by my side showing his support, but I caught his curiosity about my explanation as well, and I knew I was in for it.

"So," the officer began. "Tell me what happened. How did you know she had a gun?" The officer was thinking that, from all the other accounts, no one knew she had the gun until after I zapped her with my stun flashlight and the gun went off.

"I saw her come in," I began. "She looked out of place, so I watched her closely. She... um... took an interest in Michael and Billie, so I knew something was up. That's when I took my stun flashlight from my purse and started in her direction. When she pulled the gun, I was ready and zapped her."

By then, Billie had joined us, and she added her two cent's worth. "If you want to know the truth, Shelby has premonitions. That's how she knew." She jabbed me in the arm with her elbow. "Right?" Noticing my grimace, she continued. "It's okay Shelby, you can tell him. Most of the cops already know, so it's no big deal."

I knew most of the cops knew something like that about me, but I couldn't say the same thing about all the reporters who stood there gawking. "Okay... it's true I had a feeling that she was dangerous, so I was ready just in case. And it all worked out in the end. So that's it. That's what happened."

A few brows rose at my admission that I had premonitions. But after what they'd witnessed, the explanation made sense. In fact, most of them had to agree that I must have known ahead of time, and the only explanation seemed to be my psychic ability.

Before anyone could ask me another question, Michael came to my aid, surprising me. "Thank you Shelby." He spoke to the officer. "If that's all, I think we need a moment. Please contact me if you need anything else."

He took my elbow and steered me through security and back toward the elevators. I followed willingly, picking up his thoughts about the Channel 2 News van that had just pulled up outside the building. He didn't like that they'd get the scoop for the five o'clock news, and he wasn't about to let them interview the star witness and hero of the hour before he did.

Of course, that person was me.

CHAPTER 2

Billie ran to catch up with us, not about to let Michael take me away without her. Another reporter came along, hoping for a chance at the story. While we waited for the elevator, Michael glanced his way and nodded, thinking Billie was on a deadline and couldn't do both stories.

"Thanks for joining us, Henry," Michael said. "Did you get everything that happened?"

"Yeah. I was there. I saw it all."

"Good. What about Jeff? I noticed him taking photos. Was he there the whole time?"

"We were both headed to lunch when it happened, so yeah. He started shooting right away. I think a few others might have gotten some video on their cell phones, but I won't know how good it is until I check with them."

Michael nodded, relieved to have that much. Now he just had to get the upper hand on the story. He knew he'd have to deal with why she'd targeted him, but the real story was about me stopping her. They needed to focus on the fact that a tragedy had been averted because of Shelby Nichols.

Whether I wanted to admit to my psychic abilities or not, I'd still stopped a shooting. That was huge.

Holy hell! This was just getting worse. I didn't want to be the center of the show, so that meant I'd have to figure out something else. It would help if I knew what the woman had on Michael. Maybe I could negotiate if I knew what he was hiding.

That sounded a lot like something Uncle Joey would do, but I was desperate and willing to do anything to avoid the spotlight.

The Channel 2 news people didn't waste any time. Coming inside the building, the reporter stepped in front of the camera and began her spiel. Luckily the elevator doors opened, and we all jumped inside, heading to the third floor.

Even though we rode in silence, everyone's thoughts came at me loud and clear. I had to close my eyes and concentrate on my shields to help lower the voices. It reminded me of the woman with the gun, and I hoped the voices I heard in my mind didn't drive me crazy like her.

I picked up that Billie wanted this story so badly it hurt, but she knew Michael would go with Henry. Henry was thanking his lucky stars that he'd been in the right place at the right time, and I tried not to roll my eyes.

Michael's thoughts flashed back to the look on the woman's face, and how close he'd come to death. He knew she blamed him for her husband's death and, if he was honest, he had to agree. Wilson was targeted because Michael broke the story before telling him, and he'd died because of it.

Sure his killer was behind bars, but if Michael had handled it right, Wilson would probably still be alive. Today, his wife looked like she'd lost her mind. She needed help. Since no one had been hurt, maybe she could plead guilty by insanity and get help that way.

So that was it. Now that I knew what this was all about, the knot in my stomach unfurled. At least it should help me negotiate my part in the story, right? Not that I didn't like being a hero, but having a newspaper article all about me wasn't what I had in mind.

The doors opened, and we stepped out. Michael led the way to a large corner office. He took the seat behind his desk and motioned for us to sit in front of the desk. There were only two chairs. Since Billie didn't want to be dismissed, she hung back a little, letting Henry take the chair.

Michael glanced her way and raised his brows. "Aren't you on a deadline?"

Her shoulders fell. "Yeah. But... Shelby and I go way back. If you need me for the story, I'm sure I can help."

"I'll let you know."

Defeated, Billie glanced my way. "Uh... come see me before you leave." She wanted to plan a strategy for Claire's story that included my help. I sent her a nod, and she exited the room.

"I get the feeling you don't want to be in the spotlight," Michael said. "But I'm afraid that can't happen. You stopped that woman from killing a lot of people, and it's going to get out."

"Boss," Henry interrupted, glancing at his phone. "It's already out. We need to get an update online now. The reporter got Shelby's name from someone and just broadcast it as a breaking news story. She's asking for an interview with Shelby."

My phone began to ring. I checked the screen and saw Chris's name. "Hey there," I answered.

"Shelby! Are you all right? The news... they're saying there was a shooter at the newspaper."

"Yeah. I'm fine. I stopped her with my stun flashlight." My phone began to chirp with an incoming call. This time it was from Uncle Joey. "Oh crap! Uncle Joey's on the line. I'll call you back." Without waiting for his reply, I pushed the button to accept the call. "Hey Uncle Joey," I answered.

"Shelby. What the hell's going on? Are you all right?"

"Yeah, I'm fine." My phone chirped again with another call, this time from my best friend, Holly. "Everything's fine here. Uh... they arrested the shooter and no one was hurt. Crap... people keep calling me." Holly's call went to voice mail, and another chirp informed me that my mom was on the line.

"Don't answer them. I don't want you in the spotlight. I think you should come to my office before this gets out of hand."

"Okay, but I have to take this call. It's my mom. I'll call you back." I quickly accepted the call from my mom, but I'd waited too long, and it went to voice mail. Another call came through, this time from Ramos, and I answered his call right away.

"Hey Ramos, I'm fine."

"You just hung up on Manetto."

"I know. I'm sorry. Tell Uncle Joey I'll call him back in a minute." My phone chirped with my mom again. "Uh, I've got to take this."

I pushed the button and answered. "Hi Mom. I'm fine." Between her questions, I quickly explained what had happened. "Will you let Josh and Savannah know?" Since it was June and school was out, Josh and Savannah were on their own. Assured that I was fine, she agreed, and I disconnected.

Out of breath, I glanced up to find Michael speaking with Henry about what to post on the newspaper's website. Henry rushed out of the room, and I realized that Michael's phone had been buzzing for quite some time. As Henry left, Michael's secretary came in.

"Sir," she said. "Rosie from Channel 2 News wants to interview you and Ms. Nichols. What should I tell her?"

"Tell her we'll think about it." With a nod, she shut the door.

Michael sighed. "I should have known. I don't know why I thought I could get ahead of this. Stopping a shooter is too big a deal." He glanced my way. "I don't mean to keep you, but I have to ask. How did you know she had a gun?" He wanted me to tell him exactly how I knew, and not just blow it off as a feeling or intuition. "Do you really have premonitions like Billie said?"

"Are you putting that in the paper?"

He shrugged. "Honestly, I don't know. You've been in the paper before, so this is nothing new, and it might even be good for your private investigator business." He was dangling the carrot in front of my nose, hoping I'd take it.

"Uh... sure." I had to smile. "But right now, I'd rather not have the attention."

"So, how would you want me to explain it?" he asked, giving me the opportunity to put my spin on it as a courtesy for saving his life.

"You can just say that sometimes I have a sixth sense about things. Because of that, and the way she looked, I knew something was wrong. I think that about sums it up, right?"

His mouth twisted to one side. He wasn't ready to let it go. "So, do your premonitions come to you like a vision, or is it more like a feeling?"

"A little of both." Since hearing thoughts was a lot like that, it was close enough to the truth. Plus, it was also vague enough that it didn't bother me to tell him.

He pursed his lips, wishing I'd give him more details, but from my short answers, he knew it was a lost cause. Still, he wasn't writing me off completely. If he played his cards right, there was still a chance he could do a follow-up article on me, especially with the attention I was sure to get. He'd continue with that idea after a day or two. Until then, he'd have to be satisfied with my short answers.

"I don't know if I properly thanked you for saving my life... but saying thanks doesn't seem like enough."

"Hey," I said. "I was just in the right place at the right time, and it all worked out. So no worries." I stood to leave, ready to be on my way. "What about Rosie? She's probably still in the lobby."

He smiled. "Try to avoid her if you can. I'd rather not give her the scoop, although it sounds like someone else already has. If you want to talk to her, it's up to you." He was thinking that most people liked being in the spotlight, so he didn't want to ruin it for me if I was like them.

"To be honest, I'd rather not."

"I get that. Why don't I have our security guard escort you out of the building and make sure you get to your car safely?"

"That would be great."

"Okay. Give me a minute, and I'll call him."

While he put the call through, I scrolled through my messages. Since I'd hung up on him, I needed to call Uncle Joey back, and probably Chris, too. Then I remembered that Billie wanted me to stop by her office to figure out a strategy about Claire.

I should probably head to the police station and see how that was going, but what about Uncle Joey? First, I'd ditched him, and then I'd hung up on him, so I knew he wasn't too happy with me.

Then there was Chris, my kids, my mom, and Holly that I should call as well. With all of that on my plate, it was enough to make me want to drive into the sunset on the back of a motorcycle and leave it all behind.

"Okay, he's on his way up," Michael said, hanging up his phone. A knock sounded at the door, and Henry poked his head in.

"Sorry to interrupt, but we need to get all the details worked out for the story. Rosie is pressing to know why the shooter called you a murderer. We have to address it."

Michael sighed and nodded. "I know... come in and we'll get this worked out."

As he entered the room, the security guard appeared behind him. "I'm here for Shelby," he said.

Michael nodded and came around his desk. He held out his hands to take mine. "Shelby. Thanks again. You saved a lot of lives today. If there's ever anything I can do for you, don't hesitate to ask."

"Thanks. I'll remember that."

I picked up from Henry that he'd already looked at some pictures of the incident. Several of them were of me, and he was hoping Michael could help him decide on which one to use.

Yikes! I suddenly wanted to ask Michael to make sure I looked good in the photo they used, but that wasn't the right kind of favor to ask. I did a mental head slap and let it go. Besides, who knew? Maybe I'd need a real favor from him in the future, so it was always best to keep my options open.

I walked out the door and smiled at the security guard. He nodded, but couldn't quite meet my gaze. He'd come so close to shooting me that just thinking about it made him break out in a cold sweat. Thank goodness Michael had been there and taken control of the situation.

Hearing that, the same relief poured through me, but I kept my mouth shut and followed him to the elevators. I debated about finding Billie like she'd asked, but with everything that had happened, I just wanted to get out of there. I'd call her later.

After reaching the lobby, I caught sight of the news team taking up most of the space. They were interviewing one of the witnesses, so I hoped to get around them before they noticed me. Since Rosie didn't know what I looked like, it could happen, right?

Taking a step toward the lobby, I felt my stomach do a little flip-flop. The guard glanced my way, ready to keep everyone at arm's length if that's what I wanted. I sent him a nod. "Yeah... uh... I'd like to avoid them if possible. My car's in the parking lot across the street."

"I'll make sure you get there safely," he said.

"Okay. Just a sec." In case we were spotted, I ran my fingers through my hair, wishing I had a mirror to make sure my hair and makeup looked all right. Then I rummaged through my purse for some lipstick and managed to glide some on my lips. "All right. I'm ready. Let's go."

The security guard hid a smile and stepped purposefully toward the doors. I walked behind and to the side of him, keeping him between me and the reporter. I'd almost made it to the doors when the reporter spotted me and rushed over. "Shelby Nichols?"

Hearing my name alerted the crowd, bringing a sudden movement of people rushing my way, including the guy with the TV camera. They effectively came between me and the guard and stopped me in my tracks.

Before I knew what to do, the reporter shoved the microphone in my face. "How does it feel to be a hero?" I blinked. What was I supposed to say to that?

"A lot of people are alive because of you," she continued. "Tell us what happened. How did you know the woman had a gun? People are saying that you have psychic abilities. Is that true? Did you have a premonition that she had a gun and was going to use it?"

"Uh... well, I occasionally get premonitions, but I think it was a combination of things... and my intuition kicked in. You know how you get a feeling that something isn't right? That's how she looked to me. Anyway, I'm just glad no one got hurt. Now if you'll excuse me, I have to go."

"What about Michael Lewis-Pierce? Do you know why she called him a murderer?"

"Uh... that's his story to tell. You'll have to ask him." I caught the guard's attention and he pushed through to my side.

"But do you know? What do your premonitions say?" I picked up a note of mockery in her tone and narrowed my eyes. Did she really say that out loud?

"I'm sure it will all be explained in the paper tomorrow." I stepped out of her reach. This time the guard did his job and cleared a pathway for me to leave the building. He stayed by my side until we reached my car, and I opened the door to slide behind the wheel.

"Thanks," I told him.

"I'll make sure they know to let you out without charging the parking fee."

"Oh... that's great. Thanks." I watched him walk to the turnstile where he spoke to the person manning the booth. A moment later, he gave me a thumbs-up and made his way back to the building.

Before I had a chance to start my car, my phone rang with "Here Comes the Bride." Just hearing that tune was starting to give me a headache. Reluctantly, I answered, ready to hear her complain that I'd left without talking to her. "Hello?"

"Hey Shelby. I thought you were going to stop by before you left."

"I know, but things are pretty crazy right now and I—"

"That's okay," she broke in. "I understand. I just wanted to thank you for stopping that woman. I'm so glad you were there. Otherwise, I'd probably be dead."

"Oh... well, I'm glad it all worked out."

"Me too. Hey... do you think you could stop by the police station on your way home? I just want to make sure Claire is all right. Chris was going to help her, wasn't he?"

"He said he'd send one of his junior attorneys over, but I can stop and check on her. If they're willing to let her out on bail, do you want to cover the cost?"

"Uh... sure."

"Okay," I said. "I'll head over there and let you know." We disconnected, and my fingers hovered over Uncle Joey's number. Since I didn't want to talk to him yet, I put my phone away, deciding to wait until after I stopped at the police station. Hopefully, he wouldn't be too mad at me.

I started my car and drove out of the parking lot. The attendant lifted the bar and let me out with a friendly wave. If nothing else, at least that had gone right.

After parking at the precinct, I slipped the lanyard with my ID badge over my head and hurried inside. I went straight to Dimples's desk, and relief flooded over me to find him there. He stood with a big smile, turning his Dimples into swirling whirlwinds that always lightened my mood.

"Hey Shelby," he said, giving me a quick hug. "How does it feel to be a hero?"

"Uh..." I shrugged. "I'm not sure I want the attention, you know?" He sat back down, and I sat on the chair beside his desk. I leaned in and spoke softly, so only he could hear me. "But I'm glad I was able to stop her. When she came in, I thought she looked a little crazy, but then she started thinking about the gun, and I knew I'd better do something."

"I can't imagine," he agreed. "Thank God you were there to stop her." He didn't even want to think about losing Billie. She'd been shot before, and he'd almost lost her then. Going through that again was more than he could handle, so he changed the subject. "Billie mentioned that you'd come to help her out. What did she need?"

I quickly caught him up on her story about Claire and the DNA evidence. "It doesn't make sense. From her thoughts, I know she's the real mother. Anyway, Billie asked me to stop here and check on Claire." I leaned toward him and whispered. "Get this. Did you know Billie almost got arrested?"

"What? No."

I filled him in on that part of the story, and he shook his head. "I guess I have you to thank for keeping her out of jail, too."

"She saw reason once I reminded her of your wedding." Dimples huffed out a breath, and I continued. "Anyway, I need to see if Ethan made it over to represent Claire."

"Okay. I'll walk you down." We took the stairs. Dimples wondered if I knew why the shooter had targeted the newspaper. So far, they hadn't gotten much out of her, and it might be helpful to know. He glanced at me and raised his brows, knowing I'd heard his unspoken thoughts.

"I know why she did it. I guess she blames Michael for her husband's death because of a story he did in the paper. She's got some mental issues, which is part of the problem. I think she hears voices, so it's obvious she needs help."

"Did you hear them?"

"Yeah... but they sounded more like unintelligible whispers. They went quiet when she saw Michael and thought about shooting him." I shivered. "To be honest, it kind of freaked me out."

"I'll bet."

"So is she here?"

"Yeah. They're holding her in a psych cell for now." We reached the basement, and he turned to face me. "It looks like we're here." He glanced at me with gratitude that I'd saved Billie. "Thanks again, Shelby. I'll catch you later."

I nodded, grateful it had worked out, and turned toward the holding cells. The officer in charge pointed me in the direction of Claire's cell, and I started toward it. I found Claire sitting on a wooden bench, wearing an orange jumpsuit and crying. Ethan sat beside her, but it didn't look like he was having any luck calming her down.

Claire saw me and jumped up. "Shelby, you came. Can you get me out of here?" She held onto the bars with panic-filled eyes, and my breath caught. I'd been in her position once, and I knew just how trapped she felt. I also knew that she was innocent, so I capitalized on that.

"I'm sure this is all a mistake and we can straighten it out." I glanced at Ethan, catching his dismay that I'd make such a promise. He thought there was no way we could fight DNA evidence. With my encouragement, I was just making it worse. He wanted to focus on the fact that she had no idea she was committing welfare fraud and hopefully plea a deal that way.

"Thanks Shelby," she said. Glancing at Ethan, she continued. "He thinks I need to make a deal, but that just makes me look guilty, and I'm not."

I nodded. "I know." I caught Ethan's gaze. "Can we talk?"

"Sure," he said. We called the guard over to let him out and found a secluded spot down the hall, away from everyone.

"First thing you need to know," I began, "is that she is the mother of that baby."

"But the DNA—"

"I don't care what it says," I interrupted him. "It's wrong. I need you to handle this case like it's wrong, okay? Let's see if we can get the judge to set bail, and figure out how this happened."

He shrugged. "Okay, I'll do what I can." He didn't think the judge would set bail with the evidence against her, but he'd do his best. He also didn't understand why I was siding with Claire. He didn't like being on the losing side, and I was just making it worse. But what could he say to his boss's wife?

Of course, who knew what would happen to Chris now? A shiver of dread ran down his spine, knowing it was too late to stop what he had set in motion a few hours ago. It would get him off the hook with Strickland, but Chris had been good to him, and he hated his part in the scheme. If there had been any other way... but it was too late now.

"What have you done to Chris?" Alarm tightened my chest. Strickland was the prosecuting attorney who held a grudge against Chris.

Ethan's eyes widened, and shock rippled through him. There was no way I could know anything. "I don't know what you mean."

"Did you set Chris up?"

"What? No. I would never do that." But he was lying, and sweat popped out on his brow.

"You're lying. We're going straight to Chris's office and you're going to tell us exactly what you've done."

He closed his eyes and rubbed his face, letting out a groan. "I can't do that. I'm sorry Mrs. Nichols. I had no choice." Clenching his jaw, he turned his back on me and rushed out the door. I stood there in shock. What the hell? What had he done? I'd only picked up some of it, but it was enough to send my heart racing.

"Ethan, wait!" I opened the door and hurried down the hall to the stairs. Seeing no sign of him, I doubled back toward the other exit at the end of the hallway. Opening it, I ran up the stairs and past the intake officers to push open the outside door to the parking lot. With my chest heaving, I finally caught sight of him backing his car out of the lot and pulling into the street.

CHAPTER 3

As Ethan left, my first instinct was to go after him, but, with his head start, I knew I'd never catch up. Besides, I could just call Chris and tell him my suspicions. Once Ethan got back to the office, Chris could make sure he didn't leave until I got there, and we could question him together.

That calmed my racing heart, and I pulled out my phone. I waited for Chris to pick up, but it went to voicemail, so I left a message to call me. Next, I put a call through to his office. His executive assistant, Elisa, picked up with a cheery greeting. "Office of Christopher Nichols. How may I help you?"

"Hi Elisa, it's Shelby. Is Chris available?"

"Oh, hi Shelby. He's in a meeting with a client. Can I give him a message?"

"Do you know how long he'll be?"

"Probably half an hour or so. Do you want me to have him call you?"

"I think I'll just stop by. What's his schedule like for the rest of the day?"

"Hmm..." she said. "It looks like he's pretty busy, but we can probably squeeze you in after this appointment for a minute or two. Why don't you come in half an hour?"

"Thanks. I'll be there." I disconnected and closed my eyes. Could this day get any more complicated? Now I had to head back downstairs to talk to Claire because Ethan had rushed off.

Inside, I asked the officer in charge if they had what they needed for Claire's case. He found the paperwork which listed Chris's law firm as her attorneys, and assured me that they would be in contact when she was called in for her arraignment.

With that taken care of, I asked to see Claire one more time before I left. In her frightened state, I managed to calm her down. "Please try not to worry. We'll get this straightened out."

"I'll do my best," she replied. "But it would help to know how my baby's doing. Ethan told me the arraignment might not be until tomorrow, and I'm sick with worry. Can you find out what's happened to her?"

"Sure," I agreed, knowing she needed to hear that, above anything else I could say. "Between me and Billie, we'll make sure she's well taken care of, so you don't have to worry. Okay?"

"Thanks so much." All the fight went out of her, and she shrank in on herself. "I don't know what I'd do without you and Billie."

I smiled. "Hey... we'll figure this out. You'll see. I've got to go now, but I'll be back for your arraignment."

She nodded and, after giving her a reassuring smile, I turned to leave. I did my best to block out her emotions, but it wasn't until I had made it to the other side of the door that I could think clearly. My heart broke for her, and I sure hoped Billie could fix this.

I reached my car and slid inside, letting out my breath and taking a moment to unwind. A few seconds later, I put a call through to Billie. "Hey Billie, it's me. I have an update for you. I just spoke with Claire, and she needs to know how her baby is doing. Ethan's taken her case, but I'm not sure he has the social worker's information. I told Claire we'd make sure the baby was okay. Could you find out and let Claire know?"

"Sure. I think I have the lady's information right here. I'll give her a call and then call the station."

"Great, thanks." We said our goodbyes and disconnected. That taken care of, I knew it was time to put my call through to Uncle Joey.

"Shelby," he answered, his tone a little frosty.

"Hey Uncle Joey," I said. "Sorry I didn't get back to you, but things have been a little crazy."

"You hung up on me."

"Yeah... I'm real sorry about that. Did you find my notes?"

"Yes I did. Now about this incident—"

"I've got it handled. I had to mention my premonitions, but I don't think it's going to be a big deal. I have something worse to deal with."

"What's that?" he asked.

"I think Chris might be in trouble. I'm on my way over to his office right now, but I think there's a possibility that someone's set him up to get arrested. I think the guy who set him up is in cahoots with the prosecuting attorney. I know the guy, so once I talk to him, I'll have more details."

After a moment of silence, Uncle Joey spoke. "Do you think it has anything to do with me?"

I clenched my jaw. "Yeah," I said, stating the obvious.

"I see. Come to my office after you talk to Chris." Before I could say another word, he hung up. Did he know this was his fault? Probably. I mean, why else would Chris be in trouble with the law?

I checked my watch, surprised that it was nearly four in the afternoon. Of course, it had been a hectic few hours. I'd met with a mob boss and his minions, helped a journalist with a story, stopped a shooter from a killing spree, and found out that my husband might be in trouble with the law. Could it get any worse?

I did a mental head-slap and hoped I hadn't just jinxed myself.

At Chris's office, Elisa greeted me with a smile, telling me that Chris was still in a conference with his client.

"That's okay, I can wait." I took a seat on the small couch outside his office and glanced around, hoping to see Ethan. "Have you seen Ethan since he got back from the precinct?"

"No. But he might be in his office. Do you want to check there?"

"Sure."

Happy for a break, she led me down the hall to an office door. She knocked, then opened the door to reveal a cramped space that was barely big enough to hold a desk and a chair. A filing cabinet stood in one corner, and several folders were scattered across the desktop along with a framed photo. To my disappointment, Ethan wasn't there.

Elisa asked a couple of people if they knew where Ethan was, but they hadn't seen him since this morning, and didn't know where to find him. An uneasy chill ran down my back, and my stomach clenched. Had Ethan bailed? Would he risk losing his job? Had I missed my chance to talk to him?

We got back to Chris's office just as his client was leaving. Chris smiled, surprised to see me, and grateful I was there after the shooting. "Hey honey," he said, coming to my side. "I'm glad you're all right."

"Me too. We need to talk."

His brows rose. "Okay. Come on in." He closed the door behind us, and I fell into his arms. He was thinking that the experience with the shooter had rattled me and I'd come to him for a much-needed hug. Too bad his next client was due any minute.

"Chris... I did need a hug, but that's not the reason I'm here. It's Ethan. He's done something. I don't know what it is, only that you're in danger. I was hoping to find him so we could talk."

"What do you mean? What has he done?"

I sighed and sat down on the couch, pulling Chris with me. "When I went to the precinct to see how he was doing with Claire, I picked up that he was feeling guilty about you. He was thinking that something he'd put in motion couldn't be stopped. It even sounded like you could get arrested."

"Are you serious?" At my nod, he continued, "let me get him, and we'll straighten this out."

"He's not here. He didn't come back after I confronted him."

Alarm spiked through him. "What did you say to him?"

I explained the incident, and how Ethan took off before I could get more out of him. "I'm sorry. I guess I scared him off."

"What exactly did you pick up?" Chris's brows puckered with worry.

I closed my eyes and tried to remember everything that had gone through Ethan's mind. A lot of it was jumbled in guilt, but there was one name that stood out. "He was thinking that his debt to James Strickland would finally be over. And that he'd hated his part in the scheme to take you down, but he didn't have a choice."

"Take me down? How?"

"I don't know for sure, but I think they've got something on you, and they plan to use it to arrest you and turn you against Uncle Joey."

Chris swore in his mind, but it didn't bother me since I happened to be thinking the same thing. "Did you pick up anything about what it was?"

"No, but it must be something you've done. Did you ever say anything to Uncle Joey, or anyone in his organization, about how to break the law without getting caught, that Ethan may have overheard?"

"What? No. I would never do that." He was thinking he might do something like that to protect me. But if he did, he'd make sure it could never be traced back to him by anyone, and especially not by Ethan. He was smarter than that.

"Oh honey, I hope you never have to do that. You haven't so far, right?"

"No. I haven't."

"Good." I let out a shaky breath, knowing we both walked a thin line when it came to Uncle Joey. "Then it must be something else. Try and think if there's anything you would have done as Uncle Joey's lawyer that Ethan could use against you."

Chris shrugged. "All right. But I don't think you need to worry. I've done nothing like that. Whatever he thinks he has... it can't hurt me. There's no way."

As reassuring as that sounded, I wasn't convinced. Still, I sent him a supportive smile. "Okay. We'll get to the bottom of this. I just need to talk to Ethan. Then we'll know what's going on."

"Right. I'll find him. Once I do, we'll talk to him and figure this out."

Elisa knocked on the door before sticking her head in. "Sorry to interrupt, but your next appointment is here."

"Thanks Elisa. Will you get Ethan on the phone and tell him I need to talk to him? Tell him to come to my office as soon as he can."

"Sure," she agreed, then closed the door.

We both stood, and I gave Chris another hug. "Uncle Joey wanted me to stop by after I saw you, so I'm headed over there, but call me when you hear from Ethan."

"Does Manetto know about this?"

"Uh... yeah. I hope that's all right."

"Sure. But be careful about using Ethan's name. Let me try to talk to Ethan first." He was thinking that he didn't want Uncle Joey roughing him up, since that would just confirm whatever Ethan had against Chris.

"Oh... right. I'll make sure he understands."

"Thanks." He kissed me lightly on the lips before opening the door. We said our goodbyes, and I hurried toward the elevators.

After making it back to Thrasher Development, I found it hard to believe that I'd just been there a few hours ago.

Jackie greeted me warmly. "Shelby! I heard about the shooting. How are you doing?"

"Oh, I'm good."

"It's a good thing you were there. Do you know why that woman did it?" It always fascinated her to know what motivated someone to take such drastic measures. "They were saying she called the newspaper editor a murderer."

"Yeah, I think she blamed him for her husband's death. But, more than that, I think she has mental issues."

"Oh... well, I guess that makes sense. I'm sure all the details will be in the paper tomorrow. Maybe they'll even have a picture of you." Since I was the hero of the day, she thought it was a done deal.

"Yeah, I guess they probably will." Why did that make me so nervous? I'd been in the paper before, so it shouldn't bother me too much. I mean, after a day or two, no one would even remember my name, right?

"Joe's in his office. You can go on back."

"Okay. Thanks."

I knocked before opening Uncle Joey's door. He sat behind his desk, but stood when I entered. "Shelby. Come on in and sit down." He moved to the small cabinet against the wall and motioned toward a crystal decanter of amber liquid. "You've had quite a day. Would you like something to drink?"

"Uh... no, but thanks."

With a nod, he opened the bottom of the cabinet and pulled out a diet soda. "Then how about this?"

"Yes!"

He smiled at my enthusiasm and filled two glasses with ice, setting one in front of me and the other on his side of the desk. To my surprise, he pulled out two cans of soda and handed me one, keeping the other for himself.

"I didn't know you drank diet soda," I said, popping open my can and pouring it into the glass. Just hearing those tiny sizzling bubbles sent a wave of relief through me. I guess that made me a true diet-soda junkie.

Uncle Joey poured his with a sardonic twist of his lips. "I never liked the stuff much, but ever since you've been around, I've developed a taste for it." He held his glass up in a silent toast. I did the same, and we both took a few swallows.

"Thanks." For the first time today, I relaxed. It felt good to sit in this office drinking a diet soda with Uncle Joey. I used to dread coming here, but today, it felt like a safe place. When did everything change?

"Tell me what's going on with Chris."

"Well, I was at the precinct checking on a client. Chris sent his junior attorney over to help her, and I picked up that he'd set something in motion with the prosecuting attorney's office. I feel bad because this isn't the first I've known about it. A few weeks ago, I picked up something like this, but I never got the chance to follow through. Now it looks like I waited too long."

"What do you mean? What happened before?"

I explained that I'd been working on a case with the police, and Chris had sent the same attorney over to help out. "I think the prosecuting attorney has something on the junior attorney, and he's coercing him to spy on Chris. But, until today, it was just an idea. Now it sounds like the junior attorney turned over some real information that could get Chris arrested."

"And it's about me?" he asked.

Our gazes met. "Yeah. I think so."

"And the prosecuting attorney is James Strickland."

It wasn't really a question, but I nodded anyway. "Yeah. He never liked Chris, but now that Chris is your attorney, he likes him even less. He's setting Chris up, but I don't know how."

"And Chris knows all about it?"

"Yes," I agreed, letting out a sigh. "I would have questioned the junior attorney while I was there, but he never made it back to the office." I picked up Uncle Joey's concern and quickly continued. "But... as soon as he shows up, Chris will let me know, and we'll find out exactly what he's done. Then we'll know what to do."

Uncle Joey nodded, but he was thinking I'd been careful not to mention the attorney's name. Chris must have told me to keep quiet about it. But if he was going to help Chris, he needed to know. "I think we both know I can be of more use to Chris if you tell me this person's name."

"Yeah, you're probably right, but Chris was worried that your involvement might backfire." Oops. I hoped I hadn't just insulted Uncle Joey by telling him the truth, but he'd plied me with a diet soda, so it wasn't my fault.

"I see." Uncle Joey tamped down his initial anger at my misplaced allegiance and let out a breath. Didn't I know by now that he was good at what he did? I could trust him to be discreet, and he wasn't about to kill the guy before he knew more.

Yikes! No matter what Ethan had done, I didn't want him dead. "How about this," I began. "If he doesn't show up at Chris's office by the end of the day, I'll tell you his name so you can find him for us. How does that sound?"

"Sure," he agreed. He checked his watch. It was nearly five o'clock. "How late is he usually there?"

"You're right, he should have come back by now. Let me call Chris one more time just to make sure." I quickly put the call through. Chris picked up right away. "Hi honey. Did Ethan ever make it back?"

"No."

"Did Elisa talk to him?"

"No. He didn't answer his phone, and he hasn't come back. I guess I could stop by his apartment on the way home and see if he's there."

"Uh... why don't you let me do that? I can go over there right now. What's his address?"

"Shelby—"

"Just give me the address. We need to take care of this now."

"Fine. Just a minute while I look it up." He came back with Ethan's address and phone number, which I wrote on a pad of paper from Uncle Joey's desk.

"Are you at Thrasher?" At my affirmative answer, Chris continued. "Okay, but go alone. I don't want Ethan to freak out. He's harmless, so if he's there, you'll be fine."

"Uh... sure. Okay. I'll call you." We disconnected, and I caught Uncle Joey's frown. I held up the paper. "Chris gave me his phone number and address, so I'm good to go." I stood, sending Uncle Joey a smile. "I'll let you know what I find out."

"Sit down. You're not going alone," Uncle Joey ordered. "I don't care what Chris said. People who are in a bind tend to do stupid things, and I'm not willing to risk your safety." He picked up his phone and put a call through to Ramos. "I need you in my office," he said, then hung up.

"But we don't want to scare him off."

Uncle Joey clasped his hands together on top of his desk. With a shake of his head, he said, "Sometimes that's exactly what we need to do."

I could understand that, but what if Ethan was the informant? Wouldn't that just confirm his suspicions? I picked up that Uncle Joey had ways to make people cooperate that were a lot worse than anything the prosecuting attorney could do, so I shouldn't worry.

I swallowed. I guess he had a point. For some reason, I'd forgotten just who Uncle Joey was.

Ramos pushed the door open. Seeing me, he stopped. What had I gotten into now? "What's up?"

"I need you to accompany Shelby to visit one of Chris's junior attorneys. She'll brief you on the way. Just make sure you don't leave without the information Shelby needs."

"Got it." He glanced at me with sympathy, but behind that was the steely resolve to get the job done, no matter what it took.

Between the two of them, I was outnumbered, so I grabbed the rest of my soda and chugged it down. Finished, I set the glass on Uncle Joey's desk, resisting the urge to wipe my mouth on my sleeve, and gave him a nod.

As much as I didn't want to admit it, somewhere deep inside I was grateful that Uncle Joey cared enough to send Ramos with me. How crazy was that? Of course, if I were honest, it was hard to object to having Ramos at my side for any reason. I knew that made me a bad wife, but it wasn't enough to stop me from going with him.

I followed Ramos to the elevator, easily picking up his unwavering conviction that I was a trouble-magnet. That was the only thing that explained it. No one else he knew ever got into as much trouble as me, and that was saying something.

"Hey, it's not my fault... this time anyway."

His lips creased into a small smile since he enjoyed giving me a hard time, but today had to be one for the records.

Since he was right about that, I couldn't argue and just kept my mouth shut. After we stepped into the elevator, he said, "So tell me what's going on."

"Okay, here's the deal. Ethan is Chris's junior attorney at the law firm. The prosecuting attorney has something on Ethan, and today at the precinct, I picked up that Ethan put something in motion to get Chris in trouble with the law. Before I could determine exactly what it was, Ethan took off. He didn't show up at Chris's office, so that's why we're headed to his apartment. I need to know what he's done."

"And it involves Manetto?"

"I'm afraid so."

Ramos nodded, easily picking up the prosecuting attorney's plan to get Chris to turn on Uncle Joey to save his own skin from some trumped-up charges.

The elevator doors opened. "Want to take the bike?"

"You know it." I couldn't help the big grin that creased my lips. Since it might be the only good part of my day, how could I pass it up? Riding on a Harley behind Ramos was definitely my guilty pleasure. "Hang on while I get my leather jacket. It's in my car."

Ramos nodded, smiling at my enthusiasm. Had I left my jacket in my car on purpose? Just in case I needed it for a ride?

I sent him a smile over my shoulder. How did he know? At my car, I took off my black, dress jacket and exchanged it for the sleek, leather, motorcycle jacket, wishing I'd been wearing this at the newspaper office when they took my photo, since it totally rocked.

Ramos opened the trunk of his car and took out a couple of helmets. After taking Ethan's address, he handed me the smaller helmet. Until now I'd just assumed he always carried an extra helmet in his trunk, but today I picked up that he'd bought it just for me.

How had I missed that? Of course, he'd given me the motorcycle jacket a few months ago, so I should have known. Still, my heart gave a grateful thump that he'd done that for me.

Soon, I sat behind Ramos, holding on tight while we roared out of the parking garage and onto the street. We headed away from the downtown area toward a hub of apartment buildings on the west side of the city. The apartment building Ethan lived in was older and a little run-down.

After parking the bike on the side of the road, we entered the building and took the elevator to the fifth floor. I glanced at Ramos, taking in his dangerous, hitman vibe, and swallowed. "Uh... why don't you let me do the talking?"

He grunted, thinking that was fine to begin with, but if I really wanted to help my husband, I'd let Ramos do his job. I nodded. How could I argue with that?

We stepped out of the elevator and traversed the hall to Ethan's door. I rang the bell and knocked. We waited but could hear nothing from inside the apartment.

Ramos pulled a small pouch from his pocket with his lock-picking tools. My eyes widened. "Wait... you can't do that. What if he's in there?"

"Isn't that why we're here?" He didn't wait for me to comment, and bent quickly to his task. I swallowed and glanced up and down the hallway, hoping no one would catch us. The lock clicked, and Ramos opened the door. At least he wore leather gloves.

He glanced at me, thinking I should be careful about what I touched, and I nodded my agreement. We quickly entered the apartment and shut the door behind us.

The living room area held a couch and coffee table with a large-screen television on one end that connected to a small kitchen. It had that lived-in feeling, with a few dishes scattered here and there, along with a laundry basket of clothes waiting to be folded, but no Ethan.

"Hello," I said, not wanting to scare Ethan to death. "Anybody home?" Silence prevailed, so I glanced at Ramos. "Guess he's not here. What now?"

"We take a look around. I'll take the bedroom, you take the kitchen."

"What are we looking for?"

"Check for notes or lists, anything that will tell us more about his activities or where he would go."

"Okay."

Ramos padded down the short hallway to the bedroom, and I turned to the kitchen nook. A flush of guilt swept over to me to invade Ethan's privacy, but I pushed it away and examined the counter. Finding a stack of mail, I carefully looked through it.

With nothing out of the ordinary, I continued glancing through the other items on the counter-top and, using a tissue, opened a few drawers. I glanced at the fridge, noting a couple of business cards stuck on the outside with magnets.

One had Chris's law firm with Ethan's name as a junior attorney on it, and the other had James Strickland's name and contact information. Besides those, there was a coupon for a discount at a nearby gym, but nothing else. I needed something that would tell me what Strickland had on Ethan. Maybe Ethan kept a journal?

I hurried to the bedroom, finding Ramos searching through Ethan's drawers. He glanced my way and shook his head. Then he froze and slowly pulled a gun from under the clothes. He looked it over, noting that it was a .38 special. It wasn't loaded, but he found a box of bullets in the same drawer.

After putting them back, he turned my way. "There's nothing here."

"What about a journal? Did you see anything like that?" I checked the tops of the drawers, then the closet, and finally under the bed. Nothing. Now what?

"Do you want to wait for him?" Ramos asked. I caught an image in his mind of sitting in the dark and scaring Ethan half to death when he came in. He thought that was always a good strategy to make someone talk.

"Uh... no. He should show up at work tomorrow. I'll just talk to him then."

Ramos nodded, thinking that he could always come back later if he needed to. "All right. Let's go."

As we closed the door behind us, I glanced up and down the hall, hoping we wouldn't get caught. Ramos was thinking that I should stop looking so guilty and act like I belonged. I relaxed my shoulders and let out a breath.

"You're right," I said. "I'm just not used to living on the edge like... uh... you." I glanced up at him, hoping he didn't take that the wrong way. He raised his brow. Oops. I smiled, hoping that would pacify him, and decided to change the subject. "So... did you decide what days worked best to visit Javier?"

Because of Ramos's job as a hitman to a mob boss, he'd planned to stay out of his brother's life, wanting Javier to continue to believe that Ramos had died all those years ago.

To make up for it, Ramos had asked me to deliver a large sum of money to his brother, telling him that it was from an anonymous benefactor. That had gone smoothly, and I'd kept in touch with Javier, updating Ramos with bits of Javier's life.

But recent circumstances had led Ramos to have a change of heart. Tired of going it alone, he'd decided to let Javier know he was alive after all. That meant it was up to me to set it up.

So far, I'd had trouble finding a date that worked for both of their schedules. Javier was excited to meet his mysterious benefactor, and I knew it was sure to be a shock to find out it was his long-lost brother. Still, I was excited for them, even if Ramos was having second thoughts.

Ramos twisted his lips. The last time I'd set something up, we'd both been whisked off to Washington D.C., and he'd had to cancel. Since we'd nearly died there, and he'd basically saved my life, he wondered if I could stay out of trouble long enough for him to leave me again.

"Of course I can," I said, disgruntled that he'd even think that.

"Okay, then I think the weekend after this one will work best for me."

"Good. I'll set it up." I glanced at his strong, chiseled features. "I'm sure it will work out this time."

He snickered, then caught my gaze and schooled his expression. "I'm sure it will."

We reached his bike without spotting Ethan, and I climbed on behind Ramos. Since this was the highlight of my day, I decided to forget about everything else and enjoy the moment. Luckily, Ramos had the same idea and took the scenic route back. I couldn't complain that he knew me so well.

As we reached his parking space at Thrasher Development, I let out a sigh and dismounted. Handing him my helmet, I said, "Well, thanks for going with me. We might have to go back tomorrow, on the bike, but I'll let you know."

His lips twisted. I hadn't fooled him. He knew I loved riding his bike with him, and talking to Ethan was a good excuse to get what I wanted. "Sure. Anything else you need?" His velvet voice sent shivers up my spine, and my heart galloped.

I let out a little huff. "Uh... no. I'd better get going. Tell Uncle Joey I'll keep him informed." At his playful grin, I shook my head and hurried to my car.

It took me longer than usual to get home because of rush-hour traffic. I opened the back door and entered the kitchen, surprised to find a beautiful bouquet of flowers on the table. My thirteen-year-old daughter rushed in with a big grin on her face. "Hey mom!"

"Wow, when did this get here?"

"Isn't it totes awesome?" she asked. "It came about an hour ago." Savannah was dying to know who'd sent it. She'd taken a peek at the card, and knew it wasn't from her dad, so who could it be? Would I know? "There's a card." She pointed it out. "Open it up and see what it says."

I took the envelope from the arrangement, pulled out the small card, and read it aloud. "It says, *'To Shelby, From, A secret admirer.'* There's no name." I turned the card over just to make sure nothing else was written on the back. "I wonder who sent it."

"I know," Savannah agreed. "But it must have something to do with what happened today. Why didn't you call and tell me about it? I had to hear it from Grandma."

Oops. I knew I should have called her, along with Holly and everyone else. "I'm sorry, sweetie. There was just so much going on, but you're right, I should have called you."

"So tell me what happened. I only got the short version from Grandma."

Since I was famished, I grabbed a cookie and sat down at the table. In between bites, I told her the whole story, including the reason I'd gone to help Billie in the first place.

"Wow. If you hadn't been there, they'd probably all be dead." She was thinking that if anyone doubted my premonitions before, they'd be convinced now. "That makes you a hero."

"Oh, I don't know about that. It's more like I was in the right place at the right time. But I'm a little worried about the press coverage. I'm sure there's going to be a story in the paper tomorrow, which might include pictures. And, as I left, a Channel 2 news reporter cornered me, and I had to make a statement. It's probably already been on TV."

"Oh my gosh!" she squealed. "You're like a celebrity. We'll have to be sure and watch the news tonight. They'll probably play it again."

"Yeah." I sighed, not sharing her enthusiasm.

"Mom?" Savannah wondered why I was so down. "You should be happy. You saved people's lives. That's a big deal."

"Oh... I know... it's just a lot to take in." My phone buzzed with an incoming call. It said "private number," so I told Savannah I'd better take the call. "Hello?"

"Is this Shelby Nichols?" The deep voice had a British accent, and didn't sound familiar.

"Uh... yes."

"Good," he answered. "My name is John Brown, and I'd like to hire you. I saw your interview on the news, and I think you're just the person I need for a job. I hope you're not too busy. This is time-sensitive, but it shouldn't take long. Because of that, I'm happy to pay double your rate, whatever it may be."

"Oh... uh... sure. I've got a lot on my plate at the moment, but I could probably schedule an appointment for a short consultation tomorrow. Will that work?"

"Excellent. May I ask you a quick question?" Before I could answer he continued, "I saw your interview on the news earlier. In it, you said you have premonitions. I'm just wondering how it works. Did you know there would be a shooting at the newspaper before you arrived?"

His question took me off-guard, and I answered truthfully. "Uh... no."

"Then how soon before the incident did you know it would happen?"

"Not long."

"So your premonitions only work if you're involved? Hypothetically speaking, let's say that a plane will crash tomorrow. Would you know about that in time to stop it?"

This line of questioning sent a wave of unease over me. "No. I'm afraid not."

"Interesting," he said. "I apologize if I've made you uncomfortable. I'm just trying to get a feel for what you do. I hope you understand. What time shall we meet tomorrow?"

A sudden foreboding caught in my throat. Did I really want to meet up with this guy? "Your name is John Brown, is that right?"

"Yes. I'm a real estate accountant for JB Sizemore Consulting. Perhaps you've heard of us? Our offices are downtown, not far from the city center mall."

"Oh... yes. That sounds familiar." Although I'd never heard of the company, it helped to know that he had an office and a job. Plus, meeting him in person would clear up any qualms I might have, since I'd know his real motivations for hiring me. Still, I felt a little bit railroaded into it, but that didn't mean I had to take the job. "I can probably make it to your office sometime tomorrow morning."

"Excellent. Shall we say eleven? I'll text you my address and office number."

"Okay. That should work."

"Very well. Until tomorrow then." He disconnected. A few seconds later, my phone jingled with his text message giving me his address.

That settled, I checked the time, finding that I should probably get dinner started. With Savannah's input, we decided to grill some burgers, and I got them out of the freezer.

Josh came home from his lifeguard shift at the country club. This was his second week on the job, and he'd insisted on riding his bike there and back. I noticed that his eyes sparkled with accomplishment at his newfound independence, and I picked up that he looked forward to getting his first real paycheck.

When had he grown up? At fifteen, his voice still cracked occasionally, but it had dropped to a lower, manlier, register. As he told me about his day, I noticed some hair growing along his jaw and above his upper lip. Oh my gosh! He was getting facial hair! My breath caught with emotion. My baby was growing up right before my eyes.

"Mom? Did you hear anything I just said?"

"Uh... yeah. Of course." I blinked back the sudden moisture in my eyes and listened real hard to his thoughts.

"So... what happened?" he asked.

I picked up that he was asking about the shooting. "Oh, right." Nodding, I began telling him the same version of the story that I'd told Savannah. He basically thought the same thing as she did, namely, that I was a hero. Then I picked up that he was glad I had premonitions, otherwise I'd be dead.

"Way to go, Ma." He gave me a one-armed hug, which didn't last quite long enough. "So when's dinner? I'm starved."

"I thought we'd have burgers. Do you want to grill them up?"

"Yeah, sure."

Chris got home earlier than usual, wrapping me in a warm hug before setting down his briefcase. He noticed the flowers on the table, and his brows drew together. "Who sent those?"

I shrugged. "I have no idea. The card says it's from a secret admirer."

He rubbed his fingers through his hair and shook his head, thinking the events of today had given me some unwanted attention, like I was a celebrity or something. He didn't like it one bit.

"Hey, it might not be so bad. They're just flowers, right? They are kind of nice."

He studied me, wondering if I was telling him that he should send me flowers once in a while. I smiled and pulled him back into my arms. "I'm glad you're home. Josh is cooking burgers, so we can eat in a few minutes."

"Good deal. Did you talk to Ethan?" he asked, reminding me that I'd never called to tell him one way or the other.

"Oh... no, he wasn't there. Did he ever come back to the office?"

Chris shook his head, thinking we'd just have to wait until tomorrow to confront him.

"If he shows up," I said.

"He will. Don't worry. We'll get this figured out."

As much as I wanted to believe him, I was pretty sure it wouldn't be that easy.

CHAPTER 4

I pulled myself out of bed the next morning and hurried to the kitchen to tell Chris goodbye before he left for work. I made it just as he opened the door to leave. He paused, giving me a quick kiss before walking out. "I'll call you about Ethan."

"Okay." As the door closed behind him, I picked up a fleeting thought from his mind. He was hoping I wasn't too upset with the picture. Huh? I glanced at the kitchen table to see the newspaper, and my stomach dropped.

The headline read, "*Unsung Hero Stops Killing Spree,*" with a picture of me standing over a woman. She lay sprawled on the floor with the gun lying beside her.

My hair was swept to one side of my face, and my lips were parted like I was out of breath. My narrowed eyes held determination and a flash of vehemence that I hardly recognized.

I stood over the woman with my feet planted firmly in a superhero stance. If I hadn't known better, I'd think I'd posed for that photo. Holy hell!

The caption read, "Shelby Nichols, private investigator, and Lori Wilson, alleged attacker." I quickly read through the article, and my heart pounded harder with each sentence.

"In a timely encounter, private investigator, Shelby Nichols, foiled an alleged shooter, Lori Wilson, yesterday at the Triad Center housing the newspaper's offices, saving countless lives. According to eyewitness reports, Nichols approached Wilson, who had just entered the building, and zapped her with a stun gun. The shock caused Wilson to discharge the gun she was pulling from her jacket, which fired harmlessly into the floor. Wilson then dropped to the ground, where she remained unconscious until police arrived. As they took Wilson away, she yelled expletives at the paper's editor-in-chief, Michael Lewis-Pierce, who was in the lobby at the time. The motivation for the attack appears to be an article published a few months ago by Lewis-Pierce about Wilson's husband, who was killed at the hands of a known criminal after the article was released.

"In response to her quick action, Nichols explained it by stating that she sometimes has a sixth sense, or premonitions, about people around her. She credits this psychic ability as the reason she anticipated Wilson's intent to start a killing spree. 'I've learned to trust my intuition,' she said, and stated that she just happened to be in the right place at the right time to thwart this deadly tragedy.

"According to our records, Nichols is no stranger to these types of incidents. As previously reported by this paper, she has helped the police numerous times, most recently in the apprehension of the escaped murderer, Leo Tedesco, whom she helped capture, and who is now back behind bars. Sixth sense or not, everyone at this newspaper is grateful she was here."

I sat back in my chair and closed my eyes. This article made me sound like I was a candidate for the loony bin. I should have just told everyone I saw the gun. It might not have explained how I knew she was going to use it, but that seemed more believable than saying I had a psychic ability.

But there it was in black and white for the whole world to see. Shelby Nichols has premonitions. Of course, after I'd admitted as much in my interview with Rosie on Channel 2 News, I couldn't take it back. We'd watched it last night, and I still cringed this morning just thinking about how she'd managed to throw in the premonition part.

I hoped it didn't mean that crazy people would start calling me for my psychic services. Who knew what kinds of things they'd ask me to do? My gaze landed on the bouquet of beautiful flowers. Who had sent them and why? I wasn't sure I liked having a 'secret admirer.'

I took a couple of deep breaths to calm down. Getting upset wouldn't help. Besides, the bouquet could be from someone who'd been there, and this was their way to anonymously thank me. That was probably it. After a few days, people would forget all about me, and that would be the end of it.

My phone rang with "Here Comes the Bride," and I let out a breath. At least I knew it was Billie and not some random secret admirer. Hoping she'd made some progress on the case, I answered. "Hey Billie, what's up?"

"Did you see the article?" she asked.

"Yes. It was kind of hard to miss, since it was right there on the front page."

"I just love that picture. You look pretty bad-ass."

I chuckled. "Yeah, I hardly recognized myself." Wanting to change the subject, I continued, "So, did you get ahold of the social worker who took Claire's baby?"

"Yes. Riley's in a good home and she's doing fine. I called the precinct and told them to let Claire know."

"Good. So how's the story coming? Did you make some progress?"

"That's why I'm calling. I think I might have the answer, but we won't know for sure until Claire's relatives are tested. That might take some time, but I was hoping we could get Claire out of jail first. Do you know when her arraignment is?"

"Uh... no." Since I'd dropped the ball on that, I quickly continued, "Why don't I call Chris and find out what's going on and call you back."

"Okay. But don't forget to call me. Tomorrow was supposed to be my last day on the job. Now I can't leave until this story is done."

I sucked in a breath. "That's right. You're getting married Saturday!"

"I know!" she squealed. "I can hardly believe it."

"Don't worry. I'll call you right back." We disconnected, and I called Chris's cell. Unfortunately, it went to voice mail, so I called the office number. Elisa picked up and told me Chris was in a meeting. "Do you know if Ethan is there?" I asked.

"Yeah. I saw him earlier. Just a minute." She put me on hold, and my heart soared. He was there. At least something was going right. She came back on. "I guess he's not here after all. I think he might have gone over to the jail to meet with a client."

"Oh, that's okay. Maybe I can meet up with him there. Just in case I miss him, have him call me when he gets back." She agreed, and I called Billie. "I think Ethan's meeting with Claire right now. I'm going to head over there."

"That's great. I'll need to talk with him too so he can work on her defense. You'll never believe this, but I think this is a rare case of chimerism. It means Claire could be her own twin. It's actually been documented in another case similar to hers, but we won't know for sure until her relatives are tested."

"Wow. That sounds weird. You'll have to explain it to me later. Right now I've got to get ready, but I'll be sure to let Ethan know you found something. In fact, I'll give him your number so he can call you."

"Sounds good."

We disconnected, and I rushed to my room to get dressed, grateful I'd taken a shower last night. I threw on a pair of jeans and a cute, white, capped-sleeve shirt with a shimmery gold geometrical pattern on the front. Instead of sandals, I opted to wear my comfortable running shoes. Who knew? I might be chasing after Ethan for most of the day, and I didn't want to be slowed down by two-inch heels.

I applied some blush and mascara and brushed my long golden locks into a semblance of order. After waking my kids and getting our schedules for the day organized, I was ready to head out.

I arrived at the precinct and slipped my lanyard around my neck before walking inside. Instead of going to Dimples's desk, I took the elevator to the lower level and the holding cells. The officer in charge told me that Claire had been taken to the courthouse for her arraignment. "If you hurry, you can probably make it."

I rushed outside and across the street to the courthouse. Since I'd recently been to the courthouse where they held the arraignments, I knew right where to go. Stepping inside the courtroom, I quietly took a seat in the back and searched for Ethan.

The prisoner standing in front of the judge was denied bail and sent back to the holding cells. They soon brought another prisoner forward, and I recognized Claire's slight figure and blond ponytail. Was Ethan here? Where was he?

Ready to defend her myself, I relaxed as Ethan stood before the judge. He entered the plea of not guilty and asked for Claire to be released on her own recognizance. He argued that she'd never been arrested before, and assured the court that she was not a flight risk. With her baby held by child services, she was determined to get this resolved so she and the baby could be reunited.

I thought he made a good argument. The judge took in Claire's young, frightened face, and decided jail was no place for her. With a tap of his gavel, he released her from custody, admonishing her that she needed to make sure she appeared at every court hearing if she wanted to stay out of jail.

She quickly agreed, and it was over. I made my way toward them, hoping to reach her before the officer took her away. She turned to Ethan and asked him what would happen next.

The officer stepped forward to take her back, but Ethan requested a short visit with Claire first. As they followed the officer to a consultation room, I made it to Ethan's side. Claire caught sight of me and smiled. "Shelby! Did you hear they're releasing me?"

"Yes. That's great news." I glanced at Ethan with raised brows.

"Uh... hi Mrs. Nichols." Ethan's face flushed with guilt.

"I'd like to join you. I have some information you both need to know."

"Sure." He nodded, but didn't quite meet my gaze. Inside the room, he closed the door and motioned toward the chairs. We sat down at the desk while the officer waited just outside the door.

"Let me explain how this works," Ethan began. "They'll take you back to the holding cell at the precinct where you'll be processed out. You'll be given back your clothes and other personal items. Do you have someone who can come and get you?"

"Yes. I spoke with my mom yesterday. I'm sure she'll come."

"Good. It might take a few hours before you're released, but you'll be out today." At her nod, he glanced my way. "What did you find out?"

"Billie's pretty sure she's figured out what's going on with the DNA. She called it something like chimerism... yeah... I think that's it. But it means that Claire could be her own twin. Apparently, there was another case a lot like this one, and they figured out how the DNA came back different. I guess it's pretty rare, but it answers the DNA question satisfactorily."

"How do you prove it?"

"Billie said you needed to get DNA samples from Claire's relatives. I have Billie's number. You should call her. She can explain it better than me, and she'll be happy to tell you what to do next."

"Okay."

I found Billie's contact information in my phone, and he wrote it down. Then he pulled his business card out of his wallet and handed it to Claire. "I'll get started on this right away. Why don't you give me a call tomorrow, and we'll meet at my office?"

"Great," Claire said, taking the card. "Thanks so much. Both of you." She had hope for the first time that this was the answer, even if it sounded weird. How could she be her own twin? It didn't make sense, but she'd believe it if it meant getting Riley back.

We opened the door, and the officer took Claire back to the holding cells. I walked to the exit with Ethan, picking up his discomfort to be with me. He needed to come clean, and guilt about what he'd set in motion swamped him.

Since he was full of remorse, I figured now was a good time to grill him. "I wasn't sure I'd see you after you ran off yesterday."

He grimaced and ducked his head. "I know, sorry about that." We reached the exit, and he held the door open for me. "I'll give Billie a call and get to work on Claire's case, but I should head back to the office now."

"Sure, but first you need to tell me what's going on with Chris. Did you set him up?"

He swallowed, thinking that waking up in the middle of the night with a hitman standing beside his bed had scared the crap out of him. Did I have something to do with that? "You don't need to worry. I'm taking care of it."

He glanced down the street, wanting to get away from me. Yesterday had freaked him out. I knew stuff I shouldn't, and he didn't want to be around me more than he needed to. "I'll tell you about it sometime, but not right now. Okay?"

"So you're not going through with it? Chris isn't in danger?"

"No." It would cost him, but he didn't have much of a choice now. He'd just have to pick up the pieces afterward.

"Okay. Thanks Ethan." As he scurried away, relief washed over me. I guess Ramos had gone back and done what he did best. Watching Ethan's hunched shoulders sent a pang of remorse over me. I didn't like intimidating him. But, on the other hand, I didn't want Chris in trouble either.

At least I didn't have to worry about that anymore, and Ethan was mostly telling the truth. He was taking care of the threat, but it wasn't a done deal. I picked up that by refusing to do Strickland's bidding, he might make someone else unhappy, but since they went way back, he hoped they'd get over it. I wasn't sure what that meant, but I guess I'd find out soon enough.

Walking back to the precinct, I put a call through to Billie and gave her the good news about Claire's release. "I'm not sure what time she'll get out, but I'm headed that way, so I'll see if they have an estimated release time. It might be nice if you could talk to her for your article before you wrap it up. And I gave Ethan your number, so he should be calling you."

"Okay," she said, then blew out a breath. "I wish that solved my problem, but now I'm having trouble finishing the story. I mean... how do I end it before we have the test results from her relatives that prove my assertion that she's her own twin?"

"I see what you mean," I agreed. "But since your article is a series, can't you put this part of it on hold until you get back? I'll bet Michael will be good with it, especially when you tell him your findings. I mean... being your own twin is kind of crazy. Do you think he'll believe it?"

"Well... he'll definitely want proof of chimerism, which I won't get until the DNA test results come back. Since we haven't even figured that out yet, I'll probably be back from my honeymoon by then. I'll talk to Michael and give him a heads up. I'll just have to make sure Claire and her family get the testing done as soon as possible, so the results will be back by the time I get home."

"That should work out. I'll find out when Claire will be released and let you know." We said our goodbyes and disconnected.

At the precinct, I took the stairs to the holding cells and asked the holding officer when he thought Claire would be back from her arraignment. "They're supposed to release her today."

"It'll be later this afternoon because they have to process her out," the officer said. "Why don't I tell her to call you?"

"Sure. Here's my number in case she needs it."

He took my business card and clipped it to Claire's file. He lifted his gaze to mine, thinking about the rumors that I was a psychic. He'd heard all about my quick thinking in disarming the shooter yesterday, especially since he'd had to deal with the woman. She'd ranted and raved like a crazy person, and he was grateful she'd gone into a psych unit after that.

"So she's not here? The crazy person?"

His eyes widened. "No. Not anymore."

"That's good... I mean... I think she could use some medication."

"Yeah. You're probably right."

"Well. I've got to go. Thanks for your help."

He nodded, and I picked up that I made him nervous, so I sent him a quick wave and hurried out the door. Heading upstairs, I decided to see if Dimples was around. It would be nice to know what he thought about my sudden notoriety.

He sat at his desk, finishing up some paperwork. I caught his thoughts about getting done before the big day. With the big push for Billie to get her article finished before the wedding, he worried that she'd be too busy to take care of all the last-minute details. She might even consider postponing the wedding if the article wasn't completed in time. She wouldn't do that, would she?

"She won't," I said, sitting beside him.

He jerked and swore a blue streak in his mind. Then his eyes widened, knowing I'd heard that too. "You shouldn't sneak up on me like that."

"Sorry," I said, a big grin on my face. "But at least you know you don't need to worry about Billie blowing you off, right?" He shook his head and let out an exasperated breath, so I changed the subject. "Did you see today's paper?" At his nod, I continued, "What do you think about the article?"

"Looks like you made it on the front page." He was thinking that I probably hated it. "But it was nice. It gave you the credit you deserve, and I liked the picture." He grinned, and his dimples did that little dance that always lightened my mood. "Take a look at your desk. The chief got you a computer."

I glanced at my new desk in the back corner. It finally fit in with the rest of the desks in the room now that it had a monitor and keyboard. There was also a beautiful bouquet of flowers sitting beside the monitor. "Wow. Nice."

"Yeah. After the shooting went down yesterday, I think he was really impressed with your "hero" status. He wanted me to show you how to set up your own account, which will give you access to the police database. That should come in handy, right?" He was thinking that was a real concession on the chief's part, especially since I hadn't even asked for it.

"Yeah, for sure. If it got me a computer, I guess it was worth it. Did he get me the flowers too?"

"Uh... no I don't think so. They were delivered this morning. Why don't you open the card and find out who sent them?"

We both stepped to my desk and I reached for the card. Pulling the envelope open, I read, *"To Shelby, Thanks for your service. From: A Secret Admirer."*

"What does it say?" Dimples asked. I handed him the card. "Hmm... looks like you caught someone's attention."

"Yeah," I agreed. "I got another one yesterday. At home. It basically said the same thing. Do you think they're from the same person?"

His brows drew together. "I wouldn't think so." He looked at the card. "You could check with the florist. It looks like it's from Brown Floral." He handed the card back. "They'll have records, so it should be easy to find."

"Okay. I'll do it." Glancing at the card, I realized there was a shop nearby. "I'll check it out on the way home." That helped settle my stomach. If both arrangements were from the same person, I could make sure they weren't some whack job, and politely tell them thanks, but enough was enough. It also didn't hurt to know I had a hitman at my disposal to back me up. It had worked pretty well on Ethan.

Dimples nodded, thinking it might not be a good thing to get so much attention about my psychic abilities. Too bad I hadn't told them I'd seen the gun, instead of saying I had premonitions. Then he thought about Manetto and hoped I wasn't in trouble with him. He raised a brow. Was I?

I frowned. "I don't know what you mean."

"Uh-huh," he said, not believing me for a minute. "You'd tell me if he threatened you, right?" Dimples knew I worked for Uncle Joey. So far, Dimples hadn't been successful in getting me to turn on Uncle Joey, but he still held out hope that I'd come to him if I ever changed my mind. Needless to say, it was a sore spot between us.

"Did Billie tell you about her article?"

He knew I was changing the subject, but he let it go for now. "She said she had a good lead. Did she find out more?"

"Yes. It's really interesting." I explained her findings and asked, "Do you think someone can really be their own twin?"

"I guess it's possible. We'll see if that's what it really is when they're tested, but right now, Billie needs to finish up so we can get married."

"I just talked to her. I think she's resigned to completing the series once you get back from your honeymoon."

"Oh good." His shoulders relaxed. "I'm working until Thursday and taking Friday off because that's when most of the family is flying in." He licked his lips. "It's hard to believe we're getting married this week. I hope I'm ready." He was thinking how everything in his life was about to change.

"You'll definitely have to make some adjustments," I said. "But it will be worth it. Billie's great."

"Yeah, she is." Dimples knew she could be a handful, but he wouldn't have it any other way.

"Hey Harris," Detective Bates called. "You still coming with me?"

Dimples checked his watch, noting it was almost eleven, and stood. "Sorry I've got to go. We have to talk to an inmate out at the prison. Hey, do you want to come? It might make my job easier."

"Did you say it's almost eleven?" I jumped to my feet, grateful for an excuse not to go. "I've got an appointment." I took a few steps before turning to wave at him. "I'll get the flowers later. Have fun!"

"Yeah right."

I gave him a big smile and hurried to my car. Since John Brown's office was close to the city center mall, I drove there, parking underground, and took the escalator up to the plaza.

The Randolph Tower stood on the northeast corner of the property, and I made it inside the sliding doors right at eleven o'clock sharp. A few ladders and plastic tarps were hanging throughout the lobby. Men in white coveralls, with all kinds of tools dangling from their utility belts, worked behind them.

I took the elevator to the top floor, exiting to find more evidence of construction work. Panels of stacked sheetrock lined one side of the hallway, and several open offices held sheets of plastic to keep the dust from spreading.

I checked my phone for the office number, grateful to see it was on the other end of the building away from the workers. At the end of the hall, I spotted the door with the right number on it, but nothing else to say who it belonged to.

A chill of unease ran down my spine, and I slowed my step. What was going on? Looking at my phone, I checked the office number one more time. This was it, but there was no sign of people anywhere. Not even the construction workers. This whole floor was empty.

I stepped to the door and reached for the knob, only to find the door slightly ajar. It squeaked open with the pressure of my hand. I stood on the threshold and peered inside the room.

Amid the clutter of renovations, the open space was empty except for a desk that sat in the center of the room. A piece of paper lay on top, and I stepped closer to see what it said. Seeing the letters of my name at the top of the page, I immediately picked it up to read.

Shelby, I see you made it to my office. So sorry I couldn't be there. Now you've left me to wonder why you didn't already know that. I think someone with real premonitions would have known. I'm not sure what you're playing at, but I'm more intrigued than ever. In fact, I have a proposition for you. Please meet me at the food court in the plaza. I'll be sitting at an outside table reading a newspaper and enjoying the sunshine. I'll explain everything then. Yours, John Brown.

What the freak? Was this just an elaborate ruse to test me? I glanced around the room, hoping to spot anything that would tell me more about him. But, besides the desk, the place was completely empty.

A window faced the food court, so I stepped beside it and moved the plastic to take a look. From here, the people were too far away to see clearly, but I thought I could make out a man sitting at a table reading a newspaper. Was that him?

With growing trepidation, I carefully stuffed the note into my purse. If nothing else, at least it was evidence that he'd contacted me. But why was he playing this little game of cat and mouse? To answer that, I needed a face-to-face with him. I'd know immediately what he was up to, and what I needed to do to put an end to his shenanigans. Using determination to quiet my fear, I hurried out of the office to confront him.

After taking the elevator to the main floor, I made my way out of the building and to the food court. There were several tables spread around the plaza. I glanced toward the area I'd seen from the office above, looking for the table with a single male occupant reading a newspaper.

Finding it, I headed in that direction, keeping my mind wide open. The man sitting there held the newspaper in front of him, so I couldn't see his face. With his attention on the written words, I didn't have a chance to find out what he was thinking.

Dammit! Now what? Steeling my resolve, I walked toward the table, hoping he'd look up so I'd catch something in his mind. It wasn't until I reached his table and slid into the seat across from him that I caught his attention.

His surprised gaze found mine, and he immediately lowered his paper. "Hi," he said. "Do I know you?"

The voice was different from the one on the phone, and I picked up that he didn't have a clue who I was. My brows dipped together in confusion. "Uh... are you John Brown?"

He shook his head. "No."

Just then, a girl carrying a tray of food set it down in front of me. "Are you Shelby?" At my confused nod, she continued. "Great. Here's your order." She turned to leave, but I stopped her.

"Wait. I didn't order this."

"Oh, it's okay. Your boss was here earlier, and he ordered it for you."

"What did he say?"

She shrugged. "He said something about you never eating properly... and he wanted to surprise you with something good."

A chill ran down my spine, but I tried to smile at her. "Oh... uh... thanks."

She smiled. "Sure. Have a nice day."

I glanced at the man across from me. "I guess you didn't order this?"

He let out a huff, thinking that was a dumb question. "No. Didn't she say it was from your boss?"

"Yes... of course." What was going on? Why was I sitting across from this guy who had nothing to do with me? Was this some kind of joke? "How long have you been sitting here?"

He checked his watch. "About ten minutes."

"Did you notice anyone else sitting here at this table before you?"

"No," he said, a little exasperated that I kept interrupting him. Straightening in his chair, he continued, "If you're waiting for someone, I can move somewhere else."

"Oh... no. You're fine. I guess he left."

The man thought I was talking about my boss, so he cut me some slack. "Well... at least he ordered your lunch."

"That's right," I agreed, trying to sound normal. "But it wasn't my boss I was meeting, it was someone else." The tray held a delicious-looking turkey croissant sandwich with fries and a soda that said 'diet' on it. Besides the napkin, there wasn't a note, or anything else on the tray. "I wish he would have let me know."

"Maybe he had to leave in a hurry."

I nodded, but couldn't push away the feeling that this was another test of some kind.

"I'm Jerry, by the way. Jerry Mortensen." He held out his hand.

I shook it and responded. "Shelby Nichols."

"Nice to meet you," he said, smiling. Then his eyes widened, and he turned the paper back to the front page. His gaze went back and forth from me to the photo a few times. "That's you."

"Uh... yeah," I admitted.

"You're a bona-fide hero. So do you really have premonitions like it says?"

"It doesn't look that way. I mean, the person I was supposed to meet didn't show up, and I had no idea, right?"

He chuckled. "You make a good point." He wondered what was going on. For someone with premonitions, it didn't make sense. And why did I join him at this table? Did he look like the person I was supposed to meet? Or was this just a random encounter?

That caught my attention. Did John Brown set this all up for me to meet Jerry Mortensen? Why would he do that? This was starting to freak me out.

"Are you going to eat that?" he asked, eyeing my sandwich.

Even though the food looked amazing, I'd lost my appetite. "No. You can have it if you want. I think I'll take the Diet Coke though." I took the drink and pushed the tray toward him.

"You sure?"

I nodded. "Please, help yourself."

He picked up the sandwich and took a bite, happy to eat it, but feeling a twinge of guilt that it wasn't his. Maybe he should have tried to talk me into it a little harder, especially since my boss thought I never ate right.

"Do you come here often?" I asked.

He swallowed his bite and wiped his mouth with the napkin. "Yeah. I come out here most every day to read the paper. It's nice to be outside, and the courtyard is beautiful."

"Yeah, it is. Do you work around here?"

"Oh no. I'm retired." He smiled, flattered that I thought he looked young enough to still be working. "I bought into one of the new condos above the mall." He pointed to the building above us that held elegant, high-class apartment condos.

I'd always wondered what they looked like inside. "Nice. Do you like it?"

"I do. It's great to be living downtown. Everything I need is within walking distance. I don't have yard work or house maintenance to take care of, so I love it here."

I nodded, knowing this guy had nothing to do with me. John Brown had played me. He'd used the empty office, and then set me up to come here. But why? Was he watching me right now?

I opened my mind, hoping to pick up anything that would sound like the inner dialogue of someone watching me. With so many people around, it was like standing in a crowded room with everyone talking at the same time. Because of that, I had little hope of finding the one mind I needed.

My phone rang with an incoming call. It read "private number," just like the last time John Brown had called me. With rising unease, I answered. "Hello?"

"Shelby. I see you met my friend, Jerry. I'm disappointed that you let him eat your sandwich."

"I wasn't hungry." I glanced around, hoping I could spot him. "Where are you? Why are you doing this?"

He sighed. "Did I upset you?" When I didn't answer, he continued with a small chuckle. "I'm sorry. I hoped the sandwich would make up for it. I suppose I was wrong."

"No kidding. Look... I'm done playing this little game with you. Don't call me again."

"But what about Jerry?"

I glanced Jerry's way, then ducked my chin. "What about him?"

"He might die if you're not there to save him."

My breath caught, and the line went dead. What the freak? I glanced at Jerry, who'd been listening to my side of the conversation with rapt attention. He dipped the last of the French fries into his ketchup, caught me staring, and froze. "Did you want some?"

"No."

"Who was that anyway? It sounded like the guy you were supposed to meet. Is he coming?"

Sudden panic turned my stomach into knots. Jerry had just finished off the food meant for me. What if something was wrong with it? Is that what John meant? "Uh... yeah it was him, but he hung up on me."

"Is something wrong?" Jerry asked, noting the panic in my eyes.

I let out a breath. "Uh... no. At least, I hope not."

"Did he say something to upset you?"

"Yeah, kind of. I'm afraid it's given me an anxious feeling that maybe something isn't right."

Jerry's eyes widened with sudden understanding. "You mean like a premonition?"

"Yeah. Are you feeling okay?"

He swore in his mind, and his stomach suddenly curdled. He'd just eaten the food meant for me. "You think there's something wrong with the food? Was it poisoned?"

"Uh... probably not, but I don't know for sure. Just try not to panic. I'm sure it's nothing."

Terror clawed into Jerry's chest. What was going on? This was getting weird, and he didn't like it one bit. He slowly got to his feet, ready to get as far away from me as he could. "Uh... it was nice meeting you and all, but I gotta go."

Right at that moment, I heard someone shout, *Now*, in his mind.

Without waiting, I lunged at Jerry and managed to grab him around the waist. As we tumbled to the ground, a big crash sounded behind us. Half lying across Jerry, I rolled off him, shocked to find a huge clay pot had shattered across the table and chairs we'd just left. Dirt with flowers and shards of pottery had tipped Jerry's chair over, missing his feet by mere inches.

"What the hell?" Jerry said. "How did that get there?" He glanced my way as the realization hit him. "That could have killed me. How did you know?"

I blew out a breath and rubbed my arm where I'd scraped it on the concrete. "Are you all right?"

"Yeah. I think so." His shoulder hurt, but he could still move it. "Did you get a premonition? Is that how you knew?" The thought crossed his mind that this was all a set-up for my benefit. More free press for me by saving another person's life. It made him slightly ill.

I pursed my lips, not liking where his thoughts had taken him. Did it really look that way? "Uh... it was a premonition, but please don't tell anyone. Let's just say we were leaving when it happened, and we got out of the way in time. Okay?"

He nodded, but he wasn't sure he could do that. What if I was in on it? People should know.

"Please," I begged. "You'd be doing me a big favor."

"Okay, sure." Since I'd told him to lie, he didn't think I had anything to do with it, but how could it be a coincidence? There had to be more to it.

"Thanks."

By now, several people had gathered around us, most of them looking up at the building to see where the planter had come from.

"Are you okay?" A woman asked, coming to my side. "That thing almost killed you both. What idiot would have a planter that big on his windowsill?"

I got to my feet and looked up at the high rise apartments above the retail businesses. From here, I could see an open window in the apartment directly above the table. And there was no windowsill involved.

I thanked my lucky stars I'd heard him in time. That sick bastard. He'd set me up. This whole thing was part of some diabolical plan. My legs began to shake, and anger burned in my chest. I wanted to go after him, but only people with keys could get inside the apartment building.

That meant Jerry could get in. I grabbed his arm. "Do you know who lives in that apartment?"

His startled gaze found mine. "No, but I could get us inside, and we could find out."

Before we could head that way, two men with mall security arrived. We couldn't get out of talking to them, and I clenched my teeth in frustration. Of course, John Brown was probably long gone, but that didn't mean he hadn't left another calling card.

One of the guards began to ask questions, while the other gathered bystanders who'd witnessed the event for their statements. Since Jerry and I were the obvious targets, we were first on the list. After assuring him that we were okay, I gave him my version before Jerry could say anything. "We were just walking away when it fell. I can't believe we almost got hit."

By now Jerry was on my side and nodded his agreement. I thanked him with an encouraging nod and a smile. Just then, the police arrived and took over. We had to give our version of the events again, and I tapped my foot with impatience. Before we were done, one of the officers had asked the security guard to take him up to the apartment.

"It looks like we're too late," I said to Jerry.

"It's probably for the best," he said, thinking it wasn't a good idea to go chasing after an attempted murderer.

I couldn't agree with him, and let out a frustrated breath. "Maybe if we wait around, we'll find out who was up there."

The other police officer was still taking statements, and the crowd had grown. Word spread of an accident in the food court, bringing out plenty of curious shoppers. From the crowd, I caught sight of a newcomer and groaned. It was Henry, the same reporter who'd written the article about me for the paper. Damn.

I took Jerry's arm and pulled him away. "I've got to go. There's a news reporter here. Whatever you do, please don't tell him my name, okay?"

Jerry nodded, but concern tightened his brow. "Are you in some kind of trouble?"

"Uh... I don't know. I hope not. But don't worry. I'll get to the bottom of it."

"I hope so." He didn't say that just for my sake. He realized he could have been collateral damage to whatever was going on, and he didn't want anyone else to get hurt.

"Can I get your number so I can call you later? Since you live there, you'll have the inside scoop."

"Sure." He pulled his wallet from his pocket, took out a business card, and handed it to me. "I'm retired, but the number is the same."

"Thanks Jerry. Try not to worry too much." I tilted my lips up in what I hoped was an encouraging smile. "I have premonitions, remember? I'll do my best to make sure no one gets hurt."

That brought a quivering smile to his lips, and I quickly walked away. As I headed to my car, dread spread through my chest like a disease. Sure I'd put on a brave face for Jerry, but knowing someone was out there to set me up scared me to death.

CHAPTER 5

I sat in my car trying to decide what to do. I wanted to go to Chris's office, but who knew whether I'd be able to talk to him. It made more sense to go straight to Dimples. He had all the resources of the police department. But he was probably still at the prison and, right now, I didn't want to involve anyone else on the police force.

So it had to be Uncle Joey. I knew he'd move heaven and earth to help me, and I'd be a fool not to ask. He had resources too, and I could still go to the precinct once I knew what to look for. But I wasn't sure where to start. I needed a plan.

What could I do to find this guy? He'd called me, but the number was blocked. I still had his note, but I didn't have much hope that it would help me find him. He'd set up an elaborate trap to test me. Since I didn't really have premonitions, I'd mostly failed. What did that tell him about me, and how would he use it next time?

I shivered. He wasn't done with me yet. He could even be watching me right now. I glanced out the windshield, noting a few people heading to their cars. As long as he stayed behind closed doors, he could be anywhere, and I wouldn't know.

Was this a joke to him? What motivated someone to do something like this? Was he trying to prove me wrong? Or was he trying to prove me right? Why did he even care? One thing was certain; he was flexible and had money, so he probably wasn't tied down to a regular job.

He'd set up the phony company in the office, so he knew something about the building. He'd also gained access to the apartments above the mall. So he either had a friend who lived there, lived there himself, or had stolen an access card.

But that would have taken a lot of planning for someone who'd just found out about me yesterday. Could he be someone who'd heard about me before now, and yesterday's incident had spurred him into action?

What kind of a person did that?

My phone rang, startling me, and I checked the number. It was blocked, just like before. Letting out a breath to steel my nerves, I answered. "Yes?"

"Shelby," he said. "That was close. For a moment, I was afraid you wouldn't come through."

"What do you want?"

"There's no need to be upset."

"Are you freaking kidding me? You almost killed Jerry. That's not cool. You need to stop this nonsense at once, before someone gets hurt."

He inhaled sharply, then huffed out a breath.

Oops, had I just made things worse? Maybe I should appeal to his ego instead. Sweat popped out on my brow. Talking to a nut job like him was way out of my league. What if I made it worse and he killed someone to spite me?

"Hey," I said, in a more friendly tone. "I thought you wanted to hire me for a job. If you still want to do that, I think we should meet."

"Oh, I look forward to meeting you. I have to go, but I'll be in touch. And just in case you decide not to answer my phone calls, just remember that someone might die if you don't. It could even be during a wedding. You wouldn't want that, would you? I'll call you soon." Before I could say a word, the line went dead.

I clenched my teeth and let out a strangled groan. He knew about Dimples's wedding? Holy hell! Why was he doing this to me? I wanted to throw my phone out the window and bang my head against the steering wheel.

Instead, I took a deep breath and counted to ten. Right now, I needed to get out of here. He wasn't going to get the best of me. I could deal with this.

I pulled out of the parking garage and headed straight to Thrasher Development. Calmness settled over me just knowing that Uncle Joey had my back. This crazy person had no idea who he was dealing with. I had some things on my side that he didn't, namely, a mob boss and a hitman. It didn't get any scarier than that.

Pulling into the parking garage, I got out of my car with my shoulders back and my step confident. Inside the elevator, I pushed the button for the twenty-sixth floor, marveling at how just doing that lowered my anxiety. Stepping through the doors into Thrasher Development even brought a smile to my lips.

Jackie sat at her desk and greeted me warmly. "Hey Shelby. How's it going?"

I opened my mouth to answer, but the warmth in my chest turned to ice. There, on the corner of her desk, sat a beautiful bouquet of flowers.

Jackie noticed my gaze and smiled. "Aren't they lovely? They're for you. They just came a little while ago. I'm dying to know who sent them."

Holy Hell! Not here too. And why did she have to say dying? It suddenly clicked that this was all part of John Brown's plan to freak me out. He'd sent the flowers to my house, to the police station, and here as part of his little game to get under my skin.

Dammit! It was working.

It also meant that he knew where I lived, and he knew I had ties to both the police and Uncle Joey. My hope that he'd run away scared because of my ties to a mob boss shriveled right out of existence. If I went to Chris's office, would I find another floral arrangement there? Dread tied my stomach in knots and sent my heart racing.

"There's a card," Jackie continued. "Why don't you open it?"

I moved to the flowers on leaden feet and plucked the envelope from them. Just like the others, I read my name, before pulling the tiny card out.

"What does it say?"

I licked my lips and swallowed before I managed to get the words out of my mouth. "It says, *To Shelby, You are a true hero. From, Your Secret Admirer.*'"

"Oh how sweet. Maybe it's from someone you saved yesterday and they want to remain anonymous."

"Yeah, maybe so," I agreed, barely holding it together. "Is Uncle Joey here?"

"Sure, he's in his office. Go on down."

I let out a relieved breath, not realizing until that moment how much I counted on him to help me out. "Thank you."

"Shelby, are you all right? You seem a little shaken."

"Oh... well, to be honest, I guess all the attention is a bit overwhelming. But I'm sure in a day or two it will die down." I cringed at my stupid choice of words.

"Yeah, that's true." She wasn't convinced that I was telling the truth, but she didn't want to pry.

I sent her a smile. Then, since she thought it looked strained, I let it drop and turned down the hall to Uncle Joey's office. At his door, I knocked before turning the knob and stuck my head inside. Uncle Joey sat behind his desk, and Ramos sat in a chair in front of the desk. Just the sight of them calmed my trembling nerves.

"Shelby," Uncle Joey said, surprised to see me. "Come on in. Ramos and I were just discussing his visit with Ethan last night."

"Oh, right." For some reason, I'd totally forgotten all about that. "I saw him this morning, and he told me he would take care of the problem, so I guess your visit worked."

I slid into the other chair in front of Uncle Joey's desk and closed my eyes. As the tension drained from me, I picked up that both Uncle Joey and Ramos wondered what was going on. I should be happy Ethan was cooperating.

"Has something happened?" Uncle Joey asked.

"Yes." I wasn't sure where to start. I knew he wouldn't like any of it, but I also hoped he'd know what to do, because I had no idea. "I think I have a crazy stalker after me."

Surprise rippled through them both. "What? How do you know?" Uncle Joey asked.

"Well, first of all, he started sending me flowers. That bouquet out there is the third one I've gotten. The first one came to my house yesterday afternoon, then another was sent to the police station this morning, and now there's one here."

"Oh, yeah," Uncle Joey said. "It came about half an hour ago."

Just hearing that sent little shivers down my spine. Half an hour ago, I was nearly killed by a potted plant. He must have been pretty sure I'd survive.

"What else?" Uncle Joey asked.

"After the news broke yesterday about the shooting, I got a phone call from a man who said his name was John Brown. He had a British accent, but I'm pretty sure it's fake. In fact, in his last phone call, I hardly heard it at all." That had to be a clue, right? If he was trying to sound different, maybe he was someone I'd met before.

"Go on," Uncle Joey said, snapping me from my thoughts.

"Uh... he wanted to hire me, and we set up an appointment to meet in his office at eleven today. But when I went to his office, all I found was a note telling me he wasn't there. It said that if I had real premonitions, I would have known that."

I pulled the note from my purse. "Here it is." I set it on Uncle Joey's desk where they could read it. After I heard a few curse words in their minds, I continued, "That's when it got weird."

I explained what had happened next, and went into detail about meeting Jerry, the food, hearing the 'now' thought, and barely getting out of the way of a potted plant. "Then he called me again just before I came over here."

"What did he say?" Ramos asked, his tone edged with anger.

"Well, he was kind of gloating, and I told him to knock it off before someone got hurt. I don't think he liked that much, so I changed tactics and told him we should meet up."

Uncle Joey's brows rose, so I continued. "I need to meet him in person so I'll know exactly what he's thinking."

Uncle Joey heaved a resigned sigh, knowing I was probably right, no matter how much he didn't like it. "What did he say then?"

This was the part that creeped me out. Unable to sit still, I jumped to my feet and began to pace. "He said he was looking forward to it, and I'd better make sure to answer my phone when he called or someone might die. He even spoke about something bad happening at a wedding."

I caught Uncle Joey's gaze, barely keeping my panic at bay. "That means he knows about Dimples's wedding this weekend. Even if I don't go, or answer my phone, he threatened that someone might die because I wouldn't be there to save them. I hate this! I need to find this nutcase before anything else happens."

"You're right," Uncle Joey agreed. "From what you've said, he knows too much about you for my comfort. And sending flowers here to my office shows a certain disregard for me." He was thinking the guy had balls, but he'd learn soon enough that he was messing with the wrong man.

Ramos glanced my way. "You said he's called your cell phone, maybe we can find him through his phone number."

"It's always been blocked," I answered.

"Then how about the florist? They should have a record of who bought the flowers, especially since he had it delivered."

"Yeah... unless he paid cash."

Ramos raised his brow at my negativity, but he understood. "We should check it out just to make sure."

"You're right," I agreed. "The one at the police station was from Brown Floral. Since he said his name was John Brown, maybe he owns the shop. Could it be that simple? I know I'd recognize his voice if I ever met him."

Ramos didn't have much hope that he'd give himself away so easily. "He could have used that florist shop just because of the name. Or he could have chosen his name based on the florist shop to give you a clue. This sounds like a game he's playing."

"Either way," Uncle Joey said. "It looks like your idea of meeting him has the best chance for putting an end to it... and him... if need be."

My eyes widened. He'd said that out loud, so I knew he was serious. Instead of telling Uncle Joey that killing him was wrong, I nodded my head in agreement. A sudden stab of guilt hit me in the chest. What did that say about me? How could I be okay with murder? "Uh... yeah... but let's see what we find out first."

Uncle Joey smiled. He'd been a little surprised at how quickly I'd agreed, but from my remark, his faith in me was restored. It just went to show how upset this fellow had made me, and it angered him enough that he wouldn't have any qualms about ending the man's sorry life, no matter how I felt.

His gaze caught mine, knowing I'd heard that as well, but he wasn't going to apologize or assure me it wouldn't happen. It was different for him, and I needed to remember that.

Ramos was thinking about the other parts of my story that could give us some clues. "I think we should visit the office he sent you to. Why did he pick that place? He'd need some kind of connection to the building, don't you think?"

"Yeah," I agreed. "There was some construction going on. Maybe he's a member of the construction crew or something."

"We can ask around. Too bad you don't know what he looks like."

"The girl who brought my lunch to me at the food court must have seen him. Maybe we can get a description from her."

"Good thinking, Shelby," Uncle Joey said. "What about the man you met at the food court? Did you say he lives in the apartments?"

"Yes. I got his number. I'm sure he'll let us inside and we can take a look at the apartment the plant came from. At the very least, we can find out who lives in that apartment."

Uncle Joey caught my gaze, thinking things weren't as bleak as I'd thought. "Good. Why don't the two of you get started, and I'll see what I can find out about the office building. The Randolph Tower, right?"

I nodded, suddenly overcome with gratitude. "Thanks Uncle Joey." It came out as a strangled whisper, and I cleared my throat in an effort to gain control of my emotions.

Uncle Joey came around his desk and pulled me into a fatherly hug. "We'll find him." He was thinking that I was part of the family, and I didn't need to thank him. Under that, I picked up a coil of hot anger that this man had threatened me, and he wasn't about to let him get away with it. That calmed me more than anything else I'd heard, and I pulled away, giving him a tremulous smile.

Uncle Joey turned his gaze to Ramos, sending him an unspoken command to keep me safe. "Let me know what you find."

Relieved to have a plan, I opened the office door and stepped into the hallway. Ramos followed me out, and we stopped at Jackie's desk to look at the flowers. Sure enough, they were from Brown Floral, just like the others. Taking the card, I slipped it into my pocket and turned to leave.

"We'll be back," Ramos told Jackie. She knew something was up, but nodded respectfully, knowing she could find out all the details from Uncle Joey after we'd left.

We rode the elevator to the garage in silence. Ramos sensed that my nerves were strained, and he knew better than to offer sympathy for my predicament. What I needed right now was a show of strength, and he was happy to provide that. None of that sissy, sentimental stuff from him. He had my back, and this guy didn't stand a chance.

A smile curved my lips, pushing the stress away. We stepped out of the elevator and turned toward the corner where he parked his bike. "You look like you need a ride."

"You know it." I grinned. "Let me grab my jacket."

With more enthusiasm than I'd had all day, I snatched my jacket from the trunk of my car and slipped it on. Joining him, I asked, "So where should we go first?"

"The florist shop." He held his hand out for the card. I handed it over, and he noted the address. "The shop isn't far. After that we'll head to the office building, and then Jerry's condo."

"Sounds good." I slipped on my helmet and straddled the bike behind him like a pro. Since this was about the only time I got to hold onto Ramos, I took advantage of the moment and wrapped my arms firmly around him.

I felt his stomach muscles tighten and let out a contented sigh. He was thinking that I was holding onto him pretty tight—but he wasn't about to complain. That brought a smile to my lips, and the surge of power as we roared up the ramp sent butterflies through my stomach.

At the florist shop, I told the worker I was a consultant for the police to gain her cooperation. I even showed her my ID badge to prove it. "We received some flowers at the precinct from an anonymous source this morning, and I need to know who sent them. The card was addressed to

Shelby Nichols. Flowers were also sent to her home yesterday afternoon and to another office today."

Since nothing this interesting had ever happened in the shop before, the woman was more than willing to help us out. "And you don't have a name?"

"They weren't signed, but from what we know so far, the name John Brown might work."

"Okay. Let me look." She toggled the computer to search the orders from yesterday. "Oh... here it is. John Brown. He ordered all three yesterday to be delivered at different times. All to Shelby Nichols." She clicked on the purchase order. "It looks like he paid cash, and there's no address below his name. I'm afraid that's all I've got."

"Did you take the order?"

She shook her head. "No. I wasn't here." She glanced at the work schedule. "According to this, Alyssa took the order. She's a high school student who only works here a couple of days a week."

"When will she be here next?"

"Looks like Saturday."

"Okay. Thanks for your help."

I left the shop a little deflated. "Guess that was a dead end." Before Ramos could respond, my phone rang, and alarm tightened my chest. I pulled it from my purse, finding a number I didn't recognize on the caller ID, which meant it wasn't from John Brown. I let out a sigh. "It's not him," I told Ramos, then answered the call. "Hello?"

"Is this Shelby Nichols?" a woman asked.

"Uh... yes."

"My name is Stacey Sherwood. I'm the producer of Good Morning America. The reason I'm calling is because we heard all about your heroic actions yesterday. Stopping a mass shooting is big news. Let me tell you, the interest for this story is off the charts. People want to know the real

Shelby Nichols, and we'd love to have you appear as a guest on our show. Could we schedule you for an interview in the next few days? All expenses paid, of course."

"Uh... uh... I don't know." What the freak! How was this happening? Good Morning America? No way.

"I understand, but you would be doing the American people a service by appearing on our show. We need some good news, and your heroics are worth celebrating."

Since I was basically tongue-tied, all that came out of my mouth were a few unintelligible mutterings, so she quickly continued. "We pride ourselves on bringing heartwarming stories and the people behind them to our show, because everyone needs to know that there are great news stories worth talking about. Yours is definitely one that the people need to hear. In this day of mass shootings, I hope you can understand how necessary it is to know that at least one of them was thwarted."

She paused, waiting for my response. In the silence, I took a breath and began. "Well... I'm really busy right now. Thank you for asking, but I'm going to have to decline. Uh... but thanks anyway."

"Wait," she said, disbelief in her voice. "I'll give you some time to think about it. All right? I'll call you back in a day or two. Maybe you won't be so busy then."

"Um... well... okay."

"Great. We'll talk soon." The line went dead. I glanced at Ramos with widened eyes. "That was Good Morning America. They want to interview me on their show."

Comprehension glittered in his gaze, and he swore a blue-streak in his mind. "Holy hell." He said that out loud. It blew his mind that I was getting so much attention. "You're not going to do it are you?"

"No way," I said. "I tried to tell her that, but she wouldn't let me. I don't think she expected me to turn her down."

"Yeah. I'd bet money that you're the first person who has ever said no." He shook his head. How did these things happen to me?

"Well, at least the next time she calls, I'll be better prepared, and she won't catch me by surprise."

Ramos nodded, hoping I could withstand the fame and glory coming my way. With the amount of trouble I got in, it could be tempting to have a spot in the limelight to balance it out.

"I'm not tempted. Not even close." Even as I said the words, I had to admit that I'd already thought about what clothes I'd wear, and how cool it would be to sit on the set in Times Square. Would I wear my leather motorcycle jacket and my black boots, or something more conservative?

"You ready to go?" Ramos asked, yanking me out of my reverie. His raised brow confirmed that he'd guessed right that it would tempt me, and a small smile tugged at his lips.

I huffed and nodded, pushing that dream out of my mind. Because I'd been in the local news, a stalker was now putting people's lives in danger. Who knew what could happen if my name and what I did went nationwide. It could be catastrophic.

We mounted the bike and, a few minutes later, we entered the Randolph Building. A couple of workers stood in the lobby, and Ramos asked them about the construction. One of them explained that they were remodeling the lobby and a couple of empty floors.

"We'll be done in a month. I don't know if the owner has leased those floors out yet, but you can give him a call if you're interested."

Ramos got the name of the construction company. After thanking him, we took the elevator to the seventeenth floor. Nothing had changed since I'd been there earlier, but at least it wasn't as creepy with Ramos by my side.

I'd left the door wide open, and it was still that way, so it looked like no one else had been there. Ramos stepped inside, looking for things that I might have missed, like a security camera, or a wastebasket with a discarded receipt that might hold a clue.

I snapped my gaze toward the ceiling and let out a relieved breath to find nothing of the sort. Thank goodness. It gave me the creeps to think of John Brown watching me like that.

Ramos stepped behind the desk and pulled it open, finding the drawers empty and no sign of a wastebasket. "There's nothing here."

That didn't surprise me, but I couldn't help the disappointment rolling over my shoulders. "Well, at least Jerry isn't far. I'll give him a call and see if we can meet up."

After a few rings, he answered, happy to hear from me, and more than willing to show me the building. "I found out which condo it was, so I can show you where it happened."

"Great. I'm close by. Can I come now?"

"Sure. I'll meet you outside." He disconnected before I could ask about bringing a friend. Hopefully, he wouldn't mind too much.

He waited by the table where we'd nearly been killed, waving to me as I approached. As he realized that the big guy following me was my companion, a wave of unease washed over him. It was the scowl on Ramos's face that did it. Hoping to quell Jerry's alarm, I introduced Ramos as a good friend. The quick nod Ramos gave him only heightened Jerry's fear, and I worried that he wouldn't let us in the building.

"Is this where it happened?" Ramos asked, glancing up at the windows.

"Yes," Jerry answered. "The top window right above us."

Ramos nodded, but didn't say another word, so I spoke instead. "Shall we go inside?" I knew Jerry had news he was dying to tell me, but he hesitated because of Ramos. I took his arm and smiled. "I can tell you know something, and I can't wait to hear what you've found out."

He glanced at me, and his face cleared. I'd saved his life, so I had to be one of the good guys, even if I'd brought someone who looked like a killer with me. Maybe I'd hired a bodyguard? If that was the case, he could understand. "You're right. Come with me."

He led us inside the door, then used his key card and a pin number to gain access to the building. "I'm on the third floor, but the apartment where the pot was dropped is on the eighth floor. We'll go there first."

We boarded the elevator, and he told us that the apartment's occupant was out of town. "I found out that the owner of the condo doesn't live there. He just uses it when he comes to town for business."

"How often is that?" I asked.

"I don't know. All I know is that he's not there now." We exited the elevator and turned down the hallway toward the door. "The police went inside, but I don't know if they found anything. They didn't stay long, so I don't think there was much to go on."

At the door, Ramos took out his lock pics. Jerry's brows rose with alarm, but he kept his mouth shut. This might be illegal as hell, but it was the most excitement he'd had in years. Plus the owner was gone, so maybe it wasn't so bad.

Ramos held the door open before Jerry could blink. We hurried inside, all of us heading straight for the window. Ramos unlocked the clasp and pulled the window open, taking note of the railing around it.

If the clay pot was as big as I'd believed, getting it up and over the railing would take some muscle, but it was possible. Ramos examined the carpet, noting a round indentation that looked exactly like a clay pot. That meant it was already here, and not brought in by the stalker. It also meant that the stalker knew the occupant, or actually lived here. He could have told everyone he was out of town, even if he wasn't.

I turned to Jerry. "Do you know the name of the guy who lives here?"

"No," he said. "Why?"

"It could be him." I caught that Jerry didn't think that was possible, so I continued. "Or someone who knows he was gone, and knew about the plant. Could it be one of his neighbors?"

"Maybe," he said. "From my experience, most people tend to let their neighbors know when they're not around."

After examining the rest of the condo, Ramos joined us, thinking that, if there was a clue, the police had most likely taken it. He'd heard our exchange and spoke. "Let's talk with the neighbors."

He also thought that one of them could be our mysterious John Brown, although he highly doubted it would be that easy. Still, it was worth a shot to ask. Even if the neighbor didn't admit it, I'd know it was him with my mind reading skills.

Leaving the condo, we locked the door behind us, and I rang the bell at the apartment next door. No one answered, and Ramos brought out his lock picks again, but I stopped him. "Let's see if the other neighbor is home first."

Ramos shrugged and went along with me, even though he didn't see a problem breaking in. I rang the bell at the other door, and an older lady opened it up. Not recognizing us, her brows drew together. "Who are you?"

"Hi, I'm Shelby Nichols. We're just wondering if you've talked to your neighbor recently."

"Are you with the police? I already told them everything."

"Yes. I'm a consultant with the police," I answered, holding up my ID badge. "I'm just following up. What is your neighbor's name?"

"Tim Kitley. He's been gone since Sunday, and he won't be back for a couple of weeks. I think he lives in Chicago, but he's here a lot on business." She was thinking he was a successful salesman, but she couldn't remember what it was he sold. Was it pharmaceuticals? No... it had something to do with dental equipment... yeah... that was it.

"Oh, I see. What about the neighbor on the other side? Do you know who lives there?"

"Sure. That's Stella Chapman's place. She and her boyfriend live there. But they both work. If you want to talk to them, you'll have to come back later."

"Okay. Well, thanks so much for your time." I gave her a little wave and stepped away from the door. After she closed it, I turned to Ramos. "My stalker's not Tim Kitley."

Jerry didn't think that was too hard to figure out, even for someone without premonitions. He wasn't even here at the time. "It's got to be someone who knows him though, otherwise how did they get into his apartment?" Then his eyes widened, and he realized whoever pushed the pot out the window could have entered the apartment the same way we had.

"And," he added. "It's possible that he lives in the building. Why don't I snoop around a bit and see if I can meet the people who live on this floor. I might even be able to get some names. I'll let you know if anyone seems suspicious."

"Okay," I agreed. "That would be great."

"Sure." Jerry smiled, happy to help.

Ramos glanced my way, thinking he wanted to break into the other neighbor's apartment for a quick look around. It could be the neighbor's boyfriend, right?

I wasn't so sure that was a good idea. "Let's wait and see what Jerry comes up with."

"Huh?" Jerry asked. "What are you talking about?"

Oops. "Oh, I was just thinking out loud... you know... about taking a look in the other apartment? But it might be better to give you a chance to find out more about them first."

"Yeah," Jerry agreed. "I don't want to get in trouble."

I nodded. "Exactly. But you'll call me, right?"

"Of course." We boarded the elevator, and Jerry got off on the third floor, promising to let me know if he found anything.

Once the elevator doors shut, Ramos shook his head. "Good save." He thought I probably messed up more often than I was willing to admit.

I huffed out a breath. "Most of the time, I'm fine. It's just that I've gotten into the habit of answering your thoughts, so this time it was your fault."

He chuckled, knowing I was only half serious. He stifled the impulse to reach over and massage my tense shoulders, but... he didn't want to cross the line. Who knew where that could lead?

I knew he was teasing me, but before I could form a response, the elevator doors opened. Dang! I would have loved a shoulder massage. "Uh... I might take you up on that sometime. But... not more than that, of course."

He smirked. "Right."

I pulled my gaze away from his sensual lips and stepped out of the elevator, shaking my head to clear it. "There is one more person we need to talk to."

"Who's that?"

"The worker who brought me my lunch."

"Right," Ramos agreed. "Let's find her."

With so many eateries, it took circling the food court a few times before I found the right one. Would she still be there? As I spotted her, hope leapt in my heart. She'd slipped a purse over her shoulder and was just leaving the eatery.

I waved to get her attention and she stopped, her brows twisting in confusion. I rushed to her side and quickly explained who I was. "Oh right," she said. "You're the one who nearly got killed by the potted plant."

"Yeah, that's me. Hey... I know this sounds funny, but I need to know what the man who ordered my food looked like. Do you remember him at all?"

Her brows lifted. Wasn't it my boss who'd ordered the food? Why would I want to know what he looked like?

"It wasn't my boss. I've never met the guy. He lied to you. That's why I want to know what he looks like."

"Oh. Okay. Let me think." She'd taken so many orders that it was hard to remember one face. They all blended together in her mind. "I don't know for sure. I don't think he was wearing a suit, you know? Um... and maybe he had brown hair and eyes?"

As she tried to recall each face, they all came out a little blurry in her mind, so even my mind reading skills didn't help much. Discouraged, I let out a breath. "That's okay. Thanks anyway. Here's my card. If you remember anything about him, please call me."

"Sure." She took my card, glanced at my name, and stashed it in her purse, convinced she'd never call me. Unless someone stood out, she never remembered them.

Glancing behind me, she caught sight of Ramos and forgot all about me. She swallowed, trying her best not to stare, but she'd never seen a real live man who looked like someone from her wildest dreams before.

His chiseled features, along with his dark hair and smoky eyes, held her captive. Her gaze took in his exquisitely toned body, sending her pulse racing. He was perfection. No way could she stop staring at *that*. It simply wasn't possible.

Ramos finally noticed her stare, and a slow smile curved his lips. Her breath caught, and I thought for sure she was going to faint... or drool. I picked up that she wanted to touch him, just to make sure she wasn't dreaming. Before she could do any of those things, I thanked her again and took Ramos by the arm to pull him away.

He held back a satisfied smirk, thinking that he always enjoyed having that effect on unsuspecting females. It kind of made his day.

"Oh, please," I said. "You just happened to catch her at a vulnerable moment."

"What do you mean by that?" he asked.

I shrugged, not sure how to answer. How did I tell him that it wasn't every day a woman got to look at a man like him? "She's young and impressionable, that's all. It's like seeing a movie star in real life. The shock makes your brain freeze, and you can't help staring at such perfection."

"Oh," he said, smiling and lifting his brows. "So I'm perfection, huh?"

"No. I didn't say that."

He snickered, thinking that was exactly what I'd said, and no amount of denying it was going to change his mind. Perfection... he liked that. Before I could smack him, he turned that sexy smile on me and chuckled.

How could I be mad now? It was nice to hear a little laughter after the day I'd had. Plus, he'd learned not to take his good looks too seriously, so I couldn't hold that against him. "So what now?" I asked. "We got nothing."

He didn't think that was entirely true. We knew my stalker had a connection to the office building and the condo. We had Jerry and Manetto looking into things, and Ramos had other resources he could tap into.

"But what about the wedding? Do you think he'll try something there?"

"When is it?"

"Not until Saturday."

"I guess it's a possibility, but with all the cops and reporters sure to be there, I'm not certain he'd try anything. Maybe he just said that to upset you. He's playing a mind game with you. He wants to make you sweat."

"Well... I'm sorry to admit that it's working."

Ramos nodded. "It seems like he's got a grudge against you."

"Probably because I told everyone I had premonitions. It's as though he's testing me to prove that I'm a fake, and he wants to expose me to the world."

"I'm sure that's part of it. But why would he do that? It seems more personal. Are you sure his voice didn't sound familiar?"

"Not really," I said. "But he did try to cover it at first with a British accent. The last time we spoke, the accent was hardly noticeable."

"Maybe you should start looking at some of your old cases and see what you can come up with."

I glanced at him with widened eyes. "That's a brilliant idea."

He smiled and handed me my helmet. "Good, but for now... I think you need a distraction. Want to go for a ride?"

I grinned up at him. "You know it!"

CHAPTER 6

I arrived home in a happy mood until I noticed the bouquet of flowers sitting on my kitchen table. All the helpless rage I'd suppressed came flooding back, sending my blood pressure to a new high. Not wanting the flowers anywhere near me, I picked them up and carried them to the garbage can outside.

Admiring their bright colors, I hesitated, knowing it wasn't reasonable to take my anger out on a bunch of flowers. They were beautiful but, as another wave of frustration over-rode my sensibilities, I threw them in, relishing the sweet moment of victory over my enemy.

Just like that, I vowed that he was going down. I wasn't going to let him upset me, and he'd be sorry he ever tangled with me in the first place.

Back inside the house, I let out a relieved sigh. Without the flowers, I could forget about him for the moment. Concentrating on the many demands of my family, I pushed him and his threats to the back of my mind.

Savannah came into the kitchen and greeted me with a smile. "Hey mom," she said. "How was your day? Did you see the paper? That picture of you looks so awesome. I think we should cut it out and laminate it. I even called Madi and Ash and told them to save a copy for us."

"Oh, good thinking. Thanks honey." I smiled at her enthusiasm, picking up that she was proud of me, and I was the coolest mom ever. My heart swelled with love for her, and I pulled her into a quick hug.

"So," she began. "When are we going to go swimming at the country club? Josh said we could come any time."

"That's right," I agreed. "After the last couple of days I've had, I wouldn't mind spending some time relaxing at the pool. Maybe we can go on Friday?"

"Sure," she said, a little disappointed that we couldn't go sooner, but she still had New York to look forward to. "It's hard to believe that Miguel's opening night as Aladdin is next month and we're going. I can't wait!"

I smiled at her enthusiasm, picking up that it had seemed like ages since she'd seen him last, and she was more than ready to see him again.

Good grief. It hadn't been that long. Wasn't it just a few weeks ago that we'd been over to Uncle Joey's house for a graduation barbeque?

Now with Miguel settled in New York, it meant the time was soon coming when I'd have to introduce my husband and kids to the New York Manettos. Because of a lie Uncle Joey insisted I tell them, they erroneously thought we were related. I even had a mother that I'd just met for the first time.

Of course, his sister, and my supposed mother, Maggie, knew better, and I'd had to tell her the whole story. It had been a relief to tell her the truth, and I looked forward to seeing her again. But now my kids had to go along with the lie and call her grandma, even though she wasn't. I knew asking them to do that wasn't right, but what was I supposed to do?

"Mom? Did you hear what I said?"

Oops. I'd done it again. My kids were going to think I was getting old if I kept zoning out like this. I listened real close to her thoughts and picked up one word. "Dog? What about a dog?"

"The dog we're going to get." She pursed her lips, thinking I wasn't listening, even if I said I was. "I was saying that we'll have to wait until we get back from New York to get a dog."

"Oh, right. Good thinking." I'd recently helped a man who'd been arrested for murder. We'd kept his dog for him, and my kids had fallen in love with her. I'd basically promised them we'd get a dog after he took her back. Savannah could hardly wait, but I'd put it off. Now I realized that having an affectionate animal might do wonders for my stress levels. Plus, it would make my kids happy.

"Okay. We'll get a dog when we get back."

"Saweet!" Savannah said, pumping her fist in the air.

I spent the next hour looking through my casefiles for someone from my past that might hold a grudge against me. That's when I found out my file keeping was lousy. Sure I kept purchase orders for clients, but not a lot of information about the individual people. I had to rely on my memory for that. Some were easy to remember, but others drew a blank. Still, I only had about a year's worth to look through, and nothing stood out. Discouraged, I put everything away to fix dinner.

After Chris came home, I held him for several seconds longer than normal. As I pulled away, he glanced at me with raised brows, worried that something wasn't right. Not wanting to talk about it, I smiled. "We'll talk about it later. Okay?"

"Sure," he agreed. But he was thinking, *oh great, now what?* Did he really have to wait to hear about it? I shrugged, and alarm tightened his chest. "Is it about Ethan?"

"No. In fact, Ethan's had a change of heart, and he's not going through with whatever it was he had planned."

"Oh. That's good news. I wonder what changed his mind."

I glanced at him and winced. "Uh... you can thank Ramos for that. I guess he showed up in the middle of the night next to Ethan's bed and woke him up. He must have convinced Ethan to change his plans. Since I don't know exactly what his plans were, I'm not sure how he's going to do that, but for now, I'm happy to let him handle it."

Chris wasn't sure Ethan warranted the 'big bad wolf' treatment, but he couldn't deny the relief that filled him to know it was taken care of. "Well, okay. Good. So what else is going on? Are you really not going to tell me?"

"Oh fine," I said, letting out a dramatic sigh. "Let's talk out on the deck."

He let me pull him through the kitchen and out the sliding doors to the deck. I plopped down on the deck swing and lolled my head against the cushion.

Chris sat beside me, trying not to smile. So much drama. It was like my life was over or something. What could be so bad? Maybe this was about the case Ethan had taken, and I was disappointed that it wasn't going so well. Or maybe it was about the wedding, and Billie was having second thoughts. Whatever it was, it couldn't be worse than anything else I'd ever been through.

If only that were true. "Are you done?" I asked.

"Hey," he said, a little hurt. "I'm just waiting for you to explain."

He was right. I needed to stop feeling sorry for myself and figure this out. "There's someone stalking me."

Chris froze, that was not what he'd expected. "What?"

"It's true. He almost killed me today." Maybe that was a tiny exaggeration, but it could have happened.

"What the hell. What happened?" He sat up. His eyes filled with worry and anger.

I filled him in, starting with my appointment with John Brown and covering everything that had happened until I got home. I ended with Ramos's idea that it might be an old client of mine. "It's not much, but Ramos thinks it might be personal. After I got home I looked through my files but nothing really stood out to me."

"Maybe you should look again, when you're not so upset." Chris's brows tightened with worry. "I think you should talk to Harris or maybe the chief. They need to know what's going on. They have resources you could use, and it wouldn't hurt to have more help than what Manetto and Ramos can offer."

He didn't mind too much that I'd gone to them, but it hurt his feelings that I hadn't come to him first. He may not be a mob boss, but he loved me more than Manetto ever would.

"Oh Chris, I'm sorry. I thought about calling you first, but it shook me up so bad that having a mob boss on my side made it easier to deal with. I didn't mean to hurt your feelings."

"It's okay. Don't worry about it. I didn't mean for you to hear that." He pulled me into his arms and held me close. He concentrated on my news that someone was actually stalking me, and he could hardly believe it had happened so fast. It didn't make sense. Whoever it was must have been watching me for a while.

"You think so?" I asked. "That's just creepy."

"I know, but it's got to be true. And with the fake accent, I think it must be someone you've met before. Are you sure you can't place his voice?"

I shook my head. "I've thought of that. But no, I don't remember hearing it before. It doesn't even sound familiar to me, and it's driving me crazy."

"Okay... we'll just have to dig a little deeper. I still think you should look through your files again. It has to be related to someone you've helped in the past."

I nodded, not sure I should tell him that I thought meeting the guy was the best way to know what was going on. Uncle Joey agreed with that option, but I was pretty sure Chris wouldn't like it. "I'll go through them again tomorrow. Maybe something will pop up that I missed."

"Good." He pulled me close, hating that someone was targeting me. I'd saved a lot of lives yesterday, and this was the thanks I got? That some crazy person, coming out of the shadows, was threatening me? Why couldn't he just leave us alone? His jaw clenched with anger, and he let out a pent-up breath.

"Chris, we'll figure this out."

"I know. It's just... getting to me. You know?" His gaze caught mine. "It's crazy, but I don't think you realize how much our lives have changed, how much you've changed. I mean... you've always been kind and giving and funny and wonderful, but now you've turned into this... superhero. You've done things I can't even imagine. I'm grateful for how you've helped people... but I hate it at the same time."

He had a point, but it kind of hurt my feelings. "Well, if I'm being honest, on days like today, I'm not sure how much I like it. But then yesterday... stopping that woman from shooting everyone... I have to believe that it's totally worth it. So, for good or bad, it looks like we're just going to have to deal with it and do the best we can."

He nodded and squeezed me tight. "You're right. As long as you're by my side, I can roll with that... and whatever it brings."

I snuggled against him and laid my head on his shoulder. "Good, because it looks like we're getting a dog after we get back from New York." He chuckled, and I relaxed in his arms, knowing that, whatever I faced, Chris was right there with me.

Later that night, after everyone had gone to bed, I climbed under the covers and curled beside Chris's warm body. It worried me that John Brown, or whoever he was, had threatened Dimples's wedding, and I didn't know what to do.

"You need to tell Harris all about it," Chris said, after I told him my concerns. "I think he should know what's going on."

"But I don't want to ruin his wedding."

"Honey... if you think something might happen, isn't it best to go in prepared? You're not doing him any favors by keeping him in the dark."

"You're right. I'll talk to him first thing in the morning. Then I'm coming to your office to talk to Ethan. I know he said he'd take care of the problem, but I want to make sure. The only way to do that is to find out exactly what he's done."

"Sounds good to me," Chris said. "Now I think you need to relax, or you'll never get to sleep. Turn over and I'll give you a back rub."

Not about to miss out on that, I quickly complied. As his fingers did their magic on my bare skin, it wasn't long before I forgot all about having a stalker, Ethan's betrayal, Claire's DNA, and just about everything else that had happened recently.

Totally relaxed, I turned to face him. He began nipping at that sensitive area on my neck. Then he trailed kisses along my jaw to finally capture my lips. After a long kiss that left me breathless, he pulled away and groaned out some of my favorite words.

"Oh baby, oh baby."

As I walked up the steps into the precinct, the morning sunshine warmed my skin. It was another beautiful day in June, and I was determined to enjoy it. Today I was in charge, and I was going to find my stalker and put an end to his plans.

Dimples sat at his desk, and relief coursed through me. It was time to tell him what was going on and see what he could do to help. Chris had convinced me that Dimples needed to know his wedding could be a target, so I tried not to let guilt that I was ruining his day change my mind.

Sure, I hated to be the bearer of bad news, but what else could I do? Before I got to his desk, my gaze landed on the floral arrangement sitting on my desk in the corner. Just looking at it firmed my resolve to tell Dimples. It wasn't my fault some crazy person was stalking me.

"Hey Shelby," Dimples said. "Did you come for the flowers?"

I jerked my attention to Dimples and nodded. "You might say that. But I'm afraid it's more complicated."

"Why? What's going on?"

I slumped into the chair beside his desk. "Somebody's stalking me, and I need your help." His surprised gaze caught mine, and I tried not to flinch. "I think it's all because of the article in the paper yesterday."

I told him everything that had happened, only leaving out the part where I'd gone to Ramos and Uncle Joey for help. After I told him about the threat to his wedding, Dimples's brows drew together, and a blanket of anger fell over his face. "So you think he's setting you up?"

"I don't know what to think. He doesn't like me, that's for sure. I just wish I knew why."

Dimples nodded. "I wonder if it's someone we've dealt with, maybe even one of our old cases. He's obviously planned this for longer than a few days, right?"

"Yeah. I was thinking it might be someone I knew from my consulting business, but you're right. It could be something we've worked on together." This opened a whole new world of possibilities, and gave me hope, since nothing from my files had clicked.

"We need to get into that apartment the plant came from and take a look around," Dimples said. "We can look at the police report, too, and see if they found anything." He was wishing I'd called him right after it happened, so we could have done that yesterday. Why hadn't I talked to him before now?

"You were gone, remember?" I said, answering his thoughts. "You had to go interview someone at the prison."

He nodded, thinking he would have come back right away if I'd called. Didn't I know we were partners? And I could count on him?

My heart sank. I'd let him down, and dismay caught my breath. "Uh... I didn't think... what happened threw me. And then... you're getting married, and I didn't want to spring this on you."

Dimples shook his head, his lips twisting into a frown. "It's okay. I didn't mean to make you feel bad. Don't worry about it."

It hit me that he wasn't the first person who'd said that to me recently. Hadn't Chris and Uncle Joey both thought the same thing? I needed to toughen up or quit listening to their thoughts.

"Here's the police report," Dimples said, motioning to his computer. "It looks like the condo owner is Tim Kitley, but they didn't find him at home."

"Yeah, he's out of town."

Dimples's left brow rose. "How do you know that?"

Oops. "Uh... I went over there later and met with Jerry... the guy who was with me when the pot fell? He lives there and let me in. We talked to the lady who lives next door, and she said he was gone."

"Huh," he said, rubbing his chin. "So, if you already did that, what else did you do?"

"I went back to the office at the Randolph Tower where he left the note. But I couldn't find anything."

Dimples narrowed his eyes, thinking that was pretty brave of me to go there all alone unless... someone went with me. Who was it? Ramos?

Not wanting to answer that, I kept talking. "I also spoke to the girl who took the food order to see if she remembered what he looked like, but she didn't have anything. Then I checked out the florist shop, like you suggested, but he paid in cash, so that was a dead end, too. It's like he doesn't exist."

Dimples's lips twisted. He knew me well enough to know that I would have denied going with Ramos, if it weren't true.

"I doubt that John Brown is his real name," I said, wanting to stop Dimples's thoughts of Ramos. "But it wouldn't hurt to look him up on the police database, right? Maybe you could help me get set up on my new computer and we can check it out?"

"Sure."

We stepped over to my desk, and I contemplated throwing the flowers into the waste basket, but I couldn't do it. They were still beautiful, even if a crazy person sent them.

Dimples slid into my chair. The seat sank and tipped to the side, nearly throwing him off. He grabbed at my desk to keep from falling on the floor, and sat sideways before he managed to straighten up. The chair was still listing to the side, but at least he wasn't on the floor.

"Are you okay?" I asked, doing my best to hold back a chuckle. "I thought I was getting a new chair."

"Uh... yeah, you did, but someone switched it." Dimples stood, surprised and embarrassed that he'd forgotten about the switch.

"So who took it?"

"I told him to put it back," Dimples said, glancing over at Detective Bates's desk. "I guess he forgot."

Angry, Dimples pushed my broken chair to Bates's desk and traded for the new one. I noticed a few smiles directed our way. One of the guys even looked forward to watching Bates sit down when he came back. That brought a smile to my lips, and I hoped he came in before I left so I could watch it myself.

Dimples sat down and turned on my computer. He went through the prompts with me and, soon, I was inside the police database. He entered "John Brown." There were several hits, and I studied each photo that came up, but none of them looked familiar.

Dimples was thinking the same thing. "I think we should look over some of the cases we've worked together and see if anything pops up."

"Do you have time to do that?" I asked.

"Actually, I do. The chief hasn't given me anything new because of the wedding, and I'm just finishing up some paperwork. So I've got time, unless something big happens."

"Great. Then let's get started."

He led me to a filing cabinet. "These are all my cases. As you go through them, just look at the ones you helped me with." I took several files to my desk, and he took a few others.

I lost track of time perusing the files. After separating the ones I'd been involved with from the ones I hadn't, the stack shrank to only seven. Out of those, most of the perpetrators had ended up in jail, or been exonerated because they were innocent. Not one of them would be out to get me. Maybe Dimples would have more luck.

Before I could take the files back, my phone rang, sending a chill down my spine. I relaxed to find the caller ID had a phone number, so I quickly answered. "Hello?"

"Hi Shelby. This is Claire. My mom and I are meeting with Ethan, and I wondered if there was a chance you were going to be there."

"When are you meeting with him?"

"We just got here, but it's not for another ten minutes."

"Okay. I'm not far, so I'll come over. Just don't wait for me to get started because I might be late."

"Great. Thanks Shelby. See you soon."

I didn't think Claire needed me there to talk with Ethan, but since I wanted to know if Ethan had taken care of the problem with Strickland, it gave me a good excuse to go.

Picking up the files, I took them to Dimples. "The files on top are the ones I helped with, and nothing stood out to me. Have you found anything?"

"Not yet. But I've got a few more to look at."

"I'd stay and help, but I have to go to Chris's office to meet with Claire and Ethan. Will you call me if you find anything?"

"Sure, as long as you call me if you hear from him, or if you remember anything. This involves me now, and I don't want to be left out." This time, he wanted me to call him before I called Ramos.

"I know. I'll call. I promise."

He nodded, appeased that I was serious about his involvement, and wished me luck.

Inside Chris's building, I took the elevator to the fourth floor, deciding I'd stop by Chris's office before finding Ethan.

I walked around the corner and froze. A beautiful flower arrangement, just like the others, sat on Elisa's desk. My heart picked up speed, but I tried to shake it off. I'd known this might happen, but why now?

Elisa caught sight of me and jumped up with enthusiasm. "Hi Shelby. Look what just came for you!"

"Wow. Have they been here long?"

"Just a few minutes. You probably passed the delivery guy in the hall."

With a rush of anticipation, I hurried back to the elevator doors. As they slid shut, I turned to the fourth floor receptionist. "Did a delivery guy just get on the elevator?"

"You mean the guy who brought the flowers?" At my nod, she continued, "Yeah."

I pounced on the call button, pushing it like a crazy person. Why hadn't I noticed the guy? Several people had gotten off the elevator with me, but I didn't remember passing a delivery guy.

The other set of elevator doors finally opened, and I jumped inside, then waited forever before the doors closed.

As the doors swished open in the lobby, I ran out and turned toward the exit, hoping to catch sight of him.

I looked for a man wearing a brown shirt and a baseball cap that I'd picked up from Elisa's mind, but no one matched that description in the lobby. Pushing open the outside doors, I glanced up and down the sidewalk, then across the street. Nothing.

Opening my mind, I listened real close for any thoughts about me, but no one even glanced my way. Dang! Of course it probably wasn't my stalker anyway, but it would have been nice to question the delivery person.

Discouraged, I headed back inside. Reaching Elisa's desk, she sent me a quick smile, wondering why I'd run after him, but she was too polite to ask. Still, she was excited about the flowers. It occurred to me that, after this, I would never feel the same about getting flowers again. Sudden anger filled my heart. I held onto that anger so I could deal with the fear and stepped toward them.

"I wonder who they're from," I said, mostly to appease Elisa. She was thinking that she'd already looked, but had to act surprised so I wouldn't know.

"Yeah, me too," she said, playing her part. "Open the card and let's see."

I kept from rolling my eyes, but it was a stretch. All at once, I wanted to tell her I knew she'd already opened it. Then maybe yell at her for lying, and then end by telling her off for a few other things she'd done.

Instead, I plucked the card from the arrangement and opened it up. *"Dear Shelby,"* it read. *"You are my hero. XOXO, Your Secret Admirer."*

Whoa, he was getting a lot bolder with the XO stuff. I glanced at the envelope, finding the same "Brown Floral" name as the others. Elisa gazed at me expectantly. Letting out a huff, I read it to her so she'd back off.

"I guess it's not Chris, so who do you think it is?" she asked. "Do you have any idea?"

"Nope." I figured since she was lying, I could do it too. Chris wasn't in his office, and a fresh wave of disappointment rushed over me. "Where's Chris?"

"He left for lunch to meet a new client."

"Oh yeah? Who's the new client?"

"Let me look." She brought up the calendar on her computer. "Someone named John Sizemore. He's the CEO of JB Sizemore. I think they're an accounting firm or something."

A chill ran down my spine. JB Sizemore was the name of John Brown's supposed company. Why hadn't I mentioned that to Chris? "When did Chris set it up?"

"It was just yesterday. Kind of a sudden thing, but Chris had an hour for lunch, so we scheduled it in."

"Do you know where they went?"

She glanced back at the calendar. "Yeah. They're at that fancy Italian restaurant. Lugano's."

I felt the blood drain from my head. The last time Chris and I had been there, he'd nearly died from strychnine poisoning. What the freak!

"I've got to go."

Once more, I hurried out of the building. This time I wasn't going to let a chance to find out what was going on slip through my fingers. This person, whoever he was, had to be tied to John Brown somehow. The only way I'd know for sure was to show up at the restaurant and find out.

CHAPTER 7

I took a deep breath and stepped inside the crowded restaurant. After the hostess greeted me, I told her my husband was already there, and I'd find him.

I wound around the seats down one side of the restaurant, then circled to the back. There wasn't an empty table in sight, and nervous tension filled my stomach. I finally spotted Chris at the other end of the diner.

He sat alone at a side table next to the window, glancing between his watch and the crowded room, obviously waiting for someone to approach him. That had to mean my stalker hadn't made it yet, and relief coursed through me.

As I hurried toward Chris, he caught sight of me and his eyes widened. "Hey," he said. "What are you doing here? How did you find me?"

I took the chair across from him and leaned forward. "I just came from your office." I glanced around the restaurant, hoping to spot my stalker. Was he here, watching us? Had he set this up?

"What's going on?" Chris asked.

"I guess I left this little detail out when I explained things last night, but my stalker said he worked for JB

Sizemore. When Elisa told me you were out to lunch with a new client from JB Sizemore, I rushed over here as fast as I could."

Chris swore under his breath. "Do you think he's setting you up again, with me as bait? Is something going to happen now?"

"I don't know, but if I had to guess, that's what I'd think."

"Maybe we should go."

"Let me listen for a minute and see if I can pick anything up first. I really want to catch this guy."

Against his better judgement, Chris nodded and sat quietly. Sitting back, I closed my eyes and focused on the minds around us. Sifting through all that noise was bound to give me a headache, but I wasn't about to let that stop me.

The piercing sound of a fire alarm sent a jolt of fear through my heart. Several patrons jerked to their feet, looking for smoke or signs of trouble. A few others began leaving their seats. A loud pop, followed closely by a second one, sent people scrambling for cover. Screams began, along with a surge of bodies dashing for the doors.

I crouched in my chair, hoping to see what was going on. Chris grabbed my arm. "Let's get out of here."

As I nodded, I caught sight of a balloon floating to the ceiling. In my search for Chris I'd passed three balloons tied to a corner table. What had happened to the others? Was that what had popped?

Chris kept low and pushed me in front of him, but I wasn't ready to leave yet. My stalker might still be here watching us, and I wanted to get a look at him. "Hang on," I told Chris. "I think those pops were balloons and this is a sick prank."

"We can't take that chance. We've got to get out of here."

An older couple a few feet ahead of us couldn't move quite as fast as the people behind them. A passing man knocked the woman into her husband, and she went down to her knees. The husband lost his balance and flailed dangerously.

Chris rushed to his side and steadied him before he fell. I reached the woman and put my arms around her to help her stand. She leaned on me, and I steadied her until she could get to her feet.

"Are you okay?" I asked. "Can you walk?"

She nodded, but she was too shaken up to speak. I kept my hold on her and helped her around the fallen chairs toward the exit. Chris and her husband followed behind. Soon, we stood outside the restaurant with most of the crowd. Several people were still running away, but most had stopped to see what was going on.

The sound of sirens eased the tension, and everyone watched as the police officers jumped out of their cars. I helped the woman to a bench outside the restaurant and lowered her onto the seat. The man Chris helped had recovered enough to hurry to her side. He put his arm around her and held her close while tears ran down her cheeks.

A surge of hot anger filled my chest. This was too much. Other people were getting hurt. It wasn't just me anymore, and I wanted to rip this guy's head off. Before I ran back inside like a crazy person, I tried to shut out the audible noise and focus on the inner dialogue of those in my vicinity.

I listened closely, trying to sort out the thoughts of the victims from those of my stalker. Wouldn't he be thinking about me? I did my best, but nothing stood out. No one thought about the woman standing there as still as a rock with her eyes shut.

I let out a breath and opened my eyes to find Chris blocking me from view. He'd stood protectively beside me, knowing what I was trying to achieve. At the negative shake of my head, he enfolded me in his arms. From his mind, I picked up some of the same thoughts I'd had about the sick bastard, and it helped calm me down.

"Shelby?"

I pulled away to find Jimmy Falzone standing beside us. He was the owner of the restaurant, and one of Uncle Joey's men. "Jimmy." I threw my arms around him in an impromptu hug. He hadn't expected that, but he hugged me back, grateful I wasn't blaming him for this mess. "This is terrible. I'm so sorry."

His brows drew together. What was I apologizing for? I had nothing to do with this.

"Do you know what happened?" I asked.

"No. But I will. I still have all the security surveillance Ramos set up, so I'm sure I'll find something on them. Then whoever did this will pay." A police officer beckoned him into the restaurant. "Excuse me."

Instead of watching him leave, I followed behind, wanting to hear what they'd discovered. Before I could get inside, an officer at the door held out his hand to stop me. "Sorry ma'am. You can't go in there."

I reached for my purse so I could show him my honorary police badge, but realized I'd left it inside. Still, I wasn't about to give up. "I'm Shelby Nichols. I'm a consultant with the police. I need to go in there."

My name rang a bell, and his eyes narrowed. Was I the person who'd stopped the shooting at the newspaper office? And here I was at another shooting? In his book, that was more than a coincidence. "Sure. I know who you are. What are you doing here?"

Good grief! Didn't he hear the part about me being a consultant for the police? "Who's in charge?" I asked. I'd missed watching the police arrive, so I had no idea. He was thinking that it was Detective Bates, and I cringed. Great. Why did it have to be him?

"Will you go inside and tell Detective Bates that Shelby Nichols is here? I'm sure he'll want to see me."

The cop frowned, wondering why I'd asked who was in charge if I'd already known that. "Just a minute."

I turned to Chris. "I think my stalker's long gone, but I want to tell them about the balloons."

"Are you sure that's what those pops were?"

"Yes. Pretty sure. I mean, if he'd wanted to shoot anyone, it would have been me or you, right? And we're okay, so it was just another stupid test. I guess I failed."

"Maybe not," he said. "He was supposed to meet me. Since you showed up, that would send the message that you had a premonition about it, right?"

"Oh yeah, I hadn't thought of it that way. But I still should have stopped him."

He shook his head. "How? By standing next to the fire alarm? Because that's about the only way you could have intervened, and even for a person with premonitions, that's stretching it."

That helped me feel better. Then Bates came to the door with a scowl and motioned me inside. "What's going on, Nichols?" he asked.

My first thought was to tell him to leave my new chair alone, but that probably wasn't a good idea. "I was here with my husband, and I saw something that I thought you should know."

At his raised brows I continued. "I don't think there was a gun involved. I think the pops were a couple of balloons. You should look for that... and one of the balloons got away, so it's on the ceiling somewhere. Maybe you can get a couple of prints off it?"

"Thanks for the tip. I'll look into it." He was a lot more interested in the surveillance tapes that Jim had told him about, but he'd see if there was a balloon. "Is there anything else?"

"Yes. Can I get my purse?"

With a shake of his head, he told me to go ahead and get it. "But then you need to go back outside with the others and give your statement to the police officers out there."

It was crystal clear that I'd get no special treatment from him, and it hurt my feelings. Since I didn't want him to know that, I just smiled and grabbed my purse.

Back outside, we had to wait our turn to give our statements to the police. To pass the time, Chris and I spoke to the older couple, grateful they were doing better. The color had come back into their cheeks, but it saddened me to know it would be a long time before they went out to lunch again.

"Do you think John Brown would have met with you if I hadn't shown up?" I asked Chris.

"No. I don't think he had any intention of doing that. It would have given him away."

"That's true."

"What were you doing at my office anyway?" he asked.

"Claire called and asked me to meet with her and Ethan. I thought it was a great excuse to find out more about Ethan, and what he's doing about that problem of his." I checked my watch. "The meeting's probably over by now."

"True, but you can still come back and talk to Ethan. What concerns me now is JB Sizemore, and the kind of company he runs. There must be some connection to you. When I get back to work, I'll see what I can find out about the company."

"That's a great idea."

"Do you have any 'premonitions' about this guy's next step?" Chris grinned at his pun, and it relieved the tension in my neck.

"He usually calls to rub it in after something like this happens."

Right on cue, my phone began to ring, sending my heart into overdrive. I glanced at the caller ID. There was a number displayed, so I relaxed and answered. "Hello?"

"Hi Shelby. This is Stacey Sherwood from Good Morning America. How are you doing today?"

"Oh, I'm fine." I caught Chris's gaze and shook my head. "I'm at lunch with my husband right now. Can we talk later?"

"Of course. I'll be happy to call you back. Did you have a chance to think about my offer?"

"Uh... yes. I don't think I can do it. But thanks for asking."

"We could fly your husband out with you. Why don't you talk it over with him, and I'll call you tomorrow."

"Uh... okay."

"Good. I'll talk to you then." Disconnecting, I caught Chris staring at me with raised brows. He wondered what else I had forgotten to tell him.

Oops. "That was Good Morning America. They want me to come on their show. They called yesterday. I guess I forgot to tell you."

"Are you serious?" Chris shook his head and exhaled. "You're not doing it are you?"

"No. I even told them no, but they keep telling me to think about it."

Chris smirked. "I guess not too many people turn them down."

"I know. Right?"

"Well, at least it wasn't your stalker calling."

"True." But why hadn't he called? Was he still here watching us?

"Did you tell Dimples about him?"

"Yes." I spent the next few minutes telling Chris about our conversation and how Dimples had taken the news.

Then it was our turn to give our statements to the police officer. A minute later, we could finally leave. "I think I'll follow you back to the office for that conversation with Ethan."

Before Chris could respond, my phone rang again. Fear sent my pulse into overdrive. I glanced at the caller ID, and relaxed. "It's Dimples." I pushed the button. "Hey. I guess you heard."

"Heard what?"

"About the restaurant. You know... the supposed shooting?"

"Yeah, but how do you know about it?" he asked.

"I'm here. It was my stalker."

"Holy hell! Are you okay?"

"Yes, I'm fine." I proceeded to tell him all about Chris's lunch with JB Sizemore and how I'd found out about it. "I think the whole thing was a set up for my benefit." I told him about the balloons, and that I'd told Bates about them too. "Oh... and it's the same restaurant where Chris was poisoned."

"Sounds like he must have known about it."

"Yeah. I don't think it was a coincidence."

"Well, I have some good news. I think I found a connection. Can you come back to the precinct?"

"Of course, I'll be right there." I disconnected and glanced at Chris. "He found something. I guess I'll have to postpone my chat with Ethan."

"That's okay. Right now this is more important. I think that while you're working on that, I'll check out JB Sizemore. I'd like to know if the company really exists."

"Sounds good. I'm sorry I didn't mention the name. For some reason, I forgot all about it."

"It's okay. We'll figure this out." He pulled me in for a quick kiss, and we said our goodbyes.

My heart filled with hope that Dimples had found a connection. Maybe this was my lucky break. I hurried inside the precinct and went straight to Dimples's desk. He smiled, sending those dimples of his into overdrive, and warmth crashed into me just to look at them.

"I'm ready for some good news. What have you got?"

His eyes gleamed with satisfaction, filling me with anticipation. "Do you remember that case with the debt merchant list and the lawyer?"

"Yeah, sure. Lincoln Montgomery was killed over that list. He used to work for Chris's firm. What did you find?"

"Remember the ex-con that worked for him? The one who took the list after Lincoln was murdered?" At my nod he continued. "His name is Dalton Sizemore."

"Holy hell. That list was worth a lot of money, and he had to give it up because of my premonitions. That sounds like a motive to me."

Dimples nodded. "Since Dalton's on probation, I have all of his information. I know where he is right now. Want to have a chat with him?"

"You know it."

We took Dimples's car to Dalton's place of employment, which turned out to be a furniture company with a delivery service. Since it wasn't far from the restaurant, he could have hurried over, done the dirty deed, and gone back to work.

"He's out loading a truck right now," the manager told us. "Is he in some kind of trouble?"

"No," Dimples answered. "We just have a few questions to ask him."

"Okay. Come with me." The manager led us to the back of the building where the loading docks were located. Dalton stood inside the back of a truck, loading a plastic-covered couch for delivery. Once it was secure, the manager called him over.

Getting a good look at him, I recognized the hardness in his eyes and the diamond studs in his ears.

He spotted us and hesitated, then walked slowly toward us, wondering what the hell was going on. He knew exactly who we were, and his back stiffened. I'd ruined everything for him last time. But this time he'd been real careful and followed all the rules. His cousin had promised that nothing could be traced back to him, so how could I know anything?

He studied me, hoping to get a feel for what I might be doing there. He usually frightened women like me, but he knew I wasn't intimidated in the least. I'd known things just by talking to him, and it gave him the creeps. But he knew we had nothing on him, so he needed to play it cool.

My hopes sank. That didn't sound like my stalker. Dalton was up to something, but it didn't have anything to do with me.

"Hello Dalton," Dimples said. "We just have a few questions for you." Dimples glanced at me, noticing my crestfallen expression and let out a sigh. "Shelby?"

I gave Dalton a thin smile. "Do you know anyone by the name of JB Sizemore?"

That caught him by surprise, and his eyes widened. "JB Sizemore?" At my nod, he glanced at Dimples. "Is this a joke?"

"Just answer the question," Dimples said.

"No. I've never heard of him." He was telling the truth. None of his relatives had those initials, and it baffled him that we'd seek him out just to ask a question like that. "Is that it?"

Unfortunately, it was, but I hated to let him get away with something. "I don't know what you've got going on with your cousin, but we're watching you. Sooner or later, you're going to get caught. Is it worth going back to jail for?" I wanted to say "punk" and push on his chest with my finger, but I just hardened my gaze instead.

He swore under his breath, but didn't take the bait. "Are we done?"

"For now," I said, hoping to sound tough.

He frowned and shook his head, thinking I was a little crazy. But as he walked back to the truck, he thought it was time to lay low for a while and quit helping his cousin. Still, how did I know? It gave him the willies.

Dimples thanked the manager, and we left the building. Inside the car, Dimples turned to me. "I guess it's not him, but what was that cousin stuff all about?"

I shrugged. "I don't know. He was just thinking about his cousin and how nothing could be traced back to him, so I went with it."

"Oh," Dimples said, smiling just a little.

"That was disappointing. I thought for sure it would be him."

"Yeah, me too. Why don't you come back to the precinct and look at the rest of the files? There's about nine of them you haven't looked at. Maybe you'll see something I missed."

"Okay."

"And," he added, "Since I'm getting married in a few days, maybe we can think up a strategy in case he shows up at the wedding."

"Oh right." I glanced his way. "I'm so sorry this is ruining your big day."

He shook his head. "Don't worry. My wedding will be fine. But I think it's time to tell the chief, and the others who are coming, about your stalker and his threat to me." He shrugged. "With everyone on the look-out, nothing's going to happen."

"What about telling Billie? I hate to ruin it for her too, so I'm not sure we should tell her."

"I know, but... she needs to know. I've been thinking about this a lot and, to be honest, I don't think it will upset her. You know how she is with a story. The idea that you have a stalker who might show up at our wedding could be pretty exciting for her. You have to admit, it would make a great story. She'd probably want to tell all her fellow reporters. If we caught him there, I don't think she'd mind in the least."

"Yeah, unless someone gets hurt."

"That's not going to happen. You'll be there. You'll know, just like you did before."

Wow. Talk about pressure. "Okay. But let me be the one to tell her, all right?"

"Sure."

Inside the precinct, I took the remaining files to my desk and sat down, doing my best to ignore the flowers. The next hour crept by without a single clue coming from the files. I couldn't see a connection to any of these cases, and my frustration grew.

I handed them all back to Dimples and told him it was a dead end. "I'll look over my files again tonight. Maybe something will show up." He nodded, but was disappointed as well.

"You still want Billie to know?" I asked.

"Yes."

"Okay. I'll stop by the paper. I just have one more question." This was something I wasn't going to budge on, and I hoped Dimples would agree. "For your plan to involve the chief and the guys here, I need them to report everything to me. Do you think they'd do that?"

His brows rose. "Sure. They know you're the one with the premonitions, but if you're worried, why don't we tell the chief about it right now and see what he has to say?"

At the moment, telling the chief wasn't something I wanted to do. "Uh... how about you tell him when it's closer to the wedding. It's just that... there might be a chance I'll figure it out before then, and I'd rather not involve anyone else unless we absolutely have to."

Dimples's lips twisted, but he understood my reluctance. "Sure. But if you haven't figured it out by tomorrow, I'm going to tell him."

"Okay. That should work." I sighed. What should be a happy and exciting time for him was ruined because of me. I hated this. "I'll look through my files again tonight, and if I find anything, I'll let you know."

"Sounds good."

I left the precinct with a heavy heart. What a mess. Now I had to tell Billie, and hope that she wouldn't be too upset. Dimples had a point that she might be okay with it, but this was her big day. I wasn't sure his reasoning applied to their wedding. I put the call through, and she answered right away.

"Hey Billie, are you busy?"

"What's up?"

"I just need to talk for a minute. Can I come to your office?"

"Hmm, that sounds serious," she said. "Is it about Claire? Did you talk to Ethan?"

"No it's not them, although they were meeting today, so that's good. This is something else entirely, and it's personal."

"Oh... that sounds juicy. Come on over. I'll let the receptionist know you're coming so she can send you right up."

I could practically hear her curiosity over the phone. Maybe Dimples had a point, and Billie wouldn't be too upset. I guess I'd find out soon enough.

I entered the building, remembering it was only the day before yesterday that I'd stopped the shooting and here I was, back for more. The receptionist waved me through, and I stepped in front of the metal detectors. The security guard did a double-take, surprised to see me again so soon.

"Oh hey," he said, thinking I was quite a celebrity around here. "How are you doing?"

"I'm good, thanks." That was a big lie, but I wasn't about to tell him about a crazy stalker that was out to get me. As my bag went through the machine, he looked for my stun flashlight. Smiling to see it inside, he was grateful that I'd had it the other day. That thought cheered me up, and I smiled at him as I took my bag.

I rode the elevator to Billie's floor and stepped out to find her. Since I couldn't remember where her cubicle was, I took a moment to look around. A few workers noticed me and started clapping. Hearing the commotion, the rest of them stopped what they were doing and joined in. Mortified, I felt my face turn red.

Michael came out of his office and hurried to my side. "Thanks everyone," he said. "It looks like she's embarrassed, so good job." At their laughter, he took my arm and guided me toward his office. "This is a pleasant surprise. What brings you here?"

"That would be me," Billie said, coming to my side. "She has some information about my story." She sent a pointed look my way, hoping I'd go along with it. Michael was nice and all, but talking about her wedding while at work wasn't part of her job description.

"Yes," I agreed. "Every little bit helps, right?"

Michael wondered if it was something he could get in on, but he didn't want to come between us. It was important that my relationship with Billie remained close. That way, when she asked to do a special story about me, it would be hard to turn her down.

"Good," he said. "I'll let you get to it then."

Billie grabbed my arm and pulled me toward a small conference room. I waved at Michael and hurried inside. The door shut, and I sank into a chair, grateful to have the door silence all those thoughts about me.

"So what's going on?" Billie asked. She perched on the edge of the table, and her brows rose expectantly. She didn't think for one minute it was about her wedding.

"You'd better sit down," I said. "This might take a while." Totally intrigued, she slid into the chair beside mine and waited.

"After all the publicity directed my way from the shooting, I got a phone call from a man who wanted to hire me. But since then, I've discovered that there's more to it. It's turned into some sick game, and now he's stalking me.

"I don't know if it's because he's trying to prove I don't have premonitions, or that if I do, he wants to know if they're real. Either way, he knows details about my life that make me nervous. Like where I work and who my friends are."

I explained that I'd tried to meet him and what had happened in the food court. I also told her about the flowers that had been sent everywhere. "Then there was the restaurant business today."

"You were there?" She'd heard all about it and could hardly believe it was all about me. "What else has happened?"

"So far, that's it. He's been calling me, but the number is always blocked. Anyway, the main reason I'm telling you this is because, last time he called, he mentioned your wedding." Her brows rose with shock. "Yeah. And he made a threat that something bad might happen if I'm not there to stop it."

"Oh my gosh! He knows about my wedding?"

"Yeah. I told Dimples about the threat, and he thought it was something you should know too. That's why I'm here. I'm really sorry about this. I don't mean to ruin your wedding. I'm not even sure anything will happen, but, after the stunt he pulled today at the restaurant, I can't take that chance. I hope you're not too upset with me."

After the initial shock, she shook her head. "If he's targeting you, what does he get out of it?"

"I don't know. Making me squirm? Proving my premonitions are bogus?"

"It's got to be a former client or someone you and Drew put away."

"Yeah, that's what we thought, so we began looking through all the cases we've worked on together. We only found one lead, and that turned out to be a dead end. With your wedding so close, I thought you should know."

"Thanks," she said. Her brows creased together. She wasn't too worried, mostly because she was convinced my premonitions were real. I'd know if something was going to happen before it did. "Wow. This is crazy. A stalker who wants to prove you're a phony. What a story."

In her mind, she was already making up the headline. "Stalker - No Match for Psychic," or "Stalker Jailed Before Committing Crime." Maybe not that one, but something like it could work.

"I don't want you to be worried about this on your wedding day," I said. "You should be focused on Dimples and your vows."

She glanced at me and smiled. "I know, but I'm not really worried. It was just a threat, and you'll be there. You have to admit, it's a great story. What did Drew think we should do? He didn't want to cancel the wedding did he?"

"Oh no. That thought didn't even cross his mind." Oops, maybe I shouldn't have said that. "Uh... he's going to tell the chief, and all the cops who are coming, about it. That way, they can watch for the stupid jerk and be on the lookout for anything unusual."

"That's a great idea. Would it be all right if I told Michael? He's going to be coming, along with a few of my co-workers." She was thinking that he'd be excited to watch me in action, and since he'd spoken with her about doing an exclusive on me, this would be a great way to start the story on a personal note.

Damn. Could this get any worse? I couldn't exactly tell her no, since it was my fault her wedding could become a circus, but a story about me? No, and hell no.

"Uh... I guess if he's coming it might be helpful if he knew about the threat."

"Great." She jumped up to get him. I opened my mouth to stop her, but shut it again. How could I object? At least I had some time before she actually asked me for an exclusive interview, and I could think up an excuse. Then it hit me that she could always say I'd ruined her wedding, so I owed her. Crap.

She brought Michael into the conference room, and I had to explain the whole thing again. A spark of fascination filled his eyes. He didn't like going to weddings much, but now he could hardly wait.

"You both realize this could be dangerous, right?" I reminded them. "It's not a game."

Michael glanced at Billie, surprised at my tone, and nodded his agreement.

"And if nothing happens, you're okay with that too?" I had to ask.

Michael's brows rose. "Of course."

Billie huffed out a breath. "Nothing *is* going to happen." She didn't add *because you'll be there*, but that's what she was thinking.

"We need to find the story behind the story," Michael said, in full editor-in-chief mode. "I think if we do that, you'll come closer to knowing who he is. It will tell you what motivates him."

He began to pace. "Just off the top of my head, I can think of two reasons he's doing this. One, he believes you're a fake and he wants to expose you. Or two, it's much more personal. You may have worked on a case he was involved in, and he's fixated on you because he believes you've ruined his life." He smiled widely. "That's a good place to start."

Before he could tell me how to begin my investigation, I held up my hand. "I've already been doing that."

"Oh. Good, good," he said, realizing that he'd overstepped a little. I was a private investigator, much like a reporter, and he needed to remember that. "I'm sure you have. Well, if I can help you in any way, I'm happy to offer my services."

"Thanks. That's nice of you to offer." I wasn't about to accept his offer with all the strings attached.

"What should we watch for at the wedding?" Billie asked.

"You are not going to watch for anything," I said forcefully. "That's my job. I just wanted you to know, in case there's a sudden change of plans. Like—if someone offers you a drink that you didn't ask for, or some stranger tells you that you need to get in a car with them and go for a ride, you know—something crazy like that."

She chuckled. "All right. I get it." Then it hit her that this was a real threat, and maybe it wasn't so glamorous after all. Her family and friends would be there, and she didn't want anyone to get hurt.

"It will be okay," I said, glancing at Michael to include him. "We'll all be watching for anything out of the ordinary. He'd be a fool to try anything with all the cops there in the first place. So I don't think you need to worry."

At her nod, I continued. "Maybe tomorrow you can give me a rough outline of when everything is scheduled to take place, so I'll know what's going on."

"Oh, I can do that now." She pulled out a pen and paper and wrote down the approximate times of the ceremony, cocktail hour, dinner, toasts and dancing.

"Thanks. This will help." I took the schedule, realizing that it was going to be a long night. "I'm going to work on finding this guy. Who knows? Maybe I'll figure out who it is before the wedding, and you won't have to worry about it."

"That's right," she agreed.

"Well, I guess that's it. If I don't see you before the wedding, I'll see you then."

"Sounds good. Be sure to let me know if you find him beforehand."

"I will." I gave her a quick hug, and we said our goodbyes.

On the way to my car, I fervently hoped I could solve this before the wedding. I didn't want anything bad to happen, and the pressure was starting to get to me. Thank goodness I had some time before the big day to figure it out; otherwise, I might go crazy.

CHAPTER 8

In my car, I laid my head back on the seat and wondered what to do next. I'd totally missed talking to Ethan, so I should head back to Chris's office. Then there was Uncle Joey. I hadn't spoken to him all day, and I should probably stop by to tell him about the restaurant fiasco.

On the other hand, it was nearly four, and I really wanted to go home. I could just give Uncle Joey a call and talk to Ethan tomorrow. Besides, with school out, I needed to check on my kids. I'd neglected them the past couple of days, and guilt, plus the fact that I needed a Diet Coke something fierce, decided the matter.

As I pulled into my driveway, I waved at Josh and his friends who were outside playing basketball. They quickly moved out of my way while I parked in the garage. Inside, I dropped my purse on the kitchen counter and opened the refrigerator.

Soon, I had a glass filled with crushed ice and fizzing soda. As I took my first swallow, Savannah popped into the kitchen, and we spoke about her day. Just being home with her relieved some of my stress. I opened the container of brownies we'd made on Sunday, and set them out on a plate for her, Josh and his friends.

After nibbling on the crumbs, I worried that they'd all get eaten before I could have one. While Savannah told Josh and his friends to come in for brownies, I snuck one into a napkin and hid it in the cupboard behind the chips.

It didn't take long for the brownies to disappear, along with several glasses of milk, and I was glad I'd saved one. After the boys went back outside, Savannah reminded me that we had an Aikido class to attend.

Instead of feeling overwhelmed by so much on my plate, it gave me something to look forward to. Throwing people around was sure to do wonders for my stress levels. Plus, in my line of work, knowing how to defend myself had come in handy more than once, so how could I pass that up?

Since that didn't give me much time to look through my files, I hurried into my home office, determined to go over everything, paying attention to each little detail. The link to my stalker had to be there somewhere. I just needed to find the connection.

A few minutes after I got started, my phone rang. My heart picked up speed, and I took a deep breath to confront my stalker. I'd read up on tracing phone calls, and I was ready to push star-five-seven when the call ended so I could track his number.

But it was all for nothing, and the tension left my shoulders. It used to be that a call from Uncle Joey sent my blood pressure to record highs. That wasn't the case anymore, and I hoped that was a good thing. "Hi Uncle Joey. How are you?"

I guess he didn't think I'd be so perky, because he took a moment to respond. "Did something happen to you today?"

"Oh crap! I was going to call you. Sorry. How did you know?"

"Jim called me after the police left. Ramos is over there right now looking through the security tapes."

Oops. "Oh... that's great. I had to get home to make sure my kids were all right, but I should have called you before now. Sorry."

"Tell me what happened."

I quickly explained the whole story at the restaurant, but left out the lead I'd followed with Dimples since it didn't pan out. Uncle Joey didn't like that I worked with a cop, so the less I talked about him the better.

"JB Sizemore must be the key to this," I continued. "But so far, I haven't been able to link that name to any of the cases I've worked on."

"I might be able to help you with that," Uncle Joey said. "I did a little digging into the building records of the Randolph Tower. That name, JB Sizemore, is listed as the owner of the building. But I just found out that it's not a person's name. It's the name of a shell company."

"What does that mean?"

"A shell company is a business that's created to hold funds and manage another entity's financial transactions. It's like a shield for security reasons, which could include hiding money from an ex, or as a tax haven... that sort of thing."

"Right," I agreed, knowing I'd heard of them before. "And other activities, like money laundering, right?" Silence greeted me, so I quickly continued. "Uh... not that you'd know anything about that."

Uncle Joey huffed with annoyance, but continued. "I found out who owns the shell company. It's part of the Patton family conglomerate. Have you heard of them? They made their first millions with a chemical company and branched out to other businesses after that. "

"That name sounds familiar."

"The Patton Family Foundation has contributed a lot of money to the arts and several charities."

"Oh yeah, sure. I know who they are."

"So I take it you haven't done any work for them?"

My brows rose. "No. I think I'd remember if I had."

Uncle Joey sighed, like I'd let him down. "It wouldn't necessarily be for the foundation, but someone in the family."

"Right. I should look up the names of the family members and see if one of them matches someone in my files."

"I think that's a good place to start. Let me know if you find anything."

"Okay," I agreed.

"And Shelby," Uncle Joey said sharply, "that means call me right away."

From his tone of voice, I knew he wasn't happy I'd forgotten to call him about the restaurant. But this seemed more serious. Was there more to it?

"Sure. I'll let you know."

"Good. I'll be expecting to hear from you." He disconnected before I had a chance to question him further, and I swore under my breath. If I'd gone to his office like I should have, I'd know more about his connection to the Pattons. Now, I worried that this had more to do with Uncle Joey than I realized.

Was that possible? My stomach twisted with dread. This whole thing suddenly got about ten times worse. If it involved a mob boss, how deep did it go? My stalker had already threatened innocent people, and he'd targeted the wedding of my friends. What else did he have planned? I needed to figure this out before someone got killed.

I woke up my computer and googled the Patton family. Along with the foundation website, I found the names of the family members. Charles and Meredith Patton were the founders and had both died fifteen years ago. They had six children.

I found all of their names, but got lost when it came to their children's names. There were just too many of them and not as much information available. I wrote down what I could find, and hoped that I could look them up on the police database tomorrow.

That brought a smile to my lips. Having my own computer at the precinct was a major boon for me. And, after everything else that had happened lately, I needed something to be happy about.

I had to take a break for dinner and Aikido, but I got back to my search around nine that evening. Chris had stayed late at work and came in after grabbing a quick bite to eat.

"What's going on?" he asked.

"Uncle Joey found a lead." I quickly explained what he'd told me. "So now I'm looking through my files for anyone related to the Patton family or their chemical company."

Chris nodded, but he'd gone a little pale. He was thinking that there was a connection to his firm through his partners, John Larsen and Gary Pratt.

"What do you mean?" I asked.

"Larsen and Pratt have the account for the Patton Foundation. I don't know if they do work for the individual family members, but it's likely that they do."

"So?" I asked. "How is that bad?"

He shrugged. "If there's bad blood between the Pattons and Manetto, it could be another reason you were targeted, since I'm Manetto's lawyer."

"Oh... right. Maybe that's why Uncle Joey sounded a little tense when he suggested I look into them."

Chris pinched the bridge of his nose and closed his eyes. I stood up and gave him a hug. His arms snaked around me, pulling me close, and I leaned into him, breathing in the light, woodsy scent of his cologne that I loved. Savoring the moment, I caught his amazement that a simple hug from me somehow made him stronger.

I smiled, pulling away to look into his eyes. "I agree. That felt wonderful." Our lips met, and I tasted chocolate. My eyes flew open. I thought the brownies were all gone. "Did you just eat a brownie?"

His eyes got big. "Maybe."

"You found it?"

His lips quirked sideways, and he knew he'd been caught, especially since he was sure I'd hear in his mind that he'd found my hiding place a long time ago. Damn! He couldn't keep anything a secret from me.

"So you knew I was hiding it, and you ate it anyway? I didn't even get one earlier."

"Hey, I didn't get one either." He figured that was a good excuse since I hadn't saved him one. Didn't I know those brownies were too good to pass up? Too bad he'd been caught. He'd hoped I'd think it was Josh who'd taken it instead of him. Knowing I'd just heard that, he took a deep breath and pulled me close. "I'll make it up to you."

"You'd better," I said, narrowing my eyes.

He smiled with relief, glad he was off the hook. "I will. And you'll love it."

I huffed at his smug smile, but let him pull me into his arms for another kiss. Breathless, I pulled away. "I'd love to get started on that, but right now I need to get busy, or I might be up all night."

Chris nodded and, after another kiss full of promise, he left me to get back to work, hoping I'd be motivated to get done quickly.

I plunged into my search with zeal, but two hours later, I only had one file left and nothing to show for it. What was I missing? It had to be here somewhere. I opened the last file, remembering the case clearly. It was a woman named Olivia Beal who'd hired me to find out if her husband was cheating on her.

I checked the name of the company, but it was different from the Patton family company. Still, I remembered Olivia mentioning that she owned the company with her husband, and it wasn't hard to see that she and her husband were extremely wealthy.

The name of the company was BioTech, and the husband's name was Jameson Beal. My breath hitched. JB. Could this be it? I tried to remember if this man's voice sounded like the person who'd called me, but I drew a blank.

I thought back to the experience, remembering that my first meeting with Olivia had been at her office. She'd told me her suspicions and, when she was done, she asked if I had any premonitions about her husband.

Since I needed direct contact with him, I'd asked if I could observe him for a moment. She took me straight to his lab and showed me around. He'd been there, but he was in the middle of an experiment, so she walked me through the lab, lingering over some equipment, and then took me back to her office.

I'd picked up the affair pretty quick, mostly because of his lab assistant, who'd kept thinking about his hands during the experiment, and how much she loved them, especially when they were all over her.

Back in Olivia's office I told her that, based on my premonitions, the affair was most likely true, but, to know for sure, it would be best to have a chat with him.

Olivia promptly arranged a meeting with her husband for the following week. She told him that I was a writer for a medical journal, and I wanted to interview Jameson about his research. She'd also given me some reading material to study so I'd know more about the company.

I had to admit that the research had interested me, mostly because Jameson had come up with a supplement that was supposed to improve the cognitive abilities of the brain, especially in older people. Because it was touted as a vitamin supplement, it wasn't regulated like a real drug, but they were still running tests on its viability.

It was easy to pick up that the opportunity to help people with Alzheimer's and dementia could make them a ton of money. With that much at stake, I knew exposing Jameson could hurt their business and turn things nasty fast.

But there was no question of his cheating. During the interview, I managed to talk about his research assistant and asked if she could join us. He'd quickly agreed, and though they were professional in every way, I couldn't miss those stray thoughts of their many indiscretions. I may have even blushed a few times.

Jameson was so full of himself that he didn't even suspect that I had no idea what he was talking about. Not until the interview was over. I'd opened the door to leave and found his wife waiting in the hall.

"Well?" she'd asked, stepping inside and closing the door before any of us could leave the room.

Uneasiness filled me, and I knew that this was going to be unpleasant. I glanced at Jameson before speaking. "He's having an affair with... her. It's been going on for at least six months."

Olivia's breath hitched, but she nodded stoically. "Thank you Shelby." She turned her gaze to the assistant. "You're fired. I want you out of this building in the next ten minutes. There's an escort outside this door waiting for you. Leave everything here but your personal items."

The assistant paled, then looked to Jameson for a sign that he would defend her, but instead he stared at his wife in shock. Dread pooled in his stomach, and I was afraid he might have a heart attack.

Finding nothing from her lover, the assistant huffed with fury and shoved past me. I wanted to leave too, but Olivia halted me with a touch to my arm. She stared at Jameson, daring him to deny the affair.

His face contorted with anguish. He was thinking this couldn't be happening. How had I figured it out? Had I been spying on him? Even so, he couldn't think of one time he'd messed up. Not once. There was still a chance. He just had to convince Olivia that I was wrong.

"How can you believe her?" he asked his wife, then turned his scathing gaze on me. "She's got to be a spy from our competitors. They're trying to undermine us. Can't you see that?"

"Are you denying it?" Olivia asked. Even if she believed me over him, she wanted to wipe that smirk off his face and watch him grovel.

"Of course I am. She's just making this up, and I know how to prove it." He glanced at me with ice in his eyes. "Show Olivia the proof. In fact, I'd be very interested in seeing it myself."

They both looked my way, and I cringed inside. Olivia hadn't doubted me until that moment. She'd given my psychic abilities the benefit of the doubt, but now she wasn't so sure. What real proof did I have? So far, it was my word against his, although, deep down, she knew something had changed in their relationship. But could there be another reason?

I let out a sigh, knowing I'd been backed into a corner, and my only way out was to tell them both the sordid details of the affair. With reluctance, I met Olivia's gaze and began.

"They never meet outside the office. If you care to look, you'll find a room not far from the lab that they've been using. He's got the only key to open it, and he's furnished it quite comfortably with a sleeper sofa and other amenities."

Jameson sucked in a breath. "This is bullshit. Olivia knows I would never have an affair." He turned his pleading gaze to hers. "She's right that I have a place to sleep, but with the deadlines, you know how much time I've needed to spend here for my research. I needed a place for a quick nap so that I could keep going. That's all it is."

Olivia glanced my way, wanting to believe her husband more than anything. I turned to him, ready to call his bluff. "If that's true, then I'm sure you won't mind showing it to her. We can take a look right now."

Jameson hesitated, knowing that we'd find the bed in disarray, along with the evidence of their lovemaking just that morning. We'd also find the extra clothes they kept there.

"Or don't you want Olivia to find your assistant's clothes?"

He glanced my way, his eyes full of hate and barely-controlled anger. He was thinking that this couldn't be happening. I was ruining him and everything he cared about. This was his company. If Olivia wanted to, she could push him out, and he'd lose everything. He couldn't let that happen.

Olivia had heard enough. "It's over, Jameson. I've already spoken with my lawyers. We're done, and I want you gone." She opened the door and motioned toward the men who waited in the hall. "Please escort him out."

Looking at Jameson, she continued. "Take nothing with you. All of your work here legally belongs to the company. Don't bother going home either. Just let my secretary know where you'll be, and I'll send your things there."

"Olivia wait. You can't do this to me. This is my research, my life's work. It's mine."

"You should have thought of that before you cheated on me. It's all in the pre-nup."

"I'll fight it."

She smirked. "I would expect nothing less. But mark my words. You'll lose." With her head, she motioned the security detail to come in. We watched them take his ID badge and security clearance, then escort him out of the office. In the hall, he glanced over his shoulder, sending a look of pure rage my way. Then he was taken out of the building.

Olivia glanced at me, grateful she'd made all the necessary arrangements before confronting her husband. "I'm sorry I doubted you. I had no idea about the office. That was... what you did... how did you know?"

"My premonitions," I answered gently.

She nodded. "Of course." She believed that my psychic abilities were real, and she knew she'd have to find the room I'd mentioned, but right now, she couldn't face it. "Thank you. Your fee is at the security desk. You can collect it on your way out."

She needed some time alone, so I nodded and left. She'd given me a thousand dollar bonus, so that was a plus. I never heard from her again.

So what had happened to Jameson?

I searched the Internet for any mention of him, and found a reference in the paper about the divorce. It didn't include any juicy details, but if the divorce had been messy, with a lot of legal battles between the two of them, it made sense that he might blame me.

If Olivia had transferred all of her assets into the shell company so he couldn't touch it, he'd be pretty upset. In fact, he probably knew all about the shell company. Maybe he'd even had a hand in creating it, and it had backfired on him.

This was it. Jameson Beal was my stalker. JB Sizemore. It all fit.

Olivia was probably the only person who might know where Jameson was, so talking to her was my next step. I'd call her first thing in the morning and set up an appointment. She had to be related to the Patton family, but I'd be sure not to mention Uncle Joey during my visit.

A thrill of elation along with a wave of relief crashed over me. I'd done it. The next time I spoke with Uncle Joey, I'd know where to find my stalker.

"Mom. Wake up."

I jerked out of a fitful sleep and opened my bleary eyes to find Savannah standing over me. "What time is it?"

"It's eight-thirty. You're supposed to take me to Ash's house, remember? We're helping her mom make decorations for her aunt's wedding."

"Right. Let me get dressed, and I'll take you over."

I threw on my jeans and a t-shirt, slipped on my flip-flops, and rushed downstairs. After dropping Savannah off, I got home and called Olivia Beal.

Her secretary told me I could stop by between one and two in the afternoon. I hated to wait that long to get my answers, but I had a good feeling that she'd know where to find Beal. This whole nightmare could be over before anything else happened; even better, it could end before the wedding.

Elated, I called Thrasher Development and spoke to Jackie. Uncle Joey was in a meeting, so I told her I'd stop by between one-thirty and two.

That settled, I called Chris to tell him the good news. He'd been asleep by the time I got to bed last night. He answered right away, but didn't have a lot of time to talk. I gave him the short version and heard the relief in his voice.

"Do you really think it's him?"

"It sure seems like it, but I won't know for certain until I talk to him."

"Yeah, that's true. If you get an address from her, just promise me you won't go after him alone. Take Dimples with you."

"Oh, don't worry about that. I'm not about to go charging after him by myself." Since I hadn't said it was Dimples I'd take, I changed the subject. "Hey, is Ethan there today?"

"I think so."

"Maybe I'll stop by before my appointment. I'd really like to know what's going on with him. I thought that I could offer my help if he needs it. What do you think?"

"Sure. That's a great idea."

"Okay. I'll get ready and come over."

"I've got to be in court soon, so I might not be here, but stop by just in case. Okay?"

"Will do."

With time on my hands, I woke Josh up and fixed us some breakfast. He didn't know anything about my stalker, and I wanted to keep it that way, so I told him I had a couple of appointments today. His shift at the country club was this afternoon, but since he usually rode his bike there, he didn't need me to drive him.

"So what are you working on?" he asked.

I hated lying to my kids, but I rationalized that it was a good kind of lying, so that made it okay. "I need to help Ethan out. He's a junior lawyer at Dad's office, and he needs some help with a case." Before I knew it, I was telling him all about Claire and the DNA test. "We're hoping to prove that she's her own twin. Isn't that weird?"

"Whoa," he said. "I didn't know that was even possible." He was thinking that maybe he ought to consider becoming a private investigator. Just look at all the interesting things that I was involved with. And there was never a dull moment.

That shocked me to the core, and I had to slap my hand over my mouth to keep from shouting *no way.* Then I picked up that he thought there were some downsides, and one of them included working for a mob boss, so maybe not. But it was worth looking into.

I let out a relieved breath. At least he was being rational about it, so I didn't have to worry. Still, I decided then and there to start talking about some great careers that might interest him so it would get his mind off what I did. Besides, he was only fifteen. There was plenty of time to choose a career.

After cleaning up our breakfast dishes, I hopped into the shower. I dried my hair and put on some make-up, then riffled through my clothes, looking for something dressier than my regular jeans and a tee. Since it was June, I decided to wear a floral-print pencil skirt with my white, scoop-neck, stretchy top and wedge sandals.

For good measure, I threw my favorite jeans and t-shirt, along with socks and my running shoes, into my gym bag, so I could change into them later. After telling Josh goodbye, I hurried out to my car and drove to Chris's law firm.

I found Ethan in his tiny office pretty quick. He wasn't expecting me, and his eyes widened with shock. The dread I caught from his thoughts would have hurt my feelings if I didn't know he was hiding something.

"Mrs. Nichols. What are you doing here?"

"I think it's time we had a little chat." If anything, his dread worsened, and I was afraid he'd make up some lame excuse and run off.

Instead of using intimidation to get to him, I decided to be nice. Moving some files off the chair by his desk, I sat down and leaned forward in a conspiratorial manner.

"Look, I know you're in trouble, and I'd like to help. What can I do to get you out of this situation? I know Strickland has something on you. Maybe I can help with that?"

He shook his head. "It's too late."

"What do you mean?"

"I did something stupid when I interned for him, and he caught me. When he realizes that I'm not going through with the plan, he'll throw me under the bus. You can't stop him."

"When did this... indiscretion happen?"

"About three months ago. But time doesn't matter. He'll have me disbarred no matter what happens now."

"What did you do?"

Ethan didn't want to tell me, but I picked it up just the same. Apparently, Ethan had falsified a police report that came through the prosecuting attorney's office in order to keep a friend from going to jail. Strickland caught him and then decided to let it go so he'd have leverage over Ethan.

"Is Strickland holding something over your head? Why would he do that? Did he know you were going to work here?"

Ethan sucked in a breath, thinking how uncanny it was that I picked it up so fast. He ran a hand through his hair before catching my gaze. "Yes. I'd just gotten an offer to work here, and Strickland thought it was the perfect way to get dirt on Chris so he'd give up Manetto."

He was thinking that he'd done it too, not that it was real. The recording he'd given Strickland wasn't incriminating until Strickland had it altered. If Strickland arrested Chris, Ethan would have to tell everyone the whole damn story.

That was why he'd gone to Strickland yesterday. He'd told him the deal was off, and, if Strickland used that recording, he'd let everyone know it was falsified. Sure, it would ruin Ethan, but it would ruin Strickland too.

Strickland had been furious, and Ethan knew it was only a matter of time before Strickland 'found' the police report Ethan had altered and had him disbarred. At least Ethan didn't think he'd go to jail for it, especially if he asked Chris to represent him. But how could he ask Chris, when he'd gone through with the plan in the first place?

Too bad he couldn't take off and leave this all behind. But that would just make things worse, and he couldn't do that to his family. So, either way, he was screwed. He didn't want Manetto to kill him, so it had to be Strickland and disbarment, and maybe time in jail. He was such a stupid idiot.

Yikes! This was awful, and I had no idea how I could help him.

"Wow," I said. "So can Strickland have you arrested... you know... for what you did?" Since I wasn't supposed to know the details, I had to be careful.

"Yes."

"Okay. Uh... I'm going to see if I can help you. I can't promise anything, but let me work on it. Do you know how much time you have before Strickland makes his move?"

Ethan's eyes widened. He couldn't believe I'd help him. Not after what he'd done to Chris. Of course, I didn't know the details. If I did, he was sure I wouldn't be so nice.

"I'm sort of expecting it to hit the fan today but, if not, it will probably be tomorrow at the latest." He thought if I was smart, I'd tell Chris what I knew and have Chris fire Ethan. Yeah, maybe it was better that way. If he got fired before it all came out, he wouldn't have to see Chris's disappointment. He was such a loser.

"Look Ethan, don't give up so quickly. I'll figure something out. In the meantime, try not to be so hard on yourself. You made a mistake. Don't we all?"

He huffed out a breath. I was only saying that because I didn't know everything. "I guess so." Now he had to live with the guilt of deceiving me. Maybe he should tell me to stay out of it, but he couldn't bring himself to say the words. It was nice having someone on his side, even if it was misguided.

Sheesh. Talk about a downer. "Good. Now tell me about Claire's case. I missed out on that."

He explained what he'd done, happy that he'd helped someone before the end of his career. He just hoped I was right about the chimerism. But, on the bright side, if it didn't work out, someone else would have to tell her, since he'd probably be in jail.

"Thanks for helping her. We'll get this figured out. I'll see what I can do. In the meantime, don't give up hope."

He smiled. "Thanks Mrs. Nichols. You're a good person." Then he ruined it by thinking *even if you work for a mob boss.*

I smiled back and left his office. Wow. What a mess. It seemed the only way to help Ethan would be to get some dirt on Strickland and threaten him with it. Uncle Joey could probably do it. He might even have something on him already. But did I want to go that route? I needed to talk it over with Chris and see what he thought.

With that in mind, I made my way to his office.

"Hi Shelby." Elisa greeted me with a smile, thinking that I looked good for a change. I'd actually made an effort with my clothes and make-up, and what a difference it made. She couldn't understand why older women let themselves go. Didn't they know their husbands, and men in general, would get bored with them, especially with all the younger, sexier girls they had to choose from? It was a disgrace to all females everywhere.

Holy hell! I wanted to strangle her. The nice greeting I'd been ready to speak died on my lips. "Is Chris back?"

"No. He's still in court." She checked her watch. "But he shouldn't be long. Do you want to wait?"

"Sure. I'll wait in his office." Without giving her another glance, I opened the door to his office and stepped inside. The lights came on automatically, and I sat down behind his desk, in his comfortable chair, and made myself at home.

I didn't have a lot of time before I needed to leave for my appointment with Olivia, so I found a legal pad and began writing down what I'd picked up about Ethan. He'd altered a police report, got caught by the prosecuting attorney, who'd then coerced him into spying on Chris to bring down Uncle Joey.

Those tactics sounded more like something a mob boss would do, not the law-enforcing, prosecuting attorney.

I wasn't sure what Ethan meant about a recording, but Chris might know. Still, how would someone go about altering it? That seemed risky. I mean... wasn't it just as illegal as altering a police report? Maybe that was a good angle to use against Strickland.

I wrote all of that down, along with a few question marks since I had no idea what to do about it. Then I wrote a more intimate note, with lots of XO's, and signed my name. With a few minutes to spare, I took advantage of his personal bathroom and freshened up.

When he still hadn't arrived, I folded the paper on which I'd written everything and tucked it into his top desk drawer. Having Elisa come in and read it was the last thing I wanted. On a sticky note, I told him I'd been there, and to call me when he had a minute.

I left, giving Elisa a friendly smile, even if she didn't deserve it.

"I'll tell Chris you were here," she said.

"Thanks," I answered. "See you later."

CHAPTER 9

The drive to BioTech took close to twenty minutes, and I arrived a few minutes before one o'clock. After signing in for security purposes, the receptionist took me to Olivia's office.

Olivia stood with a smile to greet me, wondering what I wanted. It had been several months since I'd helped her, and she'd just read about me in the paper. Did I have a premonition about her that I wanted to share?

"Thanks for seeing me on such short notice," I said, hoping to put her at ease. "I'm here because I'm looking for Jameson, and I hoped you could help. Do you know where I can find him?"

Her face lost that sparkle, and her lips turned down. "What's he done this time?"

"Oh. It's nothing for you to worry about. I need to find him for a client." Sure it was a lie, but not if I was the client.

She nodded, thinking that he'd probably fleeced someone out of their money, and they'd hired me to get to the bottom of it. "I haven't kept in touch with him. When he left, he stayed with his lab assistant for a while. But I know she kicked him out."

"Is he still here in the city?"

"Oh yes. I don't know where he's living, but, in the divorce settlement, he did manage to get one of our properties. The building's not worth much, but I think he rents out the office space to a couple of businesses. He might even be living there in the back offices, or maybe the basement, but I'm not sure."

"Thanks. That's a good place for me to start. Can I get the address?"

"Of course." She pulled out a pen and paper and wrote it down. "It's a brick building on Main Street, number six-forty-four. I think one of the businesses is an insurance company, so you might look for that."

"Thank you so much." I smiled and took the paper from her.

She nodded. "I hope you find him."

We said our goodbyes, and I left the building, bursting with hope that the search for my stalker would soon be over. I drove straight to Thrasher Development. Chris may have wanted me to take Dimples as my backup, but, since Uncle Joey was involved, Ramos was the better choice.

Besides, Dimples was getting married, and I didn't want anything bad to happen to him before the wedding. I sighed, knowing that was an excuse. When it came right down to it, Ramos was my first choice. What did that say about me?

Not wanting to think too hard about that, I flipped on my play list and listened to Jodie McAllister sing "Devil Rider." Since I'd recently met her, and this song was all about Ramos, it always made me smile. It also reminded me that I hadn't sent Ramos's brother, Javier, an email about the two of them finally meeting up. How could I let that slip from my mind?

Of course, it had been a pretty busy week. I'd stopped a mass shooting, found out I had a stalker who'd tried to kill me, helped Billie with a client who could be her own twin, and... what else? Oh yeah, now I had to figure out a way to help Ethan, because he'd been coerced into getting Chris arrested so the prosecuting attorney would have leverage to go after Uncle Joey.

Yeah... my plate was kind of full. Today, I hoped to solve at least one of those problems. If I could stop Beal now, my life would be a whole lot easier, and I could concentrate on all those other things. Of course, I didn't know if it was Beal for sure, but who else could it be?

I grabbed my gym bag with my extra clothes, and added my motorcycle jacket to the mix before heading upstairs to Thrasher Development. Sure, Elisa had approved of my outfit... and I looked hot, but I'd learned from experience that, when going after a crazy person, it was best to wear suitable shoes in case I had to run. Plus, I couldn't ride a motorcycle in this tight skirt.

Jackie greeted me with a smile, and we exchanged pleasantries before she told me Uncle Joey was waiting for me in his office.

"Thanks," I replied. "I'll put my stuff in my office and head down." Opening my office door, I breezed inside, somewhat amazed that this space was actually mine. After depositing my gym bag and jacket behind my desk, I slipped my purse into a desk drawer and sat down for a minute, happy to have a chair that didn't try to throw me out.

The beautiful painting on the wall reminded me that, although there were times when Uncle Joey seemed a little gruff around the edges, he still cared for me. That was pretty amazing coming from a mob boss.

I needed to tell him what I knew about Ethan's problem. He'd know how to help Ethan better than I could. Besides, if Strickland was using Chris to get to Uncle Joey, it was Uncle Joey's problem, too. It bothered me that Strickland wasn't any better than the criminals he put away. What was up with that? He was supposed to be a good guy.

With a sigh, I left my office and knocked on Uncle Joey's door before entering. Ramos sat in front of Uncle Joey's desk and stood to greet me. He was dressed in full hitman mode, with dark jeans, black t-shirt, and a black, leather motorcycle jacket and boots.

His brows drew together at my outfit. Then he thought that I'd have to hike my skirt up a lot to sit on the back of his motorcycle. It would be downright indecent.

"I brought a change of clothes," I said, wanting to set him straight, but he just grinned, pleased that he'd rattled me. Again.

"Come in Shelby," Uncle Joey said, thinking Ramos and I sometimes acted like a couple of kids. I wanted to tell him it wasn't my fault, but that would just validate his opinion. "Did you find anything?"

"Yes. I found a connection to a past client of mine. But, before I get started on that, I need to update you on the Ethan situation."

I sat down and proceeded to tell him everything that I'd found out, including the recording that was now in Strickland's possession. "Apparently, Strickland has doctored it to make Chris sound guilty. I guess, at some point, I'm going to have to talk to Strickland and see if I can pick up where that recording is."

Uncle Joey nodded. "Yes. Getting that recording would solve all our troubles. I'll see what I can do about that. In the meantime, let's get back to this client of yours. Who is it?"

His quick change of topic made me realize he had something up his sleeve that he didn't want me to know about. "Right... uh... do you know who Olivia Beal is? She owns a company called BioTech."

Uncle Joey's brows rose. He knew Olivia well. She was a granddaughter in the Patten family. Could this have something to do with his investment in BioTech? "What about her?"

"A couple of months ago, she asked me to find out if her husband was cheating on her."

"And was he?"

"Yes."

Uncle Joey sat back in his chair, finally understanding the reason for BioTech's recent problems. "What happened to him?"

"She told him he was done and to clear out. I think he signed a pre-nup, so he basically lost everything. He had to leave all his research and patents behind. It was something about intellectual property belonging to the company."

"Now it makes sense," Uncle Joey said, thinking that, with Beal gone, plans for releasing the pills had stagnated. That's why putting pressure on the company to show results for his investment had gone unanswered. "Do you think he's the one targeting you?"

"It makes sense. He probably blames me for losing everything. I asked Olivia if she knew where I could find him, and she gave me an address to a building that Jameson got in the settlement. If he's there, we can ask him all about it. Want to check it out?"

A pleased smile curved Uncle Joey's lips, and he glanced at Ramos. "Take Shelby, and make sure you don't leave until you've had a nice, long chat with him."

Ramos nodded and glanced my way, looking me up and down. "You'll have to change if you want to take the bike."

"I'm planning on it. What about you? Did you find anything useful from Jim at the restaurant?"

"I went over the tapes from the surveillance cameras with him, but the guy must have known about the cameras, because he wore a hat and always kept his face down. The police couldn't come up with a positive ID. But you were right about the balloons. The popping wasn't from a gun."

"Well, at least he wasn't trying to kill anyone."

"True," Uncle Joey said. "And now maybe we can find him and put an end to this."

I smiled, inordinately pleased to have a mob boss on my side. "I'll go change." I hurried out and returned to my office. Locking the door behind me, I figured this was a good place to change. It was lots roomier than the bathroom, and it was private. I kicked off my shoes and pulled my shirt out from the waistband of my skirt.

My neck prickled, and I froze. It was private, right? I hadn't bothered to glance at the ceiling and corners of my office for a surveillance camera, and I jerked my gaze upward. There was nothing that I could see, but it would be just my luck if a camera was hidden somewhere.

Before I changed my mind, I went back to Uncle Joey's office and stepped inside. Uncle Joey glanced at me with raised brows. Ramos sat in the same chair as when I'd left. They both took in my bare feet and untucked shirt and wondered what was going on.

"Uh... there's not a surveillance camera in my office is there?"

Uncle Joey glanced at Ramos, since that was his department. Ramos shook his head. "No." He was thinking he might like giving me a hard time, but he would never spy on me like that. It offended him that I'd think so.

"Oh... no... I'm sure you wouldn't... it was just... I didn't mean... uh... sorry. I'll be ready in a minute." I backed out the door, my face flaming red with embarrassment. Great. I'd just insulted Ramos.

It took a few minutes to change my clothes, but longer to get over my mistake. I knew Ramos wouldn't have put a surveillance camera in my office to spy on me, but putting one there for security purposes wasn't a stretch. So I wasn't that far off, and I didn't need to apologize for that.

After slipping on my motorcycle jacket, I slung my purse over my shoulder and left my office with my head held high. Uncle Joey's door was open, and Ramos stood inside, waiting for me. He caught sight of me and told Uncle Joey I was ready and we'd be back soon, then he joined me in the hall.

He sent me a smile, thinking that, as much as I rocked the dressy outfit, he liked me best in jeans and a motorcycle jacket.

"So you're not mad?" I asked. "About the cameras?"

He chuckled. "No. I take it as a sign that you're getting better at this. A year ago, it wouldn't have crossed your mind."

"Well, you're probably right, although, if it had crossed yours, I would have known."

"No doubt. You're a force to be reckoned with."

My response was cut short by the ringing of my phone, sending panic into my heart. Since I hadn't heard from my stalker after the restaurant business, I'd been expecting him to call. I pulled my phone from my purse, but found a number on the caller ID.

"It's not him," I told Ramos, relieved. "Hello?"

"Hi Shelby. This is Stacey Sherwood again from Good Morning America. I hope you've had a chance to talk to your husband about coming to New York to appear on our show. We'd like to schedule you next week if possible. What day works best for you?"

"Oh... actually... I don't think that will work for me. I have a friend's wedding going on, and I need to help out with that."

I heard a sigh, signaling that she finally seemed to get the picture. "Well, I'm sure you're busy. Why don't I put you on the list for a later time? I'll call back in a month or so, and we'll see if we can work something out."

"That would be better for me. Thanks." We said our goodbyes and disconnected. I let out a big sigh and slipped my phone back into my purse. Since we stood by Jackie's desk, she'd heard my part of the conversation and wondered what the call was about.

"Oh, that was Good Morning America. They want me to come on their show because of the shooting. I've told them no every time, but they keep calling me back."

"Really? Are you serious?" Jackie asked. "Wow. What an honor. Why don't you want to go on the show?"

"Oh... you know... who wants all that attention? Not me! They just don't like taking no for an answer."

Ramos arched a brow and twisted his lips, thinking that I hadn't said no this time.

"Well, I can see your point," Jackie continued. "But, it's not that big of a deal, I mean... they have people on all the time, but I usually don't remember their names the next day. They always have someone new, you know? Hey, maybe you can go on the show when we're in New York for Miguel's opening night. That would work."

"Yeah... maybe," I said, hating to let her down. "But I'm sure by then they will have forgotten all about my story, like you said, and moved on to more current things. Uh... we'll be back."

She nodded, thinking I was just making excuses. How could anyone forget that I'd stopped a shooting spree? That was huge. In fact, it might be worthy of receiving a medal of some sort from the president of the United States or, at the least, the governor. On the other hand, Joe wouldn't like it much, so it was probably better to forget about it. He'd hate all the—

The elevator doors slid shut, blocking out the rest of her thoughts, and I slumped against the side of the elevator. Ramos took pity on me and kept his thoughts to himself, but it didn't take a mind reader to know he didn't approve.

"Don't worry. I'm not going to do it."

He just nodded, and I caught his thoughts that it had to be hard to be me sometimes. He appreciated that I did my best, and I usually did more than I should to help people, but I didn't have to help everyone. He didn't like that I let people walk all over me.

That cracked me up, and I let out a huff. "You mean like Uncle Joey?"

That brought a smile to his lips, and he shook his head. He thought that we'd both reached the point of no return with Manetto. Hell, I was even posing as his niece. What was I going to do in New York when I took my family to meet the New York Manettos? I'd have to tell my kids the truth at some point.

"I already did," I said. "They know Uncle Joey is a mob boss and that I work for him. But they don't know I can read minds, and I hope they never find out."

"You shouldn't count on it. At some point, they'll figure it out. You just need to decide what you'll do about it when the time comes."

On that cryptic note, the doors slid open into the parking garage, and we headed toward his bike. He was right, I did need to plan for the future, but, right now, I only wanted to think about how great it would be to catch Jameson Beal and put an end to this awful game of his.

The ride to Jameson's building went by way too fast. Ramos parked the bike out of sight on a side street. We locked our helmets on the bike and walked toward the building. "Let's cross through here," Ramos said, indicating the alley along the back and thinking that we didn't want to give ourselves away by going in the front doors.

A few cars were parked behind the buildings, along with some garbage bins and various unwanted items. The building we wanted was at the end of the alley next to another street. Ramos studied the back entrance, looking for a surveillance camera, but couldn't see one.

We approached the glass door and found it open for business. Entering, we stood inside a long hallway that separated a couple of offices. A staircase going both up and down was to our left. Ramos tilted his head toward the stairs, thinking that we should look in the basement first, and I nodded my agreement.

Heading down to the shadowy basement, my chest tightened. What if he was down there? What were we going to do then? At the bottom of the stairs, we found a couple of steel doors on either side of the hall close to the front of the building that looked like the entrance to some storage space.

The door to the right of us was different. It was made from wood and had frosted glass framing the top half, making it look more like an office door. Cautiously stepping to the door, Ramos tried the knob. Finding it locked, he took out his lock pics and went to work. A second later, he had it opened, thinking *stay behind me.*

I held my breath and followed him inside. Ramos glanced around the room, searching the dark corners, and ready to attack whoever might be there. Finding it empty, he straightened. "Close the door."

I started to breathe again and shut it quietly. Light from a couple of small windows at the top of the back wall allowed us to see without turning on a light. A large desk with a chair in front took up the space between the windows. A computer monitor sat on top, along with a printer and other office supplies.

An old couch sat against one side of the wall, with a blanket and pillow strewn haphazardly across the cushions. But it was the wall on the other side of the desk that drew me closer. It was covered with computer print-outs, and in the center was a photograph of my face.

The hairs on the back of my neck stood on end, and my breath hitched. The entire wall held pictures of me, along with articles from the newspaper. On the left, the date from a year ago last April was circled in red. Pinned underneath it was the article about the bank robbery at the grocery store where I'd been shot in the head and had gained my mind reading powers.

Beside that was a newspaper clipping with a photo of me standing in a parking lot, gazing with shock at Uncle Joey's burning car. In the grainy photo, I wore my black wig with the bangs. The next print-out showed a photo of me accepting a plaque and my ID badge from the mayor at the Museum Gala. I didn't even know there was a picture of me from that night.

Further along, the next print-out showed me standing with the bank manager in a cemetery beside a casket. The person taking the photo was too far away to see much, but the headline said it all, and the article revealed my name, stating that I'd helped the bank recover the stolen money from a long-ago robbery.

It shocked me to see so much information about me. Swallowing, I turned my gaze to a few shots of me at the courthouse. I recognized one from the time I'd been accused of murder, but there were several others, some of which I didn't remember at all.

There were a few news stories that didn't have my name in them, but they contained news reports of things I'd been involved with, like Uncle Joey's nightclub where a judge had been arrested and I'd been shot. Another one told about the serial killer who'd left a note naming all of his victims before he'd committed suicide.

Beside it, another article was pinned with a photo of me standing beside Dimples and several police officers. It showed a crime scene near a freeway underpass. My name wasn't mentioned in that one, but I was easily recognizable in the background.

Another article mentioned me and how I'd helped police find the remains of a couple of kids in the crawl space of a basement, and solving the mystery of what had actually happened to them several years earlier.

My breath hitched to see a clipping of me and Ramos floating in the Potomac River. It wasn't clear who we were, and our names were never mentioned, but there it was, pinned to the wall. Beside it came the story about the poisoning at the restaurant, stating that two people had been taken to the hospital and had barely survived.

The next article had a picture of the fugitive, Leo Tedesco, in handcuffs as he was led away by Dimples and Marshal Gerard. I wasn't even mentioned as helping to bring him in, but it was still there on the wall. In the center of it all was the most recent article of the newspaper shooting, with the photo of me looking down at the woman and holding my stun flashlight. Every single thing I'd been involved in was represented on that wall.

But that wasn't all. Interspersed among the print-outs were photos of me entering or leaving the police station. Others showed me driving out of the parking garage from

Uncle Joey's building, and there were a few of me walking into Chris's office building.

It wasn't until my gaze rested on the photos of me at home that I started to get light-headed. A few showed me coming or going from my house, but there were others of me outside with my kids. The last photo sent shards of ice through my veins. I was sitting on my deck swing with Chris, and it was taken just day before yesterday.

"Shelby?" I must have made a noise, because Ramos put his arm around me. He helped me sit in a chair and pushed my head between my knees. "Breathe slowly, in and out. In... and out. That's better. You're doing fine."

My ears rang so bad that I could hardly hear a word he said, but I focused on his voice and started to feel better. A moment later, I sat up and closed my eyes, resting my head in my hands. Ramos left my side to prowl around the room, looking for anything that would give Beal's plans away.

He shuttered his thoughts for my sake, but the anger came flooding through loud and clear. This guy was going down, even if he had to kill him to do it. That sort of shocked me out of my stupor, and I came back from my meltdown.

Taking my phone from my purse, I took photos of the wall, zooming in to get the details. I had no idea what to do next, but I wanted to make sure this was documented. Finished, I glanced toward Ramos. "What should we do now?"

He came to my side. "I'm taking you back to the office. I'll take care of this."

"How?"

"You don't want to know." He closed his mind off to me, but the grim set of his lips told me just what he had in mind.

"You're coming back to wait for him." It wasn't a question, and the tightening of his lips confirmed it. Relief swept over me so strongly that I thought I might faint. I glanced back at the wall, suddenly wanting to tear it to shreds. How dare he do this to me?

"Come on," Ramos said. "Let's get out of here before he comes back."

I let out a breath before nodding. I stood on shaking legs and grabbed the back of the chair for support. Ramos slipped his arm around my waist and tugged me against him. Embarrassed at my weakness, I wanted to tell him I was okay, but his arm felt so good around me that I leaned on him anyway.

At the door, I felt strong enough to manage on my own. "I'm good now. You can let me go." He peered at me with indecision before agreeing.

Leaning over, I rested my hands on my knees, taking a couple more deep breaths. Something shiny on the doorknob caught my attention. "Wait. What's that?"

I pointed at a thin wire hanging from the handle. Ramos took one look at it and froze. He swore several times in his mind, then shook his head in dismay.

"What is it? What's wrong?"

"It's an alarm." He searched for the other side of the wire, finding it on the floor attached to a small electronic switch of some kind. "When we opened the door, it broke the wire which tripped the switch. I'm sure it sent an alert, telling Beal that someone had entered this room."

"Is he on his way?"

"Since we tripped it when we first came in, he might already be here." He thought that the sophistication of the wire might also mean something else.

"You mean like a trap?" I asked.

He sent me a nod, grateful that I'd seen it before he'd opened the door. If Beal was smart, he'd have something ready and waiting on the other side. Beal wouldn't be out there now, but if he'd known we were here, he could have set something up while we searched the room. Opening the door would trigger his booby trap.

"What should we do?"

He glanced at the windows. "We might have to go out that way."

"Should I call Dimples?"

Our gazes met. He thought that, with the threat to me and my family, along with the threat to the detective and his wedding, we might not have a choice. But if the police got involved, his plans to kill Beal were shot.

"Oh, right. Maybe we should wait." Did I just say that? When had I become so jaded that I was willing to let Ramos kill someone for me? "Uh... until we get out of here." I caught Ramos's gaze and shrugged. "It's best to keep our options open, right?"

He grinned, thinking we had more in common than he thought. Before I could respond, the glass in one of the windows shattered, and a flaming bottle sailed into the room.

The bottle hit the cement floor and exploded. Ramos pulled me against him and lunged out of the way. He took the brunt of the fall onto his side and continued to roll toward the back wall. We came to a stop, and Ramos jumped to his feet.

The flames danced on the cement and began spreading toward the couch and the wall with all the photos. Ramos acted quickly and tore off his leather motorcycle jacket to beat out the flames heading toward the wall.

I hated to see his jacket ruined, so I rushed around the flames to the desk and grabbed the bottle of water I'd noticed earlier. "Stop. You'll ruin your jacket. Use this instead."

I chucked the bottle to him, and he caught it one-handed. He quickly slipped his shoulder holster and gun to the ground behind him and pulled his black tee over his head. Saturating it with water, he slapped at the flames with the wet shirt.

My jaw dropped open, and I stood there like a dummy, transfixed by the scene of Ramos without a shirt. As he worked, his muscles rippled, and I couldn't tear my gaze away, even if my life depended on it.

"Get away from the window," he yelled, still beating at the flames, and thinking that Beal could be out there waiting to ambush us.

My muddled brain woke up to the danger, and I eased back toward Ramos and the door. The flames had spread to the couch, and I couldn't get around them. I quickly grabbed the blanket and started beating at the flames.

They licked the edge of the couch and began to climb up the side, so I threw the blanket over the flames and slapped at them with my hands. The blanket began to smoke, but the flames died down. I kept at it, slapping and beating at them until they were nothing but smoke.

Breathing heavily, I sat back on my heels and glanced toward Ramos. He continued to slap out the last of the fire with his now-smoking shirt. Thankfully, most of the smoke had dissipated, leaving the last of it to curl from his shirt and the blanket.

As the flames died out, Ramos straightened. His chest heaved and glistened with sweat. With his legs braced apart, he looked like a Roman gladiator. The heat of anger blazed in his eyes, and his chest muscles tightened, mirroring his rage. He looked ready to yell, and I braced for a primal roar.

It never came. Instead, he tamped down his anger and glanced my way. I was panting from my exertion, and more than a little scared. It brought his anger back, and it shot out on a tide of vengeance. I picked up that he wanted to kill Beal more than he'd wanted to do anything in a long time.

The surprise of what we'd been through, and the irony of his thoughts, struck my funny bone. I choked out a strangled laugh. His brows rose, so I quickly explained. "Kill Beal... get it?" I laughed again, then snorted, which made me laugh even harder. "Oops. I don't usually snort." I knew I sounded a little crazy, but I couldn't help it.

Ramos shook his head, grateful his anger had passed and that he was back in control. He thought I was in shock, but he'd rather see me laughing than crying. He picked up his gun and holster, then slid the holster over his bare shoulders, knowing that his t-shirt was a lost cause.

My breath caught, and I gasped on another snort. With a chuckle, I blurted, "Whoa! I like that look." A snicker escaped my lips, and I blurted, "You should wear it like that all the time."

His lips twisted, and he shook his head, then spoiled my view by slipping on his motorcycle jacket. Seeing his bare chest beneath a black leather motorcycle jacket was like a dream come true. Wowza. I was never going to get that image out of my mind. On the other hand, why would I want to do that?

"You'd better call your detective," he said, pulling me from my daze. "It's time."

"What about killing Beal?" Disappointment turned my lips into a pout. Ramos's brows rose, and I threw up my hands. "Fine. You're right. I should call Dimples. Besides, you can still kill Beal... uh... later... if you have to."

My purse was still slung over my shoulder, so I grabbed my phone and put the call through before I could think about it too hard. Dimples answered right away.

"Hey there. I found my stalker, but I... uh... we... need your help." I explained the situation, telling him we were in the basement of Jameson Beal's property and had managed to beat down the flames of a Molotov cocktail.

"By we... do you mean you... and Ramos?" he asked, his voice flat.

"Uh... yeah." He let out a breath, and I knew he didn't like that part. "We think the door might be booby-trapped, or we would have left by now, so be careful." After another short pause, he said he would and disconnected.

I slipped my phone back into my purse and glanced at Ramos. He didn't relish the thought of running into Dimples, especially without a shirt. But what choice did he have? He couldn't exactly leave the room.

My lips turned up in a big smile, and I shrugged. "I guess you can always zip up your jacket." He nodded and moved to do just that, but I let out a strangled noise. "But... uh... not yet. I mean... I'm sure it's hot in here. So you can wait until he gets here. In fact, you could even take off the jacket if you're too hot."

He shook his head, thinking *Shelby... what am I going to do with you?*

My smile widened. "Just think of it as payback for teasing me about calling you Romeo."

A chuckle escaped his lips. "I guess I deserved that." He offered his hand to help me up.

I placed my hand in his, then let out a hiss and pulled it back. "Ow." Looking at my hand, I found a couple of blisters forming on my palm where I'd slapped at the flames. I glanced at my other hand, but it was fine.

"Let's see," Ramos said.

"It's just a couple of blisters." Ramos took a knee beside me and examined my hand. Satisfied that it wasn't bad enough to need a doctor, he helped me up.

A rustling noise came from outside the broken window and my heart jumped in my chest. Ramos slipped his gun from his holster. I caught sight of black running shoes and dark jeans.

Ramos raised his gun to take a shot, but the person outside took off. Ramos cursed and ran to the window, still hoping to shoot him in the leg, but he was out of sight. Then we heard the siren and knew that was what had scared him off.

Ramos thought about going after him, but the window was a little on the small side, and he wasn't sure he'd fit. Then an idea occurred to him. He realized that Beal had known more than he should have about us.

Somehow, he'd known we'd figured out the door was booby-trapped. That's why he'd gone to the trouble of throwing the Molotov cocktail through the window. After we'd put the fire out, he'd come back, but had been scared off by the siren. That meant there was a bug or a surveillance camera somewhere in the room, and Beal had heard everything we'd said.

Once again, Ramos prowled around the room, looking in all the places he thought it might be. Studying the computer monitor on the desk, he brushed his fingers around the surface and found the bug. Setting it on the floor, he crushed it under his shoe.

We heard footsteps in the hall, and Dimples called through the door. "Shelby?"

"Yes."

"I'm here. You're right. It looks like the door is booby-trapped." A few seconds later, he continued. "There's a wire hooked up to a device. I have no idea what it does, but it looks like it releases a spray of some kind. It might be something flammable."

"That would make sense since he threw a Molotov cocktail through the window," I answered. "I think he's a scientist, so that might explain the device."

"Okay. Give me another minute or two."

I heard someone talking to Dimples and realized there was at least one other officer with him, maybe more.

Ramos leaned down to whisper in my ear. "Is it okay if I zip up my jacket now?"

His breath against my ear sent shivers down my spine. I sucked in a breath and stepped back for one last look at his bare chest. He was thinking that I could touch him if I wanted. A chuckle escaped my lips along with the temptation to call his bluff.

Cocking his brow, he grinned, daring me to do it and thinking, *I know you want to.* My gaze jumped to his face. As a flush crept up my neck, I rolled my eyes. "Uh... no... I mean... yes... zip it."

His mouth tilted into a lopsided grin. "You're sending mixed signals."

I huffed out a breath. "Argh! You're driving me crazy."

"Yeah, I can tell." He liked it too.

Before I could punch him, Dimples spoke from the other side of the door. "Okay. We've got it. Go ahead and open the door."

I glanced at the door. Without noticeably turning my head, I moved my eyes to take one last look at Ramos's chest and hoped he wouldn't notice. Of course, he did. A low chuckle escaped his lips before he zipped his jacket together.

Letting out a breath, I grabbed the door handle and quickly let go, wincing from the blisters on my hand. Ramos reached around me and pulled the door open.

Dimples entered, taking in the black burn marks and glass on the cement floor, and thinking we were lucky to get the fire out before it spread. "In the rush, I forgot who you said owns this place."

"It's Jameson Beal," I answered. "He owns the building, but there's more. You need to see this." I motioned him toward the wall covered with the pictures and articles about me.

"Holy hell." It shocked him to see the extent of information Beal had gathered about me. He also noticed some of the photos featuring him as well, and a chill swept down his spine.

"What's the connection?" he asked.

"One of my cases. His wife was a client. She wanted me to find out if her husband was cheating on her. It didn't take long to figure out that he was having the affair right under her nose. There was a lot of money involved. Because of the prenuptial agreement, he basically lost everything. I guess he blames me for it."

Dimples thought that was an understatement, but he refrained from saying it out loud. "How did you know he was here?"

"I went to see his ex-wife earlier, and she told me he got this building in the settlement. She gave me the address, so I thought I'd stop by and see if he was here."

Dimples's brows rose. Why I hadn't called him?

I hurried to explain. "With your wedding so close, I didn't want to bother you, so Ramos said he'd come with me."

Dimples glanced at Ramos, and his jaw tightened. It upset him that I'd gone to Ramos, especially when he was the one whose wedding had been threatened. If anything, he deserved to know before Ramos.

"Uh... I wasn't even sure you'd be at work today," I continued, hoping he'd cut me some slack. Having him mad at me wasn't something I liked and, given the circumstances, it didn't seem fair. "But... I'm glad you were. Thanks for coming. What should we do now?"

With a sigh, he let go of his anger and answered. "First, I need to document this so I can file a police report. Do you know where he might have gone?"

"No. I don't know anything else about him."

"Okay." He motioned toward the police officer who'd come with him, and told him to call in a team to document the incident. After he'd taken care of that, he turned to me and Ramos. "I need to make a note of some details, and then you can go."

While I gave him Olivia's name, and the name of her company, Ramos wandered over to the computer. He was itching to turn it on, but he didn't think Dimples would approve. He did it anyway, but it was password protected, and he couldn't get inside.

Dimples glanced up to find Ramos at the computer and hustled toward him. "What are you doing?"

"We need to find this guy. He tried to kill us. I thought there might be something on his computer, but I can't get in."

"I'll take it from here." Dimples glanced over his shoulder at the police officer, thinking it wasn't a good idea for the police to know Ramos was involved with this. "You should go. I'll get my people on this and let you know if I find anything."

My heart swelled with gratitude that Dimples wanted to protect Ramos. "Thanks. I'll stop by the precinct in an hour or so."

Dimples's brows rose. He hadn't meant that I should go, just Ramos. His lips flattened that I'd misunderstood... probably on purpose. "Okay. Be careful out there."

Oops. Not sure what to do, I glanced at Ramos. He tilted his head toward the door. With a sigh, I followed him out. Guilt that I had turned to the bad side churned my stomach. I knew I should stay and help Dimples, but, to be honest, I wanted to get out of there. Besides standing around, there wasn't much I could do anyway. I just hoped he wasn't too mad at me.

Ramos was thinking that Dimples had sounded upset, but I shouldn't take it too hard. He was sure the detective knew his limitations, since he had to follow the rules. Ramos didn't have that problem. Now he needed to find Beal, and he had an idea of where to start.

"You do?" I asked, surprised.

"Yeah." He smiled. "Remember Jerry? Maybe we should pay him another visit. Beal might have a condo in that place after all. Now that we have his name, we might get lucky."

I nodded. "You're right. Great thinking."

Standing beside the motorcycle, I put the call through to Jerry, and he picked right up. After exchanging pleasantries, I told him the reason for my call. "I have a name, and I wondered if we could come over and check your condo's building registry."

"Sure. I'll meet you outside at our table."

"Great. Thanks." We said our goodbyes and disconnected.

After relaying his answer to Ramos, I slipped on my helmet and climbed on the motorcycle behind him. The ride didn't take near as long as I wanted, but it was enough to help clear my head. This might be the break we needed. We'd find him and... then what? Ramos could kill him? No, that wasn't going to happen. But it would be nice to scare him a little before calling Dimples to come and arrest him.

At the food court, we approached the table, finding Jerry watching for us. He'd figured when I'd said "we" that I meant the scary looking dude, and he tried to hide his discomfort as we approached.

"Hey Shelby. Good to see you. So what's going on? Did something else happen? How did you find out his name?" Jerry wanted to know all the details and had been excited that I'd called him. He'd been wondering if anything more had happened and couldn't wait to hear my story, thinking it was just as good as reading a book or watching a TV show. But this was even better because it was real.

That brought a big grin to my lips. I caught that Ramos didn't want to go over the whole story again, but how could I disappoint Jerry when he was so helpful? "A lot has happened since the potted plant incident."

I told him about the restaurant and the threats to Dimples's wedding, then wrapped it all up with the connection to an old case, along with finding the room holding the wall of photos from which we'd just escaped.

"This guy's crazy," Jerry said. "What was the case about?"

"His wife was a client of mine, and I caught him cheating on her. He lost everything, so I think he blames me for it."

"What's the guy's name?"

"Jameson Beal."

"Got it. Come on, let's go inside, and I'll ask the manager about him." Jerry was thinking that he'd have to come up with a story to tell her, but that shouldn't be too hard. He let us into the building, and we followed him to the manager's office on the first floor.

"Hi Nadine," he began, giving her a friendly smile. "I think there's been a mix-up. I got a package earlier that was meant for someone named Jameson Beal. Is he a person who lives here?"

"Let me check," she said, happy to help Jerry. He was one of her favorites, because he was so nice and polite. He was also one of the few men who knew how to treat a woman, and she always enjoyed the attention he gave her.

She got to work on her computer and pulled up the directory. "How do you spell the last name?"

Since Jerry had no idea, he glanced my way and I answered. "B-E-A-L."

That was the first she'd taken a good look at me, and her brows drew together. Was Jerry doing this for me? Who was I? Just then, Ramos stepped to my side, and her heart kicked up a notch. She drank in his perfect face and body like she was dying of thirst.

I refrained from rolling my eyes and repeated the letters a second time since I knew she'd totally spaced it. She jerked her attention back to the computer and typed in the name. "Uh... I'm not finding a Jameson Beal. Sorry."

Jerry's lips turned down with disappointment, but I caught the other name she'd found. It was Jason Beal, and he lived in number eight-twenty-two on the eighth floor. It could be an alias for Jameson, and I couldn't help the happy smile that spread across my face. "Okay. Thanks anyway," I said, tugging Jerry away.

He sent Nadine a nod and a smile over his shoulder and followed me out of her office to the elevator. As I pushed the call button, he whispered, "What's going on?"

"Uh... I just got a premonition that we need to check out the eighth floor, number eight-twenty-two. Isn't that the same floor as the condo with the potted plant?" At his nod, I continued. "Another person there has the last name of Beal, but he goes by Jason. It's close enough that I think it's worth checking out."

Jerry nodded, amazed that I'd gotten so much from her. No doubt about it. I was a real psychic. We stepped into the elevator, but refrained from speaking since there were a couple of people already inside. Luckily they weren't women, so I didn't have to listen to all the *ooos* and *ahhs* about Ramos.

We disembarked and followed the hall until we stood in front of number eight-twenty-two. It wasn't too far from the condo with the plant, so it was possible that they knew each other. This had to be the link.

"Now what?" Jerry asked.

I had no idea, so I glanced at Ramos. His lips twisted with amusement, and he shrugged. "We knock and see if he's home."

"Oh right," Jerry said. He could picture Ramos shoving the man inside once the door was opened. "Why don't you knock, and I'll stand over there out of the way."

I hid a smile. Jerry was a perceptive man, and I liked him for it.

Ramos knocked and we waited. He knocked again, but there was no response. "Guess nobody's home." With that, he pulled his lock-pick set from his pocket and got to work. A second later he had the door opened, and he cautiously slipped inside.

"Uh... I'll stay out here," Jerry said, uncomfortable with the whole breaking and entering thing. "Just make it quick."

I nodded before following Ramos, allowing the door to click shut behind me. The condo was a lot like the other one, a spacious living room area with tall windows and a gas fireplace. The open kitchen stood on the other side of the room with a granite counter top separating the space.

Ramos looked through the mail sitting on the counter, while I glanced at the framed photographs on the mantle. My heart jumped as I recognized the woman in the photo.

It was Olivia Beal. Beside her stood a young man in a cap and gown, and next to him was Jameson. Jason had to be their son.

Maybe Jameson lived here, and it was in his son's name because of the divorce? I hurried to the short hall and found two doors. The first door opened into a master bedroom with a huge closet and bathroom. I couldn't tell if this was Jameson's room or Jason's. A receipt sat on the dresser, so I picked it up. It was from a dry-cleaning service and had Jason's signature on it. That meant the second bedroom must be Jameson's.

Steeling my nerves, I opened the door. A large desk with a computer took up the space along the wall. A filing cabinet stood on one side, along with several binders. Most of the papers on the desk had Jason's name on them. So if Jameson ever stayed here, it meant he had to sleep on the couch.

Ramos came down the hall to join me, and I filled him in. "It looks like I need to talk to Jason. He might know where his father is."

Ramos nodded. "You should probably involve the detective with that. I think you'll have more success. It might also help you get back on his good side."

I couldn't fault his thinking on that. "Okay. I'll let him know."

"Let's go."

In the hall, Jerry let out a relieved breath to see us. "Find anything?"

I nodded and told him it looked like Jason was Jameson's son. As we stepped inside the elevator, I continued. "I need to talk to Jason, but I'll probably get my detective friend to help with that."

"That's a good idea," Jerry agreed. He was grateful we hadn't been caught, and totally relieved that I was going to do this the right way. Since I was a PI, he knew I did some unconventional things, but he worried that the big guy was a bad influence on me. Hopefully, I knew where to draw the line.

I smiled. If he only knew the truth... that it was a lot worse than he thought. Balancing between helping a mob boss and the police was tricky business, but I always tried to stay on the right side of things. It was confusing at times, especially when the bad guys were supposed to be the good guys. Still, it touched me that he cared.

On the first floor, he walked out with us. "It was good to see you again. Uh... be sure and tell me what happens. Okay?" He wished he'd been more helpful, but at least we'd found a link to the building.

"Sure," I said. "And if you see anything, don't hesitate to give me a call." That made him happy, and he gave me a big hug.

"Here's my number too," Ramos said, handing him his card. "In case you lose hers." Jerry's eyes widened, and he wondered if that was a veiled threat. With a good natured nod, he took the card, thinking it might come in handy to have a strong guy like Ramos on his side.

We said our goodbyes, and I followed Ramos outside.

"I think he has a crush on you," Ramos said, thinking he'd given me a pretty long hug for someone he'd just met.

"Hey, we faced death together. It's different."

He couldn't dispute that. It had definitely brought us closer together. In fact, the only times he'd ever had a kiss from me was when he'd saved my life. Since that was the case, he probably deserved a kiss right now.

I snickered and shook my head. "Nah. I don't think it was quite that life-threatening."

He huffed out a breath, thinking it had been worth a try, even if I got the better part of the deal.

"What do you mean?"

He lifted his brow, thinking that I'd seen him without a shirt. Had I forgotten that part already?

"Oh... right... not hardly." My face flushed, so I turned away to focus on the shops. Right in front of us stood a t-shirt shop, and I hesitated, looking at the display through the window. "Hey, maybe we should get you a new shirt."

Ramos paused to consider it. His shoulder holster chafed against his skin, and he knew it would be red and sore by the time he got home. Besides that, with his leather jacket zipped up, he was uncomfortably warm.

"I've got time before Dimples gets back to the station," I said, happy for a diversion. "Let's get you a new shirt. Maybe something that isn't black."

He raised a brow, but followed me inside. I went straight to the men's section and glanced through the shirts. A lot of tees had comic book characters on them, and I couldn't picture Ramos wearing anything like that. Plus, the only color I could see Ramos wearing was black, or maybe white, navy, or grey, but nothing bright.

Then I found it. A black shirt with white printing on it that read, *"I'm here to drink milk and kick ass, and I just finished my milk."* I chuckled, then imagined how Ramos would look wearing it, and I laughed even harder.

"No," he said. "Don't even think about it." He held a black, super-soft tee shirt in his hand and took it to the sales clerk. Forty dollars seemed a little steep to me, but it did look nice and comfy... and probably form-fitting to show off his abs.

Ramos bought it on the spot, certain of the size without even trying it on. After explaining that he wanted to wear it, the clerk cut off the tags and showed him to the changing room.

While Ramos disappeared inside, I kept looking through the shirts to keep busy. He came out a minute later with a smile, thinking it was perfect. With his jacket now unzipped, I tried to see it better, mostly to check out the form-fitting part. I couldn't see much, but what I could see was totally worth the effort.

As we walked through the food court toward the escalators and the parking garage, my phone rang. I jerked to a stop and pulled my phone from my purse. Dread caught in my throat to find the number was blocked. "Oh no. It's him."

I stepped away from the crowd toward a more secluded spot by the wall and answered. "Hello?"

"Hello Shelby. It's been awhile. You've been busy the last couple of days."

"Look, I know who you are, so cut the crap."

"You don't know anything. But you'll learn soon enough."

My heart pounded, and I wanted to yell at him. I took a deep breath and let it out to calm down. I knew he wanted to rattle me, so I had to make sure he didn't. "What do you want?"

"I just wanted to let you know that I have another test for you. You may have escaped from my trap today, but I'm not convinced it had anything to do with your premonitions. I can't decide if it's because of the company you keep, or if it's just pure, dumb luck. Either way, we'll see how well you do at the wedding."

His breath sounded a little raspy, so I swallowed my worry and steadied my voice. "What do you mean? What's going to happen at the wedding?"

"See. That's what I don't understand. With your premonitions, you should already know. But... since it seems your premonitions don't always work, I thought I'd give you a proper warning. Things have changed. I'm not holding back anymore."

He paused to let his words sink in. "Let me put it this way. I hope your premonitions start working better, because, if they don't, someone you care about will die."

The line went dead, and I squeezed the phone so hard my knuckles turned white. Ramos put his hand over mine. His touch brought me back from that dark place, and I turned to face him.

"He said he wanted to warn me since he didn't believe in my premonitions. He said he wasn't holding back anymore, and he threatened the wedding again." I caught Ramos's gaze. "Then he said someone I cared about would die, and he wasn't joking."

Ramos's face turned hard. "When is the wedding?"

"Day after tomorrow. I need to go to the precinct." I slipped my phone back into my purse. "I have no choice. I need to tell Dimples to postpone the wedding."

"You can't let this guy win," Ramos said, grabbing my shoulders.

"But I don't know if I can stop him. If someone dies—"

"Stop. Take a deep breath and relax." Our gazes met, and he continued. "No one is going to die. He's just threatening you. It's part of his game to get into your head. Don't let him win."

I closed my eyes and nodded, feeling the tension fall away.

Relieved, Ramos released his hold and let out a sigh. "I think it's a good idea to head over to the precinct and talk to the detective. I'm sure he'll know what to do."

"Okay."

"In the meantime, I'm going to see if I can find him."

"How?" I asked.

His mind closed off, and his stony expression sent a spike of worry through my chest. Then his lips turned up, but it wasn't the smile I was used to. It looked downright predatory, and I knew his plans included something I didn't want to know.

Resigned to let it go, I nodded and headed toward the escalator. Ramos followed, and I caught his relief that I hadn't questioned him, but worry tightened my chest. Sure, it was great to have him on my side, but what had I gotten him into? This wasn't his problem, but now that he was involved, what if he got hurt or arrested because of me? Could I live with that?

I worried about it all the way back to Thrasher. After getting off the bike, I pulled the helmet from my head and handed it to Ramos. As he turned to put it away, I caught his arm. "I don't know what you have planned, and that's okay, just... promise me that you'll be careful. I don't want anything to happen to you because of me, especially since this isn't your problem."

This time his smile filled with tenderness, and he thought that it was nice to have someone care about him, even if it was unwarranted. "I'll be fine, Shelby. You know that." He waited for my nod before he continued. "Are you coming up?"

I shook my head. "No, I need to tell Dimples about the phone call. You'll let Uncle Joey know what happened?"

"Sure."

"Okay. I'll let you know if we find anything. You do the same, okay?" He nodded again, and I hurried to my car.

CHAPTER 10

I pulled into the precinct fifteen minutes later. With my badge around my neck, I rushed into the building and through the doors to the detective's offices.

Dimples sat at his desk, and I picked up that he was searching the police database for Jameson Beal's last known address. A wave of relief swept over me, and I hoped he wasn't too mad. I took a seat in the chair beside him, and he barely glanced my way.

Still upset with me, he was thinking that I was his partner. Why hadn't I called him? The last time we'd spoken, I had made a promise that he'd be the first person I'd call. I'd let him down.

He closed his eyes, knowing I'd just heard all that, but it bothered him more than he let on. I was walking a fine line with Ramos. He was a bad guy... a hitman for Pete's sake. Didn't I realize the danger that put me in? He couldn't always cover for me like he had today. What if there came a time when he had to arrest me? Did I ever stop to consider that?

My breath caught, and shame for what I'd put Dimples through stuck in my throat. I hadn't meant to put him in this position. From his anguish, I finally realized how hard this was for him. And now, with the threat Beal posed to his wedding, it was even worse. It was all my fault.

"Hey, I'm sorry... for everything," I said, my throat tight. "If you don't want to be my partner anymore, I'll understand. It will kill me, but I get it."

He lifted his gaze to mine, and his eyes shone with an intensity I'd never seen before. "Shelby. We're not just partners. We're two people who care about each other. I can't change your circumstances, and I won't apologize for worrying about you, but I'll never stop being your partner... or your friend."

Unbidden tears sprang to my eyes, and I shook my head. "You deserve better. This whole mess is my fault."

"No. You can't believe that. Don't even go there. We're in this together, and we'll figure it out together. Whatever it takes."

"But... things are worse than you think. Beal just called me with a warning and a threat."

Dimples's brows rose, and alarm ran down his spine. "What did he say?"

With a pang of regret, I explained Beal's threat that he was upping his game and someone was going to die at the wedding. "I'm so sorry. Until we catch him, I think you should consider postponing. Or maybe you should get married somewhere else and have the celebration another day."

"What? No way. I'm not letting this creep ruin my wedding."

"But what about Billie? If she knows—"

"She'd agree with me," Dimples said. "You know that, right?"

I sighed. "Yes... but—"

"No buts. We're in this together. We'll figure it out." His eyes darkened with fury. "Tomorrow's Friday. That gives us plenty of time to set a trap. If anyone's going to die, it will be him."

Whoa. I'd never heard Dimples sound so mad. But I couldn't blame him. This was his big day, and it was totally ruined. "You know I'll do everything I can, but this is a test to him. He's testing my premonitions. Since I don't really have them, I'm worried that I won't know what he's planning in time to stop him."

"I get that, but you're not the only one involved. Look around you. Most of these guys are coming. You think we can't outsmart one man? He's the one who ought to be worried. It's time we told the chief what's going on."

"Okay, but, before we do, I need to tell you something else. I... uh... just discovered that he has a son. His name is Jason, and he lives in the new condos above the city mall. Jason might know where we can find Jameson. I think we should talk to him."

Dimples lifted his right brow and studied me, wondering how I'd come across that information. Was that why I'd left so quickly with Ramos? So I could go to this guy's condo without telling him?

"Uh... not exactly," I said. "You know Jerry? The person in the food court who almost got hit with the potted plant?" At his nod, I continued, "We've been in touch. He owns a condo in the building, and I thought maybe he could find out if Jameson lived there. But instead of Jameson, it turned out to be his son, Jason."

Dimples nodded. "Other than his last name, how do you know Jason is his son?"

This was a little harder to explain, since it involved breaking and entering. Too bad I couldn't claim it was my premonitions at work. "Uh... you probably don't want to know. Just take my word for it."

His lips twisted into a sardonic frown, and he knew we'd broken in. "Fine. We'll go talk to him, but first we need to tell the chief what's going on." This was supposed to be his last day on the job before the wedding, but now he'd probably be there all night and all day tomorrow.

"I'm sorry," I said.

"Don't." Dimples raised his hand. "It's not your fault. With any luck, we'll get this guy before the wedding."

"Yeah." I agreed, but Dimples picked up that I didn't really believe it. He didn't either. When had anything involving me ever gone smoothly? This time wouldn't be any different.

I felt bad that my negativity was rubbing off on him. Then I picked up that he thought finding out Beal had a son was a good solid lead. So it could still work out.

"That's the spirit," I said, sending him a smile.

With an effort, he managed to keep from rolling his eyes. Then he thought *that's the partner I'm used to.* "Come on."

The chief sat in his office, filling out a report. He glanced up at Dimples's knock on the door and motioned us inside. Since he didn't like doing paperwork, he was grateful for the interruption. I hoped he felt that way when we got done.

Before Dimples could explain, I took the lead. "I... uh... we have a problem." I told him everything that had happened since the shooting, ending with the threat to Dimples's wedding.

After Dimples showed him the photos we'd found in the basement, the chief's jaw clenched in anger. Most of it was directed at Beal, but a small portion was directed my way because I'd waited so long to tell him. What was I thinking? Why didn't I trust him to help me out? I'd helped the police enough times that they owed me. Hell, I even had my own desk and computer.

Oops. I had no idea he felt so strongly about it... about me. My throat tightened up a bit, just knowing he cared, and I had to swallow a few times to keep my composure.

"We have a good lead that might help us," Dimples added. "Shelby found out Beal has a son who might know where we can find him."

Chief Winder narrowed his eyes, hoping it would be that easy, but doubting it just the same. "Okay. Why don't you have a chat with the son? If he knows anything, we'll follow up. In the meantime, I need to see the layout of the venue where you're getting married. We'll need to go over the place with a fine-tooth comb. It will be difficult to prepare, with just one day before the wedding, but I'm sure we can pull it off."

The chief glanced at me, thinking it was too bad I didn't have a premonition about what was going to happen, since that would make things easier, but he didn't want to mention that and make me feel bad. He could tell I already felt bad enough.

Dimples found the wedding site on the chief's computer, and we looked through the photos of the building, both inside and out. "Billie wants to get married in the garden," Dimples said, pointing to the yard. The beautiful patio, with stairs leading down to an arch covered in flowers, beside a man-made pond and waterfall, looked amazing.

Chief Winder nodded, thinking that, with most of his men there as guests, it shouldn't be too hard to spot trouble. "Which of our people are going to be there?"

"Pretty much everyone," Dimples said, mentioning most of the detectives and a few others who had been invited.

"Good. Let's round them up and let them know what's going on."

It was close to the end of the shift, and Dimples gathered those who were still there into the chief's office. He'd tell the others tomorrow. By then, he hoped to have a better idea about what they'd need for security.

Chief Winder took charge, taking the threats against one of their own seriously. After showing them the photos from the basement wall, he asked me to tell them about my most recent phone call from Beal and the threats he'd made to Dimples's wedding.

The heat of anger in the room rose, and I knew these guys were determined not to let anything happen to Dimples. It helped calm me down. I wasn't in this alone.

The meeting ended, and Dimples led the way back to his desk. He toggled his computer awake and began the search for Jason Beal's information. "I take it he wasn't home earlier?"

"Yeah," I agreed.

"Okay. It looks like he's currently a student at the university. His phone number is listed here. I'll give him a call and see if he can meet with us."

Dimples put the call through. I held my breath, hoping he'd answer. The line clicked, and someone said hello. I smiled with relief as Dimples explained who he was and asked if we could stop by his apartment. Jason said that he was home now, but he had to leave soon.

"We'll come right over," Dimples said. Jason said to ring him when we got there, and he'd let us in.

We drove separately to the mall parking garage, and I followed Dimples to the main entrance of the condo units. We found the intercom for Jason's condo and told him we were there. He pressed the release button for access to the building, and we got on the elevator, pushing the button for the eighth floor.

Once again, I stood in front of the condo, while Dimples knocked on the door. This time, the door opened, and a younger version of Jameson Beal stood before us. Dimples showed him his badge, and Jason invited us inside.

As we sat down on the couch, Jason asked, "What's this about?"

"We're looking for your father. We hoped you might know where we can reach him."

Jason tensed. "Why? What's he done?"

"Is he here?" Dimples asked.

"No." Jason let out a breath. "I haven't seen him for a while, and I don't know where he is. He just sort of comes and goes." He glanced at me, thinking I looked familiar. Where had he seen me before?

"What do you know about your dad?" Dimples asked. "Does he have a job?"

Jason shrugged. "Last time I talked to him, he was working on a project of some kind. I have no idea where or what it was about. You can probably find him at his building. I think he has an office in the basement. What's this about? Is he in trouble?"

"Does he stay with you often?" I asked.

"No. But I gave him a key, so he can crash here if he needs to."

"When was the last time you spoke with him?" Dimples asked.

"Last week."

I picked up enough to know that Jason had no idea where his dad was now. He might still be with his latest girlfriend, but Jason didn't want to know those details. He hated what his dad had done to his family, and recently it seemed like he'd gotten worse.

He'd made a name for himself with the company but, after the divorce, he'd dropped everything. It was like he'd become a different person. With us at his door, Jason worried that his dad had finally gone off the deep end.

Maybe he'd better try contacting him, if only to let him know the police were looking for him. He still had an old phone number he could try, but he doubted it worked. If nothing else, he'd look for him at his building.

"Thanks for your time," I said, standing. "If you hear from him, could you please let us know?"

"Sure."

Dimples handed him his card and thanked him for his time. Out in the hall, the door closed firmly behind us. Dimples glanced my way. "Did you get anything?"

"He doesn't know where Jameson is, or what he's been up to, but now that we've asked him about it, I think he'll try and get in touch with him."

"How?"

"He was thinking about an old phone number he could try. If that didn't work, he'd go to the building we just came from. Jason thought his dad had changed, and worried that he'd gone off the deep end, so that fits."

"Yeah. Sounds like our guy," Dimples agreed. "I guess Beal could go back to the building, but we've cleared it out. I'll just have to concentrate on his computer and see what we can find there. We can pull up his social media and emails, maybe get something from them."

"Okay." I checked my watch. It was after five-thirty. "I'm going to head home. Call me if you get anything."

"I will. And if you find something, I expect the same." He caught my gaze. "We're partners, no matter what." He was thinking about Ramos and hoped I knew he'd always have my back, even if he didn't like who I worked with.

"Thanks. You'll be the first to know."

He nodded. "Good."

As we reached the parking garage, I turned to him. "When you talk to Billie, tell her I'm sorry."

"She knows it's not your fault."

"I know, but I feel so bad." I glanced at my shoes, unable to look at Dimples.

"Shelby." He waited for me to meet his gaze, then continued. "We'll get this guy. With all of us working together, he doesn't stand a chance. He won't ruin anything. Have some faith." He smiled. It wasn't the big smile that made his dimples twirl around in his cheeks, but they dimpled enough to bring a smile to my lips.

"Okay. I'll talk to you later."

I appreciated his positive outlook, but I didn't know if I had that kind of faith. I knew Jameson Beal wasn't fooling around. If he set up some kind of device on the premises, and didn't stick around so I could pick it up, how was I going to know how to stop him? There were so many ways this could go wrong.

With a heavy heart, I got in my car and drove home.

It didn't take much for my kids to talk me into ordering pizza. Chris got home just in time to eat, and we sat around the table, talking about the events of the day. Listening to them talk helped me forget what I'd been through, and I finally relaxed.

"So how was your day?" Chris asked me.

Everyone glanced at me. "Uh... it was all right." I kept chewing my food since I didn't want to talk about it.

"I saw your note in my office," Chris continued. "Sorry I didn't call you. It was a busy day."

"That's okay," I answered. At first I couldn't remember what note he was talking about, then it came to me that I hadn't told him about Ethan. Crap! I'd forgotten all about that.

"Oh yeah," Josh chimed in, remembering our earlier conversation. "Did you find out anything more about the lady who's her own twin? That is just so weird."

"How can you be your own twin?" Savannah asked.

I explained the case to her, which led to an interesting discussion about all kinds of things. I even told them Claire's story about getting pregnant, and the consequences of unprotected sex. It might have been a little heavy, but I figured there was no time like the present.

By then, we'd finished eating, and the kids were quick to leave the table, and our depressing conversation, to pursue happier things. Chris narrowed his eyes, thinking there was something off with me. I wasn't usually so down and weary.

Since he was right, I didn't set him straight. He sucked in a breath, knowing something bad had happened. "You'd better start talking," he said, pulling me into a hug. "Should we go out on the deck swing?"

"No." My eyes widened, and I pulled back. "He might be out there watching."

Chris took in my frightened face, and his stomach clenched. "Who? What happened?"

I swallowed and then closed my eyes, surprised at how vulnerable and upset I felt. "Sorry. I don't know why I'm having such a hard time. I guess it's all getting to me."

Chris took me in his arms, and I relaxed. I buried my face against his neck and inhaled his clean scent. He held me close, his mind offering peace and comfort, giving me time to compose myself. Feeling steadier, I pulled away and glanced into his eyes. "Thanks honey. Let's go sit down on the couch, and I'll tell you what happened today."

He nodded, keeping his mind calm for me, even though I knew it wasn't easy. He kept thinking whatever I'd been through couldn't be that bad. I was fine, no broken bones or bruises, and, even though I seemed down, that wasn't so bad either. We sat on the couch, and he took my hand in his and squeezed.

"Ow." I jerked my hand away and held it close to my body.

"What is it? Let me see." Chris reached for my hand.

"It's no big deal. I just got a couple of blisters on my palm. They're a little tender." I held my hand out to Chris, and we both examined it. He wondered how that had happened, so I answered. "I got burned from a fire I had to put out."

Chris's calm evaporated. He'd tried his best not to get upset, but now he couldn't hold it back. I rushed to explain what had happened after I'd left his office to meet with Olivia Beal.

"She gave me the address to a building Jameson owns. Uncle Joey had some information he wanted to share with me, so I went to Thrasher afterward to tell him about BioTech and Jameson Beal. Get this... Uncle Joey's one of the investors in the company, and they're part of the Patton Family. Olivia is a granddaughter."

"So there is a connection to Manetto," Chris said. "But how does that fit with you?"

"To be honest, I'm not sure it does. I told you about the divorce, right? And how Jameson lost everything?" At Chris's nod, I continued, "I'm sure that's why he's been stalking me."

"Yeah, I got that. So did you go to the building?"

"Yes. When I told Uncle Joey about it, he sent me there with Ramos." I knew Chris wouldn't like that part, but he should be grateful I hadn't gone alone, right?

Chris's jaw tightened and he nodded, thinking I was supposed to take Dimples. He knew Ramos was part of the equation when it came to Manetto, but that didn't mean he liked how much time I spent with him. Good thing he'd had that conversation with him a few days ago.

"What? You talked to Ramos?"

Chris swore in his mind. He'd wanted to keep that from me and, now that I'd picked it up, he'd have to explain. It wasn't something he wanted to do. Shaking his head, he let out a breath. "Shelby, you know I love you and... well, you've spent a lot of time with Ramos. He's an attractive guy... not as great a catch as me, but still. I just needed to make sure we had an understanding between us."

He caught my gaze and held it. "I know he cares about you. It's as plain as day. So I just wanted to make sure we were on the same page."

"Were you checking up on me?" I could hardly believe he thought I'd cheat on him.

"Honey, I know you'd never cheat on me, but sometimes there are circumstances that test us. You can't tell me you haven't been tempted."

I twisted my lips and shook my head. He was right about that, but I didn't want to admit it. "So what did you talk about?"

"I just told him how much you mean to me and that I appreciated all the times he's been there for you. You might not believe this, but I thanked him for risking his life for you. I told him that if he ever needed anything from me— except for you of course—I'd do whatever I could to make it happen."

Whoa. That had to be uncomfortable. I was glad I wasn't there. "Okay. So how did he take it?"

"Fine, I guess. He said it was all part of his job, but we both knew it was more than that." Chris shrugged. "I'm sorry Shelby, but I needed to talk to him. This isn't easy for me, but I'm trying to accept that he's part of our lives. If I didn't know you loved me and were committed to me and our family, I don't think I could handle this."

"Oh Chris. I do love you. I'm sorry this is hard for you. It's hard for everyone. I'm doing my best, but I can't help it when things happen to me."

"I know. I get it. So what happened at the building? Did you find Beal?"

"Not exactly." I explained the room in the basement with all the pictures and articles about me. I grabbed my phone and showed him the photos I'd taken. "See that one? With us on the deck swing?"

"Holy hell." Hot anger filled Chris's chest. "Wasn't that just yesterday?"

"The day before, but yes, it's recent. Now you know why I didn't want to go out there."

Chris could hardly believe Beal had gotten so close. "He must have a telephoto lens. From the angle, it looks like he was in our neighbor's back yard." Chris jumped to his feet and looked out the window, trying to figure out where the shot had been taken.

"There's a break through the trees there," he said, pointing. "He could have been in his car, watching." Chris turned back to me, his eyes blazing with anger. "So what happened after you found the pictures?"

I told him how the door had been booby-trapped, and that Beal had thrown a Molotov cocktail through the window. I skipped over the part where Ramos took off his shirt, since Chris wouldn't appreciate it, and explained how I'd been burned putting out the fire.

"I called Dimples, and he dropped everything to come. But before he got there, Beal stood outside the basement window. At least I think it was him. All I saw were his shoes and pants. Anyway, Ramos drew his gun to shoot him, but he took off."

Chris wished Ramos could have shot him, and I had to agree. I continued, explaining that we'd talked to Jerry and had found the link to the condo because Beal's son had a place there. "After we left the condo, I got a phone call. It was from Beal."

Dread washed over Chris. "What did he say?"

"He said he was through holding back, and that someone would die at the wedding. I went straight to the precinct to tell Dimples to cancel the wedding, but he refused."

I continued, telling Chris that Dimples insisted on letting the chief and his fellow officers at the precinct know of the threat, concluding with my second visit to Beal's son with Dimples that was a dead end.

"So what's the plan for tomorrow?" Chris asked.

"Dimples has Beal's computer. He's going to look through it and see if he can find anything. In the meantime, the chief is taking charge of the wedding venue. I don't think Dimples and Billie will cancel the wedding, so we'll have to make sure nothing happens."

"That's for sure," Chris agreed, knowing Saturday was going to be a long day.

"Ramos told me he'd be looking for Beal, too, but he didn't tell me how."

"That's probably for the best." Chris squeezed me against his side. "Let's hope he finds him. This is one time we can be grateful to have a hitman on our side."

I couldn't argue with that. "There's something else that's bothering me. Beal got close enough to take a picture of us on the deck. Do you think he might target the kids?"

"Who knows?" Chris considered it. "But I don't want to take any chances. What's going on tomorrow? Does Josh have to work?"

"No, it's his day off."

"How about this—if you aren't home, why don't we make sure they're at a friend's house? Do you think they'd be okay with that?"

"Of course. Savannah spent most of the day at Ash's, so she might be planning on going back tomorrow. Let's go talk to them."

"Okay, but first, you never told me about Ethan," Chris said. "What's going on there?"

"Oh yeah. I left a note in your desk drawer at work explaining it, but I forgot to tell you it was there."

Chris's brows rose. "I'd better make sure no one finds it. So what did it say?"

"It's worse than we thought. When Ethan interned with the prosecuting attorney's office, he tried to doctor a police report for a friend so he wouldn't go to jail. This was after he'd received an offer to work for your firm. Strickland caught him and threatened him with disbarment if Ethan didn't agree to spy on you. He didn't have much of a choice, so he agreed.

"Now it sounds like Ethan has a recording of you that he turned over to Strickland. I don't know what you said on it, but Ethan was thinking that Strickland doctored the recording to make it sound like you gave Uncle Joey advice that's incriminating to you.

"I guess the plan was to use that recording to pressure you to turn on Uncle Joey. After Ethan got that midnight visit from Ramos, he had a change of heart. He told Strickland he wouldn't go through with it. He also told Strickland that if he used that recording to come after you, Ethan would make sure everyone knew Strickland had falsified it."

"Wow," Chris said. "I'll bet Strickland didn't like that much."

"No. Ethan thinks Strickland is going to "find" the falsified police report and submit it as evidence to get him disbarred. He thinks Strickland will probably go through with it tomorrow. Is there anything you can do to help him?"

"There might be," Chris said. "I need to see the police report in question. Without specific proof that Ethan falsified it, I could put forward the claim that the report could have been falsified by anyone in the department, especially after all this time. If Strickland knew about it a few months ago, he should have done something about it then. Why did he wait?"

"I like it. You'll have to talk to Ethan first thing in the morning. He was pretty depressed about it today."

"I can do that."

I smiled, grateful that at least something was going right. "Well, let's go talk to the kids about tomorrow."

After explaining the situation, they didn't mind spending the day with friends, especially since Savannah already had plans to help Ash again. Josh normally hung out with his friends anyway, so that wasn't a problem.

"It's probably not necessary," I added, not wanting them to be worried. "But it's better to be safe than sorry."

Savannah remembered opening the door to an escaped convict, who'd pointed a gun at her, and she didn't want to experience anything like that again. "Is it okay if I get a stun flashlight like yours?" she asked.

"Sure," I said. "We'll order it tomorrow."

"Sweet." With a big grin on her face, she picked up her phone to call Ash.

With that settled, Chris took my hand and studied the blisters. "I think we should put some salve on that, and maybe a Band-aid or two. Then you should take some pain killers and get into bed." Besides the pain killers, he thought of something else that would take my mind off my troubles.

My eyes widened. "Reading a book? Really? That's the best you can do?"

He chuckled. "Just testing the waters."

He led me into the bathroom, but I opted to take a nice, long bubble bath before I did anything else. Later, once we'd gone to bed, I even got a good foot rub before Chris handed me the book I'd been reading. Somewhat disappointed, I opened it, but I didn't get much further than the first paragraph.

Let me just say... Chris is a master at distracting me in all the right ways.

"Oh baby, oh baby."

I woke up refreshed from a good night's sleep. The early morning light drifted through my window, and I stretched with contentment. Closing my eyes, I tried to stay in my little cocoon of happiness, but thoughts of the previous day rushed into my mind and spoiled it.

Sitting up, I checked the time, finding it just after eight-thirty. Getting out of bed, I padded down to the kitchen and found a note from Chris. He told me that he loved me and asked me to keep him informed if I heard anything about Beal.

I smiled, grateful for the note, and decided that I wasn't going to think about any of that until after I'd had a scrambled egg for breakfast. Decidedly cheerful, I cooked enough for Josh and Savannah, along with some sausage links and toast. They always responded eagerly to the smell of cooking sausage and eggs, and it was easy to rouse them from their beds.

We were just finishing up when my phone rang. After a pang of fear, I relaxed to see that it was Chris. With a smile, I quickly answered. "Hi honey. Thanks for the note. How's it going?"

"Shelby... honey... I... I'm sorry to tell you this, but... something bad has happened."

Dread ran like ice water through my veins. "What? What is it?"

"It's Ethan. He's... he's... dead."

I gasped. "No."

"It must have happened sometime last night," Chris continued. "He didn't come into work this morning, and he didn't answer his phone when I called. Because we're due in court this afternoon, we had planned to go over everything early this morning; so I knew something wasn't right." He paused, unable to continue, and I heard him swallow a few times.

"Where are you?"

"I'm here. At Ethan's place. I came over to see what was wrong, and I ... I ... found him."

"Did you call the police?" I asked.

He let out a troubled sigh. "I was checking him for a pulse when a neighbor walked by. She called the police, but it freaked her out. She thought I'd killed him. The police are here now, but they won't let me leave. It looks like they think I had something to do with this."

"Is Dimples there?"

"No. I think one of the detectives is Bates, but I don't know anyone else."

My heart sank. "Okay. I'm calling Dimples, and I'm coming right over. Don't say anything else until I get there.

I'll be there as fast as I can." I disconnected before he could say another word, and put my call through to Dimples.

"Hey Shelby, did you find something on Beal?" he asked.

"Drew, it's not... it's about Chris. He's in trouble. He went to his junior partner's apartment and found him dead. Bates is there with another detective, but they're not letting him leave. Chris didn't do it. I'm going over right now. Can you meet me there?"

He swore under his breath before responding. "Okay. I'll head over. What's the address?"

"I'll text it to you." My fingers shook so bad that it took me longer than normal to find the information. After sending the text, I glanced at my kids, realizing that they'd heard my side of the conversation and were freaking out.

I quickly explained what had happened, and that Chris was fine but he needed me. I told them not to worry and that everything would be fine. Before I rushed off to get dressed, I picked up that they were worried, but they believed in me and my abilities to solve this.

I also picked up that this might be one of those times when knowing a mob boss could come in handy. That thought came from Josh, and I tried not to let it worry me, mostly because I'd been thinking the same thing.

"Should I still go over to Ash's house?" Savannah asked.

"Yes. That's a good idea. Text me when you get there." I glanced at Josh. "You too. Make sure you lock the back door when you leave."

"I will," Josh answered. "Go. We'll be fine."

I nodded, grateful for such wonderful kids. "I'll text you in a little while with an update."

On the way to the apartment, I focused on my driving skills and tried not to think too hard about Ethan. But it was a struggle. How could he be dead? I'd just spoken with him yesterday. I'd promised that I'd help him figure this out. How had this happened? Who had done this to him?

I made it to Ethan's apartment in one piece, but my stomach swirled with anxiety. Part of me didn't believe it could possibly be real. Another part of me dreaded what came next. I just needed to focus on Chris and being there for him. That kept me going.

As the elevator doors opened on the fifth floor, a police officer told me it was a crime scene and I couldn't exit the elevator. I showed him my ID badge. After a moment's hesitation, he let me through. Hurrying down the hall, I spotted Dimples talking to Bates and let out a relieved breath.

Bates scowled to see me, thinking that I shouldn't be there. He moved to block me from entering Ethan's apartment, but I pushed under his arm, needing to get to Chris.

"Hey, you can't go in there."

Inside, I jerked to a stop. Ethan's body lay sprawled and broken on the floor. I hardly noticed the wreckage in the room. All I could see was the spray of red blood everywhere I looked. The coppery smell turned my stomach, and I swallowed to keep my breakfast down. I stood frozen at the sight of Ethan's battered face. Was he really dead?

"Ethan?" I stepped toward him, but strong arms held me back. Voices spoke, but I couldn't understand the words. A loud buzzing filled my ears, and my knees buckled. Someone grabbed me around the waist, holding me up and pulling me from the room.

Everything tilted as I sank to the floor in the hall. Dimples sat beside me, urging me to lower my head to my knees. I followed his directions and closed my eyes against the darkness. A few moments later, my vision began to clear, and the buzzing sound left my ears. I sat up and took several deep breaths.

I glanced at Dimples, then lowered my head to his shoulder and swallowed. Every time I closed my eyes, the sight of Ethan's broken body and battered face filled my mind. Even with my eyes opened, all I could see was how terrible he'd looked on the floor.

I didn't even realize I was crying until Dimples handed me a tissue. As I wiped my eyes, it suddenly dawned on me that Chris wasn't there. "Where's Chris?" I moved to stand up, but Dimples stopped me.

"He's not here. You need to—"

"What? I told him I was coming." I tried to get my feet under me. This time, Dimples helped me up, even though he thought I could still faint. As I stood, the hallway tilted just a bit, and I leaned against him until everything came into focus.

"Maybe you'd better sit back down."

"No. I'm fine. Where's Chris?"

Dimples pursed his lips, thinking I wasn't going to like it. "He went to the station with a police officer. Bates didn't give him much of a choice."

"Why?"

"For questioning... that's all. He's not under arrest, so you don't have to worry about that."

I let out a breath, suddenly overcome with remorse. I should have picked up the danger Ethan was in and offered him some kind of protection. Maybe if I'd told Chris earlier yesterday, he could have helped Ethan and stopped this from happening.

Now it was too late. Ethan was dead. I glanced at Dimples. "I might know who did this."

Dimples's brows rose in surprise. Did I think it was Manetto? With Chris's life on the line, maybe it was the one thing that would turn me against the mob boss.

"What?" I couldn't hide my astonishment. "What does he have to do with this?"

"Come with me," Dimples said, worried that someone was listening to our one-sided conversation. He also didn't want Bates to know he was telling me things he shouldn't.

He took my arm to lead me away, then slid his arm around my shoulders to steady me. We didn't speak until we had taken the elevator to the first floor and had walked outside into the sunshine. It took me that long to realize that Dimples wasn't in his regular suit and tie. Instead, he wore jeans and a polo shirt.

Today was his day off, and I'd called him to help me with this. Tomorrow was his wedding day, and a crazy madman was planning to stage a trap that could kill someone at his wedding. Yet, here he was, holding me up. I stumbled with the realization.

Worried that I might faint from shock, Dimples helped me to his car. He opened the passenger side door and practically shoved me inside, then closed the door and hurried into the driver's seat. He glanced my way, ready to push my head between my knees if I so much as twitched.

"I'm okay. It's just been a terrible shock."

"I'm sure it has. So who do you think did this if it wasn't Manetto?"

"Is that what Bates thinks? Why would he think that?"

"After Bates arrived at the scene and identified Chris and Ethan, he called the chief and told him that Chris had been found with the body. The chief told Bates that Ethan was working with the prosecuting attorney's office.

"I don't know what Ethan was doing for them, but it involved Manetto. Since Chris is Manetto's attorney, you can see why there's some suspicion that Chris, or Manetto, had something to do with Ethan's murder."

"Is that why they took Chris to the station? I thought you said they weren't arresting him."

"They're not. They don't have any evidence for an arrest, but the neighbor saw Chris with the body, and she thought he may have had something to do with it. They're just covering all their bases in case something shows up."

"We have to go to the station. I have to fix this."

Dimples shook his head. "I don't think they'll let you in on it. You need to tell me what you know."

I swallowed, not sure what to do. Should I tell Dimples everything? Could I trust him to help me? Maybe I should take this straight to Uncle Joey and leave Dimples out of it.

I glanced at Dimples, picking up that he held his breath in anticipation of my answer. He was my partner, and he'd do what he could to help me, but, if Manetto was behind this, I had to do the right thing.

I wanted to defend Uncle Joey, but I held back, knowing it would weaken my position. "Okay. I'll tell you everything I know."

Dimples exhaled with relief. His gaze shifted to the street behind us, and I turned to see the crime scene van pull up. As they opened the back doors and pulled out a gurney, Dimples started the car, thinking that we needed to talk somewhere else.

He drove a few blocks away to a residential neighborhood and pulled to the side of the street. After he turned off the car, I began, explaining the whole sordid story of Ethan's involvement with Strickland, and ending with his refusal to go through with the plan. I left out Ramos's midnight visit, instead saying that Ethan had second thoughts because Chris had done nothing wrong.

"Ethan said that Strickland doctored the recording of Chris that he'd given him. He told Strickland that, if he used it, Ethan would tell everyone it was a fake. Ethan was the only person to dispute what Strickland did with the recording. Now, with Ethan out of the way, Strickland can use it against Chris to get to Uncl... uh... Manetto."

Dimples could hardly believe my story. How could a prosecuting attorney be capable of messing with the law? I was accusing him of murder. This was insane.

"You have to remember Strickland's goal," I said. "Strickland wants Manetto. He must think that the end justifies the means. When Ethan wouldn't go through with it, he must have cracked."

"It makes sense," Dimples admitted. "But he's sworn to uphold the law... this goes against everything he's supposed to hold dear." He shook his head and let out a deep sigh, both disgusted and amazed that Strickland had carried it so far. "If he did this, he's just as bad as Manetto."

"No," I said, anger in my tone. "He's much worse, because he's supposed to be the good guy."

Dimples couldn't argue with that. "So what do we do now?"

"I need to talk to Strickland."

Dimples didn't like it, but he knew I was right. As long as Ethan was part of the conversation, I'd know if Strickland was the killer without even asking. And if he wasn't? I'd probably figure that out too. But would it prove anything? Would it help Chris? That was another story.

Then there was the fact that he was getting married tomorrow. He had the next two weeks off, and he wouldn't be there to help me. Besides the threat to his wedding, how could he enjoy his honeymoon knowing that I was in trouble? Maybe he should postpone the wedding until this was over.

"No," I said. "I can't let you do that. Billie would never forgive me... or you. I can do this without you. I may not want to, but I can." I wasn't so sure about that, but it helped to say it out loud. "Take me back. I need to get my car and head to the police station. Even if they won't let me in, I can be there as a wife for her husband. You should go back to your plans for the wedding, and let me take care of this."

"Shelby... I don't know if I can."

"Of course you can. I have... I have other resources."

Dimples sucked in a breath. "Oh... yeah. That's right, you do."

"Exactly," I agreed, even though I hated doing this to him. "I'll be fine without you." It broke my heart to push him away, but it was for his own good. He needed to get married, and there was no way I was going to be the reason it didn't happen.

Dimples kept his gaze directed my way, but I refused to look at him. After a moment, he started the car and drove back to Ethan's apartment building. My car was parked across the street, and he pulled up behind it. "Shelby. I know what you're doing. But this isn't over. I'm talking to Billie. I'll let you know what we decide."

I shook my head. "I wish you wouldn't. I can't have your wedding on my conscience. I'll abide by what you decide, but please don't postpone it because of me."

He was thinking that there were other things he could do to help me, and postponing his wedding wasn't one of them.

"What do you mean?"

"Uh... nothing," he said, but he was thinking about talking to Bates. "Go on. You need to get to the station. I'll talk to you later."

I let out a breath and got out of his car. Across the street, police officers wheeled the gurney with Ethan's body through the doors of the building. My chest ached with grief as I watched them load the gurney into the van and close the doors. The van drove away, and I wiped the tears from my cheeks.

Closing my eyes, I gathered every ounce of determination I could find. Reaching deep inside, I vowed that Strickland was going to pay for this. Ethan didn't deserve to die for Strickland's vendetta against Uncle Joey.

CHAPTER 11

I entered the precinct and made my way to the detectives' offices. Not finding Bates anywhere, I decided to try the large room where they took suspects for questioning. Through the glass, I caught sight of Chris, along with Bates and Chief Winder. Without knocking, I pulled the door open and stepped inside.

Bates jumped up. "What the hell! You can't be in here."

I glanced at Chief Winder, hoping he'd back me up, but he just pursed his lips, unsure how to handle this. I took the decision from him by sitting down at the table. "I think I can help." I knew that sounded presumptuous, but I had to be assertive if I wanted to stay.

"How?" Chief Winder asked. "With your husband involved, I'm not sure we can trust your input or your premonitions."

"I suppose you have a point," I agreed. "But since Chris didn't do it, I don't think you have to worry about that."

Bates didn't like it, but, without proof of Chris's guilt, there wasn't much he could do at the moment. Chris had said he'd been home last night, and I could account for that, but it didn't mean Chris wasn't involved.

Bates's first order of business was to talk to Strickland about the deal he had with Ethan, and get Strickland's opinion on who he thought had a motive to kill him. I wanted to jump up and down and tell him that Strickland was his best suspect, but I held back, knowing I needed proof first.

"We're done here anyway." Bates glanced at Chris. "You're free to go."

Chris pushed back his chair and came to my side. I stood as well, keeping my expression neutral, since I needed to keep a cool head for the chief's benefit. But I wasn't done yet. I glanced at Bates. "I'd like to talk to Strickland. When are you going over there?"

His breath caught. He hadn't said anything about talking to the prosecuting attorney, not even to the chief. But I knew. Still, he wasn't about to let me come. "You're not coming with me."

"Why not?"

"Because..." He glanced Chris's way, "Because he's a suspect. Strickland wouldn't want to talk to you."

"I don't need to talk to him. In fact, I don't need to say a word. I just need to be there. What could it possibly hurt?"

"And how do I know you'd tell me the truth if you got any premonitions? This is crazy." He glanced at the chief. "She can't be involved. You know that, right?"

The chief hated to side with Bates on this, but he had no choice. "Go home, Shelby. Bates is right."

I shrugged. "Fine. But I'm going to find out who did this to Ethan. It would have been easier to work with you, but I can still do it on my own."

With that parting remark, I followed Chris out of the room. He'd been quiet, but I caught that he wasn't sure my coming was a good idea. He hated putting me in this position, and he didn't want me to lose my standing with the police. On the other hand, he'd never been happier to see me stand up for him.

He glanced my way, thinking that we needed to talk, but not here. I gave him a quick nod and led the way out of the building. The tension of holding back our emotions built between us. By the time we got to my car, Chris couldn't wait any longer. The fortifications around his heart broke, and he pulled me into his arms, clutching me close.

With his guard down, the guilt and remorse of Ethan's murder closed in on him, and I caught his self-recrimination that this was his fault. If he'd been a better mentor, he could have figured this out long before now. I'd told him about it months ago. Why hadn't he taken care of it then? Now Ethan was dead. And it was too late.

I wanted to tell Chris that it wasn't his fault, but, deep down, he already knew that. He didn't need words, he just needed me. As we held each other, both of us were overcome with grief at losing Ethan in such a violent way. After a long sigh, I spoke. "Come on. Let's go get your car."

Chris took a deep breath and nodded. Straightening, he wiped his eyes. Moving to the passenger side of the car, he got in. As I pulled onto the road, I reached over and took Chris's hand, careful of my blisters, but needing to touch him. There was so much I wanted to say, but, at the moment, neither of us could find the right words.

Reaching Ethan's apartment, I parked in front of Chris's car. Two police cars were still there, but everyone else had left. I spotted a journalist from the paper with another guy who had a camera. Luckily, they were just finishing up and began walking toward their car.

After a moment of silence, I spoke. "Tell me what happened." I knew Chris needed to talk about it, but he was having a hard time, so I asked a simple question to get him started. "What time did you get here?"

He rubbed his hands over his face and pushed his hair back. "When I got to Ethan's apartment, I knocked, but he didn't answer. It worried me, so I tried the door. It opened right up, and I went inside." He swallowed, reliving the moment he'd seen Ethan. "I found him on the floor. He looked bad, but I didn't know if he was dead. His skin was cold when I touched his neck for a pulse, and I knew he was gone.

"That's when the neighbor walked by and saw me leaning over him. She started screaming, so I told her to calm down and call the police. A few of the other neighbors heard the commotion and came running. There was quite a crowd by the time the police got there, and all of them were eager to tell the police I'd been found with him."

He shook his head. "Now he's dead. I should have been looking for clues while I waited for them to show up, but, seeing him like that... I couldn't think. After the police arrived, I told them what happened and called you after that.

"At first they told me I needed to stay to give them a statement. Then it changed to telling me I needed to go to the station to give my statement and answer a few questions. I didn't want to leave before you got there, but they didn't give me a choice. Dimples arrived as I was leaving. He told me that he'd make sure you knew where I was."

"I must have just missed you then," I said.

"How much did you see?"

I swallowed. "I slipped around Bates because I thought you were inside. I saw him... it was awful." I shook my head to clear it from that horrible vision and continued. "I also picked up why they're targeting you. They think this is all tied back to Uncle Joey."

"What?"

I nodded and told him everything I knew about why they suspected Chris and Uncle Joey. "Dimples told me all of this, even though he wasn't supposed to. Chris, I told him everything, along with Strickland's plan to use the doctored recording against you. He believes me, but, with Bates on the warpath, I need proof, which I'll only get if I talk to Strickland. Then I can find out who killed Ethan, where the recording is, and what he plans to do with it."

"You're right," Chris agreed. It reminded him of my bold move back at the precinct, where I'd told Bates I'd go with him. Too bad it hadn't worked. Now we'd have to figure out another way to see Strickland. But how? "Let's go back to my office. I called Elisa and told her I was detained, but not why. I'll need to tell them what's happened. Then we can figure out what to do."

"Okay."

Chris sent me a grateful nod before getting out of the car. I waited until he was in his car and ready to leave before I pulled out and followed him to his office. We entered his building and took the elevator to the fourth floor. Stopping in front of Elisa's desk, he asked her to come with us into his office.

Surprised that I was there, she looked down her nose at my jeans and t-shirt. But all that changed when she saw the look on Chris's face. A wave of anxiety swept over her. Where was Ethan? She knew Chris had gone to check on him. Had something bad happened?

"I hate to tell you this," Chris began. "But Ethan's... he's been... killed. I found him when I went over there."

After her initial shock, she sank to the couch. With stricken eyes, she caught Chris's gaze. "He's dead? Murdered? Why would anyone kill him?"

"I don't know, but Shelby and I intend to find out." At her shaken expression, he continued. "Look, I know this is hard, but I need to let the other junior attorneys know. I need one of them to take Ethan's place in court this afternoon. Will you set up a meeting with them in the conference room in... say half an hour?"

"Okay, sure," she agreed.

"Good." He glanced my way. "I'm going to tell Pratt and Larsen what's going on. I'll be back before the meeting." At my nod, he left.

Elisa blinked back tears, and her breathing turned shallow. "Do you... do you think... it was because... of that thing with the prosecuting attorney's office?" she asked.

"What do you know about that?" I asked her.

"Just... you told me Ethan might be spying on Chris, so I've been keeping tabs on him. I didn't know it had gotten that bad though, or I would have said something to you before now."

"It's okay. Just tell me what you know. I want to find out who killed him, and any information you have will help me figure it out."

"Sure." Now that she had something to do, she calmed down and hurried to her desk. Pulling a notebook from her drawer, she brought it into the office and sat back down. She went over all the times she knew Ethan had gone to the prosecuting attorney's office. Counting them, it added up to over ten.

"He was always volunteering to be the one to go," she continued. "He told me it was because he'd interned there and knew people. I figured it was a girl, so, when I asked what her name was, he said it was Gwen."

"Oh yeah," I said. "I met her a couple of weeks ago when I went with Ethan to talk to Strickland about a case." Maybe that was my way in. I could go over there to speak to Gwen and find a way to talk to Strickland at the same time.

"It's just so sad," Elisa said, fresh tears streaming down her face. "Who would do this to him?"

"I don't know, but I plan to find out."

"I'd better get that meeting set up." She hurried out, thinking that she needed to get all of Ethan's files on the case they were taking to court this afternoon and go over them with the junior attorney taking Ethan's place.

Chris came back right before the meeting. Elisa told him that everyone was waiting in the conference room, and that she had gathered all of Ethan's files for their court appearance this afternoon.

Chris nodded with relief that she'd taken care of things. "Thanks," he told her. "You keep me going. There's no way I could do this job without you."

She beamed and got back to work, casting a little sideways glance my way and thinking how much she enjoyed working for Chris. He appreciated her. She hoped I'd heard what he'd said, mostly because she wanted me to know how much Chris needed her.

Chris shut his office door and took a deep fortifying breath, then sat beside me on the couch. "I guess it's time to tell the junior attorneys. Will you come with me? I'd like to know if any of them knew anything about Ethan's involvement with Strickland."

"That's a good idea," I agreed. "But, before we go, tell me how Pratt and Larsen took it. Did you tell them everything?"

"Yes. They're pretty shaken. Pratt will represent me if it comes to that, but I'm hoping it won't." He squeezed my hand. At my sudden intake of breath, he apologized. "Sorry. I forgot about your blisters. How are they anyway?"

"Better. I'll be good as new in a few days." It reminded me that only yesterday I'd been worried about a stalker and his stupid threats. Now it was hard to care.

We hurried to the conference room. I sat down in a chair, off to the side, while Chris stood in front of the attorneys. He began by thanking them for being there and then gave them the bad news. "I can't give you more details than that, but I'm working on it."

I picked up some stray thoughts from a number of them. They worried that Ethan's death could be tied to his work with the firm. What case had Ethan been working on that got him killed? Could something like this happen to them?

"We don't think it's related to a case he was working on," I said. "It was something more personal. Did any of you spend time with Ethan outside of work?" Unfortunately, none of them had. After a few discreet questions, I also picked up that none of them knew anything about Ethan's connection to Strickland.

I thanked them, and Chris continued. "Now I need some help. I need someone to take Ethan's spot with me in court today. Is anyone up for the task?"

To my surprise, all of them jumped at the opportunity. They all thought Chris was a great mentor, and any of them would be lucky for a chance to work with him.

Their eagerness even surprised Chris. "Thanks guys. Logan, why don't you take this one for now. Elisa has gathered all of Ethan's files and notes. You can get them from her. We're not due in court until two, so that should give you some time to go over them. Come to my office at twelve-thirty, and give me your evaluation so we can discuss our tactics."

Logan thanked Chris and hurried off to get the files. We followed at a more sedate pace. "I guess we'll have to approach Strickland another way," Chris said.

"What do you mean?"

He shut his office door and turned to me. "I'm pretty sure Strickland will use the recording Ethan provided to arrest me, especially if he was behind Ethan's murder. With Ethan out of the way, what would stop him? So we need to talk to Strickland. Now."

He was thinking that showing up at Strickland's office would be totally unexpected and, hopefully, throw him off his game. I'd have a better chance at finding out if Strickland was Ethan's killer. I'd also know what he'd done with the evidence, and I'd pick up what his next plans entailed. It would put us in the driver's seat.

"Okay. I see what you mean." I glanced down at my jeans and t-shirt, wishing I'd worn something more presentable. "Give me a minute to visit your bathroom first. I need to make sure my hair isn't a tangled mess."

Chris looked me over, only now realizing that my casual clothes might not make the best impression on Strickland; but he didn't care, and neither should I. "You look great. I wouldn't change a thing."

I smiled and gave him a quick kiss, then hurried into his private bathroom. I always carried a little makeup kit in my purse with the essentials of face cream, lip gloss, mascara, and blush. After splashing water over my face, I got to work.

Next, I borrowed Chris's brush and combed through my hair, straightening the tangles, and fluffing it up. I came out of the bathroom a few minutes later looking better, even if I couldn't totally erase the redness in my eyes from crying.

Chris waited for me in front of Elisa's desk. He'd told her where we were headed, and she had her notebook out to fill him in on what she'd discovered. Not sure that mattered anymore, he thanked her, and we headed out.

The prosecuting attorney's office wasn't far, so we walked, each of us lost in our own thoughts. As we entered the building, I heard surprise from someone's mind and glanced up to see Bates coming down the hall. "What are you doing here?" he asked, stopping beside us.

I wanted to tell him it was none of his business, but Chris answered first. "None of your business." That brought a satisfied smile to my lips, especially when Bates sputtered a curse under his breath. We kept walking, leaving him behind, and I had to admit that it felt good.

Outside Strickland's office, Gwen sat at her desk. I listened closely to her mind and realized that she didn't know Ethan was dead. I remembered that she'd liked him when he'd interned there, but he'd never reciprocated those feelings.

Now he never would.

She smiled a greeting, thinking that I looked familiar, but she couldn't place me. Then it hit her that I'd been there with Ethan once, and she wondered how he was doing. Hearing that, I sniffed and tried not to cry.

Chris sent her his best smile. "Would you tell Strickland that Chris Nichols is here to speak with him?"

"Uh... do you have an appointment?"

"He'll want to talk to me," Chris said, his friendly smile replaced with a stubborn stare.

That was the first inkling I'd had that Chris was going out on a limb. He was thinking that Larsen and Pratt had advised him not to approach Strickland without either of them present, but he'd decided to forget their advice and come anyway.

Gwen noted the aggression in Chris's tone and quickly rose to tell Strickland personally rather than use the phone. A second later, she came out of his office and beckoned us into the room.

Strickland's surprise wafted off him. He hadn't expected Chris to show up, and a sudden wariness tightened his chest. This was all going wrong, and he needed to get a handle on it before it got out of control. He caught sight of me and froze. All kinds of swearing came from his mind.

"Nichols. You're making a mistake coming here. I just heard about your junior attorney's murder. I'm going to make sure whoever did this is brought to justice. From what I've been told, you're at the top of the list."

"Why would you think that?" Chris asked. "What reason would I have to kill him?"

Strickland broke eye contact with Chris, thinking about the recording. If Chris had found out about the recording, it would give him a motive to kill Ethan. That was the angle he'd need to use. Not what he'd planned to begin with, but, with Ethan dead, he'd be happy to put Chris away for it. He could also use the recording to get Chris to turn on Manetto for a lighter sentence. He'd have to play his cards right, but it could still happen.

"Ethan didn't deserve to die," I said, stepping beside Chris. "Did you set Ethan up? Do you know who killed him?"

Strickland inhaled sharply. Guilt pierced his heart that he had something to do with it. Then he hardened his resolve. There was no way he was going down for this. Ethan's stupid friend was responsible. He wasn't supposed to kill Ethan, just rough him up.

Now he might have to get rid of Isaac. Finding him after he'd killed Ethan might be hard, but he had time to track him down. Once that was taken care of, he could point the investigation Chris's way. It could still work out.

He turned his hardened gaze on me, then back to Chris. "I think you both need to leave."

"You know who killed him," I said, my heart racing. "If you don't come forward with that information, your career is over."

"Are you threatening me?" Strickland stepped close to tower over me, using his height to full advantage. I wanted to kick him so bad it hurt. Chris pulled me back, and I heaved out a ragged breath. This guy was the worst, and I wanted him dead for what he'd done.

"Come on Shelby. Let's go." Chris hadn't expected my outburst, and he worried that I'd say something I shouldn't.

He was right. I wanted to go full ballistic on Strickland, remind him that I had premonitions, and tell him he was toast because I knew who the killer was. I'd tell Strickland that he may not have beaten Ethan to death, but there was still blood on his hands, and he was going straight to hell for it.

I'd begin by telling Strickland that I knew who Ethan's friend was, just to shake him up. But since that would give me away, I held it in. On the plus side, I knew that Strickland was desperate enough to go after Isaac, so I needed to find him first.

With a sigh, I let Chris lead me out of the room. As we turned down the hall, my heart rate slowed, but my legs began to tremble. Chris put his arm around me, and I leaned against him. It wasn't until we were back in Chris's law office that I felt normal again.

I flopped on his couch, and Chris opened his small fridge. He pulled out a diet soda and popped open the lid, then handed it to me. I gratefully took a big gulp and closed my eyes.

"Do you know who did it?" Chris asked.

"Yes. The killer is Ethan's friend, Isaac. He's the one Ethan had been trying to help when he doctored the police report. It looks like Strickland told Isaac that he was going to jail unless Ethan did what Strickland wanted.

"Strickland thought that, since Ethan was being stubborn about it, maybe Isaac would have more luck convincing him. So it's easy to guess that, when Ethan refused, Isaac got carried away and beat him to death."

Chris absently rubbed his forehead. "We need to find this guy fast."

"Yes, especially since Strickland was thinking about taking care of him. I'm not sure how he planned to do that. I don't think he'd kill him, but, if paying him off to leave the city doesn't work, he might be desperate enough to go that way."

Chris swore in his mind and ran his hand through his hair. "When you spoke to Ethan yesterday, did you pick up anything about this Isaac person from his thoughts? Like... how long they'd known each other?"

I shook my head. "Not really. I just got the general impression that they'd been friends for a long time... like they'd grown up together."

Chris nodded. "That's a good place to start. His family could tell us who his friends were. I'll see if I can find their contact information on his employment records."

I did not want to talk to his family, especially without Dimples by my side. But there might be a quicker way to find his friends. "Maybe I can find his contacts from his email account on his computer."

"That might work," Chris agreed. "It might be password protected, but go ahead and see what you can do."

I headed to Ethan's small office down the hall. It was more like a closet without a window, but at least it was private. I sat down and turned on the computer. While it booted up, I glanced over his desk, finding the usual paperclips, notepads, stapler, and pencil holder. A small, framed photo of him and a couple of friends rock climbing stood on one side of the desk. He looked so happy, and now his life was gone, taken by a friend. It broke my heart all over again.

The computer blinked with the password prompt. Hoping I didn't need one, I clicked on it with the mouse. It didn't work. Now I needed the password, or this was all for nothing. I searched the top of his desk, under the mousepad, and everywhere I thought he could have hidden it.

Pulling open his top drawer, I checked inside, pushing through pencils, erasers, notepads, and a couple of granola bars. Under a pad of sticky notes, I found a folded piece of paper with some random numbers and letters. Hope caught in my chest. I typed them into the password prompt and pushed enter. The display screen opened, and I sighed with relief.

Clicking on the internet icon, I found his email account. The computer had saved his passwords, so it was easy to get into his account and click on his contact list. My breath caught. There he was. Isaac Hill. I scrolled through his information, but found that there wasn't a phone number or an address to go with it. Damn! How was I supposed to find him now?

On a whim, I checked Ethan's inbox for anything from Isaac or Strickland that might help me. As I checked each email, a rush of guilt that I was snooping through Ethan's personal life assailed me. I closed my eyes and told him I was sorry for snooping, but I hoped he'd understand.

As I opened my eyes, the photo on his desk abruptly fell over. The noise startled me, and I jumped in my chair. Swallowing my fear, I straightened the photo, making sure it was secure before going back to my search.

I checked some of the other email providers, to see if Ethan had another email account, but came up empty. Next, I turned to social media and clicked on his Facebook account. Before it even opened, the framed photo fell over again.

I froze. It couldn't be a coincidence. Was Ethan trying to tell me something? I picked up the photo. This time, I studied the faces of the two men on either side of Ethan. Was one of them Isaac?

Slipping the backing off the frame, I pulled the photo free and turned it over. Three names were penciled on the back. Gus, Ethan and Isaac. I turned it over and studied the face belonging to Isaac. Had I seen him before? There wasn't anything familiar about him, so probably not, but at least now I had a face to put with his name.

"How am I supposed to find him?" I said it out loud, hoping for a response. Listening for a voice to speak in my mind reminded me of the woman who'd tried to kill everyone at the newspaper's offices. She'd heard voices in her head too, and now it looked like I wanted to have the same problem.

Letting out a sigh, I stood. Maybe I'd have better luck finding Isaac in the police database. If he'd been arrested, there had to be a record of it somewhere. With my newly acquired desk and computer, I could sneak in there and use it. That might work as long as Bates wasn't around. I didn't think that was likely, but, since this was my only lead, I'd just have to take the chance.

I slid the photo into my purse and shut down Ethan's computer. I wandered back to Chris's office to tell him I was leaving and poked my head inside. Logan, the junior attorney who'd taken Ethan's place, was already there, and they were going over the case.

"Hey honey, I found something, so I'm headed over to the precinct."

Chris excused himself and came to the door where we could speak privately. "What is it?"

"I got Isaac's last name off Ethan's contact list, but there wasn't anything else. I figured if Isaac had been arrested at some point, his name would show up in the police database, so I'm going back to the precinct to take a look."

Chris's eyes widened. "What about Bates? If he's there, don't you think he'll stop you?"

"I'd like to see him try." Anger pulsed through my veins. "He can't stop me. Just yesterday, the chief was thinking that I was part of the team with my own desk and everything. If Bates complains, I'll just have to remind him of that."

"Okay. Let me know what you find." He was thinking that the timing was lousy with Harris not there to help me.

"I know, but I can do this without him."

"I'm not so sure. If you figure out where this guy is, you'll need Harris to arrest him. Whatever you do, don't confront him alone." He was thinking that trouble always had a way of finding me, so I needed to be extra cautious.

My eyes widened. "Chris... I'm not stupid, I know that. I'll call Dimples, and he can arrest him. I'm sure he'd be happy to do that much, even if it's his day off."

Chris sighed and pulled me into his arms for a quick hug. "Okay. Call me if you find out anything. If I'm in court, leave a message."

"I will." I squeezed him back, then left for the precinct, grateful to have something to do.

Just as I sat down in my car, my phone began to ring with "Here Comes the Bride," so I knew it was Billie. "Hi Billie."

"Hey Shelby," she answered. "I just got off the phone with Drew. He told me about Ethan. I'm so sorry. You don't think it has anything to do with Claire's case, do you?"

"Oh, no... I'm sure it isn't connected. But I don't know how his death will impact the case. I guess Chris will need to take over for him."

"I don't think there's a rush. Claire and her family are getting their lab work done today. After that, it's just a matter of waiting for the results."

"Okay. I'll let Chris know."

"Thanks," Billie said. "I'm sorry this happened. I'm sure it was a shock."

"Yeah," I agreed. "It was awful." I swallowed and blinked back unbidden tears.

"There's another reason I called," she said, hesitating a moment before continuing. "It's about the wedding tomorrow. You'll never believe what's happened. I can hardly believe it, but I think it's going to make a huge difference."

"What is it?"

"Well, Michael spoke with the owner of the paper. He told him about the situation with you, the stalker, and his threats to my wedding."

She let out a chuckle of surprise. "Guess what? He's sending his special security detail to my wedding. Can you believe it? Michael told him Drew was a police officer, and he was already enlisting their help, but the owner insisted on sending a few of his own men."

"Wow. That's great." On some level I'd hoped she was going to cancel the wedding, but this could be the answer we needed.

"Yeah. These guys are former military with all that special training. I just finished speaking with the head guy, and he's going to do a sweep of the facility before the wedding gets started and be there for the duration. I told him that you were an essential part of the team, and guess what?"

She paused for dramatic effect and then quickly continued, "You'll be getting an earpiece and everything. Isn't that great?"

"Oh... yeah, for sure."

"That way, if you get a premonition about something, you can let them know right away, and they can take care of it. Didn't you do something like that when you were in Paris?"

"Yes... I did."

"I thought so." I could hear the pleased tone in her voice. "This is all going to work out. You'll see. They might even catch the guy. Wouldn't that be awesome?"

"Yeah... it sure would."

"Okay. Well, I just wanted you to know. I thought it might help if you had one less worry on your mind. Just be sure to be there around three, so they can get you set up."

I told her I would, and we disconnected. On the drive over to the precinct, I had a sneaking suspicion that the owner of the newspaper might have something to do with Uncle Joey. Had he coerced the owner into sending his special security team to help with the wedding?

If he had, I was more indebted to him than ever. But instead of dread, an overwhelming sense of gratitude swept through me. It was almost like having a guardian angel to watch over me. How crazy was that?

CHAPTER 12

I entered the precinct like I had every right to be there and walked with purpose to the detective's offices. Without hesitation, I hurried to my desk, noting with relief that Bates wasn't in the room. I pulled out my chair, but stopped before sitting down.

The old chair was back, sending another wave of anger over me, but I sat down carefully and managed not to cause a stir. The flowers still sat on my desk, wilted and forlorn. With a decisive gesture, I picked them up and let them fall into my wastebasket.

Grateful my desk was in the corner, I hid behind the monitor, in case Bates showed up, and powered up my computer. It took forever for the ancient relic to boot up. Entering my password, I finally got into the police database.

I typed in Isaac Hill, and a file came up with a mug shot of the same face from Ethan's photo. He'd been arrested more than once for drug possession with intent to sell, but he'd never been prosecuted. It didn't say why, but I knew that Strickland had something to do with it.

I found his last known address and phone number and quickly wrote them down. It wasn't in an area of town I recognized, so, before shutting down my computer, I opened another window to search Google Maps and put it in.

Finding a run-down apartment building confirmed my fears that this might not be the best place for me to go on my own. I needed to call Dimples, especially since he could arrest the guy, but I hated asking him for help after everything he'd done today. Still, I'd made a promise, right?

I powered off my computer, and a couple of hands came down forcefully onto my desk, startling me. I jerked backwards, unbalancing my chair, and it tilted sideways. With a yelp, I pitched to the side, headed to the floor. Immediately, those same hands grabbed the armrest of my chair, then my arm, just barely stopping my fall.

It took a moment to push the hair out of my eyes. I straightened and glanced up, catching Bates's guilty flush. I picked up his consternation that he'd almost hurt me. Since he thought I shouldn't be there, he'd only meant to startle me. Now it looked like he'd intentionally tried to bully me.

He glanced around the room, hoping no one had seen his mistake. Two of the other detectives started toward us, murder in their eyes. "What are you doing, Bates?" One of them asked, folding his arms over his chest and narrowing his eyes.

"Uh... I was just about to ask Shelby the same thing. She shouldn't be here."

"Why's that?"

"Her husband is a person of interest in a murder case. The chief doesn't want her involved."

"And you think that gives you an excuse to push her around?" This time the detective got in Bates's face. "If I ever see anything like that again, I'm writing you up. In fact, if Shelby wants to file a complaint, I'll be happy to act as a witness."

The detective caught my gaze, silently asking if that was what I wanted to do. I wanted to say yes, but decided to wait and use this as leverage. "Thanks, I appreciate that. Let me think about it." He nodded. Then, with a disgusted glance at Bates, he went back to his work.

Bates let out a breath and shook his head. "I didn't mean to startle you."

"Yes you did," I said, not about to let him weasel his way out of it. "It wouldn't have been such a big deal if you hadn't stolen my chair again. Karma's a bitch, right?" I raised my brow, giving him my best you-got-caught look. "I'm willing to let it go... for now. But be warned, I will file a complaint if something like this ever happens again."

"What are doing here?"

"I'm following a lead on Ethan's killer." Before he could tell me to quit interfering, I continued. "When I find this guy, do you want to be the arresting officer... or should I call one of them?" I motioned toward the detective who'd stood up for me. "It's your call."

"What have you got?"

I shook my head. "No. You'll have to wait for my call. What will it be?"

He hesitated. "Fine. Call me. But you'd better have some compelling evidence, or you're going to look like a fool."

I didn't think that deserved an answer, so I stood, pulling myself up to my full height, and stared him down. He was still taller than me, but he broke eye contact first. I walked away. Keeping my head up, I continued out of the building, grateful my shaking legs didn't give me away.

Well, that was fun.

I sat in my car, wishing I had a diet soda something fierce. What a day. My phone began to ring, and I could have cried. The tune was Devil Rider, the ringtone I'd programed for Ramos. "Hello?"

"Babe," Ramos said. "You okay?"

"I am now."

"What's going on?"

"Something bad happened. You remember Ethan, right?" At his grunt, I continued, "Well, someone killed him last night. It was horrible. Worse, Chris is the one who found him. Now, if we don't find the killer, Strickland is probably going to have Chris arrested."

"What the hell."

"Yeah. When we confronted Strickland, he was thinking that he could use the recording as Chris's motivation to kill Ethan. Not only that, but he still has the recording and, without Ethan to say it's been doctored, Strickland could get away with it."

"When were you going to tell me all this?"

"Uh... I just did."

He huffed out a breath. "Manetto needs to know. Now. Where are you?"

"I'm at the precinct following a lead. I might know who really killed Ethan."

His silence let me know I'd surprised him. "Don't tell me you were going after this guy."

"Okay." A low growl came from him, and I smiled. "I wasn't going by myself. I was going to call Dimples first... unless you'd like to come with me." He growled again, only this time it sounded more exasperated. Oops. "But I think I'd better come over there first."

"I think that's a good idea."

"All right. See you soon." He sent another grunt my way, and the line went dead.

Several minutes later, I stepped inside Thrasher Development, a little winded in my rush to get there. Jackie greeted me and told me to go on back to Uncle Joey's office. "They're waiting for you."

I nodded and stepped down the hall. I probably should have told Uncle Joey about things sooner, especially since I'd involved him in this mess with Ethan from the beginning. So why hadn't I? Was it because Dimples didn't want me to? That probably had something to do with it. But honestly, between the two of them, I was getting a severe case of whiplash.

Ramos sat in his usual chair in front of Uncle Joey's desk. Sitting behind his desk, Uncle Joey sent me a smile, but I picked up his disappointment that I hadn't called him before now. He supposed it had been a hard day. He just wished I wouldn't try to do everything by myself or rely so much on the police. Didn't I know he had my back?

Stricken with guilt, I opened my mouth to apologize, but he waved me off. "I'm sorry to hear about Ethan. I'm sure it's been a rough morning. Tell me what happened."

Ramos stood from his seat and gestured at me to sit down in his place. While I sat, he opened the small fridge in the cabinet and pulled out a diet soda. Wow. My second one for the day, and I hadn't even asked. He popped it open and handed it to me.

"Thanks." After a couple of refreshing swallows, I told them both everything that had happened. Uncle Joey's brows rose at the part where I'd confronted Strickland. But at least he was grateful I hadn't spilled the beans about knowing who Ethan's killer was.

Warming to my story, I even told them about my confrontation with Bates, and that he'd given in to my demands that he make the arrest when I called. "Of course, I have to find the guy first."

Uncle Joey was impressed with my take-charge attitude. Maybe I could handle working with the police, and he shouldn't let it bother him so much. "So you're sure the friend, Isaac, is the killer?" he asked.

"He sounds like the one to me, but I won't know for certain until I talk to him." I didn't add that Ethan had a picture of him on his desk, and that it had fallen over while I'd been there. Just thinking about it sent goosebumps down my arms.

Uncle Joey nodded. "If we want to take down Strickland, you need the detective to arrest Isaac— if he's the killer. But in order to help Chris, you'll need Isaac to confess and imply that Strickland put him up to it."

"That sounds about right. But I can do it. I can use his thoughts against him. He'll confess, you'll see."

Uncle Joey's face broke into a pleased smile. "There's something else you'll be happy to know." He paused for dramatic effect. "I was able to obtain a copy of the recording."

"What?" I straightened with surprise. "How?"

"I have my ways." He cleared his mind of what those ways were, and the only thing I picked up was that he had a connection in the prosecuting attorney's office.

Since I didn't want to know more, I nodded. "That's fantastic. Did you get to hear it?"

"Yes. It sounds bad for Chris, but I took it to Alex Drake. Do you remember him?"

"Yes. Of course." He was one of my first clients after I'd begun my consulting agency. He owned a high-tech security firm that helped clients all over the world. I'd helped him recover some stolen diamonds and found the man who'd killed his girlfriend. "How's he doing?"

"He's doing well. He was happy to take a look at the recording for me, especially since it involved you. With his software, it was easy for him to find the exact places where it had been doctored to sound like Chris said something that he didn't. That means it won't hold up in court, and we could prove it."

"Wow. What a relief."

He nodded. "Yes. So now we don't have to worry about that. It would have been better if I could have destroyed the original recording, but a copy was the best I could do. Now if you can find Ethan's killer, Strickland is going down."

"You don't know how good that sounds," I said. "Ethan was... well, he wasn't perfect, but he was still a good person and, in some ways, I feel responsible for his death. You know?"

Uncle Joey nodded, thinking he knew how I felt and was grateful that I'd share my feelings with him. "We can't be responsible for other people's choices. He chose the consequences when he made the choice to work for Strickland. That it ended with his death is on Strickland, not you."

"As long as Strickland pays for it," I added.

"With you going after him, I believe he will."

That brought a smile to my lips and warmth to my heart. "Thanks. Now let's just hope we can find Ethan's killer."

"What's the guy's address?" Ramos asked. I handed him the paper, and his lips thinned. "Not the best part of town. It's a good thing I'm going with you."

Our gazes met, and I smiled. "I agree."

We took the motorcycle. For the first time that day, I didn't feel like crying. Determination that I was on the right track filled me with hope. Strickland wasn't going to get away with this. Now that I had Ramos and Uncle Joey on my side, we could find this guy and make him confess before Strickland got to him.

We pulled up in front of Isaac's apartment complex. The run-down place smelled of cigarettes and urine. As we walked up the stairs, I tried not to breathe too deeply. At the door, Ramos knocked several times before an older man pulled it open. A few of his teeth were missing, and his eyes held the vacant look of a junkie.

"I'm looking for Isaac Hill. Is he here?" Ramos asked.

The man shook his head. "He ain't here. Why do you want to know?"

Ramos leaned against the doorframe, letting his jacket fall open so the man could see his gun. "Do you have any idea where he might be?"

The man scowled, wondering what kind of trouble Isaac was in. If that skinny kid brought trouble to his door, he'd kick his sorry ass to kingdom come. Maybe it was time for the kid to leave. Isaac was nothing but trouble, and he was tired of dealing with him.

Ramos glanced my way and lifted his brow, silently asking if he was telling the truth. I gave him a nod, and Ramos turned back to the man. "Well?"

Glancing between us, the man thought that Ramos's size and hard gaze made him look like a hired gun. But why was I there? I didn't fit the mold, and it threw him. "That kid owes me money. If you find him, you tell him to get his ass over here and pay me back."

Ramos straightened to his full height and towered over the man. "Do I look like a messenger to you?"

The man backed up, fear widening his eyes. "No. No. Not at all." He reached into his back pocket and slipped a small knife into his hand, keeping it out of sight. Alarm prickled the back of my neck, but I picked up that Ramos had caught the movement and was ready.

"I don't want trouble," the man said. "You could try the bar on main and third west. Sometimes he goes there."

Ramos didn't budge. "When was that last time you saw him?"

"I don't know. A few days ago." The guy backed into his apartment. Ramos made no move to stop him, and he quickly shut the door. We heard the lock click along with the bolt sliding home.

Ramos raised his brows, glancing at me. "Not too friendly, was he?"

"No. But at least he wasn't lying about the bar."

"Good. Let's check it out."

We found the bar a few blocks away. After entering, I was grateful to have Ramos by my side. The place was dark and intimidating, with a rough crowd that made me nervous. Ramos leaned against the bar and asked the bartender if he knew Isaac. I pulled the photo from my purse and pointed at Isaac's face.

The bartender pursed his lips, thinking he'd seen the kid around. He glanced at Ramos and nodded. "Yeah, he's been here before, but I haven't seen him for a few days. Go ahead and look around if you want."

Ramos did that chin lift thing and turned around. "Stay here," he told me. He took the photo from my fingers and stepped through the crowd. The bartender caught my gaze and raised his brows, hoping I'd get the message that I needed to order a drink if I was taking up a stool.

I might have felt obligated to order something, but no one else wanted my place, so I stayed put. The bartender might have challenged me, but he didn't want to tangle with Ramos, so he let it go.

As Ramos asked around, I listened for thoughts of deceit, but no one cared enough to lie about Isaac. He hadn't been there in a couple of days, and that was all they knew.

Ramos came back. "Anything?" he asked.

"Nope."

"Okay, let's go."

Outside, I couldn't help the disappointment that washed over me. What was I missing? "Hey, maybe we should go back to Ethan's apartment and take another look around? I'll bet the police are done there. I'm sure they've collected all the evidence, but we might see something they missed."

Ramos nodded, thinking it was worth a try.

Twenty minutes later, we pulled in front of the apartment building. There weren't any police cars around, so it was safe to go inside. Still, remembering all that blood slowed my steps. Ramos started toward the building, but turned back with a questioning brow. Why wasn't I coming?

I swallowed and got my legs moving to follow him. Inside, we took the elevator to the fifth floor. Ethan's apartment door had yellow crime scene tape crisscrossed in front of it. Leaving his motorcycle gloves on, Ramos tried the knob.

Finding it locked, he took out his lock picks and got to work. A moment later, the door opened. Ramos lifted the crime scene tape so I could duck under it, and he followed me inside.

A large bloodstain marked the spot where Ethan's body had been, and the accompanying coppery smell turned my stomach. The crime scene unit had taken most everything of interest. On the kitchen counter, all of Ethan's mail was gone, along with the notepads I'd seen before. Ethan's fridge still held the receipt from the grocery store, along with the ad for the gym membership.

Nothing stood out, and disappointment crashed over me. I might have more luck going through the evidence the police had already gathered, but I didn't think that Bates would let me check it out.

"I'll check the bedroom again," Ramos said.

I nodded and absently pulled the refrigerator door open, finding take-out food containers and a carton of milk. The freezer held a small carton of ice cream, along with a couple of ice cube trays. As I closed the refrigerator door, the ad for the gym membership fell to the floor.

I picked it up and examined both sides of the ad, in case Ethan had written anything on it, but found nothing. Letting out a sigh of discouragement, I put it back.

The massive blood stain on the carpet drew my gaze. A sense of despair washed over me, and tears threatened to fall. Poor Ethan. He didn't deserve this. If only I could have gotten him to confide in me sooner, this might not have happened. Finding the killer before Strickland was the only thing left I could do for him.

"Ethan," I whispered. "I need your help. I need a clue. Where should I go next? How can I find Isaac?" I let out a breath, barely holding back my tears. "I'm so sorry this happened."

I waited for something that would tell me he'd heard me, but nothing happened. Maybe the photo was the best he could do. I hadn't picked up anything from dead people for a long time. Not since my sojourn to New York. Still, I closed my eyes and asked Ethan if there was a clue I needed.

The magnet holding the ad for the gym membership fell off the refrigerator and rolled under a cabinet. As if caught on a breeze, the ad floated lazily to the ground and landed at my feet. The hairs on the back of my neck stood up, and my heart thumped.

I picked up the ad again. This time, I studied everything on it. At the bottom of the ad, three words caught my attention. I gasped. Rock Climbing Wall. This was it. The clue Ethan wanted me to find. A shiver ran up my spine, and excitement rushed over me.

Ramos came back to the kitchen, and I could hardly contain my enthusiasm. "This is it! Look. It says Rock Climbing Wall."

Ramos couldn't understand what that had to do with anything. "Explain."

"Where's the photo?" Ramos pulled it from his pocket, and I pointed at the rock climbing gear, then showed him the ad for the gym with the rock climbing wall on it. "See? This gym has something to do with finding Isaac."

"Let me see." I handed the ad over, and Ramos examined it. He nodded, thinking that it all made sense now.

"What makes sense?" I asked.

"This gym is on a short list of drug drops for one of the gangs. If Isaac is involved with them, he'd need to keep it quiet or risk their wrath. Now it makes sense that he felt desperate enough to kill Ethan to save his own skin."

"This is the clue we needed. Let's go check out the gym. Maybe he's there."

"I'll check it out later—alone."

"What?" I asked, surprised. "You don't want me to go with you?"

"Not this time. I think I'll have better luck finding him on my own. I can call you if he shows up, but it will probably be later tonight. You should take the night off. You've got a big day ahead of you tomorrow with the wedding, and you need to be in top shape if you're going to outsmart Beal. Let me see what I can dig up about Isaac, and we'll go from there."

"Are you sure?" In a way, I didn't want him to go without me. But, on the other hand, letting him take care of this relieved me more than I cared to admit.

"Yes."

"Thanks, Ramos." The tension drained away, and I sent him a grateful smile

He smiled back, thinking that he liked having me in his debt. Maybe I'd even call him Romeo again. His brows rose expectantly.

"No."

He shrugged, thinking it was worth a try.

I enjoyed the ride back to Thrasher and held on to Ramos a little tighter than I needed to. He didn't seem to mind. In the parking garage, he took my helmet. He was thinking that I looked worn out and could use a break.

"I am worn out. It's been a rough day. But please call me if you find him. No matter how late it is."

"I will."

I sent him a grateful nod and hurried to my car. Today had been awful, and Ethan's death still weighed heavily on my heart. With Ramos looking for Ethan's killer, I could focus on the wedding without worrying that Strickland would find Isaac first.

Hopefully Beal wouldn't throw something my way to ruin the wedding that I couldn't stop. Just thinking about it made my stomach hurt. What in the world did Beal have planned? And how could I ever be ready?

CHAPTER 13

The sound of my phone ringing woke me. I grabbed it and said hello while walking out of the bedroom so I wouldn't disturb Chris.

"Babe," Ramos said. "Sorry to wake you, but I've got Isaac. He's not in a cooperative mood, so I was hoping you could help me persuade him to talk."

"You bet. Where are you?"

"I'm at Big Kahuna's bar in the basement. Come in through the back when you get here."

"Okay. See you soon." I knew Big Kahuna from a while ago. He'd saved me from a drug dealer and was a friend of Ramos's. He'd even given me my own pool cue stick, which kind of made me an honorary member of his gang, so I had no qualms about meeting Ramos there.

Keeping quiet, I slipped inside my closet and pulled on my jeans and a t-shirt, along with a zippered sweatshirt. In the bathroom, I pulled my hair back into a ponytail. Ready to go, I glanced Chris's way. Should I wake him or leave a note? Ethan's death, and the threat from Strickland, had taken a toll on him. Besides that, he'd had to stay late at work because of the court case.

Not wanting him to worry, I decided to leave a note and gently closed the door. In the kitchen, I found a sticky note and wrote that Ramos had found Isaac and that I'd be back soon. Who knew? Maybe I'd be back before Chris woke up? With my luck, it wasn't likely, but I could always dream.

I checked my purse to make sure my stun flashlight was charged and ready to go, and grabbed my car keys. I drove to the Tiki Tabu bar, spotting the sign's familiar bright lights blinking off and on in the darkness. In the parking lot, I spotted Ramos's car along with a few others.

A lone light shone down on the back door, casting a yellow glow in the darkness. With a furtive glance around me, I hurried inside. Muffled sounds of music came from the bar, and I followed the dark hallway to the stairwell.

My footsteps echoed on the wooden planks, sending little shards of nervous tension through me. It was scary to be here in the middle of the night, and the basement seemed deserted. Just before I made it to the bottom of the stairs, Ramos poked his head into the stairwell, stopping me in my tracks.

"Good. You made it. Come on in." He was thinking that Isaac was an addict and a thief, who cared for no one but himself. With that attitude, he hoped I could get something from him. Otherwise his only motivation to talk might come down to offering him another fix.

Discouraged to know that, I followed Ramos into the dank room, finding the same pool table under a lone lightbulb from my last visit. Isaac sat in a chair, his wrists tied to the armrests, and a sullen expression on his face. His upper lip was swollen and his cheek bruised.

He also sported the gaunt features and telltale tracks on his arms of an addict.

He caught sight of me and wondered how I knew the hitman. I couldn't be a cop, and Strickland worked alone, so what did I want? Then he relaxed, thinking the hitman would never kill him in front of a nice lady like me, so maybe there was a way out of this.

"Hello Isaac," I said, pacing to stand in front of him. "Do you know why you're here?"

"Look. You've got the wrong guy. I don't know what you're after, but it isn't me, I didn't do anything wrong." He was thinking he had to play dumb. There was no way I knew anything about his recent activities.

"You killed Ethan, and now you're going to pay."

Isaac's nostrils flared, but he tried to cover his surprise. "I don't know what you're talking about."

"Ethan was your friend. How could you kill him like that?"

A prickle of guilt pierced his heart, and he cursed Strickland. If Ethan would have just done what Strickland asked, none of this would have happened. He'd still be alive. Why did Ethan have to change his mind? He'd ruined everything. He shouldn't have done that. This was all Ethan's fault, not his.

"I know Strickland put you up to it. What did he promise? That you'd never go to jail? And you believed him?" I shook my head. "Did you know that Strickland is looking for you?"

Isaac's eyes widened. How did I know about Strickland? He'd never told a soul. Had Ethan told me? This was bad. Isaac's arrangement with Strickland was on rocky ground. If I told anyone about it, Strickland wouldn't protect him anymore.

"If I could find out about your deal with Strickland, so can anyone else," I said. "Now you pose a threat to the prosecuting attorney. How long do you think he'll let you live? Because of you, he's tied to Ethan's murder. He'll blame you for it and throw you under the bus. Don't you see what you've done?"

Fueled by rage, I stepped close enough to tower over him. "You killed your best friend. He tried to help you, and what did he get for it? You used him and his friendship to cover for your stupid mistakes. When he took a stand, you beat him to death."

I pulled the photo from my purse and held it in front of his eyes. "This was in a frame on his desk at work. It's Ethan with you—his best friend. You meant something to him. But what did you do? You killed him. In cold blood. You murdered your best friend."

Isaac's face contorted with pain. "It's not my fault. I didn't mean to kill him. It was an accident. It's Strickland's fault. He told me I was going to jail unless I convinced Ethan to help him. He made me do it. I never would have gone to Ethan otherwise. You have to believe me."

I had to sympathize with Isaac to get him to cooperate. It went against the anger in my heart, but I steeled my nerves and did it anyway. "I do believe you. This is all Strickland's fault. And there's only one way out. That means making sure Strickland takes the fall for Ethan's death. So this is what we're going to do.

"First, we'll meet the detective in charge of the case. You can tell him what happened and that Strickland put you up to it. Once they know it was an accident, they'll go easy on you, and you can make it right. Strickland won't be able to touch you after that. Remember, he put you up to this. It wouldn't have happened otherwise, right?"

"Yes, but... I don't want to go to jail."

Incensed, I sent him a hard stare. "Did Ethan want to die? He begged you to stop, but did you listen? Did you even give him a chance to fight back?"

Isaac lowered his head in shame. In his mind, I picked up how he'd surprised Ethan with his attack. The tire iron he'd concealed under his jacket had somehow ended up in his hand. The first blow had knocked Ethan into a stupor. He could have stopped then, but his anger was out of control. He lifted the tire iron again and again—

I shuttered my mind, not wanting to see anymore. Swallowing back the bile in my throat, I spoke. "What did you do with the tire iron?"

Isaac's breath caught. How did I know? Tightening his lips, he refused to answer, thinking that maybe he could escape before I took him to the police. He could run away and start somewhere else. I didn't have any evidence that he'd killed Ethan. He'd thrown the tire iron into the dumpster at the gym, along with his blood-soaked clothes. No one would find them there, and the dump truck would take them away tomorrow. He could still get away from here. It wasn't too late.

"You're wrong, Isaac," I answered. "It is too late." I turned to Ramos. "Let's put him in the trunk of my car."

Ramos nodded, his lips pressed into a grim line. He approached Isaac, and Isaac panicked, jumping to his feet with the chair attached to his arms. He swung the chair toward Ramos, but Ramos easily stepped out of the way. Isaac lost his balance and landed on his knees. He struggled to get to his feet, but I shoved my stun flashlight against his neck and pushed the button.

His body jerked, and he fell back to the floor, out cold. A wave of satisfaction rolled over me. I knew Ramos could have handled him, but stunning him felt too damn good to pass up.

Ramos lifted a brow my way. He understood my need to do something to Isaac after he'd killed Ethan. And he appreciated how well my stun flashlight worked without all the blood that made me queasy. It was the perfect weapon for me, plus, no clean-up for him.

I smiled. That kind of sounded like we were partners. He was the brawn and I was the brains—well, the brains because of my mind reading skills. I liked that. He bent to work on Isaac's bonds, releasing him from the chair. Then he deftly tied Isaac's arms behind him. Next, he threw him over his shoulder, and I followed him out to my car.

I popped my trunk, and Ramos settled Isaac inside, then shut the lid. Concern etched his brow. "Are you sure about taking him in alone?"

"Yes. I actually think it will be fun to walk into the precinct with a killer in tow. It should sharpen my image, don't you think?"

"Are you calling the detective first?" Ramos wondered how Bates would take it.

"Yeah. I'll let him know I'm on my way, and he'll meet me there." I was taking a chance on Bates, but I figured he'd come around soon enough.

"Okay. I'll follow behind to make sure you get there safely."

"Thanks." I wanted to hug Ramos, but I held back, not wanting to cross that line going on between us. "I guess I owe you."

He grinned. "Yes... you do." Our gazes met, and he let his thoughts wander to exactly how he'd take his payment. Unable to pull my gaze away, my heart rate spiked, sending my body temperature to at least a million degrees. Even with my mouth hanging open, I found it hard to breathe. Holy hell!

He chuckled, thinking I'd stepped into that one all by myself, so I couldn't be mad at him.

"Ah!" I slammed my shields shut, along with my mouth, and rushed to open my car door. I needed to put some distance between us before I lost control. Heaving out a breath, I jerked my seat belt into place and closed my eyes.

That was so not fair. I glanced his way, wanting to send him a dirty look, but he'd already jumped into his car. I shook my head. At least he wasn't on his motorcycle to tantalize me even more. I tore my gaze from him and focused on what I needed to do next.

Oh yeah. Call Bates. Thinking about talking to him was like taking a cold shower. I put the call through and took satisfaction to hear Bates answer with a groggy hello. "Hi Bates. This is Shelby. Can you meet me at the precinct? I have Ethan's killer, and I'm bringing him in."

"You're... what?"

"Or I can call Detective Harris, although I'd rather not, since he's getting married tomorrow."

"But you can't arrest anyone," he said. "You're not even a cop."

"I know. That's why I need you. Are you coming or not?"

He hesitated, then blurted. "Fine. I'll be right there."

Setting my phone down, I put the car in drive and pulled out of the parking lot. True to his word, Ramos followed me to the station. As I got out of my car, I waved and watched him drive away.

I leaned against my car to wait for Bates, enjoying the cool night breeze, satisfied to have caught Isaac so quickly. It also gave me the upper hand with Bates, and I couldn't help the sardonic smile that twisted my lips.

A few minutes later, he arrived. Getting out of his car, he came toward me. His brow lifted, and he wondered where the perp was. I smiled and gestured toward the trunk. "He's in there."

Bates was thinking that he shouldn't be surprised since he was dealing with me, and nothing about me was ever normal. Still, my resourcefulness unnerved him. How had I found the killer so fast? How had I managed to get him into the trunk of my car by myself? He didn't think I had a gun, and I didn't look strong enough to overpower a grown man.

Geeze, I wasn't that helpless. Sure, I'd had a hitman's help, but that was part of my resourcefulness. He should know by now that I was a power to be reckoned with, and good at finding guilty people.

"Since he wasn't cooperating, I had to stun him. But he should be awake by now." I popped the trunk open, revealing Isaac, tied up with his eyes wide open.

Bates swore under his breath, then leaned down to get Isaac out. I caught a burst of panic from Isaac, and his thoughts that he'd bolt if he got the chance. "Be ready," I said to Bates. "He'll try to bolt if he can."

"I got this," Bates said. He held Isaac firmly, then told me to shut the trunk. After I'd done that, he pushed Isaac against the car and shoved his face down on the trunk. Now that he was secure, Bates snapped his handcuffs around Isaac's wrists and threw the rope to me.

I opened the car door and chucked the rope inside, then pushed the lock button on my key fob. Bates held Isaac around his upper arm in a firm grip. Not wanting Bates to get all the credit, I took Isaac's other arm, and we marched him into the building together.

Bypassing the intake desk, Bates continued on to one of the interrogation rooms, thinking that he wasn't ready to arrest Isaac without talking to him first. From the looks of him, Isaac was an addict with nothing to lose. Bates needed hard evidence that Isaac was the killer. Anything less, and he would have to set Isaac free.

Inside the room, Bates pushed Isaac into a chair, then left to start the recording in the observation room for the interview. He quickly returned, unlocked Isaac's handcuffs, and sat across from him. He indicated the chair beside him, and I sat there. He began the interview by reading Isaac his rights, then went on to his questions.

"Isaac, Shelby told me you confessed to killing Ethan Reynolds. What do have to say about that?"

Until this moment, Isaac had hoped he could get out of this. He pursed his lips, deciding not to answer, so I pulled the picture of him and Ethan from my purse and slid it in front of him. Remorse flooded over him, along with a hefty dose of guilt. Ethan had been his best friend. What had he done?

"It was an accident," he exclaimed. His eyes held a wild gleam. "Strickland made me do it."

Bates jerked back in surprise. Strickland? What the hell?

Since he was shocked speechless, I took up the slack. "What did Strickland tell you to do?"

Anxious to put the blame on Strickland, Isaac spilled the story, beginning with Ethan's bargain to help Strickland if he let Isaac off the hook.

"Do you know what Strickland wanted Ethan to do?" I was pretty sure he didn't know, but it would look bad if I didn't ask.

"No, but I think it had something to do with Ethan's job. When Ethan refused, Strickland asked me to see if I could convince him to play his part. He told me to rough him up, and he said that, if Ethan didn't cooperate, I'd end up in jail. See? This is all Strickland's fault."

"So he wanted you to physically harm Ethan?"

"Yes."

"How did you do that?" Bates asked.

Isaac shook his head, not wanting to think about the beating. "I just hit him." Bates pushed harder, but Isaac dug in and refused to say anything. "I'm done talking. I want a lawyer."

"Fine," Bates said. "Please stand." As Isaac stood, Bates continued. "You're under arrest for the murder of Ethan Reynolds."

"Wait! What about Strickland?" Isaac's face contorted with desperation. "He's the one who told me to do it. You should be arresting him."

Bates cuffed Isaac and led him from the room. In the hall, he called an officer over to process Isaac into custody. With that accomplished, he stopped the recording and returned to my side. "Too bad we don't know where the murder weapon is."

"I do," I answered. "He threw the tire iron and his bloody clothes in a dumpster behind a gym." While Bates stood with his mouth hanging open, I told him where the gym was. "But you need to get them before the trash collector comes in the morning."

"Okay," Bates said. "What about Strickland? I'm not sure how to make the accusations stick."

I shrugged, suddenly tired to the bone. "I don't know. But you can't deny that he was involved in this. I'd be happy to help you figure it out but, right now, I'd like to go home." I checked my watch, finding that it was four in the morning.

"Sure. Go ahead. I'll take care of this and let you know if you can help me later."

"Sounds good. I guess I'll see you at the wedding tomorrow."

"Yeah," he agreed. "See you then."

I climbed into bed around four-forty-five in the morning. Chris woke, and I snuggled into his arms. "Where have you been?" he asked.

I explained Ramos's phone call and my visit to the Tiki Tabu bar. By the time I got done, it was almost an hour later.

"Wow," Chris said, relieved. "It's over. You did it. You even got Bates to help you."

"Yeah. Who would have thought? Even though we have Ethan's killer, I'm not sure what we're going to do about Strickland. But at least he can't arrest you for Ethan's murder."

Chris nodded. "The truth is bound to come out."

"I hope so." I yawned, totally exhausted. "Now I just need some sleep."

Chris hugged me tight, and I relaxed in his arms. Almost asleep, I rolled over and pulled the covers snuggly around me. As I drifted away, I picked up Chris's thoughts of love for me and smiled.

I woke to an empty bed. The clock read twelve-twenty, and I bolted to a sitting position. The events of yesterday came flooding back. With a heavy heart, I flopped back down on the bed. Ethan had died yesterday, but at least his killer was behind bars.

Today was Saturday. Dimples and Billie were getting married. Today. My stomach lurched, and I shoved out of bed. Since I needed to be there at three, there was no time to waste. I hurried downstairs to see what my family was up to.

They surprised me by having most of the Saturday chores done. Chris had even started the laundry. With things under control, I ate a quick breakfast, which was really lunch, and took a nice, long shower. By the time I toweled dry, it was time to get ready.

I fixed my hair into long wavy curls, deciding to wear it down around my shoulders. With my hair and makeup done, I was ready to slip on my dress. Billie had picked spring pastels for her wedding colors, and I knew her bridesmaids were all wearing long, mist green, sheath dresses.

Naturally, I bought a new dress for the occasion as well. I'd found the perfect glacier-blue-green color that brought out my natural skin tones. It was a silhouette style, knee-length dress with a one-shoulder, sleeveless neckline and tucked waistband. Made of light chiffon material, it floated from my waist to my knees.

After slipping on my silver heels, sudden dread tightened my stomach. I'd done all I could to get ready for this. I just hoped it was enough.

Chris came into our room and whistled with appreciation. "Whoa! You look gorgeous."

"Thanks." I smiled up at him. "I'd better get going."

Since I had to be there an hour and a half early, Chris had decided to come a little later. I caught that he regretted his decision. Maybe he should go early with me, even if it meant standing around for over an hour.

"It's no big deal," I assured him. "I'll be busy with the security team. Then I'll have to check out all of the people working there for sinister thoughts. I'm afraid I won't be much of a companion with all of that going on. I hope that's okay."

"I'm sure I'll find someone to talk with while you're busy."

"Sounds good. Don't forget to bring my stun-flashlight. I plugged it in when I got home last night, so it should be charged and ready to go."

He grinned. "I won't." He pulled me into his arms for a quick kiss. "It's all going to work out."

"I sure hope so." After another hug, I grabbed my small, beaded purse, that only had room for my phone, lipstick, and car keys, and hurried out to my car.

On the drive, I tried to think of all the things that Beal might attempt at the wedding. If he got into the kitchen, there was a chance of poison. I'd learned that all too well a few weeks ago, and I had no desire for a repeat. That meant I'd need to check the workers, wait staff, and anyone going in and out of the kitchen.

Another possibility was some kind of poison gas. He'd rigged his basement office door with something like that, so I'd need to keep a lookout for a canister and check the air flow system. What else? I guess there was always the chance of a bomb. He could totally hide it in a package, disguised as a gift, and no one would know until it was too late.

By the time I arrived at the venue, my stomach was a quivering mess. It seemed like I'd have to be everywhere at once. How was I supposed to do that? Walking to the double doors, I took a deep breath to settle my nerves and pulled it open.

Inside, I found the wait staff setting the round tables with dinnerware and centerpieces. Another group of people decorated the hall with flowers and strategically placed photos of the happy couple. I paused to observe and listen to each one of them.

Finding nothing untoward, I turned down the hall and found the dressing room with a big "Bride" sign over the top. The door was ajar, so I peeked in, looking for Billie. Her stunning dress hung on a stand, just waiting for her to put it on.

Against the far wall, I found Billie sitting in front of the vanity in a white robe. Her mother stood beside her, watching as the hair dresser styled her hair into an intricate arrangement on top of her head.

"Shelby!" Billie jumped to her feet and rushed to my side. Her hairdresser let out a distressed curse, dropping a section of hair she'd been pinning up. Billie didn't even notice. She gave me a quick hug, barely containing her excitement. "Come in. Have you met my mom?"

"Yes I have. We met after you got shot."

"Oh, that's right." Her mom joined us, giving me a polite hug.

"Don't let me interrupt," I told them. "I just wanted you to know that I'm here."

Billie took both my hands in hers and examined my dress. "Wow. You look great. I love the color."

"Thanks. I can't wait to see you in your dress." I motioned toward her wedding dress. "I love it."

"I know. It's amazing."

"Billie." Her mom motioned toward the hairdresser.

"Oh sorry." She hurried back to her chair and sat down. "I can't believe it's actually happening. I'm a little nervous, but I can't wait."

I smiled. "I'm going to see if I can find the security team you told me about."

"Right. They should be here soon. I think there are four of them." She gave me a grateful smile. "Thanks Shelby, for everything."

"You bet." As I turned to leave, Billie's mom stopped me.

"Do you want to leave your purse here?" she asked. "There's a safe in the room for our things. There's plenty of space for it."

"Oh... yes. That would be great." She opened the safe, and I tucked my small purse inside.

"Just tell me when you're ready to go, and I'll unlock it for you." She was thinking it was one of those safes where the guests got to pick their own combination, and she had already set it for Billie's birthday.

"Got it. Thanks. I'll see you out there." I gave Billie's hand a squeeze and left the room, relieved that I didn't have to keep track of my purse.

I searched the hall for the team, but couldn't see them anywhere. Maybe they weren't here yet. Deciding to check out the caterers, I found the kitchen and serving area off the main hall. Delicious smells wafted from the ovens, and the place was overrun with people busy doing their jobs.

A woman wearing a white jacket with a catering logo emblazoned on the front pocket barked out orders, and everyone scurried to do her bidding. She spied me, and her brows drew together. She was thinking that I was in the way, and I shouldn't be there.

She came to my side and steered me out of the kitchen. "I'm sorry but, as you can see, we are busy. Is there something you need?"

"Yes. I'm with a special security team. Please don't tell your workers, but the groom is a police detective, and he received a threat that someone might interfere with his wedding. I'm here to make sure nothing happens, but I thought you should know. Do you have anyone new on your staff?"

Her eyes widened. "No. Most have been with me for several months, some of them years."

"It sounds like you trust them." She nodded. She didn't think that any of them could be involved in something sinister. "Okay. Good. If you see anyone in the kitchen who shouldn't be there, will you please let me know?"

"Of course."

"Thank you. Also, just be mindful of your space. If something looks out of place, or something you didn't bring shows up, please don't hesitate to find me." That kind of freaked her out, so I smiled. "I'll let you get back to work."

That taken care of, I wandered back to the hall. I took another moment to listen to the workers for anything suspicious. Finding nothing, I stepped outside onto a large patio which looked out over a lovely grotto. Leaning against the decorative fence, I found a wide, rock-hewn staircase which led down to the chairs for the guests on the green lawn.

The beauty of the open space held a quiet intimacy. A path between the chairs led to an arched trellis, covered in vines and flowers, where the ceremony would take place. Behind the trellis, a small pond, fed by a quiet waterfall, held a few ducks and waterlilies. Surrounded by tall trees and grasses, this space was a stunning backdrop for a wedding ceremony.

I turned at the sound of approaching footsteps and found four, large men dressed in white shirts, ties, and dark suits bearing down on me. The first man was so big, I could barely see the others behind him, but they all had the same no-nonsense bearing of the military, with their straight backs and alert, sweeping gazes.

The man in front tipped his head to me, while the others stood behind him. "Mrs. Nichols?"

"Yes."

"I'm Lorin Anderton, and this is my security team." He motioned to the three men behind him. "Brett, Wade, and Alejandro."

My breath caught, and my eyes nearly bulged out of my head. Alejandro was Ramos. What was he doing here? His thoughts were blocked, and he didn't even crack a smile. Then he winked. So surprised by his presence, I missed everything the man had just said.

"Uh... sorry, I missed that." I tore my gaze away from Ramos. "What did you say?"

Lorin pursed his lips. "I said that I don't expect you to learn our names. When you need to communicate, just call us by 'security team, or sec team,' all right?"

"Sure."

"We're all armed, and we have ear pieces. I have yours right here. It's a Bluetooth communicator that connects us through our phones. Just slip it in your ear, and you'll be good to go."

"Do I need my phone?" I asked.

"No. It's a wireless system that will run through my phone."

"Okay." I didn't understand how that was supposed to work, so I didn't even try.

Standing close, he gently helped me push the earplug in my ear. Because it was wireless, it wasn't connected to anything, but Lorin held a round wire with a receiver that I was supposed to wear around my neck. His was under his shirt, but he saw immediately that my wire would be visible to everyone because of my one-shoulder, sleeveless dress. He grimaced, uncertain what to do.

"Let me." Ramos stepped forward. Surprisingly, Lorin handed him the wire. "Hold out your arm." Instead of slipping it around my neck, Ramos thought that I could wear it over my shoulder, under the fabric, and tuck the receiver under my arm where no one could see it.

He slipped it over my shoulder and tucked the wire under the shoulder material. In order to get it under my arm and inside my dress, I realized that my side zipper needed to come down a few inches. Before I could suggest I find a more private spot and do it myself, Ramos expertly lowered the zipper, tucked the wire inside, and zipped it back up.

He was thinking, *you can close your mouth now*, and held back a smile. I snapped my jaw shut and narrowed my eyes. He stepped back in line with the others, and Lorin stepped forward again, holding his phone.

"Okay. We should all be connected. Report in."

Each of the men said, "Here," in a low whisper, which came through the earpiece clearly. When they were done, I followed suit and whispered it too.

Lorin smiled. "Thanks Mrs. Nichols."

"Please, call me Shelby."

"Of course. Try not to speak too loudly, and we'll all be fine. Now if you have any concerns or see anything you need us to check on, just say it out loud. Be sure to mention 'security team or sec team,' so we know you're talking to us. Also, remember that, when you speak with anyone, we'll hear everything you say."

"Right," I said, not too happy about that. I'd have to let Chris know when he got here, so I didn't say anything personal.

"I think that should cover it. We each have a quadrant of the facility to cover, and we'll be taking circuitous routes during the evening. We're all armed and ready. Again, if you need us, just let us know."

"Okay. Uh... be sure and check the ventilation systems for poison gas, and look for suspicious packages too. I've already alerted the kitchen for sabotage, but you might want to keep that in mind as well."

"Right," he said, thinking that he knew how to do his job, so I shouldn't worry. He was a professional. Then he glanced at one of the others and told him to check the ventilation system since he hadn't thought of that.

As the men headed to their positions, Ramos thought, *I'll be staying close to you*, and I opened my mouth to ask him how he'd managed to join the team. Realizing all of them would hear me, I shut it and pursed my lips. Dang. Now I'd have to wait, unless he thought about it.

Smiling, Ramos thought, *Manetto and the owner of the newspaper are good friends. It was easy.* At my nod, he took the steps down to the lawn and began to walk along the outside edge of the property. Glancing around, I realized that people had begun to arrive, and I'd better get busy. The workers had finished setting up, and classical music began to play over the speakers.

As the guests were led to the chairs on the lawn, I listened to every thought as they passed. I also kept track of the workers, since it made more sense that Beal would disguise himself as one of them.

Michael Lewis-Pierce passed by with his wife at his side. He introduced me to his wife, telling her I was the psychic who'd stopped the shooting, and she thanked me for saving her husband's life. "I'm just glad I was there," I said.

A few more newspaper people passed me, each giving me a happy greeting. One of them raised his brows, thinking he'd be ready for anything, and I knew he was privy to the threat. My stress levels spiked, knowing that so many people could get hurt, and that it was up to me to stop it.

"Shelby," Bates said, stopping at my side. "How are you doing?"

"I'm okay."

Bates could tell I was stressed out, and guilt that he'd given me such a hard time gnawed on his conscience. "Good work last night."

"Thanks. Did you find Isaac's clothes and the tire iron?"

"Yes. They were in the dumpster, like you said. He'll be formally charged for murder at his arraignment which should be happening on Monday."

"Good. What about Strickland?"

"He's been told. But it's going to take some time to formally charge him." Bates was convinced that Strickland had something to do with it, but how much, wasn't certain.

"Yeah, but we'll figure it out."

He nodded. "I'm sure we will."

Relieved to have him on my side for a change, I focused on a couple of people who had slipped past me while I had been speaking. Finding nothing bad from them, I glanced back at Bates. "Let's just hope nothing happens here, right?"

He smiled. "We're all here to help. Let me know if you need anything. Okay?"

"Sure. Thanks." This was a new side of Bates that I could get used to.

Not long after that, the chief came to my side with his wife and introduced us. After our pleasantries, he said, "Uh... good work with Bates last night. I'm glad... well... grateful for your help. It was a difficult case." He was thinking that he was glad Chris wasn't involved because I was part of his team, and if Chris had been guilty... well... that would have been awkward.

"You're right, it was difficult."

Glad to have that out of the way, he glanced at the blue sky. "Beautiful day for a wedding, isn't it? Don't forget, I'm here to help, so let me know if you need anything."

"I will. Thanks."

A few minutes before the ceremony started, Chris joined me. "Hey beautiful," he said, slipping his arm around my waist. "How's it going? Hear anything?"

"No," I responded. "But the security team is here, and I'm wearing an earpiece to keep in touch." I glanced at him meaningfully. At his puckered brows, I continued. "That means they can hear everything I say."

"Oh." Chris nodded, then thought it was a good thing I could read his mind so he could still talk to me, albeit one-sided. "That's good. Are you going to sit down?"

I let out a deep breath, unsure if I should sit or stay where I was. Just then, Dimples and his best man came outside onto the patio.

He spotted me and grinned. "Hey Shelby. Good to see you. It looks like everything's ready." He took a deep breath, thinking this was it. "Guess I'd better get down there." With a nervous grin, he continued to his place under the trellis.

"Let's sit down," Chris said, tugging on my arm. "You can keep watch from there."

"Okay." We found a couple of empty seats, and I took the one on the outside edge, wanting to be able to jump up and do something if I needed to. I kept my mind open to all the thoughts surrounding me and felt the beginnings of a headache coming on.

I listened to each newcomer, most of whom were relatives, cops, or reporters. From most of the cops, I picked up a steadfast devotion to Dimples and his bride, along with a willingness to protect them with their lives. Along with Billie's newspaper friends, they kept a vigilant eye on the group, alert for anything suspicious. All were determined to do their part to make sure nothing bad happened. My eyes teared up, and I swallowed down the sudden lump in my throat.

Soon, everyone had arrived. I kept circling the group like a hawk, not wanting to miss anything. Where was Beal? When would he make his move? Would he do something now, or wait until after the ceremony? The suspense filled me with dread. To calm my nerves, I inhaled deeply and slowly let it out.

The music stopped, catching everyone's attention, then "Pachelbel's Canon in D" began to play. Everyone turned their gazes back toward the patio, where the first bridesmaid descended the stairs. There were only three, and they were joined by groomsmen at the bottom of the steps, who ushered them to their places near the trellis in front of the pond.

Next, a cute little girl wearing a fancy tulle dress, and carrying a basket of rose petals, hopped down the stairs. She smiled with delight and threw the petals enthusiastically all over the stairs and onto the path. As she took her place, all eyes turned to the top of the stairs, and the officiator asked everyone to stand.

Billie stepped into view. Her face shone with happiness, capturing the beauty of her smile. She stood for a moment, taking it all in. I caught her excitement, tinged with trepidation and overwhelming gratitude for this moment in her life.

Her gaze shifted to Dimples, and the sight of him looking up at her with so much love brought tears to her eyes. There he stood, waiting for her with that goofy grin, and those amazing dimples that she adored. He looked so handsome and dashing in his black tux. Love for him poured from her heart. Taking a calming breath, she stepped down the stairs toward him, hardly daring to believe that this was the beginning of their life together.

On a whim, I turned my gaze to Dimples. He was completely focused on Billie. It was as if no one else existed, and they were alone in this moment. His eyes glowed with love and wonder, that this woman was soon to be his, and he vowed to do everything in his power to keep her forever by his side.

Billie's father waited for her at the bottom of the steps. She reached him and happily placed her arm in his to finish her slow walk to Dimples's side. Her father kept glancing at her. His eyes brimmed with sudden moisture and pride for the beautiful woman she had become.

As they reached Dimples, her father placed a gentle kiss on her forehead. With solemn gratitude, he placed her hand into Dimples's firm grasp.

The officiator spoke for several minutes of love and commitment. Then the ceremony began. As they exchanged vows, I listened to the crowd and found everyone's thoughts completely focused on Dimples and Billie. What a wonderful moment. It amazed me that such a large crowd of people could be united as one in thought and feeling.

After exchanging rings, the officiator pronounced them husband and wife. With a huge smile, Dimples pulled Billie into a passionate embrace, kissing her soundly. They broke apart, breathless and happy. He whispered into her ear before they separated and turned to the cheering crowd. Everyone clapped and shouted so loudly that I almost missed the one person who wasn't focused on the happy couple.

A man in a server's vest stepped to the edge of the trellis with a potted flower arrangement. He quickly set it down and rushed off, hoping no one had noticed him. Even if they had, he'd been quick, and the two hundred dollars he'd been given to complete the task was totally worth it.

Already on my feet, I rushed toward the potted plant. "A man in a server's vest just left a flower arrangement next to the trellis. Stop him. I'm getting the flowers. Something's wrong with them."

I reached the flowers at the same time as Ramos. He picked them up, and I noticed a small, black, box-like device inside the arrangement, with a red light flashing on and off. "Look," I said, pointing it out to Ramos. At the same time, a whirring sound came from above us in the air.

"Shit." With a mighty heave, Ramos chucked the flowers away from the crowd as hard as he could. A loud, hissing sound came from above us, and a dark object shot through the air. As the flower arrangement came to the ground, the object hit it, shattering it into a million pieces. The ground around it exploded, spraying grass, rocks and dirt into the air.

Ramos turned his back to the blast and pulled me to his chest, shielding me from the fallout. Screams of panic came from the crowd, along with the shower of pelting dirt hitting the ground like rain. A heartbeat later, the dirt settled, and Ramos let me go.

"You okay?" he asked.

"Yes."

With a nod, he turned to examine the small crater and began to speak into his earpiece. "It was a drone with a small rocket. The flowers had a homing beacon for the target. The rocket wasn't military grade, but I suggest we get everyone inside."

"Roger that."

I glanced over the crowd, hoping that no one was hurt. Dimples held Billie protectively in his arms, and several people had fallen to the ground, covering their heads with their arms. Now that the danger was over, they began to stand, shaking the dirt from their hair and clothes. A few guests headed into the building, but most stood there in shock.

Lorin rushed to Dimples's side, urging him and Billie toward the building. As they began to move, he ushered more people along, telling them not to panic, but to move inside in an orderly fashion. Chief Winder spoke into his phone, telling someone about the drone and asking if they could track it.

Chris came to my side. "Are you okay?" At my nod, he continued, "Was that a drone?"

"Yes." I told him about the beacon in the flower arrangement. "I didn't see where the drone went. Do you think Beal's somewhere close?"

Chris shook his head. "I don't know."

"The range of a personal drone varies," Lorin said into my earpiece. "This one was highly sophisticated but, with a small rocket, I'd say the range is probably less than two miles."

"Okay. Thanks." I told Chris what Lorin had said. "Let's get inside. I want to check on Dimples and Billie."

Soothing music played from the speakers, and we found Dimples and Billie surrounded by family, all talking at once. The wedding hostess came to Billie's side and asked if she wanted to continue or send everyone home. Billie didn't want the festivities to end, but she wasn't sure she could ask anyone to stay if it was dangerous.

She caught sight of me, knowing I'd saved her, and tears filled her eyes. She thought that maybe it was selfish to continue.

I hurried to her side. "I don't think anything else is going to happen tonight. The police are out in force, chasing him down, so I think you're good."

Billie threw her arms around me. "Thank you Shelby. Will you stay?"

"Of course."

Billie's mother wanted to get things underway, so she took charge, getting those who wished to stay to take their places. Most of the guests wanted to stay, but I picked up that many weren't eager to stay for long. I pulled Billie's mom aside and told her they might have to cut things short, and she totally agreed.

Two hours later, with full stomachs and a few drinks, a relaxed atmosphere filled the hall. Some people were even joking about "the drone incident," as it was being called. After dinner and toasts, Billie and Dimples cut the cake, then began the traditional dancing. A few dances later, they were more than ready to leave.

I felt bad that it hadn't been the perfect wedding Billie had wanted, but it was certainly unforgettable. I'd been watchful throughout the evening, so I wasn't much of a dinner companion for Chris, but he didn't complain. Now it was almost over, and I was exhausted.

The limousine pulled up outside, and everyone lined up to wish the couple a safe journey. The driver stood beside the car to open the door for them, so I moved to his side while we waited. My last job of the night was to make sure he was the real deal, and that Beal hadn't hired him.

"Hey," I said. "Is this your limo?"

"Yeah."

"Do you have a card? I might want to hire you sometime."

"Sure." He reached into his pocket. "Here you go."

Not getting much from his mind, I knew I had to ask more questions. "So, where are you taking the newlyweds?"

His brows scrunched together, and he wondered what my deal was. "Uh... I think that's something you should ask them." He was taking them straight to their hotel. Why did I want to know? Was I a stalker or something?

The irony of that thought hit me like a ton of bricks, and I held back a chuckle. "Okay. Thanks."

I joined Chris in the line, and someone passed out confetti poppers. Soon, Billie and Dimples came out of the building with big smiles and a touch of relief. We cheered and popped confetti all over them, managing to get it all over ourselves as well.

As we watched them drive away, my shoulders slumped with relief. "We did it." I turned to Chris. "It's over. I'm so ready to go home."

With both of our cars there, I told Chris to go ahead, and I'd see him at home. I found Lorin and gave him back my ear piece. Ramos had disappeared after the drone strike, so I'd have to talk to him later.

The chief had cornered the server with the flowers, but he didn't know anything, only telling us that the delivery guy wore a baseball cap with a florist shop logo on his shirt. After that, the chief and a few other officers had stayed outside, organizing the search for Beal, and I hadn't seen them since. Maybe I could get an update tomorrow but, right now, I was done.

I needed to get my purse from the safe before I could take off. After finding Billie's mother, I ended up helping her put a few things away before we made it to the safe. She thanked me again for coming to the rescue. Slipping my purse over my shoulder, I told her goodbye and hurried to my car.

Before I turned on the ignition, my phone began to ring. Digging it out of my purse, I quickly answered. "Hello?"

"Shelby."

My breath caught. It was Beal. "What do you want?"

"I don't understand," he said. His voice held a whisper of defeat. "How did you know about the beacon? I wasn't even there when it was delivered. I didn't think you'd figure it out so quickly. That's why I used a drone. But you still got the best of me. How did you do it? I have to know."

"Look Beal," I said, suddenly tired of the whole thing. "It's a gift. There are some things you can't explain, and this is one of them. Can we call a truce? I mean... come on... everyone's looking for you. Is that the way you want to live?"

"We have to meet so I can talk to you in person."

"What? No way. You just tried to kill my friends."

"Don't be ridiculous. That tiny blast wouldn't have killed them."

"Look, I've got to go. Don't call me again." I ended the call. I wasn't sure that was the best thing to do, but there was no reasoning with this guy. Maybe, if I quit taking his calls, he'd leave me alone.

I set my phone on the consul so I could start my car, and it began to ring. I heaved out a breath and picked it up. The caller ID said it was an unknown caller, so I knew it was him again. This time, I refused the call.

Setting my phone down, I started my car. As I shifted into reverse, it rang again. My phone automatically connected to my car system, so it was easy to decline. I began the drive home. Only minutes later, my phone rang with "unknown caller" on the ID, which I quickly declined.

Five minutes later, it rang again. This time I let it go to voicemail. Needing a distraction, I hit play for some tunes from my playlist. The music calmed me down, and I unclenched my hands from the steering wheel. Suddenly, the music stopped, and my phone began to ring.

Holy hell! How many times was he going to call? When I got home, I'd have to figure out a way to block his number, because this was driving me crazy. The light at the intersection glowed red, and I slammed on my brakes, so distracted by the phone that I'd nearly run the light.

While I panted from my near miss, the call finally went to voicemail. Grabbing my phone, I decided to turn it off before I caused an accident. A car honked behind me, and I glanced up to see the green light. Unable to turn it off, I dropped the phone in my lap and pulled through the intersection.

Not halfway down the block, it started up again. This time I pulled over and put the car in park. Picking up my phone, I barely registered that it was a tune I'd set for Chris, and not my regular ring-tone. My shoulders slumped, and I quickly answered. "Hi Chris."

"Honey. Where are you? I thought you'd be home by now."

"I had to help Billie's mom with something before I could leave. I'm about ten minutes away. Is everything all right?"

"Yes. I was just worried about you."

"Can you just stay on the line until I get there?"

"Sure. Why?"

"Beal's been calling me non-stop. I hung up on him and decided not to answer his calls anymore, but now he keeps calling me." Just then my phone beeped with an incoming call. "He's doing it again." I pushed decline, but I wasn't sure if I'd hung up on Chris or Beal. "Chris? Are you still there?"

I didn't get a response. Frustrated, I let out a moan. What was I doing just sitting here? I should hurry home, but now Chris would worry about me. Before I could push re-dial, the words, *Go home. Go now,* came into my mind.

I yelped and dropped my phone. Before I could think about it too hard, I sped away from the curb. With my heart racing, I clutched the steering wheel and drove home with my senses wide open and alert. What the freak? Like a bat out of hell, I didn't care about breaking the speed limit. Luckily, no one pulled me over, and I made it home in record time.

As I drove into the garage and jumped out of my car, Chris pulled the back door open. I flew into his arms, feeling his worry and relief wash over me. We held each other tightly, and I was overcome with a raw fear that, somehow, I'd just escaped something terrible.

It took several minutes for my legs to stop shaking. While Chris shut the garage door and locked up, I found my kids and spoke with them briefly about their night. Finding that all was well, I told them goodnight and went upstairs to change my clothes. Chris soon joined me, and I told him about the phone calls and what Beal had said to me.

"I don't think you should answer his calls anymore," Chris said.

"I totally agree." I finished washing my face and pulled on my favorite nightshirt. Slipping into bed, I snuggled against Chris, knowing I needed to tell him about the warning voice.

As he flipped off the light, I let out a sigh. "Something happened after I lost your phone call. I was parked on the side of the road, and I was going to call you back, but I heard a voice in my mind."

"What?"

"Yeah. The voice told me to go home and go now. I think it might have been Ethan." Now that I'd told Chris, my eyes filled with fresh tears.

Chris's jaw dropped open in astonishment. He could hardly believe that Ethan may have saved me from something bad. He should have done more to help Ethan, but if Ethan had kept me safe tonight, maybe it wasn't so bad that he was dead. Just thinking that sent a wave of guilt through his heart.

"I know what you mean," I agreed. "If it wasn't for his timely help with the ad falling from his fridge, we never would have found Isaac. Maybe since I helped find his killer, he stuck around to help me."

Chris held me tightly. "Sounds about right. Who knows what Beal was up to? Maybe he was following you? From what you told me, it sounds like he was pretty upset." I shivered next to him, and he rubbed my back. "You're safe now. Try and get some sleep. We'll figure out what to do in the morning."

CHAPTER 14

Sunday was one of my favorite days of the week, mostly because Chris cooked breakfast, and we all spent the day together. While we cleaned up the breakfast dishes, I realized I'd left my phone in my car. I found it under the seat and carried it inside.

There were over twenty missed phone calls, all from the same unknown caller. It looked like Beal had lost his cool, and I couldn't help the tingle of alarm that ran down my spine. I plugged my phone in to re-charge and showed them to Chris. With growing concern, he figured out how to block the calls from that number.

Somewhat relieved, I got busy cleaning the kitchen. As I started the dishwasher, the ring-tone sounded on my phone, sending panic into my heart. I picked it up and let out a breath. The caller ID said it was the police station.

"Hello?"

"Shelby, this is Chief Winder. We have a situation. I need you to come to the precinct."

"What's going on?"

"We received a bomb threat. We have two hours before it's supposed to go off. The caller specifically requested that you help us, so I think it's safe to say that it's Beal. He said that you're the only person who can stop it. Will you come?"

"Of course. I'll be right there."

I hurried upstairs to get dressed. Chris followed me up, and I explained what was going on. He wasn't happy that I was going. "Are you sure this isn't a trap?"

"I don't know, but I can't sit here and let it happen. I've got to go." He nodded, then thought that maybe he should come to look after me. "No. I'll be with the police. I'll be fine. Besides, if something happens, I need you here with the kids. You know that, right?"

His lips thinned with frustration, but he nodded, knowing I was right. "Fine. But you need to make sure you have someone with you the whole time."

"I will. And I'll keep my mind wide open for anything."

The forecast for the day called for plenty of sunshine and warm temperatures, so I dressed in my jeans and a t-shirt. With my face washed and teeth brushed, I pulled my hair into a low pony-tail. Ready to go, I slipped on my running shoes and made sure my purse held my stun flashlight.

Before leaving, I told my kids what was going on and promised to keep everyone updated when I could. I picked up their worry and gave them each a hug, telling them I'd be fine. Chris held me tight, then, after a quick kiss, I hopped in my car and drove away.

With mounting unease, I pulled into the precinct and hurried inside. Going straight to the chief's office, I pushed through the crowd to his desk. He caught sight of me, and his shoulders slumped with relief. He'd never dealt with a threat like this before, and just knowing I was there to help calmed him down.

I wasn't sure if that made me feel better or worse. What if I couldn't stop Beal in time? I'd only know what his plans were if I spoke with him in person. How was I going to do that without putting myself in danger?

"Thanks for coming," Chief Winder said. "Let me bring you up to speed. The caller said the bomb would detonate at two o'clock this afternoon, so that gives us a couple of hours to find it." He caught my gaze. This was the part he hadn't told me over the phone. "He's only willing to speak to you."

The news caused my head to spin. Was this because I hadn't answered his calls? Was it his sick way of getting my attention? Anger surged through me. It looked like I was going to have to talk to him whether I wanted to or not.

Should I tell the chief about his calls to me? Making my decision, I told him everything, along with the number of phone calls I'd received this morning. "I'd decided not to answer, so I guess this is his way of getting my attention."

"Shelby, it's not your fault," the chief said. "He could have hurt a lot of people at the wedding yesterday. If you hadn't given the warning, he would have. I've seen his type before. He won't stop until we stop him. Sure, we didn't get him yesterday, but he's not going to be so lucky today. We'll find him and put an end to this."

"What do you want me to do?"

"This phone came in the envelope with the threat. It's programmed with his number, so all you have to do is push the call sign. Are you ready?"

I nodded. Taking the phone, I punched the call button and waited. It rang several times before he finally picked up. "Shelby?"

"Yes. It's me."

"Good. I wasn't sure they'd take me seriously."

"Well, you definitely have our attention. So where's the bomb?"

"That's for you to figure out. In fact, don't you already know?" He paused, giving me a chance to tell him something. "So what is it? Aren't your premonitions working today?"

"I need more to go on. You need to give me something. Talking to you on the phone isn't enough."

"Hmm. Fine. I'll give you a clue. Remember the first time you eluded my carefully laid plans?"

"You mean in the food court at the mall with the potted plant?"

"Sure. Call me if you can't find it." He disconnected.

I huffed out a breath. He was toying with me, and I didn't have much hope that the bomb would be there. Now what? With the chief counting on me, I had to tell him something. Besides, maybe the bomb was somewhere close by.

I relayed Beal's words to the chief, and he organized the team to move in. He even outfitted me with a Kevlar vest and a radio. I joined him in a police van, praying this wasn't a wild goose chase. I had a sinking feeling that Beal was setting me up to fail, and anxiety ate a hole in my stomach.

Arriving at the food court, the chief told his team to evacuate the area and begin the search. I rushed toward the table that I'd shared with Jerry and the falling plant. To my surprise, Jerry sat at the table, reading his newspaper. "Jerry?"

He jerked the paper down. "Shelby? What are you doing here?" He looked at my vest with *police* written on it and blanched. "What's going on?"

"Our friend called in a bomb threat. He told me to come to the food court. Have you seen or heard anything unusual?"

Jerry stood, clutching his paper. "No. I've been reading the paper. Is it a real bomb?"

"I think so. At least they're evacuating the area, just in case."

On impulse, Jerry glanced up at the window from which the plant had fallen. I followed his gaze and noticed movement behind the curtain. Had Beal been watching? Was the bomb up there?

I grabbed my radio and spoke into it. "Chief, there was movement in the condo above my position. I'd like to check it out."

"Wait. I'm heading your way."

He hurried to my side, and I pointed out the window. "It's on the eighth floor."

"Let's move," he said. Mall security had arrived, and they let us into the building. Several police officers came with us, taking both the stairs and the elevator. The security detail unlocked the door to the apartment, and the chief and two officers went inside. I stayed in the hall until he said it was clear.

"There's nothing here," the chief told me.

"I thought I saw someone, but I guess I was wrong."

"Was this the apartment with the falling plant?" the chief asked. I nodded, and it made more sense to him. He figured that my premonitions must have been wrong because of that. "Let's head back to the food court for another look."

My stomach clenched. This was my worst nightmare. What was I going to tell him when we couldn't find the bomb? That my premonitions were on vacation?

After thoroughly searching the area, we came up empty.

"I think you need to call him again," the chief told me. "See if you can get him to be more specific. Maybe that will help with your premonitions."

"Yeah... okay." Without much hope, I called Beal. He picked up right away.

"I see that you're not having any luck," he began. "Pity. I was hoping your premonitions would work. Now it seems like you're not any better than the rest of us. Why is that? Are you a fraud after all? You're directly involved, so why don't you know where the bomb is?"

"It doesn't work like that," I answered. "Look. If you want to talk to me, just tell me where you want to meet. Drop this thing with the bomb, and I'll come to you."

"Oh, you'll come to me, but first you have to find the bomb." The line went dead.

Dammit! Now what was I supposed to do? I glanced up, only to find the chief staring at me with raised brows. By now, he expected me to know where the bomb was. A few of the other officers were thinking the same thing. Why was I just standing there?

"Uh... give me a minute," I told the chief. "I need to think."

He nodded and stepped back, then turned to face his men. "Let's give Shelby some space."

As everyone left me alone, I listened carefully to each mind in the area, moving from one to the next. Stretching my mind as far as I could, I found nothing. Beal obviously wasn't out in the open where I could hear him.

Now what? He'd brought me to the food court because that was the first place he'd set me up. Was that a clue? From talking to him, I knew he had to be someplace where he could see my failure. I glanced up to the seventeenth floor of the Randolph Tower.

With a sliver of hope, I told the chief about the office in the building. "I don't know if that's where the bomb might be, but it's worth checking out."

His eyes lit up. I'd come through. With newfound energy, he moved our search to the building. Praying I'd gotten it right, I accompanied them to the seventeenth floor and down the hall toward the office suite. As he reached for the door knob, I stopped him, remembering the booby trap at Beal's basement office.

"Wait." Knowing I needed to phrase this the right way, I continued. "This isn't a premonition, but he's been known to set booby traps. To be safe, you need to check the door before you open it."

He nodded, taking me at my word, and felt around the door jam and knob. Finding nothing to indicate a trap, he finally turned the handle and slowly opened the door. Inside, the same, lone desk sat in the middle of the room. The plastic sheets were still in place, and it didn't look like anything had changed since I'd been there last.

Stepping inside, I glanced at the desk, and my heart raced. On a piece of paper, in bold letters, it read, "BOOM!"

Was this some kind of sick joke? Dread turned my stomach. Was the bomb here, or was it another dead end? Maybe there wasn't a bomb at all? Following the chief around the desk, I fervently hoped to find the answer, or a better clue. As I glanced at the space under the desk, I gasped in shock. Red numbers counted down the seconds inside a large mass of explosives.

The chief spoke into his radio, mobilizing the bomb squad. He also called for a team to evacuate the building and the surrounding area. I watched the seconds tick down from fifty-five minutes while everyone scrambled to their places.

Dazed that this was really happening, I left with the rest of the unnecessary people, taking the elevator to the lobby. From there, we headed to the food court, where the chief set up a command center. It was far enough away from the building to be safe if the blast occurred, but still close enough to see what was going on.

I could hardly believe that Beal had been serious about the bomb. Now everyone thought my premonitions had worked. In reality, I'd been lucky to find it. The close call sent chills down my spine, and turned my legs to jelly. Trembling, I found a table that was out of the way and sat down to wait.

From here, I could hear the radio transmissions between the bomb squad and the chief. As time ticked by, it didn't seem like they'd made a lot of progress, and nervous sweat popped out on my brow.

One of the bomb squad members asked the chief to send up a steel barrier of some kind, meant to contain the blast in case it went off. He sent for it, and several minutes passed before it was delivered. The tension around me rose with each passing minute. Would they diffuse it in time?

With only ten minutes left on the countdown, the radio squawked with an update. At that same moment, something cold pressed against my neck, and a hand grasped my upper arm. "Don't make a sound, or I'll pull the trigger."

My heart jumped in my chest. I gasped, but managed to keep from screaming.

"Come with me." He pulled me to my feet, keeping the gun pressed to my neck. He angled me away, so his body was between me and the rest of the group. With the drama unfolding in front of me, I realized that everyone had moved closer to the chief where they could hear what was going on with the bomb. No one paid any attention to me.

"Keep walking." With his body so close to mine, I contemplated using an Aikido move, but the cold muzzle of the gun against my neck left me no choice. From his thoughts, I knew he'd gladly shoot me if I tried anything.

He deftly maneuvered me toward the entrance of the condo, just feet away from my table. We disappeared inside so quickly, I doubted that anyone had noticed my departure. He swiped his key card, and the door buzzed open.

To the right, another door stood ajar, held open by a plastic wedge. He shoved me inside and moved the wedge with his foot. The door slammed shut behind us, leaving us standing in a stairwell. Instead of going up, he moved to the lower staircase that was fenced off and padlocked.

"Put your hands behind your back," he said, pushing the gun against my neck. I did as he asked, and he slapped a pair of handcuffs around my wrists. Now that I was secure, he let go of me to insert his key into the lock with his free hand.

As he pushed it open, I glanced his way and surprise washed over me. He wore the uniform of a mall security guard. Is that how he got in and out so easily? "Where did you get the uniform?"

He smirked. "I work here. Now move."

Holding the gun to my neck, he grabbed my upper arm and led me into the lower stairwell. After securing the lock on the gate, we started down the stairs. Now that we'd made it this far, his hold on me relaxed, and I picked up his intention to lock me up in the basement.

At the bottom of the long staircase, the basement floor opened into a maze of pipes and electrical equipment. He pulled me past the machinery to a door at the end of the room. Turning the knob, he pushed the door open and flipped a light switch, then pulled me inside.

Along the nearest wall, the large room was furnished with white kitchen cabinets, complete with a countertop sporting a microwave and sink. A tall refrigerator sat in the corner. Against the other wall, a cot with a small mattress held a pillow and a tussled blanket. Beside the bed, a door stood open, leading into a bathroom.

A small wooden table, with four chairs, took up the space near the fridge. Beal pulled the nearest chair out and pushed me into it. As I sat, I caught his pleased thoughts and relief that he'd pulled it off. He'd caught me, and I hadn't been able to stop him. He'd won. He'd beaten me, the great Shelby Nichols.

The elation that filled him made me sick, and I wanted to punch him in the face.

"I found your bomb," I said. "So you didn't beat me."

His brows rose. Why did I say that? Didn't I know he could kill me?

"Why are you doing this to me?" I asked. "Olivia hired me to do a job for her. It wasn't personal."

"You ruined my life," he said, his eyes blazing with anger. "I had a multi-million dollar business. Because of you, I lost it all." Struggling for composure, he clenched his jaw, and stepped back to lean against the counter. With deliberate ease, he held the gun loosely in his hand. Every few seconds, he took pleasure in pointing it at me. Each time he did it, I jerked back, and he enjoyed watching me squirm.

"I have nothing now. I lost all my patents, all my research and findings. My life's work." He straightened with growing agitation and pointed the gun my way, like he was going to shoot me.

I swallowed and tried not to flinch. I still wore the Kevlar vest. If he shot me, I'd be fine, right? ... unless he hit me in the head.

"And it's all because of you." His upper lip rose in a sneer, and he began to pace. "I had everything worked out. I'd planned for every contingency. There was no way you, or anyone else, could have found out about the affair. But somehow, you did. You ruined me." His chest heaved with anger, and his eyes turned dark with pain.

"But you're going to pay now, and so will Olivia. When the bomb goes off, her precious building will be damaged, and her stock will drop. Her shell company will lose a substantial amount of money, and it will serve her right."

He checked his watch, and his brows lifted with disbelief. "It should have gone off by now." He pinned me with his penetrating gaze. "I can't believe it. They must have stopped it. They shouldn't have been able to do that."

His chest heaved with anger. I'd done it again. But... wasn't that a chance he'd been willing to take? He hadn't wanted to kill anyone with the bomb. It was just his way to lure me out. So he needed to calm down. He still had me. That was his main goal. He'd still won. This wasn't over yet. He still had cards to play.

I may have thought him crazy before, but now I was a true believer. Worry sent shards of fear down my spine. What did he want with me? I listened to his thoughts and found him studying me and thinking it was time to get to the bottom of this.

"You're going to tell me how you did it. I don't believe you have premonitions. There have been too many times you should have known things ahead of time, and you didn't."

He put his gun into the back waistband of his jeans and moved toward the cupboard. Opening it, he pulled out a tray holding a scalpel and gauze, along with a needle and drugs he'd prepared to help persuade me.

How I'd figured out that he was having an affair had made no sense to him. So he'd made it his mission to learn my secret. He'd begun by looking into my background. There was a reason that I'd succeeded, but what he'd found defied all explanation. I claimed to have premonitions and called myself a psychic.

In all his research and scientific studies, he'd never come across anything like it. Psychics were charlatans who preyed on the misfortune and gullibility of those desperate to believe in something spiritual. They weren't real.

That's when he'd decided to test me. The incident with the shooter at the newspaper had spurred him into action. I'd had the audacity to tell everyone I'd known about the shooter because of my premonitions. So it was the perfect time to show the world I was a fake.

But all his tests had backfired. So far, I'd bested him at every turn, until now, when he'd managed to capture me. For some reason, I'd missed that, and now he had me. A sense of accomplishment rolled over him. He'd beaten me, and now I was his. He would finally find out my secret.

Terror seized my heart. He was insane, and I knew he wasn't going to stop until he knew the truth. How was I going to get out of this? I took stock of my surroundings. Sure I was handcuffed, but not to the chair. I had a Kevlar vest on, so that offered me some protection. Best of all, I'd worn my watch. It still had the tracker in it.

That meant I had to hold out until someone realized I was missing and contacted Chris. He'd turn to Uncle Joey right away. Uncle Joey would tell Ramos, and Ramos would look for me using the tracker. It could still work out.

Beal picked up the scalpel and came toward me, thinking a few cuts to my free nerve endings would put me in the mood to cooperate. I had no idea what that meant, but it sounded painful.

"Uh... what are you doing?" I asked.

"You know what I want?"

"Yes, of course I do. You're upset with me because you think I ruined your life. Maybe I did, but you have to remember that I was just doing my job. It's not my fault your wife hired me."

"I don't care about that anymore," he said, bringing the knife toward my face. "I just want to know how you did it."

"Look, I understand that you're upset. You lost a lot. It's too bad, and I'm sorry it worked out that way. But you shouldn't take it out on me. I didn't do anything wrong. You're the one who had the affair."

Beal let out a frustrated bellow and brought the knife toward my face. I jerked to the side, and he caught my throat with one hand and squeezed, lifting me from the chair. Panting heavily, he brought the scalpel to my neck, ready to cut my carotid artery and watch me bleed to death.

"Stop," I croaked. "I'll tell you... how... I do it." I couldn't get enough air. I struggled to breathe, but he held my throat too tight. "Please. Stop." Black spots danced before my eyes, and my ears started to ring.

He released me. I fell back onto the chair and bent forward, gasping in air and coughing. My throat burned, and tears flooded my eyes. He grabbed my ponytail and pulled my head back. With his face inches from mine, he growled. "Start talking."

"I can read minds," I sputtered. "I know it sounds crazy, but it's the truth."

He let me go with disgust. "You can't be serious." He let out a dismayed huff. "That's... that's not possible."

"It's true." My chest heaved. "Test me. It's easy enough to prove."

A speculative gleam came into his eyes. He thought that, if I could read minds, it opened a whole new level of scientific study. Maybe even lead to a breakthrough in thought processes. But how did something like this happen?

"I got shot in the head. That's how it happened." His eyes widened, so I told him the story, going into as much detail as possible, hoping to give Ramos enough time to rescue me.

He listened to each word, fascinated that it was true. It was still hard for him to believe I could read minds, but, because it explained everything so well, he had to believe it. "So is that when you started your own business?"

"Yes."

"What about Manetto? Does he know you can read minds?"

Should I lie? But how could I keep it from him? All he had to do was start cutting me, and I'd tell him everything he wanted to know. "Yes. He knows my secret."

Beal nodded, understanding what a valuable asset I could be to a mob boss. In fact, he might pay a pretty penny to keep me from harm. He was worth millions. A few million to keep me around would hardly be missed. With that much money, Beal could start over. He could even start a new study, with me as his test subject. That meant he'd have to keep unlimited access to me as part of the deal, but he could work that out. And if Manetto didn't agree, he'd kill me and savor every minute of it.

His gaze caught mine, and his eyes widened. Had I just heard everything he'd been thinking? "Do you think Manetto will pay a ransom for you?"

"I sure hope so."

Beal chuckled. "Why don't we ask him?" He plucked his phone from his pocket and scrolled through the numbers until he found Thrasher Development. It rang several times before it went to voicemail. His gaze caught mine. "Why didn't he answer?"

"Uh... maybe because it's Sunday and he's not there?"

He scowled. Was I making fun of him? He knew how to get around that. "I think you should call him. Where's your phone?"

"Uh... in my purse at the police station."

"What about the burner phone I gave you?"

"The chief has it."

Beal didn't believe me. "Get up." I didn't move fast enough, so he jerked me to my feet.

"All right," I said, gasping from the pain in my arm. "It's in my front jeans pocket." I turned my head and tried not to flinch while he reached into my pocket.

Pulling it out, he asked, "Do you know his phone number?"

"I wish I did, but who memorizes numbers these days?"

Beal let out a frustrated breath and swore in his mind. He believed me this time. So now he needed Manetto's number. Good thing he'd kept a few files from BioTech in Jason's condo. It should be in one of them, and he knew right where to look.

That meant he'd have to leave me here for a few minutes while he found the number and made the call, but it shouldn't take long. He set the scalpel down on the tray and grabbed my arm. Twisting me around, he unlocked the handcuffs. Leaving one on my wrist, he clipped the other one to the handle on the refrigerator.

"Stay put. I'll be back." He quickly left the room, locking the door behind him.

I closed my eyes, grateful for the reprieve. I gently rubbed my bruised throat, wishing for a drink of water. If I could unlock the handcuff, I could get out of here. I'd practiced doing that a few times, but I wasn't very good at it. I searched the room, hoping to see a paperclip or something else I could use.

The table held salt and pepper shakers, but no paperclips. If I could somehow reach the tray, I might be able to use the scalpel or the needle. Stretching as far as I could, I lifted my leg to reach the tray with my foot. I barely tapped the corner.

Repositioning my body, I stretched further, pulling hard against my wrist. This time, I managed to catch the lip of the tray with the toe of my shoe. I angled it toward me and it tipped sideways, then fell to the ground with a clatter.

The syringe rolled across the floor, and the tray landed on top of the scalpel. Damn! I stretched again, but everything was too far away to reach. Exhaling, I glanced at the counter, realizing there were plenty of drawers I could search.

I riffled through each drawer that I could reach, but all I found was a wooden toothpick. There were a couple of plastic forks, but they wouldn't help me at all.

Ugh! I opened the refrigerator. Maybe there was some butter or mayonnaise I could put on my hand that would make it slippery enough to pull out? All I found was a jar of pickles and a box of soda. No butter, no mayo, nothing.

As I closed the fridge, the knob on the door rattled. It stopped, and I held my breath. The knob turned, and the door slowly opened. I froze, then gasped with relief. "Ramos! You found me."

He quickly stepped inside, shutting the door behind him. "There's no time. Let's get you out of here." He rushed to my side, slipping his gun in his waistband to unlock my handcuff. Grabbing his lock set, he took out the one he needed and inserted it into the cuff. A second later, it popped open.

"Thanks." I rubbed my swollen wrist.

Before I could move, the door burst open. Beal rushed inside, firing his gun at Ramos. A bullet hit Ramos, and he staggered back from the impact. Managing to pull his gun from his waistband, Ramos fired two shots at Beal, hitting him in the leg and shoulder.

Beal let out a yowl and raised his gun to fire at Ramos. Knowing Ramos had been shot, I stepped in front of him. The bullet caught me in the chest, knocking the breath right out of me. Sharp pain sent me crashing backward into Ramos, and he fell, dropping his gun.

I fell to my side, facing Ramos, and struggled to catch my breath. Fighting to stay conscious, I glanced Ramos's way. Terror filled my heart. He blinked his eyes, but he couldn't seem to move. He just lay there helpless, with blood flowing from his chest. Raw panic sent my head spinning.

Beal approached, dragging his leg. His intent to shoot Ramos washed over me. Gasping for air, I desperately searched for Ramos's gun.

Holding his injured arm, Beal slowly lifted his gun to shoot Ramos. My fingers found the gun. Clasping it in my palm, I twisted to my back and fired in Beal's direction.

The bullets hit him in the chest, and he staggered back. I fired two more times, frantic to stop him. I kept shooting until there were no bullets left. The gun dropped from Beal's fingers, and he fell to the ground, unmoving.

Letting out a cry, I dropped the gun. Turning, I crawled to Ramos. His eyes were shut, and it didn't look like he was breathing. Hardly aware of my own pain, I leaned over him.

"Ramos." He didn't respond. I pushed to my knees and found the bullet wound in his chest. It looked too close to his heart, robbing me of reason. "Ramos! Don't you dare die. You can't die on me."

In desperation, I felt for his pulse. It was there, but faint. He was losing too much blood. I placed my hands over the wound to staunch the bleeding and pressed down. "Please, please, please. Stay with me Ramos. You can't die. You can't."

Footsteps sounded in the hall. I turned to see Jerry leading the chief toward me. "Jerry! Chief! I need an ambulance, quick. He's been shot. It's bad."

Chief Winder spoke into his radio. He caught my gaze. "They were on standby so they're close." He touched Beal's neck to find a pulse but felt nothing.

"Are you okay?" he asked, coming to my side.

"The vest saved me, but Ramos... there's so much blood."

The chief knelt beside Ramos, thinking it didn't look good. He glanced around the room for a towel to stanch the bleeding. "Keep pressure on it," he told me. He stood to get help, then let out a relieved breath. The paramedics came to the door.

"Hurry!" I called. "He's barely breathing."

They stepped over Beal's body and knelt beside Ramos. The paramedic moved my hands from Ramos's wound, quickly replacing them with a gauze pad and pressing down. Another paramedic came to my side and asked me to move so he could get an IV started.

I shifted out of the way behind Ramos's head. From the first paramedic, I picked up his thoughts that Ramos was in bad shape. He didn't expect him to make it. He'd lost too much blood, and the bullet looked close to his heart. If he was going to have a chance, they needed to get him to a hospital fast.

With the IV started, they loaded Ramos onto a gurney and strapped him in. Quickly rolling him from the room, they began to run, pushing him down the wide hall. I struggled to stand, intending to follow. Sharp pain caught my chest. I gasped, and the pain increased.

Unable to catch my breath sent panic through me. A soft moan escaped my lips, and the chief grabbed my arm. "Shelby, just breathe. Here. Lay back down. It will help."

"But I need to go."

"We'll get you to the hospital. Just relax. Another gurney is on its way."

I took shallow breaths to ease the pain, but it made me light-headed and dizzy. Black spots appeared in my vision, and panic filled me, causing tears to spill down the sides of my face.

"Shelby, it's me."

"Jerry?" I panted.

"Yeah. I'm here," he said, taking my hand." You're doing great. Try to relax, okay?"

"Okay."

"The other paramedics are here. They'll take you to the hospital. You're going to be fine."

They came to my side, sliding an oxygen mask over my nose and mouth. A few minutes later, they lifted me onto a gurney. As they wheeled me away, the tears continued to spill down the sides of my face and into my hair.

I couldn't seem to stop crying. I knew I'd be fine, but what about Ramos? I didn't want him to die. All the way to the hospital, I prayed for Ramos, pleading for him to live, that, somehow, he'd be strong enough to make it.

CHAPTER 15

"Shelby?" I opened my eyes to find a kind woman leaning over me. "How are you feeling? Are you in much pain?"

"It's not too bad, it just hurts to breathe."

"So none of this blood is yours?" My hands still had Ramos's blood on them. Taking stock, I noticed blood on my right arm and elbow, with more on my jeans and t-shirt.

I swallowed. "No, it's not."

"Okay. We'll get you cleaned up, but first we need to get you out of this Kevlar vest so we can take a look at your chest. Are you up for that?"

"Sure."

"Let's move you into a sitting position to take it off. We'll probably need to take your shirt off at the same time so we can see the damage."

"Okay." I moved my legs to the side of the bed and sat up. Sharp pain exploded in my chest, and my breath caught. The nurse quickly pulled the Velcro bindings from the sides of the vest and removed it. Next, I lifted my arms, and she helped pull my t-shirt over my head. I closed my eyes and panted until the pain subsided.

The nurse's brows rose at the sight of the huge bruise. "It looks like you got hit in the sternum. Probably cracked it."

I glanced down to find my chest covered in a monstrous, black-and-blue bruise that spread outward from the center. "No wonder it hurts. I thought maybe I was having a heart attack."

"No doubt," she agreed. "I think you can leave your bra on for now. But let's get you in a hospital gown." She shook out the gown and helped me get it over my shoulders to tie in front. Next, she opened a package of wet, cloth wipes to wash the blood off my hands and arm.

"There. That's better. You can lie down if you want, and I'll send the doctor in."

"Wait," I said. "Do you know how my friend is doing? The one who got shot?"

Her gaze caught mine, and pity clouded her eyes. She wasn't supposed to tell me, but what could it hurt? "All I know is that he's in surgery."

"So he's alive?"

"Yes." But, from what she'd heard, she wasn't sure how long he'd last. "I'll get the doctor now." She left, pulling the curtain behind her.

Paralyzed with fear for Ramos, I could barely think straight. The doctor arrived and quickly examined my bruise. "It looks like you might have a cracked sternum, but we won't know for sure without an x-ray. I'll order one up. How's the pain?"

"It hurts to breathe."

"I'll get you something for that, too. Let's prop the bed up to a sitting position so you can lie back. It will take a few minutes before they come get you for the x-ray."

After raising the bed, he helped me get settled. Soon, the nurse entered with some pain pills, and I swallowed them down with a glass of water. Several minutes later, she came back with a wheelchair. In a daze, I endured getting the x-ray, without much pain, and realized that the pain pills had kicked in. By the time I got back to my bed, I could even breathe easier.

A few minutes after the nurse left, she came back in with a smile. Behind her, Chris stepped inside. His anxious gaze gave way to relief. Seeing him brought tears to my eyes. I held out my arms, and he enfolded me in a careful embrace, holding me while I sobbed. Each sob hurt my chest, so I worked hard to get under control.

"Am I hurting you?"

"No... well maybe a little, but I don't care."

He pulled away, but held my hands a moment longer. Noticing my runny nose, he found a tissue, and handed it to me. "It sounds like you may have a cracked rib or something."

Wiping my nose, I nodded, but could hardly talk through my tears. The curtain parted again, and the doctor walked in. He introduced himself to Chris while I dashed the tears from my cheeks. He explained the results of the x-ray, telling us that my sternum was cracked, and I would need to take it easy for a couple of weeks.

"We'll send you home with instructions and some pain medication. I'll get them ready, and then you can leave."

After he left, Chris took my hands again. "I'm glad it wasn't worse. From what I heard it was a close call."

"Oh Chris, it was awful. Beal is dead, and Ramos got shot. It doesn't look good for Ramos, and I'm so worried. What if he doesn't make it? It's my fault."

Chris tightened his hold on my hands, wanting to reassure me. "None of this is your fault. Ramos is strong. He'll pull through." Even though he wasn't sure about that, he'd say anything to help me feel better. "Did they give you something for the pain?"

"Yes. I'm okay. It hurts, but nothing I can't handle."

The nurse came back inside. "It looks like they're sending you home. Would you like to put your shirt back on? There's a police officer waiting to talk to you."

"Okay." With Chris's help, we got my shirt over my head with only a few groans of pain from me. He cringed to see the bruise and swelling, thinking it had to hurt a lot worse than I let on.

With that done, I sank back on the bed, exhausted from the effort. The nurse left the partitioned room, and Chief Winder came inside. After a quick greeting to Chris, he came to the other side of my bed. "How are you doing?"

Chris took my hand again, offering his support. "I've got a cracked sternum. Other than that, I'm okay."

"Ouch. That's too bad."

"Yeah," I agreed. "I'm glad I had that Kevlar vest on."

"That's for sure." He hesitated, then got down to business. "I need to know what happened. Are you up to telling me?"

"Sure." Between short breaths, I explained everything, starting from the time Beal held the gun to my neck, and ending with the chief's arrival. I left out the part about where I confessed to reading minds, only telling him that Beal left to check on something, and Ramos somehow knew where I was and found me.

"They shot each other. I stepped in front of Ramos and got shot in the chest. With Ramos down, Beal was going to shoot him again. I managed to grab Ramos's gun, and I shot Beal. I'm the one who killed him." Just saying it out loud sent shivers down my spine, making me a little light-headed. Had I really killed someone?

Chris tightened his hold on my hand, and I picked up his shock. It was worse than he'd thought, and gratitude that I hadn't been killed warred with his anger at what Beal had done. He was glad Beal was dead and only sorry that I'd been the one who'd killed him.

"It was clearly self-defense," the chief said, wanting me to know he had my back. "You did well, Shelby. We found the bomb and diffused it because of you. You're a credit to the police force, and I'd like to thank you for your help today."

I nodded, and tears flooded my eyes. The chief patted my arm and continued, "Your friend is still in surgery. I hate to admit it, but he found you without any help from us. We owe him a debt as well. I hope he pulls through."

I couldn't speak, so I nodded again. The chief told me to rest up, and he left the room. The doctor came back in with instructions and a prescription. I barely heard his instructions, counting on Chris to listen for me. All I could think about was Ramos.

"Ready to go home?" Chris asked.

"No." I shook my head. "I can't go yet. I have to see how Ramos is first."

"Okay. Let's see what we can find out." He helped me up, and I leaned on him to walk out. We asked one of the nurses where we could wait to hear about Ramos, and she told us where to go.

We arrived in the waiting room to find Uncle Joey and Jackie. Uncle Joey stood, holding his arms out to me. I shuffled to him, and he held me close. His worry about Ramos warred with his gratitude that I was all right.

He helped me settle onto the couch beside him, wincing at all the blood on my shirt and pants. "Can you tell me what happened?"

I explained how Beal had taken me, and was ready to kill me before coming up with his plan to call Uncle Joey for a ransom. "How did Ramos know I was in trouble?"

"That's an interesting story," Uncle Joey said. "I'm not exactly clear myself. From what I could gather, a friend of yours called Ramos. Apparently he lives in the condos."

"Oh. You mean Jerry?"

"Yeah, that sounds right. He was there when he noticed you leaving with one of the security guards. He thought it was strange that you'd leave. With everyone so focused on the bomb, none of the cops had time to listen to him. He suspected the guard was up to no good and called Ramos." His brows rose that Jerry had Ramos's number, and he wondered how that had happened.

Instead of asking, he continued, "Jerry met Ramos on the other side of the building, and let him inside. Using the tracker from your watch, they figured out where Beal had taken you. By then, Beal had contacted me about the ransom. I called Ramos, and he hurried to get you out of there. I think he told Jerry to get the police while he went after you."

"That makes sense," I said. "After Ramos freed me from my handcuffs, Beal came in, taking us both by surprise. He started firing and... a bullet hit Ramos in the chest. Ramos shot Beal a couple of times, but it didn't stop him.

"When Beal fired again, I stepped in front of Ramos." Uncle Joey inhaled sharply and I quickly continued. "I had on a Kevlar vest, so it only cracked my sternum, but Ramos and I both went down. Beal was yelling and screaming, but what scared me the most was Ramos. He wasn't moving. Then Beal crawled closer, and I knew he wanted to kill Ramos. He would have done it too, but I grabbed Ramos's gun. I shot Beal... I... I killed him."

Uncle Joey put his arm around my shoulders and pulled me close. I rested my head against him and tried not to cry. "You did well, Shelby. I'm proud of you."

After a moment, I pulled away. "Not well enough. If Ramos dies... I don't know if I can live with it. It was my fault he was there."

"No. No. Don't say that." Uncle Joey patted my arm, and I dropped my head back to his shoulder. "None of this was your fault. And Ramos isn't going to die. He'll pull through, you'll see."

But I caught Uncle Joey's passing thought that Ramos was a warrior. He was no stranger to death. If he died saving me, well, Ramos would say it was a good way to go.

Hearing that brought fresh tears to my eyes. Maybe Ramos did feel that way. I knew he'd want me to see it like that if he died. But, right now, I couldn't bear the thought of losing him.

Time passed in slow motion. Each minute seemed like hours. Uncle Joey and Chris helped me get more comfortable on the couch, and Chris took Uncle Joey's spot beside me.

After just twenty minutes had passed, I caught Chris's gaze. He sent me a smile, but I could tell he was getting restless just sitting there. "Hey, do you think you could do me a favor?"

"Sure. What is it?"

"My purse is still at the precinct with my phone. Would you mind getting it for me?"

"Yeah. I can do that. Is your car there too?"

"Yes, but we can get it tomorrow."

"Okay. I'll be back soon."

"I think I'll get some coffee," Jackie said, thinking she needed a break. "Do both of you want a Diet Coke?" Uncle

Joey and I agreed to her offer, and she left, grateful for something to do.

With her gone, I told Uncle Joey that Beal had gotten my secret out of me, and that's why he'd decided to ask Uncle Joey for the ransom.

"I'd figured as much," Uncle Joey said. "Is that how you got those bruises on your neck?"

I absently rubbed my neck. "Yeah. He was choking me, and he really wanted to kill me. So I told him." I caught Uncle Joey's gaze. "I'm glad he's dead."

"So am I." Uncle Joey was thinking that if I hadn't killed him, he would have done it himself.

That brought a smile to my lips.

"I know you probably feel bad about it," he continued. "But you did the right thing. Just remember that, okay?"

"Okay."

Jackie came back with our drinks, and we settled in to wait.

True to his word, Chris made it back forty-five minutes later. With no word about Ramos, a sudden need to call my kids and make sure everything was okay washed over me. I told Chris and he dug my phone out of my purse.

I put the call through. Just hearing their voices soothed me. After giving them a shortened version where I skimmed over the bad parts I finished up, telling them we'd be home as soon as we could, and slipped the phone back into my purse. Guilt washed over me because of everything I put my kids through.

"How did they take it?" Chris asked.

"They're fine, but maybe you should go home. I'm sure Uncle Joey will give me a ride."

Chris nodded. "Sure, but I'll wait a few more minutes." I picked up his worry about me, and about what would happen if the news was bad. He didn't want to leave me to face this without him.

My heart burst with love and gratitude for such a great husband. After everything I put him through, I wasn't sure I deserved it. "Thanks honey." I squeezed his hand, unable to say more without crying.

A doctor entered the waiting room, and we all froze. Was this it? He wore green scrubs with a cap over his hair and a surgical mask pulled below his chin. "I'm looking for Alejandro Ramos's family."

Uncle Joey stood. "That's us."

The doctor nodded, then pulled a chair toward our little group, motioning for Uncle Joey to sit down. "He made it through surgery. We repaired the damage and retrieved the bullet. It was rough. But, if he can make it through the next few hours, he has a good chance to completely recover. That said, I have to warn you. He lost a lot of blood and he's in critical condition. I can't guarantee that he'll make it, but we'll do the best we can."

"Thank you," Uncle Joey said. "When can we see him?"

The doctor shook his head. "Not for a while. He's in intensive care. If he makes it through the night, we'll re-assess his condition. You can see him once he's more stable."

Uncle Joey nodded. "I want to be notified if there's any change."

"Of course," the doctor agreed. "I'll send someone out to get your information."

It was late evening by the time Chris and I left the hospital. Uncle Joey and Jackie stayed behind to fill out all the forms. I'd noticed that he'd put "step-father" under "relationship to patient." Sorrow filled my heart. Ramos's brother should be here. He should know what was going on. What if Ramos... I couldn't even think that he wouldn't make it. Still, Ramos deserved to have Javier by his side.

With a heavy heart, I decided to call Javier tomorrow and tell him everything. Tonight, there was nothing more we could do. I made Uncle Joey promise to call me the minute he heard anything, no matter what time it was, and Chris took me home.

The minute we got home, my chest began to hurt, so Chris left to get my prescription. Josh and Savannah were relieved to see us. I held them loosely, careful of my bruises. I told them most of the details I'd left out earlier. But I couldn't tell them the part where I'd killed a man. It wasn't something I wanted to think about.

Right then, I just wanted to take my pain pills and go to bed. After changing into my night shirt, I realized I still had blood on my hands, so I took a nice, hot shower. By then, Chris had returned with my prescription.

I took my pills and got into bed, closing my eyes. Worry for Ramos left me restless. Fear that I'd get a phone call from Uncle Joey with bad news kept me from sleeping deeply. It wasn't until the gray light of dawn lightened the sky that I finally slept.

I woke around nine the next morning. The realization that Uncle Joey hadn't called brought tears to my eyes. Yes. Ramos had made it through the night. I put the call through to Uncle Joey and waited for him to pick up.

"How's Ramos?" I blurted.

"He's hanging in there. They're hoping to move him out of intensive care today if he continues to improve, so it looks good. I'm headed to the hospital soon. Do you want to come?"

"Yes."

"I'll pick you up in about an hour."

While I got ready, I realized my chest didn't hurt quite so bad. I still had to be careful, but at least I could breathe. Chris had gone to work, but he'd left a note to update him on Ramos's condition. I sent him a quick text, then I told Savannah and Josh that I was headed to the hospital. Josh had work this afternoon, and Savannah asked to have her friend over, reminding me that I needed to get my car from the police station.

With everything settled, I still had twenty minutes before Uncle Joey came to get me. Enough time to call Javier. I swallowed my nervousness and found Javier's information. My heart pounding, I put the call through. He answered after the second ring.

"Hello?"

"Javier? This is Shelby Nichols, remember me?"

"Of course," he said. "How are you?"

"I'm good, uh... well. I'm well." My nervousness came through, making it hard to talk. "Uh... I'm calling because your benefactor needs to... uh... he needs to meet you. I know we've had to change things a few times, but, under the circumstances, I... we... need to speed things up."

"Okay," Javier responded. "Is something wrong?"

Now came the hard part. "I don't know exactly how to tell you this, and it wasn't supposed to happen this way, but it's your benefactor. He's... well... it's your brother. Alejandro is alive. He's your mysterious benefactor."

Hearing nothing from Javier, I rushed to continue. "It's a long story, but he thought you were dead all these years. When he found out that you were alive, Ramos... he goes by

Ramos now... didn't want to hurt you again, so he decided to help you anonymously."

Javier's breathing was heavy, but he still said nothing. "Javier... he's wanted to meet you for weeks now, but it was never the right time. Now I'm asking because yesterday... he was shot. He almost died. He saved my life. But he's barely hanging on, and I think he needs you. He's all alone. He has no one, no family." I held my breath. "Will you come?"

A long silence answered me before he spoke. "You're telling me my brother is alive?"

"Yes. Yes—he is."

"Then, of course I will come."

I closed my eyes and sighed with gratitude. "Thank you. I'll arrange your flight, along with everything else you'll need, and I'll call you back." Before disconnecting, we spoke for a few more minutes about the details I'd need to book his flight.

A black car pulled into my driveway. I called goodbye to my kids and walked out. I couldn't move as fast as I'd like because of the pain, but inside, my heart was bursting. Javier was coming!

Uncle Joey sat in the driver's seat, surprising me. He usually came in a limo, and I'd never seen him drive. I stepped gingerly to the passenger door but had trouble opening the handle.

He opened it from the inside, and I climbed in. "What kind of a car is this?"

"Do you like it?" He was brimming with enthusiasm.

"Of course. You always have the best cars."

"It's a Tesla."

"Oh wow, I've always wanted to take a test drive in one of these."

He smiled. "Put on your seatbelt. This thing can move."

I had to admit it was the smoothest ride I'd ever had. I guess with no engine, or gears to shift, there was nothing to slow it down. We got on the freeway and he punched it, taking it to sixty in seconds. I'd never been pushed back in my seat like that in a car before. I could get used to it.

"How's your injury?" he asked, worried he'd overdone it. "Feeling better?"

"It still hurts, but not as much. I think that it might have something to do with the fact that Ramos made it through the night."

Uncle Joey nodded. "Yeah. Let's just hope he continues to improve. I can't imagine not having him around." He was thinking that Ramos had filled that empty spot in his life. Their relationship wasn't that of father and son, but it was close.

"There's something I want to talk to you about," I began. At Uncle Joey's nod, I told him all about Javier. "Ramos will probably kill me, but I had to call him. Javier is his brother."

"Does he want to come?"

"Yes. He does." I smiled at Uncle Joey, relieved and pleased. "I told him I'd make the arrangements."

"Good. I'll have Jackie get on it right now. He can be on a plane this afternoon." He put the call through the car's speaker phone, and I spoke with Jackie. She took Javier's information and promised to call me back to finish setting it up.

After the excitement of Javier's news, we entered the hospital full of hope. On Ramos's floor, they told us he'd had a rough night. He was holding his own, but they'd had a scare during the night. I picked up that he'd stopped breathing once, and my breath caught.

"Can we see him?" I asked.

The nurse nodded, but I picked up her reluctance. She knew that loved ones needed to be together at times like this. It could help the patient's recovery to know someone was nearby. "He's still in intensive care, but we're hoping to move him out later if he continues to improve. Follow me."

As she took us down the hall, she reminded us of washing our hands, and how important our support and love could be, as long as it didn't tax the patient. She took us through some double doors to the intensive care unit.

The walls between the patient and the nurse's station were clear glass, and we could see Ramos lying motionless on the bed. She introduced us to Ramos's nurse, who directed us to use the disinfectant gel before entering.

"He needs rest and peace to get better," she said. "But he's making progress. We were able to take out the breathing tube this morning, so he can talk, but he needs to stay quiet and calm."

"Of course." I started inside, but Uncle Joey stood rooted to the spot. Seeing Ramos in this condition broke his heart, and he wasn't sure he could handle it.

I glanced back at him, and he said, "You go ahead."

I sent him a nod and went inside. Sitting beside Ramos, I took his hand. He was hooked up to all sorts of machines that monitored his heart rate and blood oxygen levels. An IV dripped into his arm, and his face had lost that rough edge in sleep. At least his color was good, not pale or sickly, and that helped push away my fear.

I didn't want to disturb him, but there was so much I wanted to say. Maybe if I spoke softly, it wouldn't wake him up. That way, I could tell him all the feelings in my heart, and he'd never know. This might be the only chance I'd ever get to do that, so I had to take advantage of it. I glanced back toward Uncle Joey, but he wasn't there. With no one around, I could speak freely.

"Hey there," I began. "I just wanted to tell you that I... well... I love you, Ramos. I have for a long time, and I will till the day I die. So you hang in there, all right? Don't leave me... us. Uncle Joey would be lost without you. We all need you. So you have to get better."

I rubbed his hand with my thumb, while tears filled my eyes. "Thanks for coming after me. You saved me again. I know you do that a lot, but if you'll just get better, I promise that I'll stay out of trouble from now on. You'll never have to save me again."

"Shelby," he rasped.

My eyes widened, and my gaze jerked to his. "Ramos?"

His lips tilted. "Yeah. I'm here."

My breath whooshed out. "Good. Uh... don't try to talk. You need to conserve your strength." He smiled again, but closed his eyes against the pain. "Do you need me to get you anything? Water? The nurse?"

He was thinking *I thought you said I wasn't supposed to talk.*

Now I smiled. "I guess that works."

Yeah, not tiring at all. Don't worry, Shelby. I'm not going anywhere. But... in the future, you shouldn't make promises you can't keep.

"You heard that?"

Yeah. His eyes closed, and he let out a contented sigh. *Hmm... it was nice to hear you say that you love me. Go ahead and tell me that... anytime.*

My jaw dropped, and my face flamed red, but Ramos didn't see it. His mind was lost in contented sleep. I sat there for a long time just watching him breathe. From the corner of my eye, I caught sight of Uncle Joey returning. He stepped toward the door, but still couldn't come inside. I gently set Ramos's hand on the bed and stepped into the hall with him.

He took in my smile and sagged with relief. "Did he talk to you?" he whispered.

I nodded. "Yes. Mostly in his mind, so it didn't tire him. I think he's going to make it. He's going to be all right. Why don't you go inside and sit down for a minute?"

"Maybe later," he said. "You need to call Javier. Jackie's got everything set up. If it all works out, he should be here tonight."

My heart thumped. Now that it was really happening, I hoped I'd done the right thing. Ramos would be happy to see Javier, right?

Under a ray of relief and gratitude, Uncle Joey and I left the hospital. I waited to call Javier until we got to Thrasher Development where Jackie had all the information. I gave Javier all the details of his flight with an open return date, and told him I'd pick him up from the airport. From there we'd go straight to the hospital, and he would stay at the hotel across the street.

"How's he doing?" Javier asked me, his voice tinged with worry. "Have you seen him today?"

"Yes. He's doing better. I think he's going to make it."

He sighed with relief. "Good. I'll see you soon."

Uncle Joey had wanted to give Javier the use of Ramos's apartment at Thrasher, but he wasn't sure how much Ramos would like his involvement. Ramos had kept Javier at a distance because of his ties to Uncle Joey, so it followed that Ramos wouldn't want Javier involved with a mob boss.

I felt bad about that, but I thought it made sense. At least until Ramos decided otherwise, we would keep Uncle Joey out of it. Of course, between Uncle Joey and me, I thought I was the bigger danger. I told Uncle Joey that, and he laughed.

Uncle Joey dropped me off at the precinct so I could get my car. I thought about stepping inside to see how the case against Isaac was going, but I was just too tired. That trip to the hospital, along with my injury and all the emotion, had totally worn me out.

I got home, took a pain pill, and laid down on my bed to rest. Managing to fall asleep, I woke up when Chris came home. He was happy to hear the good news about Ramos.

"I did something that I hope won't make him mad," I said.

Chris's brows rose. "What?"

I explained about my phone call to Javier, and that he'd be arriving at seven tonight. "I'm picking him up from the airport, and we're going straight to the hospital."

Chris nodded. "I can see why you're worried, but this is good. Ramos needs someone to watch out for him for a change." Chris was also relieved that it wouldn't be me. He knew I cared for Ramos and, as much as he accepted that, he didn't want those feelings to change into something that would threaten our marriage.

"Chris, I love you. I'm not going anywhere."

He pulled me against him, but didn't hug me too tightly. "I love you too. My world would fade into shadows without you by my side." He kissed me tenderly, branding my heart with his love. "We'll get through this, but I have to admit, I'm looking forward to taking some time off."

"I know. Me too. Just think, we're headed to New York next month. That will be a nice break."

Chris chuckled. "Yeah. Meeting the New York Manettos should be fun." I caught his hint of sarcasm, mostly because we'd have to play along with the lie that we were related to them. It could get tricky. "But, from what you've told me," he continued, "at least it won't be dangerous."

I smiled and met Chris's gaze. He was thinking the same thing as me, that somehow things always got complicated when I was involved. We burst out laughing. It hurt my chest, but, at the same time, it felt good, like the cares of the world had fallen from my shoulders.

And after what I'd been through these last few days, it was nice to laugh again.

I waved at Javier. He caught sight of me and waved back, then hurried to my car. It was a thirty-minute drive to the hospital, and I spent the time telling him how Ramos got shot. Javier took it all in, impressed that I'd taken a bullet for him.

"Does he know that?" Javier asked.

I shrugged. "I don't know, but it doesn't matter."

Javier disagreed, but he didn't say it out loud. He asked several more questions about the incident, and I explained the whole story about Beal, including everything that had happened before the bomb incident. Of course, I left out the mind reading part, only saying that he was testing my premonitions. By the time we got to the hospital, Javier was thinking that Ramos and I were pretty close. Were we lovers too?

"Uh... we're just friends," I said. "Good friends... who care about each other. I'm happily married, and Ramos... well, I guess I can tell you, but Ramos is... uh... he works for the local mob boss." I couldn't say he was a hitman out loud, but Javier got the idea.

I expected him to be surprised, but he wasn't. Because of Ramos's past, he'd anticipated something like that. I didn't want him to think too poorly of Ramos, so I told him I worked for the mob boss too. That surprised him. He wondered how in the world I juggled working for a mob boss and the police. No wonder I needed Ramos around. "You also have your own business?"

"Uh... yeah. It can get a little crazy."

Javier just smiled, thinking that was probably an understatement. Then he thought that maybe Ramos should move back to Miami. Or he could at least come and stay with him for a few weeks to recover. I didn't like hearing that much, but he was probably right. Maybe Ramos should get out of the business and away from me, where it wasn't so dangerous. I mean... he'd nearly died yesterday, and it was because of me.

We entered the hospital and took the elevator to Ramos's floor. "I think I should talk to him first, and prepare him to see you, so it's not such a shock to his system, you know?"

"You think he'll be mad?" Javier asked.

"Oh no... maybe at me, but he'd never be mad at you. So it's all good."

"Okay." Javier nodded. He could tell that I was nervous, but, if Ramos was injured, I shouldn't worry too much. What could he do in his weakened state? Nothing. Anticipation washed over him. He could hardly wait to see him. After all these years, Ramos was alive. His brother. There were too many years to make up for, and he wouldn't allow anger, or remorse, to ever come between them again.

Just hearing that calmed my jittery nerves.

We entered the intensive care unit to find Ramos's bed empty. Fear struck my heart. I turned to the nurse, who told us that he'd been upgraded and moved to a room. Sagging with relief, I hardly heard her directions to his room.

Somehow we made it to the right door. I looked through the glass to make sure Ramos was in there. He lay with his eyes closed, but he looked better than he had this morning. I turned to Javier. "This is it. Leave the door open a crack so you'll know when to come in." Javier nodded, excitement shining in his eyes.

Taking a deep breath, I opened the door and stepped in. Ramos's eyes opened, and he glanced my way. "Hey," I said, smiling. "How are you doing?"

His lips tilted in a lop-sided smile. "You're back." His voice rasped. "I could get used to this." I sat beside his bed and looked him over. His unshaven jaw seemed darker than normal, and shadows lingered under his eyes. But his dark gaze held that same intensity as before, and I knew he would get well.

"Help me raise the bed up a little," he asked. He pushed the button, and the back began to rise. His pillow fell to the side, so I fluffed it up a little before sliding it under his head. "That's better. Thanks. The doctor said I'm doing well. I might even be able to go home in a few days."

"That's great news. So the pain's okay?"

"Yeah. It's manageable. How about you? How's your chest?"

"Oh... it's bruised. I have a cracked sternum."

He shook his head. "I remember you stepping in front of me. My heart kind of stopped. I thought that we were both going to die." A shadow passed over his face. He caught my gaze. "It's kind of hazy after that, but I remember you shooting at him. Did you kill him?"

I swallowed and nodded. "Yes. I shot him quite a few times, actually." Our gazes met. "I don't feel bad about it either. Is that normal?"

Ramos's brows rose. He understood why I'd ask him. "Answer this. Why don't you feel bad?"

"Because he was a terrible person, and he was going to kill you, and probably me. I don't know if he deserved it. But I had no choice."

"That's your answer. That's why you don't feel bad. I'd be dead if you hadn't killed him, so I might be biased. But it's a good enough reason for me."

"It's a good reason for me too." I smiled, drinking in this new companionship that we shared. I didn't want this moment to end, but guilt sliced through me. I glanced toward the door, knowing I'd been a little selfish keeping Javier waiting.

"Uh... I have a surprise for you." I moved to the foot of the bed. Ramos lost his smile, and his eyes narrowed. He didn't like surprises. "But this is a good surprise. I hope." Now his brows rose. What had I done? He noticed that I kept glancing at the door. Why did I do that? Was someone out there?

"Yes, there is. Someone important to you. Uh, don't be mad, okay?" I turned to the door and raised my voice. "You'd better come in now."

Javier pushed the door open and stepped into the room. "I thought you'd never say that."

Ramos caught his breath. Javier? He looked at me, then back at Javier. What had I done?

"You said you were ready to see him," I explained. "And I thought now was a good time—"

"Javi," Ramos said. That was all it took. Javier rushed to Ramos's side, bent down on one knee, and buried his face in Ramos's shoulder. Javier's body shook as he cried. Ramos patted Javier's head, overcome with emotion. Javier was here. His brother had come. Ramos mussed Javier's hair, while tears glistened in his eyes.

Tears filled my eyes. Soon they ran down my cheeks. This tender moment eased the pain in my heart. Ramos had his brother back. After more than ten years, they were together again.

A few moments later, Javier lifted his head and reached for the tissues on the bedside table. He handed some to Ramos as well. Glancing at me, he passed them across the bed to my outstretched hand. Still a little weepy, he pulled the chair to Ramos's side and sat down.

"I forgive you for not telling me you were alive," he said. "Can you forgive me? I was a stupid boy who didn't listen to his older brother. All these years, I've blamed myself for your death. Seeing you... it's like a miracle."

Ramos shook his head and let out a breath. "There is nothing to forgive. You are alive. That's all that matters now."

Javier clasped Ramos's hand and nodded. "Shelby broke the news to me this morning, so I'm still in a daze."

They both looked my way, their dark-eyed gazes nearly identical. I picked up gratitude, as well as annoyance, and... love.

"She was afraid," Javier continued, "that you might die. So she called me. I hope you're not mad at her."

Ramos's smile held affection. "No." He glanced back at Javier. "This wasn't the reunion I hoped for but... now that you're here... I think this was probably much better. Thank you for coming. I'm sorry it took me so long."

Javier wouldn't hear of it. "It's in the past. Now we can begin again. We have a lot to make up for. I want to know all about you, everything that's happened to you, and how you found out I was alive."

Ramos glanced my way. "It's because of Shelby. It's a long story, and I'm happy to tell you, but... I'm kind of tired." Ramos's strength was flagging, and we could both see that he needed his rest.

"We'll have plenty of time," Javier promised.

A nurse came in, took one look at Ramos, and told us that we needed to leave.

"I'll come back tomorrow," Javier said. "I'm staying at the hotel across the street. I can spend the whole day with you. If you want."

"Of course," Ramos said. "I can't imagine anything better."

"Good. I'll see you then."

The nurse held the door open for us, not about to let us stay one minute longer. I glanced at Ramos and sent him a smile.

"Shelby, wait."

I raised my brows. "Yes?"

"Come here." With an apologetic glance at the nurse, I stepped to Ramos's side. "Closer." I leaned toward him, and he took my hand in his, pulling me even closer. "Thank you."

"You're welcome." I aimed a kiss for his cheek, but he turned his face, and my kiss landed on the side of his mouth.

"You missed. Since I saved your life, don't you owe me a better kiss than that?" He was thinking about the last time we'd kissed in the Potomac River. He'd saved my life then, right? Didn't he deserve another one after nearly dying?

I knew I was playing with fire, but Ramos was hurt, so it wasn't like anything could happen. Taking a breath, I leaned down and chastely kissed him full on the lips. His hand cupped the side of my face, and the kiss deepened. Lost in the moment, it wasn't until I heard the nurse clear her throat that I managed to pull away.

"There," I said breathlessly. "Thanks for saving my life. Again."

He smiled, thinking that kiss had made all the pain totally worth it. "Goodnight Shelby."

I sighed and shook my head, but I couldn't stop the smile that spread over my lips. "Goodnight Romeo."

I stayed close to home for the next few days, mostly because exhaustion had finally caught up to me. My chest hurt more than I cared to admit, but, in a way, it was a good excuse to take it easy. Ramos had asked Uncle Joey to meet Javier the very next day. The day after that, I met Javier and Uncle Joey for lunch with Ramos at the hospital.

We enjoyed our time together, and Ramos continued to improve. With Uncle Joey's considerable help, Javier made arrangements to stay until after Ramos was discharged. That way someone would be there when he got home.

Javier even got to use Ramos's car, and he checked out of the hotel to stay in Ramos's house. Ramos drew the line at letting Javier use his motorcycle, and I had to stifle a smile. I offered to help as well, and it did my heart good to know that, between all of us, Ramos had a family to take care of him.

Thursday was Ethan's memorial service. I went to the cemetery with Chris and listened to the heartfelt memories that his friends and family shared. By then it was known that Isaac had confessed to killing Ethan, and the reverberations of his crime brought a wave of shock to Ethan's family and friends.

How does one ever get over something like that? I didn't have any answers, but I did know that Ethan had helped me, and I hoped he could rest in peace.

Chris's firm created a scholarship fund in Ethan's name to help assist law students in need, ensuring that Ethan's legacy would live on for years to come.

Strickland was another matter. Although he had been accused by Isaac as the instigator of Ethan's death, he denied all knowledge and claimed he had nothing to do with it. I knew Isaac's trial would take many months before coming to an end. For Ethan's sake, I'd do what I could to make sure that justice was served.

In the meantime, the allegations against Strickland were enough to warrant an investigation, and I hoped he'd lose his position as the prosecuting attorney. At the least he should lose his license to practice law. But it didn't seem like enough to compensate for Ethan's death.

On the upside, it looked like Strickland's recording of Chris had become worthless. With criminal accusations against him, he'd lost all credibility, which was a win in any book.

Claire's day in court came a week later. Even though she'd been released from jail, social services had refused to give Riley back to her. Chris had taken her case, and we met in court on a beautiful sunny morning.

To my surprise, Billie and a cameraman joined us just before it began. Her face shone with happiness, and she couldn't wait to tell me all about her honeymoon. She also wanted to hear everything that had happened to me after they'd left.

"Can you go to lunch after this?" she asked.

"Sure. That would be great."

The judge entered the courtroom, and we all stood. The charges were read against Claire. Chris defended her with the new DNA tests from her family, showing scientific proof that, due to chimerism, Claire was indeed Riley's mother.

After the judge examined the evidence, all charges against Claire were dropped, and Riley was ordered to be returned to her mother. Chris had been working with the social worker involved, so it was only moments later that the woman brought Riley into the courtroom, and we witnessed the happy reunion.

Billie's cameraman got plenty of photos of the event, ensuring Billie's success at having a winning article in the newspaper. With a happy ending all around, Billie and I spent an hour at lunch, catching up. She'd heard about the bomb, of course, but didn't know that I'd shot Beal.

"You killed Beal?" she asked. "I thought it was Ramos."

I sighed, still uncomfortable about that part. "It was probably a combination... I mean... Ramos shot him first, but yeah, I shot him too, and I would do it again. He was going to kill Ramos... and me."

Billie nodded, thinking I lived an exciting life, and this little detail was the stuff of legends. Her gaze caught mine with excitement at the possibilities of the interview and subsequent article she could write about me... if she could get me to agree. From the look of wariness on my face, she knew better than to ask me about it today, but maybe later. If nothing else, she was tenacious, and she had no trouble waiting me out.

Oh great! Now I had to worry about that. At least she wasn't going to go behind my back and write it anyway, so that was a plus. We spoke some more, then she had to get back to work and finish her article.

A week later, I was at Thrasher Development, helping Uncle Joey with his involvement in Olivia Beal's company. After holding a conference with the investors, she announced that BioTech was finally in production of the supplement to enhance brain function in older adults. She went into detail about the tests, making it sound like a miracle drug.

We sat in Uncle Joey's office, and I filled him in on what I'd picked up from the meeting. "As you know, since it's a supplement, they've bypassed the FDA. They've still done a lot of testing, and they aren't lying about their claim that it helps brain function, but the percentage of success is kind of low. I think it was just over fifty percent of test subjects who saw any improvement."

Uncle Joey nodded. "As long as it won't harm anyone, I'm good with that." He was thinking of taking it himself. Not that he needed it, but, maybe in ten years when he was in his seventies.

I smiled. He'd added that last part for me. "Sure, why not?"

I gathered my things and stepped into the hall to find a familiar figure coming toward me. "Ramos. What are you doing here?" He'd lost a little weight, but, other than that, he looked great.

"Just thought I'd stop by." He glanced at Uncle Joey, who'd come into the hall. "I'm feeling pretty good."

"Great. You can come back to work next week," Uncle Joey said. "But only part-time. Until then, I want you to take it easy."

Ramos grimaced. He was tired of taking it easy. Three weeks with nothing to do had driven him crazy. "When are you leaving for New York?" he asked.

Uncle Joey's eyes lit up. "Next week. So I guess that means you'll have to wait until I come back before you get started. But that's good. It will give you more time to recover." Uncle Joey slapped him on the shoulder and returned to his office, shutting the door behind him.

I met Ramos's gaze. "I'm going to New York too, so you won't have to worry about me. Maybe you could visit Javier while we're gone? Have you thought about that?"

"Maybe," Ramos said. He liked having his brother back in his life, but right now, he didn't mind the distance, especially since he had a kid. Every time Ramos had spoken with Javier on the phone, it seemed like that kid was screaming about something. He didn't think he could take it for more than a few hours.

I chuckled. "That makes sense. So don't stay with them. Meet them at the beach or something fun like that."

"Now that I could do." He smiled. "Are you headed out?"

"Yeah. Actually, I'm off to see someone. Remember Jerry?" At his nod, I continued. "I'm meeting him at our table in the food court for lunch. I never got to thank him for helping us out. You want to come?"

His smile widened. "Yes. But only if we take the bike."

"You ready for that?"

"Babe, that's how I got here."

"Oh... okay. I'd love that."

We took the elevator down to the parking garage. Ramos pulled my helmet from the trunk of his car and handed it over. While I fastened it under my chin, he mounted the bike and waited for me to get on behind him.

To start the bike, he used the button instead of the kick starter, which seemed like a good idea with his injury. Not wanting to hurt him, I wasn't sure I should put my arms around him. He glanced over his shoulder at me with a raised brow, wondering why I hadn't done that.

"Uh... is it okay? I mean... it won't hurt you or anything, right?"

"Babe," he growled. "It's the only reason we're taking the bike."

I chuckled. "Oh... okay."

As we started out of the garage, I clasped my arms around him and held on tight. The thrill of roaring down the road sent butterflies through my stomach. Ramos was back. It felt good. No. It was better than good. It was amazing.

I'd almost lost him. Warmth and happiness washed over me. I knew I'd made a promise to stay out of trouble so he wouldn't get hurt again. But who was I kidding? Maybe that was a silly promise. Maybe this was how my life was meant to be. I mean... I could read minds, for Pete's sake. Still, I was determined to be more careful. And then, I'd just have to hang on and hope for the best.

In the meantime, I was determined to cherish every moment I had with the ones I loved most.

Thank you for reading **Marked for Murder: A Shelby Nichols Adventure!** Ready for the next book in the series? **Ghostly Serenade: A Shelby Nichols Adventure,** is now available in print, ebook and audible formats. Get your copy today!

If you enjoyed this book, please consider leaving a review on Amazon. It's a great way to thank an author and keep her writing!

A Midsummer Night's Murder: A Shelby Nichols Novella is available in both ebook and audible formats. Don't miss this fun novella!

Want to know more about Ramos? **Devil in a Black Suit,** a book about Ramos, and his mysterious past, from his point of view, is available in paperback, ebook and Audible.

NEWSLETTER SIGNUP For news, updates, and special offers, please sign up for my newsletter on my website at www.colleenhelme.com. To thank you for subscribing you will receive a FREE ebook.

ABOUT THE AUTHOR

USA TODAY AND WALL STREET JOURNAL BESTSELLING AUTHOR

As the author of the bestselling Shelby Nichols Adventure Series, Colleen is often asked if Shelby Nichols is her alter-ego. "Definitely," she says. "Shelby is the epitome of everything I wish I dared to be." Colleen has always tried to find the humor in every situation and continues to enjoy writing about Shelby's adventures. "I love getting Shelby into trouble... I just don't always know how to get her out of it!" Besides writing, she loves a good book, biking, hiking, and playing board and card games with family and friends. She loves to connect with readers and admits that fans of the series keep her writing.

Connect with Colleen at www.colleenhelme.com

Made in the USA
Middletown, DE
05 December 2021

54326379R00205